THE CANADIAN BEAVER LODGE

LODGE

ASSASSINS ASSOCIATION

JERRY CRIPE

FROM THE TINY ACORN…
GROWS THE MIGHTY OAK

www.acornpublishingllc.com

For information, address:
Acorn Publishing, LLC
3943 Irvine Blvd. Ste. 218
Irvine, CA 92602

Printed in the United States of America

ISBN-13: 979-8-88528-018-1 (hardcover)
ISBN-13: 979-8-88528-017-4 (paperback)
Library of Congress Control Number: 2022907547

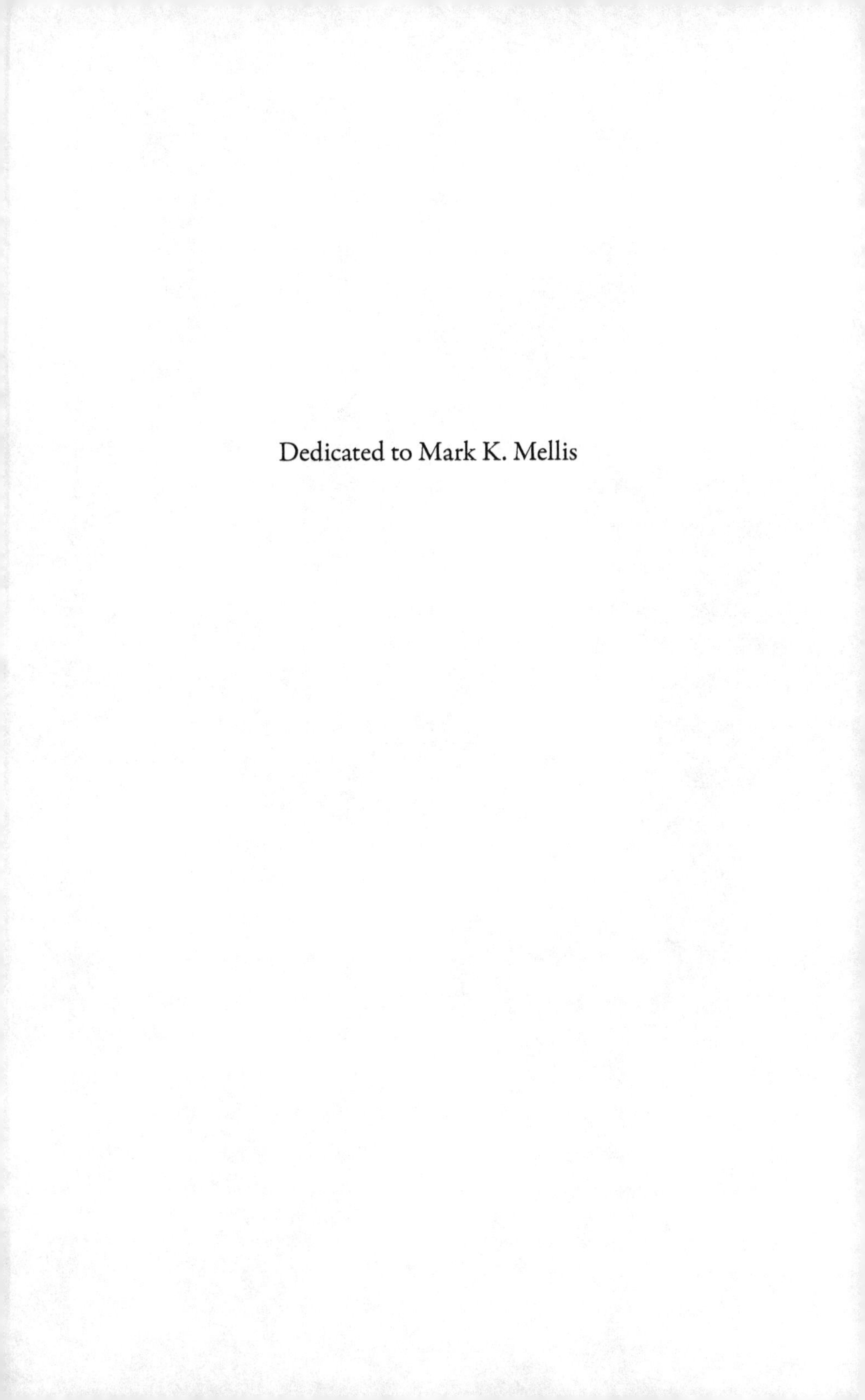

Dedicated to Mark K. Mellis

PART ONE

CHAPTER 1

Beaver Island, British Columbia
10:00 a.m. Sunday, December 31, 2017

Where Golly Gee dwelled, few could tell. Still fewer knew what she looked like. Those who did know let her get away with murder and other knavish things, on the conditions that, one, she honor a list of high-value parliamentary officials; two, she donate obscene amounts of money to charities; and three, she shut down the music and clear the island of cars by ten.

But tonight, on New Year's Eve, the shadowy scofflaw could go and go until the last ember of the pyrotechnic show sizzled in the sea. So, for her final blowout in the western hemisphere before launching the career move of a lifetime, Golly Gee wanted a guardian angel to wear to the ball—plus a dance partner not afraid of stepping on her touchy toes. Was this too much to ask for? The five-foot, filthy-rich Russian duchess frowned down at feet fated to waltz the night alone.

Golly Gee was tempted to call off the Canadian Beaver Lodge Assassins Association year-end banquet and send each employee home with a party plate and a prize. Her unseasonal funk went well beyond the invitation's hackneyed border trim of silver bells and holly berries. The twelve days of Christmas were slipping by without a shipment from her jeweler, and no four-eyed fool would make the run to Beaver

Island on the last day of December, even for her.

Or would he?

From her treetop minaret, Golly trained a monocular on someone attired in festive eggplant purple and jade green who claimed the fifteen-minute "Pick-Up and Drop-Off" space at the end of her ice-puddled, fir-lined drive. With a touch of the send key, out went the announcement. She hit print and splashed a hardcopy with *eau de parfum* to stash behind her medaled sash. Then, masking her face with a muskox toque, herringbone bandana, and orange, reflective goggles, she pumped her nine-millimeter summertime carry and, with a "Whooo!" down the beavertail escape hatch, chuted to see what fate had sent her way.

On a tight timetable to make delivery, Jaxy had already blown half the day driving in circles around Bargain Bay—a bent finger of aquamarine that parted Beaver Island, a four-hundred-hectare, bean-shaped plot of forested, algae-spotted rock from the British Columbian mainland by a wet whisker at high tide. Before an "Americans Will Be Shot on Sight" notification the California courier slouched to blend in with the Canadian woods. His Mighty Ducks jacket didn't help. He sought a way in along the frosty length of the fort's homespun fence of twining logs and branches that towered another six feet above his head and ran the mossy slope to the island's peninsular beachhead. Fresh paw prints trekking through a snowy thatch discouraged further exploration, so Jaxy turned back in his immaculate, two-toned wingtips. Between the car and fence he noticed a toy beaver atop a rough-hewn post holding a tiny sign that said: "Squeeze Me".

He stretched forth a cautious hand. *Squeak.*

Nothing happened.

On the next *Squeak-uh–Squeak-uh*, a rustling from brittle rushes a stone's throw off broke the morning crisp, followed by a disquieting stillness. At the prospect of becoming breakfast to some wild island feline, Jaxy wanted to leave the parcels with an electronic link to a goods receipt. However, the value of the boxed jewels exceeded the monetary limit for an unattended drop, so with a solid wallop to the knotty fence encompassing the Beaver Lodge, the courier called out for assistance. This brought down a snow shower on his head, and wiggles and giggles from the brushwood.

Kids—Jaxy relaxed. With a firm hand he grasped the plastic toy for a final, hard *Squeak*!!

KER-BLAMM!!! Jaxy took a shot to the ribs, reeling him against his car clutching at the bloody splotch on his side. The next blast to his fanny pack doubled him over, splattered in red. When the stinging stopped, he looked down at his superficial wounds. Paint.

"We got him! We got him!" whooped two girls in neckerchiefs and fatigues climbing out from the duck blind.

A woman wearing a khaki troop sash rushed in from the opposite way.

"Are you their mother?" asked Jaxy in anger.

With her bandana dipped in puddle slush the leader swabbed him clean. "I'm sorry. They aren't supposed to do target practice off the range, or on guests without permission."

"But then there's no surprise!" argued the sharpshooter.

"Don't fret, the color will lift. We use natural, water-soluble ingredients harvested from native, island plants. It's safe enough to eat on your salad—right girls?"

Jaxy said, "I'm not staying for lunch. I have a delivery to make from—."

"California!" the youngster raised the paintball gun in defense of Canada.

"Kits! We are not at war with Anaheim, so next time ask."

"Mister, may we *please* try again?" asked the tall one with the gun.

"Act real surprised like before—you did super!" the wiry one chipped in.

"No, you may not." Jaxy unzipped the Hawaiian print fanny pack to inspect the packaged goods for damage. They seemed okay.

"Poopy head!" the littler one unhooked the pack and over Jaxy's head it sailed for a game of keep-away until he swatted it down with his long arm span. The pack burst open and two fist-sized, gift boxes and a canvas roll of his personal music gear fell flat to the ground. The Kits dove for the wrapped fancies, and the adults for the dangerous looking hardware, landing in a heap with the lady's knee in the small of Jaxy's back, and a stringed instrument winder wrenching his ear.

"How does it work?" She cranked on it.

"Better on guitar pegs," replied Jaxy with his cheek mashed into the muck.

"And this?" she slid a stainless, triangular piece along his throat.

"Leveling fingerboards."

"And the shoe polish is for?"

"My shoes."

"Whooo! You have an answer for everything."

"You do realize I could stand up anytime and throw you over the fence with one hand, but then I wouldn't have anyone to sign the tablet," said Jaxy.

The click of a nine-millimeter safety below his ear said otherwise.

"Who sent you?" She eased up to let him nose a business card from his pack.

"I-I make deliveries for the Russian Antique Mall. Mostly local. This is my first time to Canada," Jaxy said.

The leader turned the dual use card around. "This side says you're a Rockabilly star."

"He's a spy!" charged the girls.

"Slow down. Start by asking something he should know and watch him squirm. Here. Try 'Hits from the 50's'. She typed in the search terms and handed her phone off to the Kit playing with the needle-nose pliers.

"Mister California delivery dude," led the inquisitor, "do you know 'Twenty Flight Rock'? I heard Paul McCartney wrote that."

"Don't believe everything you read on the Internet."

The youngster yanked a prime, black hair from Jaxy's nostril and held it up to his eye.

"Ouch! Okay I'll talk. Eddie Cochran co-wrote it for the movie 'The Girl Can't Help It'."

"What year?"

"Nineteen fifty . . . six."

"Wrong. Seven," she went for another hair.

"Well done!" clapped the leader praising the kits and permitting the courier to his feet.

Jaxy cleaned his thick, black rimmed glasses on a shirt tail, and returned the goods to the fanny pack. "Can we wrap-up this badge activity so I can go?"

"Already? Why not stay for the New Years' party. You can sit with the Pelt Peddlers and lead the lodge in singing 'Auld Lang Syne'."

"Lady, I'd love to, but I'm more of a blues than the bluegrass kind. So, if you wouldn't mind pointing me to the receiving dock, I have a plane to catch."

The small, but effective at pointblank gun reappeared in the lodge leader's hand. "I am receiving."

Jaxy eyed the pocket pistol pointed perilously at his beltline and relinquished the pack without ado. "Shucks lady, go on, take it. Everything's insured. Ribbons and all."

At hearing that, she combed over the packing strewn on the ground.

"Is there a problem?" asked Jaxy, itching to go.

"When isn't there. Which bow went to which box?"

To speed things up Jaxy took charge, "Hey Kits! Want to earn points toward your Shoplifting Badge? The white ribbon goes on the gold box, and the purple one with the white."

"You're positive?" She questioned the packaging before releasing the beaver kits to return to their station.

"Who would stick a white bow on a white present?" asked Jaxy.

"Ever been to a wedding?"

"Working on it. Since we're clear on colors, can I have my pack? The Antique Mall doesn't cover personal losses, and I'm saving money to build my own music recording studio by not spending it on unnecessary tool replacement."

"My mouse, if this were a mugging, I would not have asked you to my dance." The woman took the banquet invitation from her sash and pressed it into Jaxy's hand. "Should you change your mind, show this at the door."

"What door?" Jaxy looked about.

"Stand back." She fed her badge to the squeak toy. The seam of a great, hinged gate parted to reveal reinforced, steel walls with autonomous weapon stations spaced every ten bays. The unblinking, glass eye of an overhead sensor tracked their every movement. A pair of tan Belgian Malinoises with black eyes and lolling pink tongues stood at attention awaiting attack orders.

Jaxy recovered from his rattled state to watch the colony leader melt into the compound, jangling his flowery fanny pack.

"Wait! Lady—My Keys!!!" he pled to no avail. To the car Jaxy ran for his phone to lodge a frantic complaint to the front desk, but not before the vixen locked him out with the fob.

"See you at the dance, my mouse!" she waved from inside the fort's leafy shadows.

"Gaw!" Jaxy slapped the window. Then, blocking out all concerns after her he plunged, making three long and impressive strides past the sleek dogs before they overtook him like a prairie hare.

CHAPTER 2

The Beaver Lodge, B.C.
11:00 a.m. Sunday, December 31

On any other Sunday, to have a monkey-suited man with a name pin "YAN" slam Jaxy's head against the guard shack and order him to spread-it would have been the lowlight of his week. Today, however, unless the courier could give the baboon patting him down a "smaht" reason for trespassing, with but a few hours left it was about to bottom out for the year.

"Buh-but, sir, that lady not only took possession of the boxes, but my car keys too! So I'd stay and sing the midnight countdown," Jaxy unfolded the embossed invitation.

Yan lifted the note from Jaxy's quaking fingers. "You seem cold."

"A li-little."

Into the cramped and stuffy guard post they went with Yan fanning off the perfume. "Pffew! Aren't you special? I barely rated an evite. Can you describe her?"

"Under all those layers?" Jaxy warmed his hands over the oil radiator.

"Try."

"Short and top-heavy, with entitlement issues."

This succinct depiction passed muster, but Jaxy still had to supply a rationale for neglecting Beaver Lodge sign-in protocol. So, he tendered that he panicked at losing his tool roll—custom wares he would need for adjusting the public announcement levels if he was to serve justice to "Auld Lang Syne" live on stage.

"Before a crowd too hammered to care, how much sound checking does it take to knock off that old number?" asked Yan, calling up Jaxy's personnel records in the companywide database.

"Not much, but I'm still a professional."

Yan clipped a contractors' badge to Jaxy's collar. "That you are, Mr. Thrie. Take the trackway to the concert shell. I'll send your tool kit around for the assignment. Do not leave the arena unescorted and drop the badge off when you go. That clear?"

"Crystal."

By a suspended boardwalk that skirted a scopious pond of pungent bulrushes and lily pads, past an artificial dam and recirculating waterfall Jaxy descended to the lapping waters of the boathouse quay. There, a scalloped bandstand curved back at aluminum bleachers that rose up the pebbled beach. From the risers Jaxy scattered a handful of gravel across the dais as a perfunctory sound check while waiting for his gear. The clickety-clacks echoed with such astounding clarity that he reckoned a performer needed little amplification to be heard over the foaming breakers and misty foghorns. A tangle of scummy green, oxidized coax and power cords led Jaxy backstage where he discovered he wasn't the only tech in the house.

Jaxy guessed the frail frame wearing headphones and sitting motionless before the mixing board to be in its seventies, maybe more. Jaxy held out his contractor's badge and cleared his throat, but the dead man didn't twitch. Typical old guy, thought Jaxy. The aging pioneers of analog ruled the airwaves, and they could go as slow as they please.

"Excuse me?" Jaxy said in a louder voice, reaching in to lower the amplified sound but still brought no reaction. He waved in the periphery, but the stiff didn't flinch an inch. Finally, Jaxy flicked a guitar pick at the soundman's ear with enough force, so it seemed, to knock the codger off the stool! Aghast, Jaxy flew into action, administering CPR and defibrillation to shock the man back to the land of the living. In the end all attempts at revival went for naught, for the weary, old heart had stopped a full ten minutes before Jaxy arrived.

Jaxy read the name off the shirt—"Pops Lang." From a list of company extensions posted by the wall phone he dialed the internal crises response hotline to let it ring and ring until it became evident the Beavers did not budget for holiday emergencies. Jaxy looked down at the deceased. Sticking around for his music tools suddenly seemed ill-advised. He wiped the area clean, propped Pops the way he found him, and fled back up the track as fast as his long legs could go. At the beaver pond Jaxy veered right, keeping a screen of cattails between him and the guard shack to wend around to the exclusive, varnished, tri-level clubhouse with a panoramic view of Bargain Bay.

Off the wraparound deck, a single-seat skiff tied to a teal, ornamental pier with rope handrails, serenely rocked on the reedy pond. Through leaded window glass Jaxy peered at lodge associates hobnobbing over flapjacks at the company canteen. Buoyed at the prospect of finding his fanny pack alongside a pancake stack, he took the knob.

"WHAP!!!"

A loud slap cracked across the marsh. The skiff bobbed with the ripples. Before Jaxy could jump clear of the door, the diners rushed out, trampling him underfoot and dragging him by the armpits to a bomb shelter beneath the tail of a giant beaver parade float on wheels parked off the cove about fifty paces away in the lee of the north facing fence.

"Just a raid drill!" Yan doffed his yellow, safety champion's hardhat, tapping heads and taking names. At Jaxy he paused, "Wrong evacuation zone, sugar pie. Should have gone to the submersible."

"I-ahm, completed the sound check, so I came up before the buffet closed."

"Ahead of schedule and without your specialty tools?"

"I made do with what I found lying around," quailed Jaxy.

A snub-nose ground into his kidney, "Like Pops Lang?"

JAXY'S NEXT INTENSIVE INTERVIEW with colony security took place high in the executive chambers of the Beaver float head on a chair equipped with a roller chart and graphing needles. He combed back his black, wavy locks, glistening from pomade and perspiration in the one-way window with an arm cuffed and sensors clipped to thumbs and digits.

A modulated voice filtered through the scrambler, "Mister Jackson Thrie?"

"Jaxy. And pronounced 'three' as in the number."

"Yes or no."

"Yes."

"From Anaheim, California?"

"Glendale."

"A simple 'yes' or 'no', please."

"No."

"Did you take cold or pain medication, sleeping pills, alcohol, prescription, or any mind or mood-altering drugs in the last twelve hours?"

"No."

"Excellent. Do you have pets?"

"Are fish considered—?"

"Yes . . . or . . ."

"I *don't* know."

"Let's move on. Are you married?"

"Define marriage."

"Mister Thrie, have you been polygraphed before?"

"No."

"To tune this contraption and establish a baseline, you must limit your answers to yesses and nos. Are you, or are you not, married?"

"That's a complex question."

ZAP!! 12.6 volts cold-cranked Jaxy into a binary state of mind.

"No," he grimaced as needles and nerves steadied.

The balance of the exercise went satisfactorily, and at the end the unseen calibrator thanked Jaxy for his candor saying, "That wasn't so bad, was it?"

"No. But let me qualify that one by saying I'm not married yet."

"Mister Thrie: Are you engaged to be married?"

"Yes."

"For less than a year?"

"No."

"For less than two??"

"No."

"More than three???"

"Yes."

ZAP!!!

Thus far, having ascertained that Jackson Mason Thrie of Glendale, California, rockabilly musician and roustabout for the Russian Antique Mall was in a dubitable domestic relationship with approximately six fish and an attorney, Golly Gee dismissed the difficult delivery boy for a washroom break. On the retractable, gun turret she hung her bandana to dry alongside Jaxy's horrid, florid fanny pack. She inventoried his intriguing array of gadgets. Baffled by the brown shoe polish when the obvious choice for skulking was black, she also wanted to hear why he favored flat nickel wire over steel, making a note to put guitar strings and strangulation on the agenda.

Enough fantasizing—the big moment had arrived. Goosebumps ran the length of Golly Gee's spine as the she pulled the purple ribbon from the alabaster jewelry box carved with the Russian Federation, double-headed eagle. She swiveled back the lid, and from a bed of red mulberry silk lifted a palm-sized, twenty-two karat, guardian angel ringed by diamonds and sapphires fashioned a full century before by the goldsmith of renown, Peter Carl Fabergé.

To Golly Gee, a rare object of this significance demanded a thorough examination. Therefore, the university-trained scientist proceeded with a hand lens, calipers, and balance scale to take down measurements, and record visual observations in her composition notebook:

Gold: 208.98 pennyweight, alloy yellow. 6.40 x 4.01 cm. oblong. Slight taper where a 30.5 cm. serpentine chain attaches. Front surface of sculpted leaf scrolls and bellflowers. Back surface polished flat. Thickness varies to 0.9 cm maximum. Thins out to edges set with precious stones.

Gemstones: Sapphires, type 1, 6-8 mm round, appx. 2 ct. Sri Lankan. Twelve each set asymmetrically around the centerpiece. From a second chain loop off the bottom hang three gold teardrops topped with diamonds. Pear cut, clear, no inclusions, appx. 2 ct.

Centerpiece Angel: 2.4 by 3.5 cm glazed ceramic with hand-painted Guardian Angel in 19th century Russian iconographic style. Cream colored frock. White tunic. Light hair and halo. Yellow tri-bar cross in right hand. Youthful, feminine face. Round, sad, downward looking eyes.

Golly Gee turned the neckpiece over and continued making notes:

Inscription in Cyrillic: "Maria Feodorovna. Empress of ALL the Russias." Followed by a poem that translates to: "May this angel keep you and your dear children safe throughout the year."

Centered in back: 2.5 cm coin size engraving of Maria as a young woman in profile with tiara, button nose, and sharp chin and cheekbones.

Date of Manufacture: 1918 by Carl F.

Almost satisfied, Golly Gee reviewed the angel's facts and figures against those listed in the Imperial Museum's catalogue of crown jewels and everything checked out.

If angels could talk, whimsically wished Golly. The stories told of the woman who once wore this would fill the remaining the pages of her notebook . . .

CHAPTER 3

The Yellow Palace, Copenhagen
November 26, 1847

Scarcely a drop of Russian blood coursed through Maria Feodorovna's veins, the rule rather than the exception among Romanov consorts. The credentials of her father, Prince Christian of Glücksburg, appeared prestigious on paper, but as the fourth son of a low-ranking Dane, the title translated into scant money or power. Nonetheless, where the cadet lacked in leverage, he excelled in family planning. For, by taking the hand of the niece of King Christian VIII in marriage, upon the ruler's death in 1863, Louise of Hesse-Kassel and Prince Christian ascended as Queen and King of Denmark.

As the first matter of royal business the queen unloaded her brood, and in doing so she become known as "The Mother-in-law of Europe". Alexandra, she gave away to Albert, Prince of Wales, to rise as Queen of England. The national assembly of Greece elected William to fill the vacated throne in Athens, whence he took the name King George. Valdemar wed Princess Marie d'Orléans to fortify Denmark's alliance with France. The eldest son, Crown Prince Frederick, stayed put for reasons obvious, and the baby of the bunch, Thyra, made her own way in the world. Last out the door went Marie Sophie Frederikke Dagmar—Dagmar of Denmark.

Baptized Lutheran, Dagmar grew up moderately religious and modestly flirtatious, but she minded her manners, and manners she had! Her petite figure cut a wide swath in the new world of high society about which she moved with ease, and her striking presence turned many a head. One in note belonging to the Tsar of Russia who sized her up as a fine catch for his son. Having met the chief requirement of eligibility for matchmaking with a Romanov—correlative, royal bloodlines—Dagmar held no reservation about the other two expectations of church and state: the willingness to make the sign of the cross from right to left, and lots of babies.

Thereafter she went by Maria Feodorovna, and while some may judge her flair for jewelry a bit over the top, she was after all, Empress of all the Russias, and wore it well. The young Tsar Alexander lavished his bride to no end with creations by the acclaimed Carl Fabergé, who churned out more than ostentatious Easter eggs, and according to legend, a guardian angel to keep Maria safe from harm as she fled before the Bolsheviks to the Crimea.

CHAPTER 4

The Beaver Float, B.C.
11:30 a.m. Sunday, December 31

From the other jewelry box gilt with lacy weaves of sterling and tiffany beads, Golly Gee unwrapped a second, freshly minted angel. The copy came customized with a beacon embedded for her archrival who, when not in lockdown for air-hockey hustling an off-duty, Las Vegas cop, didn't stay in one place too long. The master crafter did such a fine job Golly couldn't tell the two angels apart. Now came the true test. Did it work? She hooked up her newfangled satellite receiver built to outperform any on the market to pinpoint the guardian angel to a one-meter square area and locked in the bearings to *north Lake Michigan*! Peeved at her electronics supplier for making this unpardonable mistake, the only question she had for Jaxy when he returned to the hot seat was: Could he fix it?

Answered Jaxy, "Not without my tools—."

"Yes or no."

Yan asked, "Won't breaking the seal void the warranty? The monitor box should go back to the manufacturer the way it came. Unopened. What's another six weeks?"

"I don't have six weeks." From a stainless passthrough Golly deposited the canvas roll onto Jaxy's lap with the defective GPS system, soldering iron, multimeter, oscilloscope, power supply, programming keypad, and schematics.

"No car keys?" Jaxy pressed his luck.

"Earn them, my mouse." She slammed the flowery fanny pack repeating her maxim, "All men are monsters"—not mice—and cheeky musicians the worst of all. Notwithstanding they had useful properties, so she went over the Gollygraph® charts making fastidious notes. That she had farmed out the internal hit on Pops Lang to the Southern California branch office to skirt the ethics conundrum of rubbing out one of her own didn't give Jaxy fiat to barge into her boathouse to drop Pops on the day of the big dance. If, to his credit, it came to light that by posing as a rockabilly guitarist Jaxy circumnavigated the usual channels to safeguard the element of surprise, then the finding showed he moved fast.

At this juncture, following the Beaver Lodge Operations Manual of Enquiry, she would customarily grill a new prospect over an extended period before sending him on a new undertaking, or to the bottom of the bay depending on the outputs of a decision tree that could take weeks to construct. For this commission Golly had neither the luxury of time nor a more versatile candidate to vet on short notice, so came the whiteboard.

At the corner she circled "Project Cowgirl" in blue. Lateral and descending arrows linked geometric shapes. The courier's range of exploitable abilities she captured in red: Electronics Geek – Adept Smuggler – Cool Tools and Killer Shoes – Furniture Repair and Delivery – Whiz at Locating People – Moves Quick – Martial Arts and Weapons Skills TBD. At the bottom she grouped lifestyle and interests: Detail Oriented – Big Hair and Wardrobe – Old School Musician – Trivia Buff with Fair Retention – Hockey Fan – Poor Eyesight – Good with Children – Long Term Antique Mall Driver – Engaged 3+ Years – Are Fish Pets? From the pen cup she then took black to put herself in the mix with "Made Me Laugh", but when

Golly Gee tried to change it to "Smile" the ink would not rub off.

"Yaaaaan!!" Golly banged on the glass with the permanent marker.

The second in command placed his face into the mirrored window. "Need something?"

"Who put *THIS* in the dry erase can???"

"Probably you."

"Solvent and lab wipes! NOW!!"

Yan came with the requested items. "What happened?"

"It's what did NOT," she scrubbed at the loathsome letters with rubbing alcohol and conviction.

"A toonie says it did." Yan spun the two-dollar coin and stepped the spy-cam to where the kits extracted the Rockabilly's nasal vibrissa with pliers. The same scene caught her sharing a tummy laugh with Jaxy, something no man in the colony leader's violent, three decades of existence had accomplished. Galled at her lapse in vigilance, with a firm resolve to never go there again Golly purged the video files. From the side of the eye she then caught Jaxy drumming out the "Bro Hymn" upon successful compilation of working GPS code, and she couldn't help but crack up.

Affinity Diagrams be damned. With an "*iacta alea est,*" Golly Gee excused Yan to go sit with Jaxy while she composed an internal memo to the Russian Antique Mall:

Klav,

Congrats on your latest addition to the team! Where have you been hiding him—in a Matryoshka doll? A diamond in the rough, you have shaped Jaxy Thrie into a true asset. With the retirement of Pops Lang, he shall be deployed to Nevada. Contingent on his performance there, I will recommend "Rockabilly" to the Multidisciplined Assistant Assassin Field Applications Specialist II position at the start of Q3. Do not open a req for his replacement or extend a relo to island headquarters until I reach my final decision in July.

Also, have your 2017 accomplishments in by midnight, and next year's goals ready to share Tuesday. Don't make me remind you again.
Happy New Year!
GG

On a boilerplate proposal Golly then loaded the contract particulars of "Project Cowgirl", laying out the essentials of the operation but nothing of its purpose. At the end of six months Jaxy would then report in to be handed his assassins' permit, or his ass on a platter should he fail the mission.

WHILE GOLLY FINISHED THE paperwork in her half of the beaver head office, the men buttoned up the electronics on their side of the glass sharing pipe dreams: Yan's to buy out the mobile home park that screwed him so he could screw them back, and Jaxy's to marry his high school sweetheart and start his own music recording label. He then petitioned for something to eat.

Yan rolled in a trolley of pastries and super sweet coffee. "This will have to tide you over. Won't be long."

Concerned that a hit of sugar and caffeine would amp him up, Jaxy took small sips while waiting for his invisible tormentor to quit playing with the enhanced users interface and get to work. He gave a butter tart a polite nibble and immediately spat out the lodge-baked goodie into a serviette, fearing from the flavor the pie had been poisoned.

In haste, Yan bit off half and swallowed it down with an idiotic smile, "Aren't they scrumptious?"

Jaxy made a foul face at Yan's window reflection and passed on seconds.

In a low voice Yan urged, "Take one or you'll be—."

"Would Mr. Thrie care to relate something?" asked the modulated voice.

With a poker face, Yan bowed to the speaker box, "Jaxy was raving about your butter tarts."

"Was not," said Jaxy.

"Whooo! Strap him down," flowed the order.

Yan buckled tight the subject's rangy arms and legs. Then, upon clamping noise-cancelling earmuffs on his own head said, "Hope you put extra gonchies in that purse, sugar pie.

"HAD YOU MET POPS Lang before today?" The first one landed.

Jaxy braced himself. "No."

"Did you ever communicate by any means on any matter?" Followed in rapid succession.

"No."

"Do you recall him visiting the Russian Antique Mall?"

"Not to my knowledge—No."

"Give the man water, Yan, and keep going. Did Lang work alone?"

Jaxy took a drink. "Yes."

Time passed before the next. "Same question: Did you detect the presence of anyone other than Pops at the boathouse?"

"No," Jaxy replied, gaining confidence.

"Did you bludgeon, shoot, stab, suffocate, or electrocute him?"

"No."

"Inject, poison, or expose him to a lethal drug, chemical or gas?"

"No."

"Jesus Murphy! Did you excite, scare or bore him to death???"

"No."

"Did he take long to expire?"

"I cannot say."

"I respect that. Is that your car I see in the fifteen-minute slot?"

Since it belonged to a rental agency Jaxy answered, "No."

"Who then parked it there at ten o'clock this morning?"

"Can you couch that for a simple Yes or No, please?" Jaxy tightened his grip.

"Answer the stupid question."

"Then stop changing the stupid rules!"

"Fine. In violation of the conveyance bylaws of the unincorporated community of Beaver Island, British Columbia, did you leave a vehicle beyond the time allotted in a fifteen-minute limit zone thinking no one would give a cranberry if it sat there all day?"

"Yes."

Zap!!

"Not fair!" Jaxy pointed to the reversal in zapping policy.

"Life's not fair, Mister Thrie. Learn from your mistakes. Yes or no. Would people say you're a good dancer?"

Electroshocked for admissions of truth as well as falsehoods, he went with the trend: "No," he lied.

The styli took off in wild swings of magnitude, but no current flowed through the chair.

"As good as Michael Jackson?"

"Better." The needle nearly broke off the drum and hit the wall.

"Do you like butter tarts?"

He had only tried the one so guessed with "Yes." Jaxy's sphincter puckered as the pens gave erratic and mixed results.

"I'll rephrase: Do you like *my* butter tarts?"

Come what may, Jaxy could not bring himself to lie on the money question. To hell with it, he thought, and in defiance pronounced them "atrocious".

"Yes or no."

"No." The chart fell quiet as Jaxy dug his nails into the cushy armrests expecting to have his sorry ass singed to Singapore for that one.

After a lengthy and stressful pause the garbled voice said, "I cannot tell from your biometrics if you are a decent dancer, Mister Thrie, or if you just think you are. I must see you at the New Year's Eve party for further assessment."

"Thank you, but my fiancée is waiting for me in Vancouver. We're catching a flight to a show in Las Vegas, and I'm cutting it close."

"Is that a 'no'?"

"Yes."

ZAP!!!

CHAPTER 5

Beaver Island, B.C.
12:00 p.m. Sunday, December 31

On the elevator ride from the Beaver Head office to the ground floor Yan paid Jaxy a high compliment, "Man, dissing those tarts took beaver balls—and to walk away from the Gollygraph on your own power? That's a first. About the boathouse now—I want specifics."

"I can't believe I wasn't charbroiled right there in the chair for leaving the poor boy flopped over on his. Did he get looked after?"

"Autopsy's underway. The 'why' I get: Last month the Lodge intercepted Pops passing coded messages to a foreign entity, so contracted out the hit and you came through! Nice to have made your acquaintance."

"It's how I found him," Jaxy brushed aside the compliment, anxious to set the record straight that he had nothing to do with the soundman's death.

"—and left him, so anything more you can contribute we would appreciate. If competition sensitive or pending patent I can have legal draw up a non-disclosure. But if you developed a technique on the company dime, you are bound to submit an abstract to the Assassins Innovation and Engineering Symposium. It's a nuisance, but you'd be a shoo-in for the Eminent Keener Award."

Jaxy scuffed with his toe. "Looked to me like a heart attack."

"Naturally, you sly dog. No toxins, no marks, no nothing. You're good."

"Just lucky."

Yan scratched his head at the vacant Pick-Up and Drop-Off slot. "Or not."

Short of time, Jaxy stood on the drive berating the beaver brats that hotwired his car for a joyride.

"Not this time." Yan detached a citation from the parking sign. "Looks like the Island police towed it. Don't sweat it—we'll spring you free Tuesday. Meanwhile, Beaver lodging comes with Wi-Fi, premium movies, mud baths, and all the butter tarts you can eat."

"I need a ride NOW! And I'll thumb one if I have to!"

"I'll see what I can do," Yan hopped on the hotline, and in seconds the Beaver Island Airport Shuttle was on its way.

Before he could see it, Jaxy felt the Ural M70 flat twin motorcycle rumble up from the parkade. The zebra-striped, winter bike shifted to a stop, and the cyclist in an aviator jacket pointed down to the sidecar. With the other hand the shuttle chauffeur held out for double-time, holiday pay.

"That's highway robbery!" protested Jaxy, but neither did it surprise him, for these island brigands had him over the barrel. He emptied his wallet into her greedy paw and squeezed in accusing, "Didn't you assault me once today?"

"Don't you wish," the pint-sized rider stood high and wide on the pegs to cram the fare down her leather chaps.

"Sure act the same."

"If so, you wouldn't have enough change left over for a lift to Francis Point," she said, then hinging forward as out the gate they throttled towards Hopkins Landing.

On the ferry ride, Jaxy tried to find time alone, but the helmeted cyclist tagged along going off on women's pro motocross and how, in no way could she scrape by these days with the young hot-snots riding away with the endorsements. So, with injuries piling up she quit the circuit and found humanitarian work with the Beaver Lodge that offered private health coverage with a free, trial drug program for chronic pain. Unaware that this philanthropic, tax-exempt foundation sheltered the activities of a wanton band of hooligans, once inducted she had to change her name to "Chaps" and sever ties to the outside. The way out always ended badly for those who tried to leave the island—straight off the backend of a watercraft into sixty feet of brine.

Her struggles struck a sympathetic chord with Jaxy who told of his frustrations as a twenty-first century, fifties songwriter trapped in a dead-end job at a moldy warehouse with bad ventilation, and by a woman married to her work. While he droned, the shuttle driver divided a rice burrito between them, then walked off mid-sentence to eat and journal alone. As they made landing a black helicopter hovered off starboard. Chaps jumped up to curse at it, but it wouldn't move on until she gave the pilot the one-finger salute.

"What was that about?" asked Jaxy at the railing.

"Yan. Rocks his socks when I do that." She tore two pages from a composition notebook and then walked him back to the sidecar where she stuffed them into a bulky, bubble mailer.

"I see what you mean. There's no escaping."

"Like the girlfriend," she flicked a paint fleck from his Mighty Ducks logo.

Jaxy moved the hand off. "Careful, it's her special Christmas present."

"When she's not looking, trade up for a red rebel jacket. But I adore the shoes. They're keepers. And take *this* treasure," Chaps fondled the fanny pack, "back to the bargain bin."

"Remove your hand or I'm telling."

She turned away to raise the faceguard and wash down a pain pill. "And who do you think Yan will believe?"

"I see. What's with the cloak and dagger anyhow?" Jaxy tapped the opaque shield.

"Beaver regulation. I took it off at an outlet to try on a turtleneck and the witch gave me three days in the glue trap! You never can tell when or from where she watches—even in the changing stalls. I swear to you Jaxy, if I ever escape this shithole I'll show you my bellybutton ring. But to earn that, you have to get this guardian angel to my big sis in Las Vegas. Make sure she wears it. It will guide me to her." The cyclist pushed the mailer on Jaxy.

"What? I'm not touching that again."

"You said you're headed to a concert there."

"Buick Slick and the Stud Nuts."

"So . . . I thought maybe . . ."

"You're not serious."

"Am too. It's a peace sign. Sticks out like this," she wiggled a pinky on her navel.

"Not that—this! Can't you mail it?" Jaxy gave it a once-over.

"Jillian moves a lot. You're a professional. Follow the directions I put inside and you'll find her. But we have to act before the Beavers know it's gone and Gollygraph *me*!"

"You're too trusting. I could turn it—and you—in for a reward."

"As big as this?" the cycle chauffeur flashed a Beaver Island Credit Union money card with Jaxy's name printed on a red nosed reindeer. "How does ten thousand in U.S. sound? Five now, the rest after the job's done."

Jaxy shoved the gift card with the mailer and two pages of delivery instructions into the fanny pack. "Like the start of a beautiful, new recording studio."

The stretch to Vancouver International Airport went without incident. As he disembarked Jaxy asked about the object of value inside the bubble mailer, "What do I tell customs?"

"What you said coming in."

"Going out's not as simple."

"Jesus Murphy! It's a phony. Lose that godawful belly bag and wear it."

"Specifically mine? Or do you hate all fanny packs in general?"

"Whooo! That's a complex question," Golly Gee flipped him a butter tart and roared down the road to Beaver Island.

CHAPTER 6

Vancouver International Airport, B.C.
3:00 p.m. Sunday, December 31

Guinevere Hill Esquire; Attorney-at-Law, and Glendale City Councilmember had three functional tones of voice: Business-friendly for everyday commerce at home, work, the gym, and social occasions; scorching-bitchy for hammering home a point when other lines of logic failed; and saccharine-sweet reserved for the jury, her father when she needed something, and Jaxy in BIG trouble.

"Who was that?" Guin poured it on as she came up to Jaxy at the airport curbside.

Jaxy slumped against a luggage cart muttering, "Holy mother of Christ."

Guin shaded her eyes at the stuffed beaver growing smaller in the distance, "Didn't look like her to me."

To remain impartial till she had the facts, Guin allowed her man his opening statement as to why a leather clad biker rode him to the airport after locking himself out in a tow zone. Rather than cane the scatterbrain for mislaying his keys, she granted a continuance for the compelling reason that she couldn't wait another second to tell the wonderful news! Due to a last-minute dropout, the mayor summoned her to represent the city of Glendale in the Rose Parade, and tomorrow she'd be waving to the world from her mother's '68 convertible! The downside? The freshman councilmember had to head straight back to wax the whitewalls and could not ring in the New Year at the Stud Nuts concert.

Consequently, Jaxy could return home with her, or go it alone to Las Vegas. After kicking it around they kissed and parted ways on the promise that he would make it in time for the Rose Bowl party by bus or plane, *but no motorcycles*! This brought a genuine smile to Guin's face. Jaxy always found a way.

FRAZZLED BY FUSILLADES OF parties and parades, and drained by the longest day of his life, Jaxy didn't think about the fanny pack before dropping it on the conveyer. As a consequence, airport security thought about it for him, and the last day of the year got longer.

With shoes hanging from his fingertips Jaxy proclaimed his innocence, "Honest, I'm a courier for the Russian Antique Mall. The tools are for guitar repair, and they meet boarding standards."

The presiding official said, "We don't give a fig about the hardware. Where do you intend to take this?" he indicated the guardian angel.

At the sight of converging uniforms with black garrison belts and batons, Jaxy's tongue went thick and his mind blank, "On . . . an airplane?"

To the collecting crowd the head official translated: "What Mister Thrie wants to say is that he carried this one-of-a-kind Fabergé into Canada on company business and didn't claim it coming back because it originated in America. Fact is—it didn't. Six months ago, professionals lifted *The Guardian Angel of Maria Feodorovna* from the Romanov Imperial Museum in Denmark."

An ogler asked, "What's the worth?"

From a cheat sheet he read, "A hundred million crowns, but

according to the curator the symbolic value beats that by an undefined amount. Needless to say, the safe return of this hot potato is an Interpol priority."

"Put that in dollars," requested another.

"Twenty million give or take, depending how bad a person wants it, or wants to keep someone else from having it. But to the one who nabs the thief?" he threw Jaxy a pleasant smile, "the Romanov Guild has promised a fully loaded Gran Coupe."

On the brink of a breakdown, Jaxy rolled out his defense: "I haven't left the continent since the Rio Olympics."

"No one says you did."

"Then this must be a reproduction. A legit one."

"It's your word against the experts, so unless you produce a paper trail that says otherwise, plan on seeing the new year in Canada."

Hope rose as Jaxy called up the tablet purchase order for one copy of a Fabergé angel milled from 3-D images. Line-by-line he walked them through the invoice, but when he opened the waybill, his chest went into a freefall. Rather than putting the originator's name and address on the docket, the underhanded artisan sourced a Siberian, precious metals refinery, pricing out the deliverable commodities on a single line for twenty-two million euros, marked for delivery to a non-existent, shell company in Glendale, California.

To the ground Jaxy dropped with hands behind his neck, believing he had lost all. And well he might, if not for the timely arrival of Border Services Agent Pierre de Chavoie known to Jaxy in a different context as "Yan".

"Whew! Glad I caught up!" Superintendent de Chavoie addressed the group from a balancing, two-wheel scooter. "I trust sugar pie didn't throw any bullshido at you."

"No more than the usual." They formed a line to shake the Mountie's hand.

"Good, because the man you're about to take downtown is a bona fide, Carl Fabergé, Subject Matter Expert from Moscow, and damn good with balalaika too, aren't you, Gospodin Thriesky?"

From his knees Jaxy affirmed with a slight nod and huge relief.

"So, my good people, if the novelty you found in the ambassador's possession is bogus, then it stands to reason he has bogus paperwork to go with it! Da?" Yan delivered an inconspicuous kick.

"Da," said Jaxy.

"But the real 'hockey puck' recently surfaced and the Mounted Police impounded it at a restricted camp. That phony angel he's taking to Las Vegas is for a sting operation. Black marketeers will come from far and wide to bid, not knowing he set them up. Now, if you'll give back his shoes, there's a vodka and ginger beer on a plane with his name on it."

And with that Yan laid the question to rest, confiscated the guardian angel, and scootered off.

THRILLED TO HAVE THAT millstone off his neck, Jaxy scuttled to the gate in time to watch his plane back onto the tarmac. "Gaw!" he clapped his shoes together, checking the next departure.

"Always fly WWA. They have the best cookies," said Yan rolling up on his scooter. Down the mezzanine they then buzzed to the Wild West Airlines counter. Before Jaxy could count down the top ten reasons for leaving Canada as fast as possible he stood at the jetway with a new pass on the glass.

"Put sugar pie on the aisle with lots of leg room." Yan ordered the comely flight attendant with arching, apple green eyes.

The crewmember cocked her white Cowgirl hat over a dirty-blonde ponytail. "Huu, Superintendent! The plane is stuffed, and everyone's boarded."

Yan pointed at her aviator vest tag, "It's first class or your ass,

Avlon—I know your husband."

"Aye, aye!" Aviator Avlon snapped to attention while the men engaged in a sidebar.

"I appreciate the gesture, 'Superintendent', but I thought you came to keep an eye on the shuttle driver—not me," said Jaxy while waiting for his first class seat reassignment.

"I'm following the puck. Keeping it in play." Yan forced the mailer into Jaxy's hands.

"The heck??? No way!"

Yan clamped a hand on Jaxy's mouth. "Like I said. This isn't *the* Fabergé. Just a good look-alike."

"So good it almost landed me in the penalty box."

"Hockey sticks. I could have whistled the play dead anytime. I wanted to see how far down ice you could work it shorthanded. You almost poked it through! Hard part's over. Give up that stutter and how you killed Pops Lang—and you'll do alright."

"I didn't touch Pops."

Yan took a note: "'Did not touch Pops. That's a start."

Jaxy held the bubble mailer over a trash receptacle saying, "I don't get your game, but it ends here unless you can guarantee that Chaps retires unharmed for sneaking this off the island for you."

"Hell, I'm not sure I'll see my bed tonight or wake from it if I do. But if it helps you sleep—I'm her bodyguard." Yan patted his pit holster.

"Then what gives with the twenty-four surveillance, confinement, and pain pills?"

"We take those measures for her own good because in her racing days Chaps took one helmet hit too many, and if the woman hasn't figured out by this time that that bellybutton piercing transmits, she never will. And not to rain on your Rose Parade, but you hadn't a realistic chance at seeing it to begin with. Now, I don't give a rat's patootie if you make Vegas on time, but when I saw the Wild West manifest, I pulled strings to put you on her sister's plane for you kids to get acquainted. Careful though, when lit, Avlon's hubby is one mean hombre."

Jaxy looked over to the green-eyed attendant. "You mean that's *her*? Chap's sister?"

Yan nudged Jaxy. "Go get her tiger."

With grateful sarcasm Jaxy said, "How thoughtful, Yan. But married or not, I would never flirt with a woman at work. Besides, my fiancée wouldn't stand for it. Which brings me to the Rose Parade. Chaps didn't mention it—*Guin did.* So, where did you plant my bug—in my bellybutton too?"

From Jaxy's fanny pack Yan dug a green, alien face guitar pick, and crushed it underfoot. "There. You're wire free, so you owe me. How *did* you kill Pops?"

"With a balalaika."

"Smart aleck." The henchman of many hats clipped on his earphones, hopped on the two-wheeler and careened down the colonnade to the helipad.

Jaxy gave him a ten-second start, then on a hunch that Yan crushed the wrong guitar pick cupped the fanny pack to his mouth and yelled, "Yan! Heads Up!!!"

Startled out of his wits, Yan ripped off the headset, lost grip of the handlebar, and took out a kiosk with his head held high.

"Watch out for what?" Aviator Avlon asked, separating the backing from an adhesive stub.

"Flying bugs," Jaxy tossed the remaining guitar picks in the trash.

"Profanity, sir, is not tolerated in my cabin." She knelt to tag the backpack.

"You mean I can't take it on? It always fit before!" Jaxy clung to the soft frame as a baby joey.

"We're full! Do I have to spell it?" Her eyebrows arched to the sky.

"Can you?" Jaxy arched his.

"*F. U.* double L. Hug a pillow."

AS IT TURNED OUT, Wild West Airlines hadn't booked the flight close to capacity leaving an abundance of compartment space. Aviator Avlon was simply a brat. Even so, Jaxy could not help admiring her eyes while not giving his permission to wander. For, engaged to a well-positioned lawyer with an address in the Verdugos, despite Guin Hill's periodic paroxysms, he had a good thing at home. His opinion of Aviator Avlon dropped another notch when she passed him over for drinks. Not that he wanted a ginger beer with his name on it, but she could have asked.

At a touch and go in Portland, a passenger built like Johnny Bravo took the window and dropped off in the bat of an eye. Jaxy sacrificed shoulder room, snugged in the earbuds to the "Restless" sounds of Rockabilly Rat, and unfolded his legs and the letter from the mailer scrawled in cribbed, choppy longhand.

Dear Jaxy:

In your bag you will find a guitar pick wired with a one-way sending, peace sign antenna. The transducer is sensitive and prone to distortion so use your inside voice to sign-in when you land. My device will recognize the waveforms and pair them through a firewall the Beavers can't hack.

The scope of "Project Cowgirl" is simple. Deliver the package to my twin sister Jillian by Valentines, or I may never get off the island. Do what you must to persuade her to accept the gift short of crossing her husband. No dalliance is worth that.

Forever yours,
Chaps

Clipped to the cover sheet came the recipient's dossier. Jaxy couldn't decide if it read like a dating personal, a sports profile, or a rap sheet:

Jillian "J.D." Avlon. Thirty-two years, five foot one, 34-24-38, green eyed, occasional blonde, WWA Flight Attendant. Colorado State University Class of 2008 graduate on a softball scholarship. B.A. in PoliSci. Southpaw. Undefeated at air hockey in her last four dozen matches, also enjoys Frisbee, art, petting zoos, and the racetracks. Served six months in County for fixing competitive games of wager. Reinstated by the airlines, but banned from employee housing, lives out of Las Vegas hotels and country bars. Married three years. Prefers older men. Enjoys conversation. Non-smoker. Light drinker. Picky eater. Not into music.

Not into music!—despaired Jaxy. What on earth could they converse about? Polo? Politics? Pruno? Air hockey they had in common, but the best of small talkers couldn't carry that far.

"Cookie?" Aviator Avlon came by with a sampling of snacks.

"No, I'm Jaxy. Cookie's asleep at the window. And you are . . ." Jaxy craned at her tag to make sure he had the name right.

"Busy." Jillian turned a shoulder.

"Jackson Thrie, actually. Shall we start at the top?"

"Let's not," she laced tight the Wild West uniform vest.

"That's not what I meant. I'm not that kind."

The WWA attendant spun on a bootheel. "There's only one 'kind' of you. And just because you happen to know some border collie who says he knows my husband, don't assume you know me, and I have no qualms in asking 'Cookie' to help you off the plane this minute if you as much as look at my top one more time."

"Down, Jillian, down. Peanuts if you got them," said Jaxy with dampening hands.

"Huu! We're on first name?!?"

The drowsy, window traveler disagreeably grunted with an

attention-grabbing burp.

"Oh no, Ms . . . Ms . . .!" Jaxy pushed the overhead panic button.

Through an array of sparkling dental work she bared, "Avlon?"

"Avlon, right! He's about to . . ." Jaxy thumbed at his partner.

Jillian arched her brows at the placid, window passenger mulling the drink menu.

". . . order?" Jaxy meekly finished.

"Horny Bull on ice, and fizz water with an antihistamine for my friend."

"I'm not airsick. But thank you."

"Something's got you rattled. When's the last time you ate?"

"It's not that. Women make me nervous. Not all, just some—like that one."

"You want to meet her?"

Mildly embarrassed, Jaxy said, "Yeah. I would."

"Then your approach is ass-backwards."

"So, act cool like you? That's the problem. I can't."

"Nah. That's bullshit. A cutie like that can only be won over by sympathy."

Jillian returned with the items and a barf bag. She patted Jaxy's head, "No reason to be ashamed. Try not to miss."

"Lookie there! Didn't I say? Warming up to you already. Now convince her."

"How?" asked Jaxy.

The man demonstrated the move.

"Like so?" Jaxy placed a finger on his own tongue.

"Further back."

Jaxy tried but nothing came up. He then thought about the butter tart in his coat pocket and refluxed. On the unappetizing morsel Jaxy meditated, weighing the cost, but Jillian was one tough nut and he may not get another shot at cracking her defenses.

He took a bite. It was worse than he remembered.

"Oh mercy, mercy," Jillian hustled with towels and antiacids to help Jaxy to the water closet, telling him to take his time.

Until he tried with the door folded shut to kneel, Jaxy did not appreciate how tight an inflight lavatory could become. As the walls closed in, every heave of rice burrito and butter tart illustrated how one bad choice after another had boxed him in. As he flushed the chunks along with his noble speech out the vacuum pipes, he vowed never again to flirt with anyone but Guin. Still, he had accepted an appreciable amount for a delivery job, so Jaxy squared his moral compass and sallied forth for a forthright way to pass the gift to Jillian, to find Jillian passing the time with his ruggedly handsome seat partner!

"Win some. Lose some," the beefcake rubbed it in with the offer of a breath mint while showing off Jillian's number already listed with his favorites. "On record the name's Rory—retired marine—but if duty calls? I'm combat ready! Friends call me 'The Captain'."

"Jaxy. Jaxy Thrie."

"What kind of wussy name is that—can I call you Jack?"

"Some do," Jaxy slouched, energy spent.

"Don't take it to heart, son," the Captain polished off his tequila and orange juice with a Hollywood smile. "That Cowgirl's my wife."

CHAPTER 7

Beaver Island, B.C.
5:00 p.m. Sunday, December 31

On the last ferry boat back Golly Gee watched for Jaxy's signal of a safe landing in Vegas, but picked up nothing but a nag mail from her godfather. With Epiphany around the bend, the time drew nigh for the great blessing of the Beaver Pond, and every year she had to come up with a new excuse for putting it off: The dam leaked. The kits were holding a bake sale. The ISO audit had come due. She had run out of ideas! Furthermore, the priest hinted that too much time had lapsed since her last confession. Hmm—should she rubout the California courier before or after? Decisions-decisions. Golly Gee reviewed her calendar and said she'd get back.

Home and safe inside the Beaver Lodge motor pool, Golly removed the helmet, peeled off her chaps . . . and breathed. She checked the incoming messages for the umpteenth time. Nothing. Against sound practice she attempted an unsecured call, but Jaxy didn't respond. Probably at the concert with HER!! Girlfriends were pushovers, and wives she could work around, but breaching the battlements of the betrothed? At the boathouse pavilion Golly Gee found distraction in arranging banquet tables and setting places by seniority, but her spirits sank when the roster showed everyone with a date—including Yan!

Not feeling well, she let him step in as master of ceremonies to excuse herself, filling a dessert plate as she left the boathouse. Favoring her lower lumbar from the rigors of the ride, off Golly Gee galumphed to the pond, passing partygoers in twos and fours along the boardwalk coming down the other way. At the dark and deserted lodge house, she unloosed her trusty rowboat, the Standart, from its moorings and cast off into the brume of night to become one with the sleeping frogs of winter.

Some New Year's dance! Golly stuffed an entire slice of lemon-frosted cake in her mouth. Fiancées ruin everything.

CHAPTER 8

McCarran International Airport, Las Vegas, Nevada
6:00 p.m. Sunday, December 31

With a heart overflowing for not having broken out the jewelry box in front of Jillian Avlon's combat-ready husband, Jaxy prepared to deplane. On the descent he listened to the Captain run off about a union bash he planned to crash, followed by a week of mountaineering. Jaxy made mention of the show he would attend after getting down on hands and knees to kiss the land of the free. Then toasting the retired marine for commendable service to his country, he raised the seat to land.

Forty minutes and two peanut tubes later Jaxy came to learn at baggage claim that his, alas, went to Flagstaff! "Gaw! You're kidding me. That no-good, little—I'm gonna—."

A wolf-whistle cut through the portico, and there went that little no-good down the escalator, twirling her hat on one finger and pretending to throw-up with the other.

"Jillian! Wait!! I have something!!!" ran Jaxy hard after, but by the time he reached the gangway too many travelers clogged the lane and he lost visual. He asked the courtesy counter where she might be headed, but WWA declined to divulge employee information. With time to kill before the Stud Nuts show, Jaxy browsed the internet for country dives that hosted air hockey and started calling.

"Hi, I made a date with J.D. tonight. Could you let her know I'm running late?"

"Haven't seen her in weeks…" "Slapped them cheeks out the door when she be messin' with my man . . ." "Try the Detention Center," back came the replies.

On the fourth attempt Jaxy got a hit.

"You probations?" asked the bar owner.

"Tell her to stay *put*," said Jaxy with authority. "I'll be there in ten."

Jaxy took an instant liking to the place, for midst the garish pageantry of Sin City, Klinnick's Bar and Grill stood out as a sanctuary of sanity, billing a rotation of country swing bands to entertain the common folk. Regulation dart lanes, a pinball arcade, and gaming stations took up every square inch unoccupied by the drinking clientele, so it mystified him as to where they staged the groups.

On the mailer he wrote Jillian's name in care of the saloon, pulled low the courier cap, and ducked under the mistletoe to approach the one person behind the bar not wearing a Klinnick's shirt. "Pardon, ma'am, I have a carton addressed to one of your workers—a Ms. Jillian Avlon. Any chance she'll clock in tonight?"

The saloon owner looked over the orange, vertical striped shirt, cuffed chinos, and Gatsby wingtips. "Ladies room. Could be a while."

"I'll wait."

As a supporter of small businesses, Jaxy tried the "Klinnickly Dead" house brew with a plate of baked beans and ribs. While his order came up he placed a quick call to his Glendale homies that he'd finally found an air hockey contender worth playing with a winning streak as long as his.

Tap. Tap. Tap.

At Jaxy's side arrived the ponytailed Cowgirl with her vest undone and stirring a pink, umbrella drink.

"You? Again?!? Fffff . . ." Jillian almost let fly the unmentionable word for the second time that day, and in a jiffy had her top laced shut.

Jaxy quieted her outspoken opinion with an explanation of his business while he dove into the ribs.

"Who from?" she studied the mailer with suspicion.

"Your sister." Jaxy smacked his fingers, "the one in Canada."

"I don't have a sister in Canada." Jillian took the pen from his ear and wrote, "Return to Sender" across the front.

Jaxy tugged at a buckskin fringe. "It came with a card."

"Got the wrong Jillian Avlon," she flicked his hand away.

"How many of you work for the airlines?"

The owner butted in, "J.D. doesn't have a sister, mister . . . PERIOD!"

"It's hard. I get it. Same happened after this fight with my fiancée over a refurbished washer I surprised her with. Didn't speak to me for a week, but I eventually got it to work—and you can too! If your sis is reaching out, why not reach back?" asked Jaxy.

"We're done here." Jillian finished off the cocktail.

"Then give Buick Slick a chance. The Stud Nuts kick off at nine and I have an extra ticket."

"Like this town can use another comedian," the boisterous bar owner said causing those around to har-har, and then left to let Jillian deal with the clown.

"Then how about a friendly game of air hockey?" Jaxy asked.

"No such thing," Jillian grabbed his lapel. "You're vice, aren't you? I'm clean, so beat it, buster!"

"I'm a professional. I play for gasoline and groceries." He slipped her a Fat Pipes business card.

In doubt, Jillian looked at the band member's faces sticking out the end of a chrome exhaust stack. "Music or hockey?"

"Both."

"Not very good."

"Don't judge a band by the logo."

"That you mention it," she took the pen and improved upon it. "Talking about my air hockey game."

"Forty-eight straight? You sound terrible."

"Forty-nine."

"You're the bomb-diggity in the basin. Handle's 'Rock-a-Billy' by the way—reigning champ at Ted's Pool Shed. I'd hoped to show the bros at home you can't make fifty."

Jillian reached for the envelope. "Thought you came to give me that."

Jaxy pulled it away with a shake. "What's inside envelope number one, she's asking?"

Jillian rang up Ted's Pool Shed. "Hello, I'm calling to authenticate air hockey chump 'Rock-a-Billy' says he's kick-ass good . . . he is . . . please describe . . . six foot . . . looks like Buddy Holly, that's him, thanks—Hold on! Ever heard of 'J.D. Avlon'? . . . *Forty-nine*!!!"

"You think I look like Buddy Holly?" Jaxy put his black-rimmed eyeglasses on with a dimpled smile.

"Huu! He's way cuter." Sweat beaded up on Jillian's lip as she pulled in close. "Round one starts at a dollar and doubles each turn, so unless you're sitting on a thick wad, I recommend you cave before my P.O. shows up, as that could get expensive for us both."

To a framed glossy of J.D. Avlon in a wet tee hanging by the jukebox Jaxy turned, "All I want is your signature on that saying I beat you in nine."

"And all I want is for you to pay up after I cleat your Rockabilly backside in seven, but I need collateral, or I bounce."

Jaxy wrapped his Mighty Ducks jacket around her shoulders. "Don't spill on it. And from you?"

Jillian placed her white, felt hat on his head. "Don't get it sweaty."

"It'll be over before I break one."

Jillian ground his knuckles in a viselike squeeze, "You got that right."

When Jillian went to raid the register of tokens Rita Klinnick pulled her aside, "Are you out of your mind? You still have four months' probation. And what's with the jacket?"

"For bragging rights."

"Who you be braggin' to—the judge?"

"Match fifty then I hang it up. Please—please—please?"

"Promise?"

"Pinky promise."

Rita flipped the "Closed" sign, lowered the shades, latched the door, and announced over the karaoke, "Cowgirls and boys, your attention please. Klinnick's Bar and Grill is closed for a special, New Year's Eve air hockey event. You are welcome to stay and root on your favorite, or if you wish to leave you may do so by the alley. We will not allow photography during the match."

Excited murmurs rippled through the hall as the patrons heard the motor whirr and whish of air, and upon winning the flip, saw J.D. take her end of the table for the first time in a year.

The owner continued, "At the south end, coming to us from Glendale, California, tonight's challenger, Rock-a-Biiiiiiiilly!"

"Boo!" jeered the crowd.

"And at the other, although she needs no introduction for her record speaks for itself, going for her fiftieth straight, Air Hockey Queen of Clark County, Jillian 'J.D.' Aaaaavlon!"

"Yay!!!" hooted the spectators clearing out tables and chairs to set up an ad hoc stadium. It was game on.

Jillian won the face-off, but Jaxy didn't roll over as expected at the crack of plastic. The clacking of mallets increased in speed and racket as he swept the puck into the goal.

"She's rusty," said one.

"Setting him up," said another.

The next points didn't come easy to Jillian, for while her strength lay in a fast and unrelenting offense, Jaxy's did in his reflexes to fight off her tricky spins and curves. They traded sides twice more, and at halfway Jillian went up by two. At the break they were kept apart to prevent even a hint of bunko. Side bets took a serious turn as some broke rank to chase higher paying odds on the dark horse from Glendale.

At the buzzer Jaxy came out mallet swinging and took three to go ahead. On a change of tactics, Jillian switched hands and smashed home back-to-back victories then got penalized for palming. Jaxy scored with ease on the unguarded goal.

"That cost me!" Jillian challenged the call. "Whose side are you on?"

"Bullpuck. You were going to give that point away to build the pot. Probations is coming and we need to wrap this up," goaded the referee, and sent the players to the opposite ends of the bar for a brief respite before facing sudden death.

Up by a grand, if Jaxy lost the thirteenth he could break out the money card, but he had a better plan. He caught Jillian's eye and felt for his wallet with a distressed look. Jillian slipped her arms into the Mighty Ducks jacket to admire the new fashion in the mirror. Jaxy shook "no" and opened the mailer to allow her a peek at the jewelry box. Jillian nodded, threw back another pink drink, and dropped the remaining token in the slot.

The ferocity and length of the final match lived long in Klinnick's lore, as Jaxy went on the defensive to drag it out. At one point Jillian slammed the puck so hard it snapped in half off the table shade while the spectators dove for the pieces. In the end her wicked sidearm prevailed, and the Clark County Air Hockey Queen laid claim to game fifty.

The cheers, backslapping, and whistles for the hometown honey were interrupted by a rude bang on the window and a blaring bullhorn ordering Rita Klinnick to open up.

"Private party! Sorry you didn't get the memo!" yelled the owner.

The officer came right back. "A Cowgirl was seen coming in off the six-thirty, so don't make this hard or I'll bust your cheeks too."

"Warm up the karaoke," Jaxy told the owner as he snagged the wet-T picture from the wall and muscled Jillian to the lady's room where he ordered her to strip.

"WHAT?????" Jillian went beet red.

Jaxy handed off the mailer inside the hat. "I can't be caught with this on my person again, so take it and go. I'll stall the cops." Jaxy faced away, unbuckling his trousers.

While Jillian disrobed, she upbraided him, "Gheck! I said don't get it sweaty. The hat's yours now."

"Good. I need it. Here," Jaxy traded back for his shirt.

Jillian pinched her nose and dropped it in the trash bucket, then zipped up the Mighty Ducks jacket over the bubble mailer clinched to her chest. "This'll do."

"Give it back! The jacket's a special inaugural season edition and not part of the bet."

"Neither was my hat."

Jaxy slid the photograph out. "Then sign this for something to hawk at Ted's for a replacement."

Across the front she penned: To Rock-a-Billy, the second-best, air hockey jock west of the river, xo J.D. "Now pucker up," she said.

Jaxy pulled away, "I'm in a committed relationship."

"Like this," Jillian formed an open pout.

"Mmm-mm," fought Jaxy with spirited resistance while she applied peach gloss to his mouth.

"How many pets do you have?" Jillian asked.

"Gah! What does it matter?"

"Stop talking so I can do this."

"You should have been a dentist."

She arched her eyebrows.

"Do fish count?" Jaxy asked anyway.

"On their finn-gers. Get it? Fingers?"

"Six. You really don't like music?"

Jillian touched up the edges replying, "Any animal song is good."

"Didn't take you for an Eric Burdon groupie."

"Done. Now you're cuter," she said, stopping momentarily to free a ladybug caught in the screen as she vaulted in cuffed chinos through the alley window, wingtips first, as the parole officer came knocking.

Jaxy lipped out to the hall in falsetto, "Can't Rock-a-Filly have her privacy between sets?"

In reply the cops busted off the knob, but instead of J.D. Avlon they found Jaxy Thrie in a fringed, WWA miniskirt and felt hat, with two rolls of toilet tissue stuffed up the vest.

"Let's go girls!" strutted Jaxy in cramped, snakeskin boots to the microphone stand, where twanging away like Shania Twain let "Man! I Feel Like a Woman" rip.

CHAPTER 9

St. Maximos the Confessor Greek Orthodox Church,
Minnehaha, Washington
9:00 a.m. Monday, January 1, 2018

The light turnout for a Monday liturgy filed forward to receive the sacrament. Last in line, a half-pint poppet in a patchwork shawl, apron dress, and snagged, mismatched cottons slouched around Chuck Taylor All Stars took her place to partake from the ruddy hand of a like-sized officiator with a silver-streaked goatee that complemented his thick, wavy hair.

The Greek priest returned the spoon untouched to the chalice. "See me at confession—and tie your shoes."

"I'll be waiting," Golly Gee wrapped her face and left for his office.

At refreshment hour Fr. Michael Klapakis caught the younger of identical twin headaches propping her unlaced sneakers atop his broad, oak desk to put drops in her eyes.

"Out of my chair," the priest knocked the hi-tops to the floor.

Golly Gee returned them. "Do that again and I'll report you to the bishop."

"Do dat again and I report you to police," he swatted them a second time.

"Help, help! A leetle woman with beeg, giant boobs is sitting in my chair!" Golly mocked into the phone, then relinquished the cracked and creaking leather to go preen the Ficus of brown leaves that were falling to the threadbare carpet between two tall, casement windows trimmed in a depressing tone of Nantucket blue.

"You won't bless pond, and you no give confession, so why come—to check on plants and say, 'Happy New Year'? Happy New Year. Now go do whatever you do when not pouring rat poison down someone's pipe," Fr. Michael jabbed at the door and broke out his tobacco kit to tend his own.

"I made good on my promise and stopped sanctioning that. I'm idea shopping for this year's resolution. Got any?"

"I do. Become better team player by pulling your family together instead of blowing it apart with leetle, letter bombs."

"Wasn't me! But if it scares my brother off, so much the better. I do love his gargoyles. Someday I'll own his entire collection—except for this—it you may keep." Golly tied back the curtain swag to shed light on the Jean Roche original painting: *The Bored Chimerae.*

"Tank you. And how do you plan to scare off beeg sister? Drag her husband down Sunnyside by your sidecar?"

Golly slipped him a gift card to his favorite golf pro-shop and a freshly baked butter tart. "To start the bonding, I want the Avlons in couples' counseling so I won't have to."

Fr. Michael bounced the pastry off the desk and caught it on the rebound. "Shape 'em into golf balls and I take dozen, but I can't make your sister stay with dat loser no matter how many you bake. She no listen to me either."

"Then have Jillian put off serving divorce papers till August. And for your rock collection," from her blouse Golly Gee whipped out a gold pendant ablaze with sapphires and diamonds, "this you may have after the coronation."

At the legendary Fabergé the priest stroked his goatee. "*The Guardian Angel of Maria Feodorovna* taken from the Imperial Museum of Art and Antiquities on the day the board of trustees announce it go to Romanov crown heir—or heiress, elect."

Her eyes flashed, "Taken, yes, but not stolen! When Rat Catcher blew my brother out of contention in Paris, the Romanov Guild staged the break-in to blame the assassination attempt on me! So, I jacked it from them and had the clock shop make a first-rate imitation with a homing device for my sister. It's a beauty! Once Jillian has it around her impeccable neck, I'll file an objection as to why I don't trust those strict, Romanov House Lawyers not to redirect the Fabergé angel to some presumptive, male claimant and took it back in support of Jillian as the legitimate Empress of all the Russias."

"And in advertising this, send Rat Catcher down the hole to do your dirty work here as he tried in France, taking home the tracker from your dead sister's head as trophy where you will hunt him down, slap him around and throw to the fishes, leaving you as the great Romanov vindicator and last Grand Duchess standing." Fr. Michael fleshed out the diabolic ruse.

"Whooo! Am I *that* obvious?"

"Clairvoyance, Golly, you do not require. But if that rat fails to take the cheese, unequally wed or not, should you not be more concerned about your reputation than the Avlons?"

"Bah, I can't even get locked up for road rage. Good Lord I've tried. And they can't deny the vast amounts for disaster relief the Beaver Lodge has raised this year alone—us God-fearing underdogs got to stick together. You should see the thank-you cards pile up. And don't forget academic scholarships, and grants for sustainable agriculture and medicines to the third world. It's all there. Food, clothing, water purification, wind and solar harnessing, educational toys, school supplies, clinic upgrades . . ."

Fr. Michael stopped listening at "God-fearing underdogs" and let Golly sing her praises to exhaustion while he replenished the jellybeans. "I look forward to your Nobel Peace Prize acceptance speech."

"You just heard it." She licked a thumb to spit shine her

Eleemosynary pin.

The priest stood to address an Astoria framed portraiture of two seated adults surrounded by four teenage girls and a younger boy in a sailor suit. "Your generosity impressive, Golly, but it exists to serve your agenda. You are nothing like your ancestors."

Golly viewed the century-old print of the Tsar's family facing back at the desk. "And Jillian is? I, at least, know a little po russki, a lot about DNA—."

"Graft, hostile takeovers, tax evasion, and making bodies disappear."

"May I finish?"

"Is that possible?"

With a graceful curtsey, across the office she waltzed the priest through a reverse fleckerl, "My way around a ballroom. All I need is Saint Olga's corset from the Ipatiev House, and I'm set."

At the killer's sacrosanct regard for a martyr's shed blood the priest gave a wistful smile and spun the medallion around, "If the copycat is that remarkable, how do you tell them apart?"

"Easy! Let's see where my new, promising recruit is today," Golly Gee fired up the powerful apparatus. According to the coordinates, however, instead of galivanting the Southwest with her California courier, the angel reproduction with the implanted chip had found its way to Minnehaha coming to rest on Golly's own breast.

"*Awwww JAXY*!!!" She ripped off the replica and flung it at the wall, then collapsed into the priest's chair devouring lemon jellybeans by the handful.

With the same respect given the genuine article, Fr. Michael cleaned, kissed, and gave her back the reject. "And the real guardian angel went where?"

"Las Vegas," moaned Golly. Then recovering her composure returned the fake to the saddle bag, tucked her tummy in the vesting mirror, and concluded their business, "Before jetting off to Reuben's clock shop, I need a recommendation."

"That is what godfather is for! How can I help?"

"What do you feed a Rockabilly?"

TUTORED BY A PROTÉGÉ of the great Fabergé, Remarkable Reuben Reisenschein not only ran the finest jewelry emporium in Copenhagen, his alarm clocks were the pride of Scandinavia. That is until Golly Gee, to suit her ever-growing fancy of global expansion, moved him at gunpoint halfway around the globe to Vancouver, Washington with the pact that someday she'd return him to Denmark a wealthier man.

Although Golly demanded to see him this New Year's morn, Reuben opted out to go experience the fair waters of Cabo San Lucas until her tizzy blew over. An urgent call from sanitation about a mice invasion, however, delayed his leave-taking. Maintenance had already opened up, so with hexagonal wireframes balanced on the tip of his nose, Remarkable Reuben scoured the storefront for droppings or destructive gnawing. Finding nothing, the pudgy watchmaker questioned the pest inspector roaming the shop in a Tyvek suit for any sign of rodent.

The exterminator deadbolted the door, dimmed the blinding track lights, and put the angel tracker to the balding man's glasses. "Just one. You."

Perspiration trickled from the jittery jeweler's hairy ear onto the beeping touchscreen. "It works, doesn't it?"

"It won't if you keep drizzling on it!" Golly Gee proceeded to demonstrate how to address signal, offer a tissue from a pocket pack, and mag load a single stack all at once. "What I want, Reuben, is to tell the master angel from the mockup without having to rely on electronics."

A bank of red and orange CCTV diodes running up a pedestal post blinked, boosting Reuben's courage. "Can't without the original. And disclosing the differentiating, physical features wasn't stipulated in the contract."

"Neither was disfiguring yours, but I'm happy to amend it."

"And this consultation is being livestreamed to a man who would rather watch golf, so you can—."

"Slap pond water? Yes, I installed the app on Father's phone." Golly threw a kiss at the camera and set the weapon down. "You are, nonetheless, required to declare the bulk properties, XRF signature, resistivity, conductivity, malleability, tensile strength . . ."

At "specific gravity" Reuben zoned, and nit-picked the purchase agreement and material certs. "The sub used nationalized gold stock so trace element analysis will not discriminate, and at your insistence I set Sri Lankan sapphires that a PhD in mass spectrometry couldn't distinguish."

"Let's start with diameter, thickness, and weight."

"Within the metrology tolerances and repeatability, when overlaid on the master, the critical dimensions are the same."

"And the serpentine chain?" Golly pressed on.

"Maria wore it so thin I replaced it." Reuben returned the original in a mini envelope.

"Whooo! Thought I had you. About the ceramic: Don't I own the fabrication rights to that?"

"Not unless you buy out the foundry. But save your cash because you can't test the surface finish or detect the microchip and battery without destroying it."

"How good is the coin cell?"

"Twenty-five thousand hours."

"So, if I'm not in Moscow by July . . .?"

"The angel will outlast you."

"Good to know. Shipping records, please."

Remarkable Reuben spread the slips alongside the packing on the glass top and in no time got tripped up in the tangle, "You say the copy came tied with purple? That can't be right."

"Precisely! Who would close a white giftbox with a white ribbon? Don't dwell too long on it, Reuben—it's not a trick question!!!" Golly Gee slammed the box on the counter.

Reuben shrugged, "We see it all the time. Baby baptisms, confirmation crosses, Fabergé forgeries . . ."

With amplifying intensity Golly drawled, "Well, let me tell ya who don't—Rockabillies! That's who! I'll bet they exchange wedding presents in recycled *birthday bags turned inside out*!!"

"Golly, if you're not pleased with my wrapping, fill out a customer complaint and I'll be back in two weeks. May I leave for Cabo?"

"You're not packing for Yakima until you straighten this mess." Golly popped the cables from the video camera and placed a call to the Russian Antique Mall.

Without the camera on, Reuben reverted to custard pudding. "Golly, I had nothing to do with it. You have to believe me!"

"Not now, Reuben I'm talking—*and stop dripping on me*!" she threw a wipe his way. When Golly hung up she peppered the jeweler with questions: Did Jaxy act suspicious, snoop, or pry when he came in? Did he hack the GPS to add spyware, or introduce an error to later debug? Did he misdirect the kits, why, and on whose order?

At that moment Reuben could think of nothing beyond covering his own roly-poly behind. "If Jaxy used Sunday's delivery to gain lodge access and terminate Pops, then to get in and out fast, he had no reason to believe that the ribbon color mattered, so he took a guess and guessed wrong."

"Jesus Reuben! Why didn't you tell him?" Golly stomped around.

"Because you, my dear, classified that Over-The-Top Secret for which Jaxy Thrie is not cleared!" Reuben pointed at the bold red letters stamped on each contract page.

Golly bent a mannequin into the fifth, ballet position, and played with a bronze music note with a garnet dangling from the foam head asking, "Do you think a Rockabilly would go for these?"

"Not sure what a Rockabilly is. But I'm confident they'd look capital."

"On me, Reuben." Golly stood tiptoe.

"Asking if almondine goes with your icy, blue eyes? Yes, I believe so," set forth Reuben his honest, diplomatic opinion. "Granting that if history repeats, this Rockabilly you expect to impress won't be for long."

Golly tried others then said, "Put them on layaway."

"The dangles or the dead man?"

"Both. I'll bring you back a corndog."

"And I'll send you a postcard."

"And a serape. Red."

"And if I can't find red?"

Golly turned off the showroom lights. "Don't—and find out."

CHAPTER 10

The Verdugo Hills, California
10:00 a.m. Monday, January 1

Jaxy awoke with a knot on his head, welts on his wrists, and Rachmaninoff playing at his blistered feet. He identified the caller by the ringtone and kicked the phone off the cushion.

Previous day events rushed in.

Up he jumped to cram back the Wild West Airlines uniform that spilled to the sunroom floor from a duffel that reached Las Vegas minutes before he departed persona non grata. Given two choices, Jaxy opted to wear the white-fringed miniskirt on a red-eye to Burbank over sporting it overnight in jail. At least he had the presence take it off in the garage before his fiancée caught him wearing it in the house.

"Guin?" Jaxy called out. Hearing nothing, he plumped the divan and went through the rambling, hillside ranch house to where he found coffee percolating with a note asking him to take down the Christmas tree and net the swimming pool of leaves.

"Oh yeah. The Rose Bowl party," he skimmed the dance favorites she wanted played in the cactus garden that afternoon.

"*Por ti seré, Por ti seré,*" sang Jaxy diving into the pool for a wakeup lap before tackling the chores with the Tournament of Roses playing in the background. By noon he had the ornaments down and the needles vacuumed, leaving the porcelain nativity scene with the saguaro, llama and donkey for Guin to put away. With one task to go, Jaxy grabbed his van keys and wound his way down the canyons above Glendale to the Russian Antique Mall for the Fat Pipes' stage speakers and drum kit.

"Happy New Year, Klav!" Jaxy came through the steel backdoor with a bang and made his way through the cluttered aisles of eclectic imports to a booth of old-world flintlocks and muskets, and a mishmash of peasant toys, housewares, and religious objects. There he found his boss in a silver tonic suit crouched before a gramophone singing the "Tra-la-las" to opus 38.

"Or is that outlawed in Russia too?" Jaxy carried on.

"New Year's No. Why?"

"I mean happiness."

Klav Lovorsky stopped the music and steered him to the safe. "It'll get happier when you put it in there."

"What in where?"

"My message—didn't you get it?"

"Which one?" Jaxy propped a wingtip on a wobbly Shaker stool, took up an overpriced, pick-thrashed, sonic blue, '62 Telecaster guitar constructed of ash and maple fifteen years before his birth, and played a riff of "Everybody's Trying to be my Baby".

Klav wrapped his fingers around the neck. "Check your *messages*, please."

"I'll be. There it is." Jaxy pressed the phone to his ear to hear his boss tell him to bring the priceless, Fabergé guardian angel to the store—pronto!

Sighed Jaxy holding up a pair of fingers, "There are two, Klav. Why? I don't know, but Yan kept the hot one and sent me on with the knockoff, albeit for a cheap knockoff it's pretty good."

"So good they got mixed up."

"Not possible. I checked them out before I left the Beaver Lodge."

"You checked the electronics box—*not the angels*. The Dam Mother says the swap happened at the front gate and she is flying in Thursday to personally take you out."

"As in . . . 'for good'???" Jaxy broke into a sweat.

"No. For a spicy hot mustard dog and sweet potato fries," said Klav with a pelvic thrust.

"Lovorsky!!!" Jaxy blew his top in fear. "What did you get me into?"

"You don't have to go, though personally I recommend the beer batter corndog with onion rings."

"And no one can make me stay because I quit!" Jaxy peeled the key from his ring and slid it across the yellowed, taped cracks on a glass case of nineteenth century, black powder muzzleloaders and lead balls.

Klav slid it back. "It's what Corndog Thursday's about. The way you snuffed the old boy at the boathouse without a scratch impressed the Beaver Board enough to fast-track you to a salaried position."

"I tried to save a man's life there, Klav, not take one."

Acknowledged Klav, "Oh, you don't have to convince me. But you got involved all the same which means you can't leave the family store or collect overtime anymore. Welcome to the Canadian Beaver Lodge Assassins Association." The middle manager handed Jaxy his corporate badge, benefits packet, ethics manual, and a Busty Beaver, stress relief squeeze toy.

"Watch me!" Jaxy roared to life, strewing pages as he tried to leave, but Klav boxed him in.

"Forgive me, Jaxy. I never wanted you to be a part of this, and I hate losing a topnotch worker over a lapse in judgement by sending you there. So, I simply ask that you to take a close look at the package. Then, if you still want out with a card and a cake, keep the true nature of this import business to yourself—and bring me the Fabergé."

"Or else?" Jaxy dragged a fingernail across his throat.

With a sick smile Lovorsky said, "Yes, but it will be my neck the

Dam Mother breaks, not yours, and she will have you to do it for your next promotion."

"No way. You're like family. I wouldn't do that to an enemy."

"You already did, taking Pops' place. So, if you don't wish to be installed as the next Antique Mall manager, where is it?"

Jaxy dug at his sock with the heel of his shoe. "I . . . I left it."

"Don't stand there. Go get it."

"In my-my-Mighty Ducks jacket."

"I noticed you're not wearing it. And your jacket is?"

Jaxy drooped his head, "Las Vegas."

CHAPTER 11

Klinnick's Bar and Grill, Las Vegas, NV
5:00 p.m. Monday, January 1

As the night crawlers emerged, and the married-with-children retired to their respective Las Vegas resorts, Jaxy made his way across the Mojave Desert to the same tawdry tavern where he hoped to take Jillian in a grudge match to win back the angel. If that didn't pan out, he would forfeit the money card and a shopping trip to the music mart. To his dismay, Klinnick's had rolled the air hockey table out by the oak pit, and in its' place Samantha Walker & The Red Canyon Rockers had set up to play.

Through the throng of country bar connoisseurs with tight jeans and loose lips Jaxy drifted to the alley passageway where he stopped to listen in on a dispute between band members:

"I just found out!" The bass player raised a Blackhawk Stetson to mop his forehead.

"But the Hotties took the tourney and expect live music. Can't anyone fill in for Sam tonight?" asked the drummer.

The bassist waved about, "Called around, but *nada*. Besides people come for her. Not us."

"Pardon me, anyone seen J.D. Avlon?" Jaxy asked.

"Rock-a-Filly!" The drummer's face lit up. "Hey guys, this queen nails Shania."

"Not tonight," declined Jaxy. "Jillian ran off with my hockey jacket. Think she'll show up?"

The bassist replied, "Hard to say. Best place to scout her out is from here. If you hit those high notes, Rita Klinnick might help—but if not, you'll likely be shopping for a new coat. Right . . . boys?"

Jaxy checked his drive-weary appearance in the wall mirror mounted to make the place, including the wet stains beneath his arms, look wider.

"'M'on, 'Filly. If we sound tight, who cares what your shirt looks like? You can take Sam's *and* my pay." The drummer sank to begging.

Jaxy passed out business cards. "Keep it. I'll be back in a jiff with Daisy."

"She sings too?"

"Duane Eddy recorded 'Forty Miles of Bad Road' on that guitar."

"Know any Maddie & Tae?" asked the fiddler.

"*Shat up and fish*—Can you play 'Train Kept a-Rollin'?"

The harmonica wailed 'get along', and it was show time.

Reserved by nature, a peculiar thing would happen when Jaxy stepped up to the stand with guitar in hand. Somewhere deep in his psyche a switch would flip on the callback to "Train", and the audience exchange brought him out of his shell. This night, however, Jaxy needed to keep the place subdued and his wits about him to scan the sea of faces and pick out Jillian the moment she showed hers, so he passed around charts for something less engaging to kick it off.

In strict fairness, how could Jaxy have known that four cymbal clashes into "Flyin' Saucers Rock'n'Roll", The Henderson Hotties would crash the door carrying the Nevada State Ultimate Frisbee New Year's Tournament trophy on their shoulders? In seconds the party was ON. Discs were flying, divas were diving, and Jaxy couldn't see a thing.

The fete pulled in passing pedestrians that in turn attracted more, as they crammed a house already packed beyond the fire marshal's limit. At the final downbeat of "Hot Dog" mobbed by booze-sloppy fans, the condition of Jaxy's shirt four hours beforehand no longer mattered.

"That was sensational!" Rita Klinnick brought Jaxy his portion of entertainment pay and a complimentary draft. "We sold more suds tonight than last. I'd like to put your legs into the rotation."

"Put me in touch with Jillian, or they walk." Jaxy blew off the foam.

"I would while you still can. She's three years married to an ex-marine. A mean ex-marine."

"And my fiancée of ten is a prosecuting attorney so we're even."

"Ten what—years? You're not serious. Do you observe engagement anniversaries?"

"Not if I don't get back the jacket she gave me for Christmas," said Jaxy, adding for emphasis, "a mint condition Anaheim Ducks first issue."

"Play the Winter Wet T Contest on Saturday and you might get lucky. J.D. took the summer cup by a nautical mile," Rita added smiling, "without cheating."

"You'd think they'd get in the way of the mallet."

"That's her secret to winning—they block your peripheral vision. So, what do you say? Seventy-five an hour, plus two percent off tap sales as an incentive to hold the house until you can't stand up, then I'll bring you a chair."

"Three and a table for promos. But score me a date with Jillian or you won't hear another note."

Rita spun a Frisbee. "You almost got her arrested. She deserves the jacket."

Jaxy pinched the disc. "She hinted she'd play again."

"If it's a pride thing get over it. There are better odds in this town."

"For a good luck charm about so big," Jaxy touched the middle finger to his thumb. "I want to win it back."

Rita laid down the law, "Not at my table! J.D. said you were playing for bragging rights, not strip hockey for a rabbit's foot. No more games for you. Either of you!"

"Then I'll make an offer. For a finder's fee, you'll receive the same," Jaxy wrote an attractive figure on a beer coaster with a rough sketch of the medallion.

Rita returned a grilling stare. "For putting the old lady's jacket on the line you're playing Sunday too with the tip jar going to new Hottie jerseys."

"Put me in touch with Jillian."

"It's a deal, baby seal!" Rita Klinnick poured another round and called it a night.

CHAPTER 12

The Avlon Home, Clackamas, Oregon
9:00 a.m. Tuesday, January 2, 2018

On her first week off from flying since October, Jillian Avlon sat cross-legged on a mound of pillows, watching cartoons with a box of dry cereal in her lap. Too irritated to talk, having come home to a patio littered with crushed beer cans and an uncovered spa with a flotilla of duck doo, she snugged her pajamas and leaned into the sofa with her feet on the coffee table (something she never let anyone else do), and blew off the call from work.

They had tried couples counseling, but Rory would understate his liquor intake, clam up, or storm off at everyone "ganging up" on him. Support groups helped, but meetings are hard to make when you're forever in the air, or hostage in a house where she never knew which Rory, the happy fun or the angry one, would stumble through the door. Not that it always went awry—Rory had his moments when he showered, shaved and swept her into the bedroom to reconcile their differences only to dash her hopes by nightfall.

Today was to be different. Rory would get no cuddles and kisses upon coming home from the union blowout. Rather, a New Year's ultimatum to shape up or ship out. But how can you deliver such a message to a man who seeing it coming, goes ice climbing?

Tick-tock . . . tick-tock . . .

It took all that Jillian had not to take a tomahawk to the oppressive, Black Forest, grandfather clock and knock a mahogany antler off. Instead she channeled her repressed anger into something worthwhile by resolving to start the new year by putting the old one with Oregon behind. Jillian unplugged the obnoxious reminder that time marches on and mustered the courage to play back the telephone message. News had traveled that she'd skipped probation, and the airlines wanted a reason to give the inveterate gambler a two-week, layoff notice in preference to canning her on the spot. Jillian cried and cried until she bitterly laughed. How could she leave her husband? The tissue box went to mush in her hands—she had no job!

Jillian got dressed and reviewed her portfolio. Against the Dow her funds had dipped. She browsed her business page and heaved a sigh. As a tax write-off "Steeds and Studs" paid off in spades, but at a rate of one pet portrait order per month, she'd reap more going door to door painting street numbers, and no way would she put Thunder Roll up for sale. What alimony she could count on wouldn't feed a gerbil, and the thought of falling back on her mom made her ill. The gems in the bank box weren't hers for the taking, and the silver, beaded box she won at air hockey was nice, but not worth flushing a career over.

The phone sounded off again. At least she had one friend in the world.

"Hey girl, Hotties took first, and did you miss the par-tee of the year!" Rita Klinnick came on in her usual, exuberant way.

"See? You didn't need me on the team. Work doesn't either," Jillian started to dump her truck of troubles when a paddle of mallards took over the yard and she went after them with a broom. "Shoo! Shoo!"

"Work doesn't what?"

"Nothing. Rory left the top off and the tub won't work. So, tell me about it."

"Rock-a-Billy came back for his purple jacket and that rabbit's foot you won.

"Believe me, Rita, it's no rabbit's foot. The greaser owes me three large and a new hat. If he wants it, that's what it will take."

"What I'm saying! It's a seller's market. Don't take less than four times that for the fancy, gold angel. Throw in the jacket and everyone wins."

"What angel?"

"Don't hit me with that shit. I'll forward his number. Don't begin the year on a bad luck foot."

"Well Happy New Year to you too, Rita! And don't you dare give him mine," cautioned Jillian. She broke open the silver beaded box. She had a fancy, gold angel to find!

THE LAST, YELLOW JELLYBEAN fell from the bag, hit the edge of a fluted, glass bowl, and skittered across the desk. Along with buckets of golf balls, and tobacco for the pipe, candy for the children topped Fr. Michael's list of life's little essentials. He nibbled the lemon tip and braced himself for the Jillian Avlon inspirational "message-of-the-day". Some mornings it would be about Typhoon Rory, on others he would hear of equestrian or art events, a pick-up game, or a sandal sale. Jillian never asked for advice or took any, so Fr. Michael did not call back unless she requested.

Jewelry dominated today's communiqué.

"Hi Father Michael! I found a real gem on a sweet deal with wording I can't make sense of. If you can't meet today that's okay, I'll work it out. Huu! The duckies are here. Gotta run."

Halfway between home and church they met at the hospital where the priest went on Tuesdays to distribute flowers to adults, jellybeans (diet permitting) to children, and hope to the drunks in the detox ward.

"How you acquire?" Fr. Michael asked, turning the tiffany beaded jewelry box in the cafeteria window to catch the reflections.

"eBay. It looked pretty."

"Pretty expensive, I tink. How much?"

"Not too. But check out the crackerjack I found inside!"

From a square of mulberry silk Fr. Michael unfolded *The Guardian Angel of Maria Feodorovna*. Catching his breath, he snapped the case shut, concealing it between his arms. "Where did this come from?"

"Told you! I didn't notice it right away, but when I pulled on the silk padding to clean the box, the angel fell out. I doubt the owner knew it was there. Can you read it?"

Away from the brunch room bustle they retreated to the meditation grotto, where, by the illumination of electric candles they studied the treasure in private. The crisp edges had been rubbed soft with time and affection, making the inscription difficult to make out, but the indentation of a dainty woman with curled hair and prim chin caught the eye.

Fr. Michael asked, "Ever hear of Maria Feodorovna?"

"The tennis player? That's the one sport I couldn't ace, so I don't follow."

"Babushka from church. I go show and bring right back, dat's ok?"

Jillian furrowed her brows, but she trusted her priest so granted permission, provided he return the fancy, gold angel by evening, translated or not.

TO A SHELF PACKED with books and devotional items behind his church office desk, Fr. Michael carried the Feodorovna Angel. He stood it against a stone collected from the Sea of Galilee, showered it with holy water, and lit a candle. After petitioning the guardian's forbearance for the indignities it may have suffered at his goddaughter's hands, Fr Michael took the angel down and blackened the indentations with pipe charcoal. Then hunched over a Russian-English dictionary and a borrowed, prep school microscope, letter by letter he worked out the dedication:

Maria Feodorovna
EMPRESS OF ALL THE RUSSIAS
"May this angel bless and keep you every moment of the year,
Hold it close and make a wish for all your children dear"
Carl
January 1, 1918.

"Maria no play tennis, that's for sure," Fr. Michael rolled back to ponder how the older goddaughter came into possession so soon after it left the younger's. No less chatty than her Canadian twin on subjects mundane, to prod Jillian about the matter would yield nothing but ornery silence—not a chalk talk. For now, he let the eBay blarney slide, knowing in time she would disclose more. Information about Jillian's lineage Fr. Michael had withheld from her as well, but since the Paris explosion left the younger brother Jean impaired in a state of shock, the Grand Duke's capacity to shoulder the Russian, double-eagle mantle had been compromised. For Jillian to shed her American skin as the next of kin to accept the Guardian Angel of Maria Feodorovna from the Romanov Guild and symbolically head the Russian nations would require crash courses in language, diplomacy, and charm school. For Golly it would necessitate the applying of brakes before she took the title literally and wooed her nationalistic subjects into staging an all-out Russian coup. Whichever way it played, their godfather needed to take stewardship of the angel, and the angel to Remarkable Reuben to make sure that *this* angel was the true Fabergé.

"Father Michael, Father Michael, how are my lovelies?" Reuben Reisenschein guided the clergyman to the back of the clock shop where oiled cubbies and smithing tools under harsh lighting contrasted with the glittering wonders that filled the showroom.

"Ladies are fine your excellency, and yours?" saluted Fr. Michael, setting the guardian angel on the craftsman's bench by a tub of butter tarts the watchmaker couldn't pay to give away. "Keeping unsavory company, I see."

"Present one included. Shall we take a gander at this bejeweled dandy?" Reuben slipped on cotton gloves and viewed the angel under a magnifying light. "Back so soon. And how did Maria's angel find its way into a pauper's pocket two days after it left mine?"

"Trade secret." Fr. Michael latched the door before proceeding in a low voice, "I too am dying to know what sets them apart besides the ribbons and bows."

"Trade secret," replied Reuben.

"And when Golly Gee learns who traded them out, and buries that secret at sea with you?"

"Then it won't matter, will it, Michael?"

"To you? No. But to Jillian Avlon it will."

"Convince me first this other goddaughter of yours is 'Dagmar the New' of Denmark, and not the latest in the line of imposters."

"Golly's convinced. What better proof can I give?"

"Convinced is she? To her a dead wannabe is better than a living rival." Reuben fixed the medallion to a gyroscope, clocked the tiara, let the gimbals come to rest, and measured the angles. "Nineteen degrees, eighteen. The secret is in the sapphires."

"Fair enough. If you still have the makings, what would a plated rendition on a pauper's budget cost? Camille's birthday is coming, and I detest shopping."

With reverence Reuben wrapped the angel in silk. "For you not a cent. I shall write it off as a raffle donation. But with all respect, Michael, as remarkable as she is, your wife hardly carriages like a Feodorovna."

"And you no look like Carl Fabergé."

CHAPTER 13

Nansensgade Street, Copenhagen
1986

Born in Copenhagen, Dagmar Jillian Nikolaevna retained faint memories of early childhood. Among the more vivid, coloring at her father's feet in Alexander Nevsky Church stood out, before an intracranial hemorrhage took his life coming up on her second birthday. Of the unpleasant doctor visits, the odors, and the needle sticks that followed, the duchess had little recollection. She could not recall her birth mother.

Raised as the sole adopted child of Adele and Ralf Anders, the director of an investigative service that conducted background checks on government suppliers, Jillian's siblings faded from a young mind preoccupied with the constant hounding of an austere, American family that moved frequently about Colorado. Subsequently, every fall Jillian started out at new primary school where she competed on the playground to stake her turf, and a different Old Lutheran Sunday school where she doodled on her visitor button.

In spite of the Anders' insistence on regular church attendance and Jillian's dominance at recess, religion and athletics fell far short of her first loves: Art and horses. Under the discipline of private lessons the gifted artist plied her hand to the pad to please her parents. All went well until Jillian entered a sketch at the state fair called "Horse Clearing Obstacle" and came home with the white ribbon. Rather than receiving praise for showing third, she had her radio sequestered for not coming in first! One by one Jillian splintered her pencils on the table edge, took up her glove, and stormed off to sign up for little league.

At the age of thirteen, Jillian "J.D." Anders found herself batting third in the line-up and carrying Fort Collins to the nationals on her compact shoulders. This led to a softball scholarship at Colorado State where she roomed with Rita Klinnick, a chemistry major whose senior project subsisted of isomerization and fermentation of barley in the dormitory. It struck Jillian as odd that Adele and Ralf took turns attending every game while showing no interest in the sport. "It is our duty," they said. The sports achievements won the tomboy no applause, but it filled her time when not scooping manure and braiding manes at the livery or attending the Greek Church with her boyfriend—the two places in town she found through trial and experimentation the Anders wouldn't follow.

One spring night, after a heartbreaking loss in the final softball game of the season, Jillian started in again on animal portraits. She fearfully hid her work until Rita turned the mattresses one summer's day and outed her to a hometown friend on leave from Iraq. Jillian's attention to detail mesmerized Captain Rory Avlon who requested one for his quarters. And she, flattered by an older military man taken more by the crispness of her illustrations than her salute, sent more.

Caught up in the flush of romance, Jillian applied for entry to the Officer Candidate School. Excluded from roles of combat for carrying a congenital, coagulation disorder, she left Fort Collins to join the Wild West Airlines—the one occupation she could do without the Anders' incessant surveillance unless they wanted to go broke buying tickets. To her delight, Rory retired and came home to ask for her hand in marriage. Pleased to pass their charge into the protective hands of a decorated soldier, the Anders threw the grandest wedding affordable, and went on a long Scandinavian cruise.

Jillian wholly gave herself to holy matrimony and set up house, while Rory treated his post-war stress with lots of tequila, and his wife like junk after the ring went on. Locked into a marriage doomed from the start, the more Rory sought escape at work, in the bottle, or on the mountains, the more Jillian found consolation at the easel, on the saddle, or in bars with other men.

Jillian drained, mopped, and refilled the tub, dropped the privacy blinds, capped her hair, and slipped into the churning water. She closed her eyes and revisited the trip to Copenhagen that previous summer upon receiving a formal invitation in Dansk and English to a reunion on her thirty-first birthday.

Thrilled out of her mind to meet actual, blood relatives, Jillian took a crash course on handy, Danish phrases, and found a passenger to help with pronunciation. However, when she disembarked, instead of a welcoming committee with signs, an intimidating woman on a walker escorted Jillian to a windowless room to inform her the card was a hoax. When done, the stalwart stateswoman handed Jillian three things: A return ticket to Portland, a stern warning to stay out of Copenhagen, and a care package from Yekaterinburg, Russia.

"Was ist los?" The Condor steward brought Jillian a pillow after the plane leveled out.

Jillian burst into tears, "American's don't like me, the Danes don't want me, and the Russians can't—make—sweaters!"

It seemed ruefully funny now, for Jillian had passed judgment by running a fast hand across the wretched garment. At home she discovered why the bulky item weighed so much when, rolled up inside an old corset she found a bracelet. Further mining produced a wealth of jewels, and a card sealed by a stamp of waxed daggers. The note read: "Dagmar—Lock these away with the corset. You will need all of it when the time comes —A friend from the Guild."

Uncertain over what to make of the fabulous find, Jillian assumed the "Guild" mistook her for someone named Dagmar to bootleg a small fortune across the waters. She thus bundled the jewels in a safety deposit box and waited for Dagmar to show up.

Done with reminiscing, Jillian dried her hands, and on the sketchpad outlined a stone tower. She flipped a page and drew it again, enlarging the top three windows. Under the keystone she placed a woman in a formal and once more turned the page. She closed on the woman's torso, filling in the scoop with black, heavy strokes. By a serpentine chain she suspended an oval. On the fourth and final scene, Jillian placed stones around the pendant's border that filled the sheet. Inside the stones she placed a face, the face of an angel, with wings spread, prepared for flight.

The angel's eyes blinked. "Liar!" accused one. "Cheat!" charged the other.

"But I won it fair and square!" said Jillian.

"Tough" . . . "Cookies!"

"Stop talking that way!"

The eyes went still.

"You win! You win!!" Jillian flung the pad. Her head flopped forward, water shot up her nose and woke her up. Jillian sneezed and shook her head, climbed out from the pool, and peeled back the sopping pages.

They were empty.

Wrapped in a towel, Jillian entered the house and dialed the telephone with shaking fingers.

"Jaxy? J.D. Remember?" Jillian came on strong before changing her mind.

"Do I?" laughed Jaxy, "didn't think I'd hear from you."

"You can thank Rita," Jillian sneezed again.

"Bless you both in bunches. Have you the item?"

Jillian blew her nose honking, "It's out getting appraised."

Jaxy groaned.

"For insurance. I need your mailing address," she said.

"Seriously?"

"If I'm to start out the year with a clean slate, I can't have this riding on my conscience." Then, as if the angel still rested on her doleful breast, Jillian looked down and sighed, "been nice knowing you."

"You too, but hey, I'm still in town. Come down and I'll play you blindfolded for a drink."

Jillian hacked back a wad. "I may be coming down with something. Do you think zinc lozenges work?"

"Right now, I don't care."

"That I'm sick?" she sniveled.

"No! I do, I do. I've never tried one. Heard they taste lousy."

"People swear by it. But what do they know? Not like you can test it by sticking a chunk up half your face. But I suppose I ought. What can it hurt?"

"Nothing, I imagine. But listen, seriously I do need it."

"You too? Try the lime and tell me what you think."

"The angel! *By Thursday*!!"

"I'll ship it."

"Too risky. Honestly, Jillian, a head cold makes no difference."

"See? You don't care."

"Believe me, I'm getting there."

"Thursday then. Out in the open, closer to me."

"Where?"

"The Sellwood Bridge. I gotta . . . gotta-*chooo*!" Jillian creamed the mouthpiece.

"Bless you again. I'll come prepared."

FR. MICHAEL'S PHONE JINGLED. "Yilli'! I about to call. We have beeg problem. Maria go play tennis all day."

"Doesn't matter. I need it," said Jillian.

"This morning you want translation, and now you don't. What changed?"

"My heart. I want to do right and return it to the owner."

"Yillianz, shouldn't you let expert valuate first? You can keep and send extra money. That make eBay even happier!"

"I had a bad dream."

"Go on."

"I saw me in a tower."

"Like Saint Barbara, yes?"

"No. It was *me*! Wearing the angel, and it called me a thief. It scared me and I want to give it back."

"You belief in dreams?"

"No . . . maybe . . . oh, I don't know. It seemed so real."

"Sometimes they do. Tell me more and I interpret."

"Alright!! I didn't buy it online. I scored it at Rita's. But you don't have to punish me . . . the airlines . . . already . . . did," Jillian choked up.

"No! Yilli'!"

"So, for my resolution I quit air hockey—never to play again."

Fr. Michael's alarm had less to do with his goddaughter getting sacked as that was bound to happen, but that her sinister sister had sent an operator to Nevada slick enough to slip her the assumed replica before anyone knew it had left Canadian airspace. "I have more bad news. Medallion old and fragile, and sapphire fall out."

"Oh no!!!"

"I find, thank goodness, so take to Remarkable Reuben to reset."

"When will he have it ready?"

"Monday."

"Monday! How long does it take a drop of glue to dry?"

"If one fall out, Reuben say more to follow, so he do them all."

"For goodness' sake. I'll be gone by then! Can't he speed it up?"

"Reuben have but one speed, my dear."

"One speed, my ass," replied Jillian—but waited until he hung up.

On her way to Remarkable Reuben's to push the repair along Jillian regrouped. Premonitions and omens belonged to the gullible, the superstitious, and the aficionados of conspiracy talk radio. Even if her priest gave it polite consideration, he saw her dream as a naïve notion. Nothing else. If guilty of anything, it was playing Rock-a-Billy to begin with, but did he not put her up to it? Tough cookies then, she would haggle for a pretty price and give Jaxy just enough to make his trip worthwhile. By hawking it with some of the other settings that found their way into her bank box she could eke by until new streams of revenue flowed.

As she fit her Mini-Cooper into an empty slot off Esther Short Park, Jillian eyed the troubled sky. Her bones felt a storm brewing. A gust blew the door into her face. Another sign? As she passed through the splendid things that filled Reisenshein's marvelous showroom, Jillian suppressed her misgivings, stopping at an amusing, programmable cuckoo clock that popped out to announce the store would close in ten minutes.

"Did a priest come in with an angel on a chain?" asked Jillian at the counter.

The salesperson waited for the quirky punch line. When none came, he took her wrist, "Ambrosial skin—I have the perfect watch."

Jillian pulled her hand away. "He did. It's mine. I want it!"

A chubby, bald man in a black apron stuck his head out from a vintage, turn-crank cash register, blanched whiter than his button-down, and closed shop immediately, sending the sales help home.

"Michael took it! I swear it's not here," quaked Reuben when they were alone.

Jillian closed her lids to a sliver. "Mended already. That is remarkable."

"You sound stuffy. Lemon drop?" The tin tremored in Reuben's hand.

Jillian cleared her nose and waved the candy off with a hanky. "It's fine if Father has it. Did he pay?"

"Not yet."

"Well, somebody has to," she dipped into her purse.

"Yes! I mean no! I mean put the gun away. You need me to get it back!"

"What in the world are you babbling about? I gave it to him to translate, not keep!" Jillian lashed out heading for the car.

Displaying uncharacteristic courage, Reuben braced the doorway. "Please don't harm him—he's just a simple priest."

"I thought so too! He's not just any priest—*He's my godfather*! My whole life I've called him every day. I know it bugs him, but I love hearing his voice on the machine and I trusted him above anyone, even the Anders, and now . . . he stole . . . my angel!!!"

Color rushed into Reuben's cheeks. "Anders? You say?"

"Ms. Anders-Avlon. Please, another tissue?" snuffled Jillian as her eyes shifted above his head to a crest of crossed daggers on the wall bearing the motto: Strike First—Strike Hard.

Remarkable Reuben unfolded the angel from his apron pocket and handed her the mulberry silk. "Use this, I have stacks. And a thousand pardons with it. I had you confused with one coming to rob you of this very thing! We want to protect, not take it from you, and to finally lay eyes on Dagmar of Denmark, Grand Duchess of the House of Nikolaevna. Look this way. Yes, to the light. You have her eyes, but green, not blue, and the same button nose too. It's you. It's really you!"

"I'd say you're the one confused! I'm the Duchess of Dumb Ideas. I don't live in fairy castles with drawbridges and moats, nor would I have the foggiest notion of what to do with a house that size except sell it."

"It's time you learned." Reuben swung the angel before her eyes by a finger cot in keeping with a clock's pendulum. "Did you know Maria—?"

Jillian palmed the pendant and saucily noted the date. "No. Did you?"

With a burnisher, Reuben traced the dowager Empress' delicate face. "She was a remarkable woman."

Why the Empress emblazoned on the back so enthralled everyone Jillian could not comprehend, when the winged invader of dreams on the front commanded her attention. She extended Reuben's magnifier for a closer look at the intricate work of a wizard with a one-hair brush. Dark brown, loosely woven curls flowed onto the guardian's shoulders over a white tunic into the folds of ochre wings, and, unlike those depicted in storybooks and Christmas cards, holding forth a cross, as to thump her on the head for being a naughty girl.

"How much would you say this is worth?" asked Jillian.

Reuben replied, "More than you can imagine."

"Name a price that I can and it's yours."

"I still could not afford it."

At this excellent yet troublesome news, Jillian scrambled to concoct a new plan to lose Jaxy for good. Therefore, she requested a small favor.

"Two in one day," he said.

"Remarkable!" they laughed together.

Continued Jillian, "I have decided not to part with this."

"Splendid idea."

"But Father Michael adores it so. Could you cast one for him?" asked Jillian, adding quiet emphasis, "but less pricey, since I can't access my Swiss account till next week. As for the original, repot the stones. Take all the time you need. I'll sit in back, and drink tea, and draw you a puppy."

"I would love to Ms. Avlon, but I took on one extra job this week.

I haven't enough time in the day to work in a second."

"Then I'll find someone who can work around the clock!" Jillian arched her eyebrows, immensely proud of the comeback.

"No. No. Let me. But I need surety."

Jillian dug into her pocketbook.

"Sorry, the store doesn't extend credit."

"Will you accept a check?"

"I'm saying your money is no good here."

Jillian's ire rose, *"Would you take a horse painting?"*

"I'd love one." On the red, silken square, Reuben drew up a binding contract in gold ink, and with a flourished stroke of a line said, "Sign here."

"I wiped my nose on this, you know," Jillian shook it by the corner. Flummoxed by the stipulations she read aloud, "In payment for one Guardian Angel I'm to let you engrave my face and relocate your clock shop *where?*"

"The Yellow Palace . . . Butter tart?"

CHAPTER 14

McCarran International Airport, Las Vegas, NV
10:00 p.m. Tuesday, January 2

Not until late in the day did Jaxy learn that the Sellwood Bridge was a long, cold road trip from Klinnick's Bar and Grill. So, to the airport he hightailed to learn that the entire northwest had fallen under the weather, grounding planes in and out of Portland. Down on options, under a full wolf moon Jaxy let Rita know he'd have to take a raincheck on the weekend, set the cruise on seventy, and broke free of Las Vegas tapping his toes to "I Don't Care if the Sun Don't Shine". Conditions permitting, by afternoon he would catnap at a roadside rest, then fare forth to claim his prize and drop it off at Reuben's shop to beat the cutoff and save his boss's neck.

And then there was the Guin.

To head north without clearing it with the fiancée carried some risk, but with luck he would be back Sunday with his jacket and a dozen long stems. Then, after she stripped the walls of paint with some choice, Portuguese parts of speech, he'd make Guin laugh with a few self-deprecating wisecracks, and all would be forgiven. Friends asked why he put up with her crap. Out of decorum he refused to elaborate and dismissed it as Brazilian foreplay.

Through the blustery afternoon Jaxy pushed on to La Grande

clearing the way for an irksome, new Malibu that paced him with brights on from Boise. At the point where the ice made it inadvisable to attempt Deadman Pass till the morrow, Jaxy scrapped his plan to chill in the van and found a budget inn, stopping to pick up a pint of Glenlivet along the way. The blue, Chevy Malibu took a room there too.

Before settling in with the Beaver Lodge benefits and ethics policy manuals, Jaxy poured a finger of scotch and texted Guin. He let her know that the saloon put up a handsome sum for a weekend show and to not expect him back for black & white movie night. That should mollify her for the next seventy-two hours, Jaxy reckoned as the malt burned its way down, for should Guin follow up, at least this story would hold water.

IN A WORSE BIND with the Learjet failing to climb above the squall, Golly's pilot proffered two choices: Together they could plummet to their deaths in the Trinity Alps, or she could try for California another day. Put that way, Golly returned to the lodge and cancelled corndogs, desiring instead to have her pet operative bring an order with sweet potato fries and the Fabergé angel to Beaver Island as soon as the storm eased. When Jaxy brushed her off, Golly Gee learned where he went and routed a call through Klav Lavorsky's Antique Mall to Klinnick's Bar and Grill.

"Hey, may I speak to the proprietor?" asked Golly.

"This is she," affirmed Rita, "who's asking?"

"Jaxy Thrie's legal counsel,"

"Lookie, if Rock-a-Billy's in hot water, I knew nothing of the hockey bet."

"Specifics please."

"Don't tell anyone I said this, but he's the better player. Why he let

J.D. run it up only to throw the match, makes no sense."

"Was he drinking?"

"Not to speak of."

"Yes or no."

"No."

"Excellent. To claim a loss, I need receipts and the tax year."

Rita lowered her voice. "New Year's Eve he put up a nifty heirloom. With the jacket he could easily deduct three thousand dollars."

"Whooo! Did she nick his fanny pack too?"

"I should consult my attorney before saying more."

"For sure. Let me talk to him."

"They went to Portland."

"On the D.L.?"

"Have a good day."

"N' you," huffed Golly. Why do sisters have to ruin *everything*???

"TIME IS MONEY," THE Honorable Judge Leroy Booker-Hill reminded his daughter every Wednesday at three when, for Guin's edification he brought by a week's worth of finance journals and a box of Whoppers to her Wilshire law office. A converted chalk blue concrete and block glass dental suite, Guin kept the Dwarf Palm and Flamingo Flower, picture window panorama to take the edge off the pain of her client's bills. The Caribbean motif contrasted with her dad's wire suspended, Hawker Hector biplanes, and soaring bookcases stuffed with leatherbound boredom. At least her Highlights and High Times got read.

"As I waste both, second guessing the Dow," Guin's forehead creased at the upward trend not sure to hold or sell while thumbing through a disarranged stack of sticky-notes. She dialed a number off one and listened to the numerical options until the bot told her to press '4' to speak to a real person.

"Rallye Resort Hotels," answered the real person, "this week we're hosting 'The Red Hot, Hot Rod Show' featuring red coupes and roadsters from the golden age of—."

"Jackson Thrie—did he take a room there? That's T-h-r-I-e."

"Hold please."

Guin cupped the mouthpiece. "'Muskrat Love'. Daddy—they're playing 'Muskrat Love'!"

"He reserved one, then cancelled," said the real person.

"'Muskrat Love'! Who plays that for a car show?" asked Guin as she shoved the receiver into the cradle. "God, I can't stand these new phones."

"I see you broke two already," Booker noted the rejects piled in the corner.

"Slamming the phone makes more than a statement, papa. It's free therapy."

"Have you priced one lately?"

"You are so right, it's time for change." She opened the door to the reception room and broadcasted her resolution to the staff: "'The Mighty Guin' will end the year with the same phone she started with!"

"Add duct tape to the supplies list!" Booker followed up, then went to filling in the crosswords his daughter couldn't get.

Guin reread the text from Jaxy and linked to Klinnick's Bar and Grill, introducing herself as 'Rose Vandervelt', the Fat Pipes' entertainment rep.

"How many attorneys does he retain?" asked the bar owner.

"As many as a rock star requires. Why?"

"Because Guin Hill called not an hour ago."

"Did she," Guin sweetened, "about wha . . .?"

"Rock-a-Billy's air hockey game. So, before I forget, to help itemize I believe he intended for Jillian to keep the necklace—not the jacket —but she ended up with both for what it's worth."

"That's worth a lot. And how many women does he retain in Las Vegas?"

"J.D. lives in Portland, actually. The other attorney took it all down."

"Thank you. I will have to confer with Ms. Hill on this. Where did she place the call?"

Rita read off the Russian Antique Mall phone number.

"Interesting. The Fat Pipes rehearse there. About this solo gig Jaxy took without informing the band. That could be a breach in contract."

"Lookie Vandervelt, I'm happy to cancel if there's a conflict. Anyway, he may not make it back from Oregon by then with the big storm rolling in."

"It's fixin' to be a whopper."

"And please don't say anything to his fiancée, it would only worry her."

"More like *piss her off*!!!"

The projectile knocked the puzzle from Booker's hand, deflected off a cushion, and recoiled onto Guin's desk. Everyone else got cordless, but her last one remained embedded in the drywall as an artsy, plant hook, from which hung a philodendron.

A THOUSAND SLOPPY MILES to the north, Jillian surveyed "Sop City", as she called it, from above. Not out the window of a 737, but on her farewell hike through the West Hills—the sole thing about Portland she would miss. She panned her phone under the umbrella, snapping shots through the drizzle whereupon, seeing a message from Rita, tripped over a root in her haste to call back.

"What do you mean Jaxy's on his way?" freaked Jillian.

"Don't yell at me—you set it up."

"But they closed the airports!"

"Not the interstate."

"He's driving?" asked Jillian.

"All the way in that fat ass van."

"But I'm not ready."

"What's so complicated? It's not like you have to get your hair done."

"This whole thing is idiotic. Jaxy can come, but I'll be in The Dalles making arrangements for Thunder Roll," Jillian said with finality.

"Oh no! Is your horse okay?"

"He's getting hard to trailer with that shin splint. I'm setting him up with a therapist before taking work leave."

"About time. Couples that play together stay together."

"Alone. To paint. I have a huge backlog."

"Then meet Jaxy somewhere other than that donut place. Telling ya' girl, you need to lay off those things before they make it hard to trailer load you."

As a rule, Jillian swore only at inexperienced umpires and truculent yearlings, but at that moment she came close to letting one fly. "Rita, I can't drop everything for some Rock-a-hillbilly!"

"Who is driving fifteen hours for fifteen minutes of your time? He wants one thing from you, if it makes a difference. He's been engaged to the same broad for ten years. And check out the Fat Pipes homepage. His songs will crack you up."

"They already have," Jillian hung up, and loped through the mud to her car.

Before confirming the horse appointment, Jillian had her socks up on the coffee table and laptop between her knees, clicking through the weather stations to see the storm breaking over Seattle. This meant Idaho would clear up with a quarter inch of irresistible new glaze for her husband to enjoy while she cleared out. Seizing upon this, Jillian compared truck rentals and concluded that the van with a tow bar made sense for short legs, but who would help? Movers cost too much.

She had no girlfriends in Portland. Any able-bodied man also knew her husband, and she dare not declare it to her priest. "Oh well," she soughed like the Little Red Hen—she'd have to do it herself.

Settled on vehicle selections, she searched for "Maria Feodorovna". Of the two, she judged the one from Denmark prettier, naturally. After muddling through a host of polysyllabic surnames, it came to her why in poli-sci, three chapters deep into *War and Peace* she went straightaway to Blockbuster to rent the mini-series. Her spine involuntarily reflexed. Dagmar again! Jillian relaxed. No big deal. A name common among Danes. A fluky coincidence.

Against sound judgment, to the other end of the social status scale she went to check out Jaxy 3 & The Fat Pipes, and midway through "Dogpatch Glottal Catch" her head nearly split in half. Drilling into the gallery of candids, Jillian enlarged the one with a hollow-body, Gretsch guitar balanced on Jaxy's gangly legs hanging out the spacious, bubbletop van with whale-tale, California plate "MOBYD3".

"Huu!" clapped Jillian, more tickled at having almost missed the obvious than the Daisy Mae Scraggs sticker on his big, white guitar. If Maria Feodorovna afforded a bus ticket out, Jaxy Thrie was the driver, and Moby Dick her ride!

CHAPTER 15

Icicle Creek, WA
8:00 a.m. Thursday, January 4, 2018

At daybreak, two climbers approached the triple ice floes of Hubba Hubba. From the sculpted, lucent waterfalls fixed in place, they chose the narrow one cascading motionless down the side of uneven dark, blocky crags. A fun, if not difficult rated incline. Not their first choice for an outing, at least the local burg of Leavenworth with its Bavarian ales heralded the promise of a good time that evening.

Out front on the pitch, lanky Brad arched with his crampons dug in. He gazed through dark glasses at the distorted pines that jutted from the crestline, and then swung his axe into the brittle surface. A chunk of fissile rock fractured to knock out a row of icicles that dripped like the terrible teeth of a giant yeti from an overhang. Rory covered to let the detritus shower off his helmet.

"Watch it!" He shook out his hood.

"You're the one crawlin' up my tailpipe," Brad yelled back.

The icy sheath shuddered with an eerie moan. The men remained stationary until it ceased. Brad then proceeded, showing more respect to Hubba's fickle ways, while Rory moved to the side, recovering anchors as they scaled.

At the summit the alpinists reclined to enjoy the lookout over central Washington with dried apricots, spiced jerky, and sunflower seeds.

"Say again why we came here instead of Twin Falls?" asked Brad.

"Same song and dance," replied Rory with weariness.

"And you can't miss a single board meeting?"

"That's what the union wants, to finalize the budget without the watchdog to hold them accountable. I pulled them from the fiscal precipice last year. I won't go through it again."

"Take a handful of this beautiful day back with you, sunshine, and surprise them with some warmth for a change." Brad removed his shades to tan his face.

Rory scanned the terrain, swiveling the dual band, radio antennae to scan for weather bulletins. "Don't let that big blue fool ya, Brad. Next one's going to be a slammer."

"That's what they said about the last."

"And sometimes they are right . . . Aw, Jesus. What do they want now?" Rory tuned in a correspondent and walked off to listen in private.

The drug dealer's voice crackled over the radio, "Cleared the port, Captain. Crossing over at six."

"Said Sunday," Rory pushed back.

"Tonight, and I knock a note off. Blow me, and the price of rock just went up."

"I'm *on* a rock, you fuckin' Canuck, in the middle of nowhere!"

"Inflation's a bitch, hey?" cackled Yan before the airwaves faded.

From his climbing buddy's body language, Brad felt a storm brewing on the early side when Rory crunched up to boot a rock off the lip.

"Watch it! There's people down there," said Brad.

"I knew it."

"Then why'd you do it?"

"The board moved the vote up because I'm here with you—not

there with them—so it's *my* fault if I don't make it tonight even though I said no more Thursdays because it screws with family night."

Brad shook out the rope. "You call taking in a ballgame at my place 'family night'?"

"You may be the biggest bunghole I know, but you made the cut." Rory clipped in.

"All because I have the wider screen," said Brad leaning into the slack to back down the fall.

IN A HURRY TO have everything set by noon, Jillian showed up as soon as the clock shop opened to collect the Fabergé original and the shiny new one starring her amazing face. Reuben placed them side by side and critiqued the work, "Compared to type-one rounds these sapphires don't sparkle the same, and the luster is too reflective."

"It's gorgeous—but where's the angel?" Jillian panicked at the duplicate's missing centerpiece.

"At a mug and T-shirt shop."

"But you said you would have it ready!"

"*You* said, Ms. Avlon, you would come for this at close of business," Reuben closed the original with a Valentine sticker. "Others may work around the clock, but I do not. Monday is the best I can do."

"Even for a Duchess?" curtseyed Jillian in a mad search for a new strategy while trying on a silver masquerade mask from the clearance table.

Reuben raised his hands in play. "Is this a holdup?"

With a forefinger at his breast, Jillian replied, "You read my mind," and thanking him for his time and effort, took the Fabergé and zipped off to her bank, clothier, and hairdresser.

CHAPTER 16

Hood River, OR
12:00 p.m. Thursday, January 4, 2018

Brilliant blue skies over the Columbia River, decorated with billowy, gray and white cloud pillows, felt warm and friendly. The slick highway under the tires, however, made lane changes tricky as Jaxy headed into the gorge rehearsing the tongue-lashing he would never unleash on the WWA agent that denied him passage on a glorious day for flying. At the Hood River waterfront, he pulled off to watch a sailboat formation conduct maneuvers.

A blue velvet Malibu stopped to watch them too.

Beneath the creaky, green truss bridge connecting the shores, a wheat barge rode the currents against a backdrop of glistening evergreens. Clapboard houses looked back from an incline on the Washington side. Jaxy snapped a picture of the idyllic scene, then sixty minutes later rolled into Portland and less than ideal afternoon traffic. Although the news said to expect the second slow-moving front by nightfall with temperatures in the low twenties, Jaxy estimated the odds at catching Jillian a day early and beating it out at fifty-fifty. With traffic merging and horns honking, Jaxy let a call go as he coasted off the freeway. The Malibu breezed by following the arrows to Vancouver.

"Jaxy! It's after three. Where are you?" Jillian spoke in haste when he rang back.

"Portland. Surprise!" announced Jaxy from the aromatic warmth of an independent hawker of exotic books, geodes, beads, and yoga mats.

"I know! Where?"

"You do?? Can you meet at Sellwood now?"

"I *said* the Pittock Mansion."

Jaxy looked at the missed voice message. "Sorry. Had both hands on the wheel."

"You don't have hands free? Of course, you don't. Never mind. Put them on and go to the White Stag, then two lefts and a right will take you to the edge of town where Burnside meets the trees. You can't miss it."

"Miss what??"

"Told you!"

"Slow down and spell it."

"P–I–T–T–O–C–K. M–A–N–."

"Got it. Address?" Jaxy flagged a cashier for a pencil and scratchpad.

"*It doesn't need one*! I'll find you on the east lawn," said Jillian, and the line went dead.

"Imperious woman." Jaxy put away the phone.

"Author?" The clerk keyed in a book title search.

"Do you sell maps?"

With a travel guide and cinnamon tea, Jaxy motored on until the promontory came into view. From the description he guessed at where the historic landmark topped out over the homes that dotted the slope and peeked through the dense foliage and could tell that the estate held a commanding view. Ten minutes later he wound his way up the switchbacks to the visitor's lot, empty except for a beat-up, long-bed, city pickup.

He cast about the grounds for Jillian in the twilight. Perhaps she waited inside. Up he skipped to the vestibule of this grand building. A sign on a chain read: "Closed for January". Under the cornices and gables Jaxy dawdled, shuddering at what a single month's heating bill would read. Beyond this wondrous, century-old sandstone and red-topped edifice, Jaxy crossed the lawn, the size of a large, oval putting green, to where it ended at a black, waist-high, chain link fence, and an impressive look down on city high-rises.

Every minute or so he checked his watch, but the little hand ignored the hurried looks of its' anxious owner as each second chipped away at his chance of getting the angel across the Columbia before closing time. To keep his mind off the time, Jaxy studied the valley topography lit by a setting sun that sent long shadows toward Mt. Hood that peaked like a frosted witch's hat through the haze. Closer in, he examined the triangular patterns where the diagonal avenues intersected those that ran up from the embankment where the watercourses met, and the less attractive, industrial complexes that cluttered the peninsulas and basin sandbars.

In the shade of an ancient, moss-covered oak, Jaxy envisioned his fiancée in an ivory train, cradling a nosegay beneath an arbor on the glade. At least he had come during a break between storms or else he would not have had this privileged view of the perfect spot for a wedding. On the way to the van for his camera, Jaxy met with a white, wooly Husky on a walk. He stooped to pat the pooch while leveling the other glove shoulder high to enquire if a pony-tailed blonde in uniform had come by. The owner couldn't say and tugged the dog away leaving the parkland to Jaxy and a strapping lad struggling through the creeping vines with power cutters and a workday of trimmings.

Jaxy's apprehension mounted with the stygian thunderheads that rolled in to obscure the sunset and blacken the land. He called back but Jillian's mailbox was full. His texts went without reply. If it pleased her to strand him, why here? Perhaps when she went to insure the parcel post, upon seeing the appraisal she changed her mind and set him up for the woodcutter to greet with a felling axe instead!

Feminine footfalls cut off such thoughts. Jaxy straightened to sweep aside the curls that fell across his glasses and deliver up a four-point lecture to himself: Keep your distance, do not get her talking, take the angel, and scram before you catch a cold.

"Hey Rock-a-Billy."

Jaxy covered his mouth and nose with a handkerchief, turned, and did a double take that dismantled his early warning system. Barefoot on the grass stood Jillian in a black, scissor-cut miniskirt and cornhusk hair that flounced about a red and white, polka-dot blouse knotted at the waist with his Mighty Ducks jacket pulled off the shoulder.

"J-Jillian?" he stuttered, completely thrown off plan.

"Huu!" she warded him off. "Are you sick?"

"You said you were," answered Jaxy in a muffled voice.

Jillian tugged at his elbow to reassure him that she was perfectly fine.

"Keep your germs to yourself," Jaxy flicked away her fingers anyway.

"Good! We're both well." Jillian clasped his neck and arched, staining the buttons to the breaking point. "Keep staring at my shmoos. We're being watched."

"Park's closed!" shouted the groundskeeper with the first spit of rain.

"This way!" she said, ducking through the bracken to the servant's cottage where she had Jaxy crouch low against the alcove's drawn, lace curtains. "We're safe here."

"From the woodsman?" asked Jaxy.

Jillian charged the air with dangerous excitement, "He's buried five they say. Least that's how many Spruce he planted equaling the number of new ghost sightings that haunt the grounds. He must recruit for them."

"Who?"

"The owners, silly. Georgiana Pittock died in nineteen eighteen. One hundred years ago. Huu! There's a coincidence. Henry followed her into the hole the next year. They lived only a few after completion but must have loved it because their ghosts stuck around to rearrange furniture, open windows to air out the place, and other curious things. The spirits of the servants and butler get in on it too."

"Are you always this fun?"

"Get down!" Jillian hooked a heel driving Jaxy to the ground, grabbing fistfuls of shirt, and burying her face in his chest. "Don't let them get me—promise!"

The more Jaxy resisted the harder she tickled until he cracked, "Promise! Jeez, did you see one?"

Jillian sat on his stomach and removed his eyeglasses, wiped them dry and squinted through them. "Not with these coke bottles."

The vision of Guin's face suddenly eclipsed the one respiring into his own, so Jaxy got down to business. "Now that we chased off ghosts and goblins—my angel. Did you bring it?"

Jillian patted the jacket, "Right here."

As the tempest cut loose the gardener yelled from the ledge, "You there! Didn't you hear me? Park's closed!!"

"He found us!" Jillian cried in faux alarm.

Out from under the one mansion attraction not pitched in the brochure Jaxy scrambled to his feet. Unable to withstand the onslaught of the natural elements, unnatural specters, and the park patrol, to the car lot they fled against a punishing wall of rain. When Jaxy opened his van to usher Jillian inside where they could close the deal without having to dodge buckets of ice water thrown their way by the capricious gods of winter, the gardener beeped his horn, and waved them on as he zipped by in his truck.

Jillian squeezed Jaxy's hand and hopped in her Mini-Cooper shouting, "Follow me to Firebreak Steaks. I'm hungry!"

"Wait! Jillian!! My glasses!!!" Jaxy waved his arms, then dropped to the ground as a rapid release of bullets whizzed by his ear deployed at close range from an Italian racing bike partially concealed by bushes at the edge of the parking lot entrance.

Jillian stomped the accelerator, spinning the teensy tires through the sharp exit turn to swamp the gun-toting assailant with a wave of water. Jaxy jumped into the cab and, hunching low, through the same puddle he hydroplaned to slide out and smack the motorbike by the fender with a solid, metallic crunch. The impact knocked Moby back onto the road, while taking the last two rounds in the rear.

CHAPTER 17

The storm turned into a whopper after all. Bumper to bumper the climbers inched their way off the slopes until through the wiper-blurred windshield the unsympathetic men noted an out-of-state Mercedes crumpled in the median.

"California drivers. You'll find one at the bottom of every pileup," Brad signaled to bypass the bottleneck.

"Too bad we didn't take the towie. Could'a hit the flashers and been home by now," grouched Rory.

"Next time," noted Brad, and having had enough of rubberneckers, kicked the Jeep into four high, and over the rise they spun, flinging muddy weeds all the way to Snoqualmie Parkway.

"Over there." Rory motioned at a cluster of small businesses.

"We're just gettin' goin'," argued Brad, reaching speed.

"Thirsty."

Except when scouting the route up a wall, Rory called the shots and Brad followed. They had enlisted in the Marines as strangers and left as lifelong friends with this arrangement that suited them both. Brad, therefore, did as commanded and idled at the handicap slot, while The Captain dashed into the market.

A minute later Rory emerged to lean against the dry side of an aluminum awning, clutching a paper bag under his coat and a radio to his head. "Jillian's in town??" he asked with startled concern.

"Not for long. She's saying goodbye to Thunder Roll!!" tattled Rita Klinnick.

Rory's angst shifted to excitement. "She's selling him?"

"No, she's taking time off from work to spend it without you, you dumb ox."

"Uh? Why would she do that."

"You tell me. The last time your wife 'needed space' she crossed the continental divide. Better get in gear and take care of business at home while you still have one!"

"Thanks for the tip, Rita. I'll be in touch," Rory snapped the radio to his leg.

Inside the jeep, Rory brushed the rain from his cargo pants and slid the sack to expose licorice twists and a silver stopper.

"Are you nuts? Put that away," Brad thumbed over his shoulder.

"Want some?" Rory dug his knife into the foil.

"Drinking and driving. You can't be serious."

"I'm drinking, you're driving." Rory uncorked the tequila and took a long swallow.

"Union meeting that bad, huh?"

"Screw the IBEW," Rory moistened a whetstone in a slurry of licorice spit. "I want an Ortega burger."

Home safe from out-of-state drivers, Brad slid four patties under the broiler, cracked a domestic, and dealt solitaire while Rory paced. After enduring ten, agonizing minutes Brad interrupted, "I brought you down from Hubba, Cap', to keep peace at the committee table. Not to hear you lose it at mine."

Rory straddled a kitchen chair. "If Steve Harvey asked, 'Name something a flight attendant does on an airplane'—'Stays faithful' wouldn't get a vote."

Brad set out the paper plates and condiments, then shuffled cards. "Twenty-one? We'll play for the last pickle."

Rory cut the deck, "You're not getting it, Brad."

"That storming your own house with a carbine is the healing touch that's missing from your marriage? No. Not quite. You two ever communicate?"

Rory bit into the burger. "She doesn't. It's like talking to Pepper."

The half-wild hybrid entered the conversation with a lazy whop of her bristly tail.

"See that? She rolls her eyes and wags, then does the exact opposite of what you say."

"Let's show him. C'mere girl!" Brad slapped his thigh.

Taking her sweet time, Pepper rose, stretched her muscular, sinewy legs, turned around, and went to gnawing a sheep's shank on newsprint, the acceptable substitute for a dog dish to a Wolador.

"To my point. I busted my butt fixing up the place too. Poured a new patio. 'Scaped the back forty into a frickin' bird sanctuary! Does my wife appreciate it?"

Brad dealt one up, one down. "Probably. Look, my ex dragged me through it too when she ran off with—,"

"Hit me."

"A cougar-chaser from the gym with mommy issues. What can you do?" Brad took a tug from his beer.

"Twist a foam roller up his ass, that's what." Rory set his cards down, "Stay."

"Nineteen," Brad swept the cards away. "J.D.'s a lifer with the airlines—you knew that going in."

"You taking sides?"

"Trying to see both."

Rory sliced the dill down the middle. "At least yours didn't split the house while you were out of town."

"Candice took the house while I was out of town."

Rory wiped the juice from his chin, "Mill said, 'A man who has nothing for which he is willing to fight is a miserable creature.'"

"Referring to Uncle Sam, I believe." Brad slurped the other half.

"'Semper Fi', goes way beyond the Marines, Brad. A lesson Jillian's going to learn."

Brad doubted that but kept it to himself.

WITH A BUM FOOT and an Aprilia road racer laid down with a punctured gas line and bent fork, Golly Gee had even fewer friends in Portland to hail than her sister on a bad luck night. Her strategically placed friend and mentor inside the police bureau, Sergeant "Tank" Pantzer, privately backed her overseas ambitions with a few of his own. Unfortunately, the cold war era, East Berlin counterspy could not publicize the fact, so permanently banned her from his westside beat. To boot, regional gangs wanted her head on a pike for infringement, and she needed to get off the hill fast in case an unfriendly caught sight of her tailing Jillian to the mansion.

Golly ran down her short list of civilian contacts. Remarkable Reuben couldn't be more useless snow-birding in Baja. Calling upon her godfather held even less promise, for going open season on his fair-haired one would be met with severe disapproval. A ride for hire might work, but why hazard exposure when she could borrow one?

Thus, she covered the trashed bike with leaves and vines and tested a tender ankle that turned in the crash. It seemed okay. With a wire coil and utility knife, off she limped to find a jalopy to jump. As the bypath grew long and snaky, Golly Gee cut through the groves toward pagoda lights and an old Peugeot. She paid for leaving the hardpack though, when her soles lost traction on the slick leaves and down a rivulet she tumbled, landing with an inelegant plop on a storm drain. No longer able to bear her body weight, back to the gate lodge she went on muddy hands and knees through the drizzle.

Soaked to the skin, in the alcove she shivered and shook while growing hot under the collar thinking of her sister, high and dry before a roaring fire, sharing a toddy with Jaxy. Facing a long and miserable night she reached out to Yan. Fortune smiled down through the rain. On account of an early Saskatchewanian batch, her right hand had left a day early for Oregon to connect with her number one drug distributor: Rory Avlon.

In an elevated mood, Golly Gee hitched her chaps, picked a banana slug from her hair, and snapping a forked stick to size with her good heel set off hoping the city parks had not the funds or foresight to alarm the mansion's upper access points. Along the masonry she shined her light for finger holds when rounding a corner, a heavy, knotted rope struck Golly square on the lips! From under of a tangle of whips and covers that fell about her shoulders and head, the frantic cripple struck with the crutch this way and that until coming to realize that her attacker was nothing more than a weighted tassel at the end of a heavy drape flapping in the wind. Elated at this stroke of luck, Golly Gee didn't have to force entry into the Pittock Mansion after all! For someone had left a ground floor window wide open, letting the curtains dance in the rain.

Strange.

CHAPTER 18

L&C Hotel, Portland, OR
6:00 p.m. Thursday, January 4

Not easy for anyone to keep up with Jillian on a clear day, the fireball drove so fast that in the downpour Jaxy lost her. When he approached downtown, he looked up the steakhouse, but from the gully-washed intersection Jaxy could only make out a blurry neon "Hotel" sign glimmering through the rain.

"Oh no, we're not! We are not lodging here together!" argued Jaxy. The sky then opened with a gale force such that he barely made it off the flooded avenue to the lee of the hotel marquee when the phone kicked in. He mulled it over. Even if she paid a goon to do him in under the cover of a January storm and ditch him for the gardener to pot, she still had the guardian angel and he needed it back.

Well, since my baby left me . . . Again, he let the ringtone play through. When Heartbreak Hotel started for the third time, he curtly acceded, "What?"

"What's taking you? My feet are freezing!" asked Jillian through chattering teeth.

"You almost got me killed up there. That's what," said Jaxy.

"Aw, those scar-wee ghosts can't hurt you."

"If they can interior decorate, what's to keep them from forming motorcycle clubs and doing drive-bys?"

"Uh-oh," Jillian grew serious, "did the road racer follow you out?"

"Not in the shape I left it."

"Huu! That bee's been in my bonnet since the jewelers. I changed our meeting location to the mansion in hopes of shaking it at the bridge."

"Or once your jeweler told you what the angel is worth, you hired a motorcycle gang to follow us there, and you're calling on my phone to see if I'm still above ground."

"My word, Jaxy. That is the meanest thing anyone has ever said, you despicable man. This angel has been nothing but trouble since the moment we met. I don't want a thing to do with it—*or you*—anymore."

Jaxy raised his voice over the pelting rain, "On that we stand united. But it's after dark and I missed my deadline so I might as well bed down somewhere in the hills and take it off your hands in the morning."

"But your glasses."

"I carry back-ups."

"And the jacket?"

"Yours for tonight. Can't have you catch a real cold."

"Aww, and that, Jaxy, is the nicest thing any person has ever. And I say person because I rescued a falcon from the dugout and made the coach take it to a shelter. Long story short, it got well and went on its happy way, then one day it brought me quail still warm from the kill, gutted and plucked and dressed to grill. So, I threw it on the coals and . . . sure you aren't hungry?"

"I was. Where's Firebreaks?"

Tap. Tap. Tap.

Jaxy looked straight out at an umbrella tip. She had been there the whole time.

"Hurry—Burr!!" beseeched Jillian hopping in bare feet.

Jaxy ran the window down to raise a staunch protest: "I am NOT spending one minute at this flea-bitten flophouse with you, so hand it over and let's wrap this up."

"And leave me to dine alone?"

"Quit stonewalling and give me the goddam angel!"

Whack! The umbrella raised a welt on Jaxy's neck. "Take it back lest I smite thee again," she said.

At a loss to the offense, Jaxy massaged the thrash mark, "Take back what?"

"What you called him." Jillian brought the guardian angel up alongside the umbrella. "Go on, apologize."

"This isn't happening . . . I'm going to wake up any second in Glendale . . ."

"I can't hear you."

To the angel Jaxy said, "I'm sorry I called you a 'goddam'—."

Whack!

Jaxy's hand shot out to snag the chain, but Jillian moved faster as she pattered to the lobby. By the time Jaxy caught up, the desk had two card keys ready for a room circled on a map.

"Second elevator to the fifth floor. Fitness and sauna stay open till eleven," the host walked Jaxy through the amenities.

Jaxy brought down a fist, "Reverse the charges."

"It's on the misses' card. Let the lady do her part."

"For a single, then."

"I should say so," the host wrapped a reassuring hand around Jaxy's wrist and gasped, "Your pulse! Breathe with me . . . that's it, slow and steady . . . not too deep. Out with the old fears . . . in with the new year. Good. Wash up, I'll have the concierge ready the bower. And congratulations—she's quite the catch."

"A catch? Her?" repeated Jaxy, in a fog.

Down a red velvet, papered hall, Jillian tripped along barefoot to Firebreak Steaks singing out, "Dry off—I'll find a booth."

Holding a straight face, the bellhop offered Jaxy a towel. "For the mud, sir."

Jaxy freshened up and joined Jillian at a posh, recessed table set with a tea rose where the host had the duo pose for a photograph.

"We have proof Daisy Mae finally got her man and it's going up in this booth! 'Shine's on us. Enjoy your honeymoon," she slipped them drink coupons.

Jaxy slapped them down. "Honeymoon! Have you lost your mind???"

Jillian ran her chilly toes up his pant cuff. "I had to say something to get us a reserved table. Huu! She's coming. Quick! Put this on."

Jaxy batted her foot away.

Without taking her eyes from the menu, Jillian showed a man's wedding band to the host sniffling, "My husband won't wear it—says it gets in the way of climbing."

The proper host said something into Jaxy's ear while Jillian spoke to the waiter: "Black tea with half ruby-red and grenadine over crushed ice with a cherry." Turning to Jaxy she explained, "I came up with that when Rita brought home a sack of overripe grapefruits. I said, 'what do I do with these?' She said, 'When life gives you a jillion grapefruits make 'Jillian-ade'.' So, I did!"

Jaxy looked dead ahead and said, "I'll take a 'Jackson-ade'."

"I'm afraid I do not know that one either, sir," said the patient waiter.

"Tennessee whiskey on the rocks with a side of peanuts." Jaxy handed over his voucher. "I made that up just now."

Between jazz sets, the flautist serenaded the newly married while Jillian rambled through bites and yums of a six-ounce cut about Henry Pittock and the Oregonian, how the property fell to ruins after his demise, and the city procured the dilapidated mansion for a song to spend many times that on its restoration. When Jaxy asked about work, through a forced smile she spoke not of herself, but of her husband's exploits coming home from the war as power line foreman, then upon building his electrical empire, rising to prominence in the union. Their combined income seemed fantastic until Rory grew cross at her for being gone weeks at a time. He told Jillian they did not need her money anymore and wanted her out of the sky and on his lap every night. This made her want to fly away all the more she lamented, "Because he loves Bonita more than me."

From that point on, Jaxy caught but a portion of Jillian's words, for he kept returning to the problems stacking up at his own home.

"Are you listening to me, or those crunchy peanuts?" Jillian arched her eyebrows and leaned farther than the required distance to try one.

"I'm sorry. Missing band practice tonight—that's all." Jaxy diverted his stare to the grand piano.

Jillian closed her blouse. "I listened to 'Glottal Catch'. Carried me right back to the Ozarks."

Jaxy livened, "'House of the Rising Sun' goes further. To the brothels of England."

"Ee-yuu. That's an awful song. Why bring that up?"

"Then which Animals song do you like?"

"I like green alligators and long-necked geese," Jillian broke out singing.

"That's the Irish Rovers."

"Whatever. But mostly I like ones about horses."

"A Horse is a horse . . ." Jaxy sang the Mr. Ed theme.

Jillian punished him in turn with "My Little Pony" and then asked, "do your fish have names?"

"They don't live long enough to get one."

Jillian gave a hard, penetrating stare.

"Whenever Guin gets stoned, she forgets to cover the koi pond. Try to see it as her way of feeding the wildlife. Do you have pets?"

In an instant Jillian bubbled over about Thunder Roll, how she purchased the thoroughbred at auction, then found a ranch in The

Dalles to board, groom and exercise him. In exchange, Thunder provided the rancher's bay with company in the stalls. Jillian tried to make it over often because time spent with her horse gave her a huge lift, kept her away from Rory—who, she footnoted, regarded one as an extravagant waste of money—and made Rory jealous of her time and attention.

Jaxy understood, "My sweetheart likes music, but hates the way it takes me away. At the same time she can't see how a two-fold career consumes her. Growing up with three brothers and one bathroom, you'd think she'd have learned a thing or two about sharing."

Reflected Jillian, "Had I a brother, I might have too."

CHAPTER 19

Paris, France

Born in Copenhagen but taught to bicycle on the plains of Pays de France, Jean Roche loved his caregivers and gave no thought to his Danish roots until his dental ones suffered prolonged bleeding when his wisdom teeth came out. Despite an abundance of home remedies and the laying-on of hands the flow, nonetheless, persisted. Away from his household of well-intentioned faith healers, tests revealed to Jean's relief that the syndrome came from chromosome pairing, and not Parisian bathhouses.

In short, the young man had hereditary hemophilia.

The mild and dutiful art student took his herbal elixir regimen by day to look good, and protein infusions by night to stay that way. Upon stabilization a physical therapist helped trace Jean's medical history. Wrapped up in the research they found more reasons to spend time together and eventually rented a luxurious le Marais studio on the Seine. As time went by, Jean's interest in his condition fell off as the Roche name on canvas surpassed his university art instructors' in recognition and remuneration. No longer caring about genealogy, showing up to class, or socializing with peers, the phenom quit school to hide out with his roommate, who modeled a faultless physique for many a Roche nude up to the day an envious art rival blew his companion to Timbuktu with a letter bomb, sending protestors into the streets and Jean Roche's reputation soaring. In his sole interview with an art gazette, Jean portrayed the overplayed attention as insensitive to the devastating loss of a lover, half a face, and most of his hearing, and refused to attend any more press conferences. Once the noise died down the recluse shuttered his windows, cloaked his face with a black mantilla, and paid the maid to collect his mail and shop for skin care products.

Jean's languor lingered for months until in the witching hour, at the precise time the one sister sat stewing inside a Portland mansion, and the other stood to pay for a porterhouse steak, a hefty matron thumped her walker on the Roche apartment. In fright, Jean called on the gendarmes to fly to his aid only to find that this slow-paced trustee came armed with nothing but a balance sheet of his assets and an æbleskiver. While Jean digested the goody and his documented holdings, the Danish administrator swept the tenement clean of electronic bugs while explaining how his state of health came by inbred lines of nobility, and the letter bomb from a Siberian hitman named "Rat Catcher"—the same assassin that murdered his biological father.

The doyenne then pitched that the Romanov diadem was the Grand Duke's to wear could he stomach marrying a prescreened, Prussian princess over that queen from Amsterdam. Elsewise, *The Guardian Angel of Maria Feodorovna* would pass to the next eligible candidate. When Jean grew wroth that this Danish stranger had knowledge of his *affaire de cœur* with the housecleaner, the executor showed him a miniaturized microphone found in the duster and said "Naughty Lotti" wouldn't be by to polish the floors anymore.

She then provided Jean with a travel visa and an opportunity to meditate in safe seclusion at a mountaintop monastery where his black kimono would blend right in. Jean pushed back, saying that he had already tried holistic medicines, and the doctors would frown on feculent animals packing plasma therapy to a primitive ashram lacking sanitized facilities. To this the custodian testified that state-of-the-art treatment was available a car ride away, and Totum, Washington had flush commodes.

CHAPTER 20

Firebreak Steaks, Portland, OR
7:00 p.m. Thursday, January 4

By the time Jaxy brought his nose up from the tip calculator, Jillian had her credit card in the restaurant check folder.

Jaxy laid his on top. "Dutch, Jillian."

"Danish tonight." Jillian made him put it away and opened her "Steeds and Studs" art gallery homepage to show off a chestnut stallion.

"Thunder Roll?" asked Jaxy.

"You remember!" said Jillian, and swept to the next, "And that's Gem!"

"Beautiful animals."

"A fourteen inch starts at twelve hundred, depending on matte and frame. I have a charcoal collection too. Think about it while I expense dinner. See? Not a date." Jillian poked at the cart.

Jaxy made a gallant effort to not choke at the sticker price and gestured toward the bar saying, "Let's take it there."

Jillian fiddled with her napkin. "Can't."

"Were sure tossing them down at Klinnick's."

"That was sparkling grapefruit juice."

"Oh? . . . Oh!" Jaxy moved his whiskey from sight onto a vacant table.

"It's not that." Jillian smoothed her front, and having a difficult time, in halting words finally forced out: "I'm going . . . to have . . . a baby."

"That's awesome!" congratulated Jaxy, inching his way along. "Your husband's right about not flying. Speaking of, put me down for one Thunder on the nine-month plan, and I'll take the angel and see how far down the road I can go. Guin's expecting too, ha-ha, but not in that way. I have to be home Sunday."

Jillian pressed his hand to the table. "Jaxy, I'm scared."

"Well yeah, it is scary—I mean it sounds scary. I'm sure they have classes."

"Of my husband."

"Why? He doesn't want a kid?"

Jillian's lips went tight. "Not if it's not his."

Jaxy collected himself and made a face at the cup. "This is coffee country. Let's go somewhere with a decent roast to sort this out."

"Let's make a cup in the room."

"You call that decent?

"I'll brew a pot at my house!" Jillian perked up.

"Whoa! That's the last place we are going."

"But you promised!" she said, attracting the uneasy notice of other diners.

"What with? When?"

"At the mansion," answered Jillian, and then with enough force to be heard in the hall scalded him with, "*to have and to hold*!"

Jaxy apologized to a nearby table and marched her to the corridor. "This is why we need to find a quiet spot."

"Like—my—house."

"Like hell." Jaxy flipped the room key up and down; a guitar pick trick he did for finger control.

Jillian balled her fists, "See? You don't care."

"To have my ass kicked? No."

"Told you. Rory's in Idaho."

"I'm not talking about *him*."

Jillian played with his shirt buttons. "I don't mean to impose, but I don't know a soul in Portland and that cycle stalker has me super scared!"

"Not one? How long have you lived here?"

"Too long," Jillian cocked her head. "What else did you have planned tonight?"

Jaxy took up her drink voucher. "To spend it watching the Ducks."

"Come watch them at my place! Gehck, they leave droppings everywhere and quack me awake each morning because Rory thinks it's a gas to feed them table scraps before work. Half the waterfowl must stop in Clackamas. We're a duck stop—get it? Truck stop, duck stop."

"I'm referring to the Anaheim . . . do I have to spell it out?"

"Try me."

"I am a man—engaged to a woman—who most surely—would not understand!"

"Since 2008? *That*, I do not understand."

No closer to the angel than when he arrived and flustered beyond words with Jillian's impetuosity, Jaxy slipped off to beg of work an extra day of grace. In seconds he came back shaking his fanny pack at the host, "See what she made me do! I locked my keys in the van!"

"I made him?" Jillian whacked his thigh with the umbrella.

"Darling—your vows!" the host pled for restraint.

Jillian patted Jaxy's leg. "Sorry, toots. Did that hurt?"

"Cut . . . it . . . out," said Jaxy, and then reviewing the limitations on his auto service cursed, "I can't believe it. My policy doesn't cover this."

"And I can't believe you don't keep a spare somewhere!"

"I do," wilted Jaxy, "under the floor mat."

"Didn't my mother-in-law teach you *anything*?" asked Jillian, offering up her travel club card.

"Not much."

"Unbelievable," the host plucked the plastic from Jillian's fingers and dialed in the mishap.

THE DISPATCHER DOLED OUT the essentials: "Got a lockout at the L&C Hotel. Some dick-fer on his honeymoon left a Ram 1500 b-frame under the rotunda. California plate M-O-B-Y-D-3. Can you make it by nine?"

"I'm in Leavenworth," said Brad Thornton.

"That's not what 'Find A Lazy-Butt Tow Operator' says. The sooner you're there, the sooner they're gone—Oregon's counting on you."

Brad shot Rory a distasteful look, "California newlyweds."

"'Frisco Hipsters. Who else would honeymoon here?".

"Let's go Pep'! Can't keep the missus waiting." Brad leashed the collar while Rory left for Clackamas to go watch basketball at home.

Under the hotel rotunda Brad found the beached whale. Poking a finger into Moby's aerated door he asked, "Run off with someone's bride?"

"Nah . . . hunting." Jaxy scratched a dog's slender snout sniffing at his cuff.

Pepper ducked around and then inched in for another taste of Jaxy's thumb while her owner jimmied the door.

Jaxy wiped away the slobber and passed Brad the membership card.

Brad dropped the smile. "Holder has to sign."

From the hotel Jillian came to authorize then stepped back saying, "Brad! Aren't you . . . in Idaho?"

"Shorthanded tonight with the California crazies on the road," Brad replied, then turning to Jaxy asked, "this the lucky lady?"

Jaxy moved away. "Nice to meet you. Should get back to the reception."

Brad laid a heavy hand on Jaxy's shoulder. "The garter can wait."

"J.D. your girl too?" Jaxy knocked it away.

Before Pepper could settle the quarrel in her master's favor, Jillian spanked the dog's nose and separated them. "Oh Bradley, this is one gigantic misunderstanding! My dear old art teacher, Jaxy, married today after the longest engagement in the 'Guin'-ness Book of Records, and I did the guestbook! Everybody dressed fifties and the sock hop was the funnest ever! I tried to make him take a painting, but Jaxy wouldn't hear it and bought one. Isn't he the best?" Jillian laid a loud smooch on Jaxy's cheek and showed Brad the order.

Said Brad, "My mistake. Best wishes to you. And do drive the missus home safe. You do not want to see me again."

Just inside the lobby Jillian hid behind a planter box until the tow truck trundled away, then up on her toes she went to box Jaxy's ear as he came in. "'*Your girl too*?' Jeepers, I can't believe you said that!"

"And you don't know a single soul in Portland! May I have the angel so you can party on with the rest of your friends?" asked Jaxy, kicking open the hotel door.

Down went Jillian's chin.

"Say, 'goodnight' Jillian." Jaxy wrenched the wedding band from his finger and held it out in trade.

With venom Jillian shot back, "Goodnight!" and removing hers, ricocheted it off his head to roll down the lobby and stop at the host's feet.

Jaxy raised his hands in innocence. "She threw it."

While the hotel redressed the groom's egregious behavior, Jillian curled up on the padded bench facing the wall to work out what to do next. To have badgered Brad for the scoop on her husband would have invited suspicion, so she would need to physically see the brown Bronco on the driveway. If Rory came home early, then onward to The Dalles they would venture where Jaxy would meet Thunder Roll whether he wished to or not. Jillian ceased deliberating when Jaxy whispered a radical change of plan in her ear.

"We're going where?" She sat up confounded.

Jaxy raised his eyes skyward. "To the top."

To incentivize Jaxy to allow his whiney wife her way on their nuptials, the L&C Hotel upgraded the couple to the honeymooner's penthouse at no additional charge. There, from a cushy, heart-shaped mattress fitted with satin sheets and dove white pillows, Jillian slipped off her underwear, took aim at the chandelier and let her powder blue bikini fly.

She stared up at the briefs snagged on a bulb. "Thank goodness they don't install ceiling mirrors. Can you imagine how unattractive a couple in bed would look from this angle? Then I'd wonder—what is he watching?"

Focused on the Anaheim Ducks' line change, Jaxy replied, "Hockey." Then swiveling to the window, he pulled aside the curtains as raindrops turned to snowflakes and asked, "Can your car make it home in this?"

"It's all-wheel, but we should leave now," Jillian shut off the television.

Jaxy flipped it on. "Yes. You probably should."

"And send me home alone? I'm telling!" Jillian reached to the nightstand to call down and allege anew that her atrocious husband wanted to kick her to the curb.

Jaxy fought back with a blistering, counter accusation, "She is the most conniving person ever, and that includes the guy who torched Burning Man four days ahead of schedule!"

Jillian nabbed the phone from his hand. "He started it!"

"Did not!" said Jaxy, at which point he leaned on the cradle and killed the call.

With what leverage he had, Jaxy set the terms: "Put the guardian angel this instant in my fanny pack and I will go anywhere you say. After that I will block your calls and forget we ever met!"

"Pinky promise?"

Jaxy ground his teeth and hooked fingers. "Pinky promise."

Jillian shoved the tiffany beaded box into the pack. "You can follow me to my house."

Jaxy looked out towards the river. "I ought to ride with you."

"I won't lose you," Jillian stressed.

"More snow is coming, and I do not want to chain the tires again. I'll call for a taxi ride back to the hotel when you feel safe."

Forced to surrender her bargaining chip and leave the cargo van behind, Jillian mussed towels and linens to make a newlywed mess while Jaxy bagged the soaps and shampoos. Set to go, she flipped the "do not disturb" hanger on the door and tugged Jaxy to the elevator where he pressed the arrow for lower parking.

"I brought a change of clothes for one night. Period," declared Jaxy in no uncertain terms, loaning out his argyles.

In an indelicate fashion Jillian pulled the socks over her bare toes. "Huu, Jaxy! You move slower than this elevator."

"On the sofa."

"Sounds tight."

"Ding!" the doors parted and up jumped Jillian to interlace her fingers through his and lead him to the slaughter singing, "Baby Let Me Take You Home . . ."

CHAPTER 21

The Avlon Home, Clackamas, OR
7:30 p.m. Thursday, January 4

Through the neighborhoods above Clackamas to a lawn lit with
seasonal decorations Rory navigated the raised, copper trim, Eddie
Bauer, Ford Bronco. He stopped to feed Bonita as he came through
the garage, then on to the master bedroom he went to puzzle over his
flighty wife's unpacked luggage.

"Jillian's not here, Brad," Rory updated his buddy over the house
phone, "but she didn't leave either."

"Not sure what you're saying Cap'."

"I'm saying I found her roller bag, so she didn't go to The Dalles.
An outbound call went to the beauty salon at ten."

"Not ten thirty? That's what this detective B.S. is about?? To find
out your wife stayed home to get her flippin' hair done for a wedding
instead of riding off like a retard into an arctic storm??"

"What wedding? Jillian didn't' say anything about a wedding."

"Bumped into her at the reception at the L&C."

Rory quieted down. "Ow, that hurts. Why didn't she ask me
along?"

"Maybe if you could go easy on the punch bowl for a night, Rufus,
she would."

"You too? You too??" Rory soured and hung up, for a greater problem was headed his way from Saskatoon. With the inconvenience of having his wife in town, Rory could not let Yan the dope man anywhere near the house, so heading out he stuck a card to the doorbell for Yan to stop at the Electric Avlon service shop.

OF THE MANUFACTURING AND sale of unregulated pharmaceuticals, turnover statistics are hard to obtain. But in general, they who hold out longest in the business consume least of the product; particularly those in the dual employ of Royal Canadian Mounted Police and the Beaver Lodge Assassins Association.

Superintendent Pierre de Chavoie became such a character when conducting a routine walkthrough of the Eleemosynary Beavers of British Columbia, Canada Day parade float entry let it be known that he had fallen from grace for gross misuse of public service computers on government time. Demoted to truck and trailer inspections, Pierre hung on the edge of losing his doublewide trailer to foreclosure and needed a second source of income to climb out. This got to Golly Gee who zeroed out his bankrupt accounts for instituting a double standard at border checkpoints. In no time de Chavoie found himself in the black and working two jobs.

Capitalizing on his gift for gab, Golly placed Pierre de Chavoie at the helm of market expansion. Since every Lodge member had a field name, and Big Nasty and Little Nasty were taken, she sized him up and said, "You're 'Average Nasty'", or YAN for short. In a Suburban loaded with the best tech and Canadian opioids, she sent Yan south to cozy up to union leaders, and a special affiliate Golly Gee had in mind: Electric Avlon.

The one restriction for wholesale markdown to preferred buyers didn't ride on bulk quantities ordered, but that they not withhold any for personal use. Distributors, therefore, had to pass random drug panels. The threat meant little to Rory since the electrician preferred to recreate exclusively with Jaliscan liquor. The requisites for Yan to keep his trailer were the same with one additional provision: Supply Rory with top shelf tequila, invent a fiction vis-à-vis his latest heartbreak, then let Captain Avlon ramble into the wee hours about his froward wife for Yan to record and relay to the Lodge.

With this objective in mind, Yan watched snow accrue on an animated Santa Claus from the comfort of the Suburban while bringing Golly Gee up to speed on his persnickety customer who objected to the latest price hike.

Out of patience, Golly Gee yapped, "I don't care. Give the drugs away at cost and pop out the third seat to make room for my bike."

"I would, but the Bronc's not here."

"Maybe Rory garaged it. Did you look?"

"And cross that grid of trip hazards?"

"Pansy."

Yan opened and closed the driver's door with a thunk, muted the phone, and plugged in his own angel tracking system pinning Golly's location to 3229 NW Pittock Drive. What is she doing there? he wondered, verifying her position on a second, global positioning receiver he had secretly shipped to his home to monitor her every move. Golly Gee's broken, electronics box he had special ordered to come with faulty software in order to force her to return it to the vender. This way she would keep both angels until the Valentine's Day raid. Elegant in simplicity, this tactic did not allow for Jaxy's expedient repair, forcing Yan to impound the rental car to buy time. When Golly circumvented that, Yan exchanged the angels at the airport to get the beacon out of Jaxy's hands and back into hers at the high price of temporarily losing sight of the Fabergé.

The slender file on Jackson Mason Thrie with no living, blood relative, and limited hobbies and work experience outside the Russian

Antique Mall made for a fast read, giving Yan nothing useful beyond how to crate a samovar or tune a guitar. But with that shrewd, rockabilly act Jaxy had stayed ten steps ahead since icing Pops at the boathouse. This presented a challenge more thrilling than bringing down Golly Gee, and Yan did not wish to gaff the little fish to let a bigger one slip away. If he could just catch Jaxy with his pants down before the Captain did . . .

Yan checked-in with a private investigator who stayed current with Jillian's travel card usage, updated the folder, and slid it under the seat before turning on the headset. "Sorry Gol', the place is deader than your last four dinner dates, but the L&C is hopping! Seems Jillian didn't make it to The Dalles after all but took a room with your boytoy. Hubby must have come home sooner than expected."

"Why that . . ."

K-BWAAANG!!!

"Ooh, that sounded bad."

"I kicked a pedal harp over with my bad foot!" howled Golly.

"Where the heck are you?"

"Shut-up and goose your lardy ass to the Pittock Mansion and pull my bike out of the weeds!"

"Given'r, Gol."

With a heave and a ho, they got the plastered motorcycle into the Suburban by yoking the fork to the rack and pulling out the back seats to let the rest hang off the end. Yan didn't question, and Golly didn't elaborate. As they passed over the Columbia, she routed them eastward to a nondescript abode while rolling out a radical change of marching orders:

"You're not peddling drugs or alcohol anymore, but religion. Tell Rory to come off his lofty peak because you met a devoted butter tart from West Van, and it's time he acted like a responsible family man and do the same. I want nothing but good news on this or your gun, badge, and trailer."

"What are you doing here?" asked Yan when they stopped at a house with a '96 Civic on the drive that had an exhaust blackened sticker that read: "Honk 40 Times If You're Orthodox".

"Watching golf." Golly Gee slammed the door behind her.

WITH SWEATY PALMS YAN accelerated the Suburban with its new shine and sound, waking up Minnehaha with "Back That A** Up" as he headed out to a brick-and-mortar book retailer. After settling on *The Bulletproof Guide to an Everlasting Love*, Yan radioed in—not to the Captain, not to the Lodge, and not to the detachment in Surrey, but straight to the top of the Force: "Going dark for 24 to surface in 73. I need the dope on a mid-nineties, Hon..zz..zp!" the frequency fuzzed out. Shit. Until then, he had to hold a successful mediation with a mean motherfucker not known for balanced self-appraisal on a topic Yan knew nothing about, or kiss his doublewide goodbye.

CHAPTER 22

The Klapakis Parsonage, Minnehaha, WA
8:00 p.m. Thursday, January 4

"Golf ees like church," said Fr. Michael from his recliner, skipping through the TV stations to the Australasia PGA finals.

"Uh-huh," replied his wife over a deep basket of purple yarn and darning needles, "your homilies and the sports channels put me to sleep."

"You see honey, at all times, and in all places, liturgy happens—and so does golf."

Camille could not knit and watch television, so to her none of this nonsense mattered. How her husband could fill his pipe, follow the leaderboard, and grade prep-school, Anatomy quizzes, she could not fathom.

"Ta-Da!" Camille sniffed at a finished shawl. "Hope the recipient can't tell tobacco from incense."

"You want to trade jobs?"

"Sure! Hand me those. I'll give them all 'A's.'"

"Why you do dat?"

"Because anyone who doesn't drop your lecture by the third week deserves one. At any rate, that pesky student called again. She missed you at the office," Camille brought him the number on a scratch pad.

"How did student get house number?" Father Michael swiped through his missed calls then at the page. "Oh. Yillianz'."

"Something like that, but with a 'J', as in *Jillian*—and the 'z' is silent," she pointed out the absent letter. Camille had long stopped trying to improve her husband's English, but every so often she couldn't help giving it another go.

"Yilli' no student. She work for airline and attend church now and then. Sits in back."

"That stuck-up thing? Never stays for coffee."

"You notice that?"

"It's my job."

"I thought it was to doze off."

"Not this Sunday." From her Bible leaf the Presbytera pulled a bulletin. "She stared at the front for the longest time, then turned it over and redrew from memory *all fourteen ecumenical fathers*! Then left it on the pew for someone to throw away."

Fr. Michael studied each saint from front to back. "Outstanding."

"To see a gift like that wasted flying here to there to nowhere. Between putts invite her for Sunday dinner. Could pay her to touch up your illustrations. The old flip charts need help."

"Now whose being pest?"

"Mike . . ."

"Okay, I call. But not this minute," he wiggled his pipe by the stem to wedge a crux, downslope chip out of the rough and onto the green.

"By all means don't have a stroke missing one," snorted Camille, and at hearing a loud car blow down the street playing rude music, peeked out the fisheye lens. "Oh dear. It's her at the door—*and she's limping*!"

"Golly!" Fr. Michael came out to lend a hand, "You have terrible spill!"

The mud-splattered cyclist grimaced, "Lovorsky's wheelman, Jaxy? Not so cute anymore. He rammed my bike at the Pittock after seizing

Jillian and taking my angel!"

"Slow down, daughter, slow down. From the top."

"In a word! They barricaded themselves at the top of the L&C saying they're on their honeymoon and have the staff pampering them like British royalty. With my messed-up leg, I can't climb a footstool to see what they're up to!"

"With hotel doting on I belief she okay. And angel too—with Reuben!"

"It is?"

"Under lock and key."

"Then perform yours and send Jillian home!" Golly stamped her sore foot. "Ouch. Ouch. Ouch."

"Mark my word, Golly. Learn lesson from this, or same test will come, over and again, until you do."

"Whooo, have I! The price for not following procedure. Snagging Jaxy is priority one."

"If you wanted to snag him, I tink you would aim higher."

"Can't Gollygraph a dead person."

"True, but not tonight. Come, let me handle Yillianz'. Remember Code of David," Fr. Michael scooped up the younger to give her exalted foot a rest.

"I *am* God's anointed," answered back Golly with her arms wrapped affectionately around his neck, and together they went inside the parsonage.

AFTER JILLIAN LEFT THE clock shop earlier in the day, Remarkable Reuben picked up two ceramic angels from the souvenir store and retreated to his work area. Satisfied with the kiln ware, by shift's end he filled the whimsical rush orders: Fr. Michael's birthday surprise for his wife, and Jillian's gift to Fr. Michael. With two more angels on the loose, to avoid obfuscation Reuben introduced glaring differences and closed-up the orders in ordinary cartons, burying them in the bangles and baubles destined for the upcoming St. Maximos feast day raffle. With command of the store handed off to the staff, he closed early to order his affairs before flying south for the winter. Alone at the vault he unfurled, in his estimation, the store's greatest treasure: The Romanov Family Tree.

Convinced at length of Jillian's pedigree, Reuben lifted the quill from the golden inkwell to include her birth name at the bottommost branch with her siblings. Aspirants who would soon enter the arena for one to triumph, and for whose head he would mould the imperial crown. With hopes riding high on Jillian, but his money on Golly Gee, Reuben rolled the scroll into a mailing tube addressed to Michael Klapakis, then arranged for a lift to the air terminal.

Through reinforced, security doors Reuben shoved his satchel to a svelte man in a twill raincoat reeking of Siberian cigarettes and cheap cologne, who received and fit the black, travel kit in the back of a blue Malibu.

CHAPTER 23

The Avlon Home, Clackamas, OR
8:30 p.m. Thursday, January 4

Through swirling mists of fine, white particulates that evaporated the instant they hit the windshield Jillian weaved the lanes to Sunnyside Road before they started to aggregate on the ground. On the mesa she made her way to a desolate lane and braked before the only residence with colored strings still up and blinking. A life-size Santa waved back at the street. Jillian went in ahead. All clear, the garage door lifted for the car to fit alongside a workout bench with an Olympic bar balancing four plates to an end, and the longest dumbbell rack to be found outside a bodybuilder's gym. Kickboxing trophies packed the corner, and against the wall in a glass tank under a heat lamp basked a twelve-foot snake digesting a rabbit.

At that moment Guin's text hit: "Wazzup in Oregon?"

Jaxy paused before responding. Over the span of time not one lie of significance had he gotten away with, so they had a policy. Don't try. There is always a first for anything, though, so with his stomach in knots he wrote: "A promoter wants to hear the Fat Pipe's demo. I came to show off what I got."

"I hope SHE'S impressed!" Guin fired off with a puking, green emoji.

"Something wrong?" asked Jillian.

Jaxy stayed in the car. "My fiancée. She's taken ill. I have to leave."

Jillian lifted a free-heel ski from the wall and shoved it through the door. "Then you better get moving if you expect to make Eugene by breakfast."

ON A GUEST ROOM, bath towel went Jaxy's comb, wristwatch, wallet, keys, toothbrush, phone, and charger to leave nary a crumb of evidence that anyone stayed the night. He had to, for the snowstorm was turning back motorists, and with another inch the Cooper wouldn't make it to the curb.

"Why don't you drive a four-by like everyone else around here?" asked Jaxy, coming up the hall.

"Why don't you?" replied Jillian from where she measured out coffee beans.

"Don't live in snow." Jaxy stopped to lower the thermostat.

From across the room Jillian dialed it back up and said, "You can shovel it for me in the morning to see what it's like."

"Or Monday, let Rory carry your car to the street."

"Can't hear you!" Jillian said over the grinder.

As Jillian set out creamers and sweeteners, Jaxy made himself at home in a living room without a hint of holidays past in distinction to the kitschy yard. The subdued, almond fabric complimented the bamboo end table holding a variety of publications and a healthy houseplant. The tiger maple sideboard near the French, patio doors, served as the liquor cabinet and wet bar. A majestic horse painting hung over the lime-washed fireplace. Photos on the mantelshelf recalled happier times. A mahogany grandfather clock with ugly chew marks at the base dominated the room and went with nothing. Vacuum lines showed on the carpet. This did not look like the jumbled living space of the abusive types that reared Jaxy, so reflecting on her husband's juvenile antics on the airplane, he suspected Jillian may have blown the state of things out of proportion to justify her own bad behavior.

"What in heaven are you doing?" she asked, arms akimbo.

At the clock base Jaxy worked shoe polish into the digs and scratches. "A hack I learned from the antique racket. There! Marks gone like magic."

"Would I disappear like magic if you rubbed some on me?"

Jaxy folded the cloth, buffing side in. "You're too damaged."

"Only a mean, rotten person would think such a thing."

"Care what else I think?" Jaxy reset the hands and plugged the clock back into the wall socket.

Jillian reached down and unplugged it. "Would it matter?"

"The baby could be Rory's. You ought to get tested," said Jaxy, leaving the clock to go fill the coffee carafe with tap water.

Jillian dumped it out to pour in bottled. "I did. At Thanksgiving. He hasn't noticed."

"Does he *have* to know it's not his?" Jaxy added more grounds to the filter.

Jillian raised the reservoir. "Oh, he will."

"Because you were in Las Vegas?"

"No," Jillian wrested away the spoon and patted her blouse with it, "because it won't look much like an Anglo-Saxon."

"Aye. Who else knows?"

Jillian sighed, "Just my mom. She had nothing to say."

"And Rita?"

Jillian arched her eyebrows. "Rita says *too* much."

The phone rang.

Jillian put her finger to Jaxy's lips and gaily answered, "Rory— how's Idaho?"

"Still there, last I looked."

"You went. Yes?"

"Union struck again, so Leavenworth. You should join us! They got a new sleigh ride. You could give some driving pointers."

Jillian laughed, "In this? No thanks. I'm falling behind on pet portraits, so I'd better stay and paint. Oh! I bumped into Brad Thornton at a wedding reception. He didn't go?"

"Pulling a double. Who got yoked—anyone I know?"

"No, but I sold a painting to a collector who wants more for his store." Jillian winked at Jaxy.

"Way to hustle! How's Thunder?"

"On the mend. So, Hubba till Sunday?"

"That's the plan."

"Stay longer if you want—nothing for you here. Huu! The washer stopped, gotta run!"

UPON HEARING THE GOOD news that Jillian had changed her mind and decided to paint at home, Rita Klinnick danced in circles around the saloon tables. "That's great, Rory! I am so happy!"

"Worry not. Jillian keeps hinting at a move to the desert, but it's all talk. Been stressing about work—that outfit's pure hell to work for. They take it out on her, then she comes home and takes it out on me. We could both use a break."

"Rory—don't get mad and hang up before I get this off my chest. I know you're trying—."

"But . . ."

"But when two people fight, they expect the other to blink first. Someone has to set the example, and if you don't take charge of your drinking, Jillian won't change. That's it—I'm done."

"Rita, can I level with you? You riled me tonight, and why? Because you can't stay out of people's shit! You mean well—."

"But . . ."

"But the more you play traffic cop, the worse the pileups. And yeah, I'll think about my drinking over a shot of Patron."

"You do that! Or try a New Year's reboot and spend it on flowers."

"Did you hear a word I said?"

"Flowers! Zipping it."

"Could pick out a rose on the way Sunday."

"Sunday! Ever heard 'strike while the fire's hot'?"

"Rita!"

"Bye!"

JAXY IMPLIED PAPER AND pen, but Jillian brought pencils and a straight edge instead.

"Are you being difficult on purpose?" he asked.

"You said you wanted to draft something," Jillian jiggled off to make something of her hair.

On a columnized table Jaxy put down the pros and cons of Jillian striking off on her own, and those for staying to work it out. Next, to discourage her from moving to the greater Los Angeles area, he broke down the cost of living to show that a single mom on a tight budget would fare better in Nevada. On the last sheet he laid out the people impacted on a social network analysis and connected them to their satellite issues.

"Huu! Where'd you learn to problem-solve like that?" asked Jillian of what looked like a complex molecular compound.

"Our marriage and family counselor."

"So, you *are* going to tie the knot!" She snugged her hair into a bun.

"Let's start with—."

"Don't see why not. Your engagement has outlasted most marriages I know."

"Your mother."

"Let's not."

"She lives in Fort Collins," said Jaxy.

"She said to call after the abortion."

Jaxy listed that as a possibility.

Jillian snatched the pencil from his hand and savagely struck out the word.

"Hey! You said it, not me."

"No way." Jillian wrapped her arms around her tummy and gave Jaxy a hurt look as if he had suggested it.

Jaxy circled the offending term and drew a diagonal line through it.

Jillian took the eraser and rubbed it out.

Step by step they added and eliminated options until a strategy crystallized. The main disagreement had to do with Thunder Roll.

"He can't come," said Jaxy.

"Viv has a trailer."

"And a truck to pull it?"

"Your van—."

"Has no hitch. Nor have I the desire to wire lights at night in bad weather. End of discussion, Thunder stays." Jaxy put the pencils up.

"Then I'm not going."

"Suit yourself. Tomorrow I'm off to Vancouver either way."

Jillian's eyes went huge. "But that's the wrong direction."

"For work. One more stop to make."

While Jaxy assembled boxes, Jillian emptied her dresser as if fleeing before a fire, exercising care to leave behind sufficient mementos, lotions, and clothing to give the impression that she had not entirely cleared out. Impressed by the quality of Jillian's artwork, as well as the mammoth stockpile of supplies, Jaxy wondered if her rancher friend had space for it.

"But Jaxy, I can't burden Viv with my stuff. Besides, barns have rats and mice and icky things!"

Jaxy collapsed at the kitchen table and gave Jillian an honest look of total stupefaction. "Then why the hell are we going there?"

Jillian returned one of equal amazement. "You don't know a thing about horses, do you?"

For the next five minutes Jaxy shut his mouth and got educated.

"So, you see," Jillian applied a gentle rub to his shoulders, "you don't up and leave one without saying goodbye."

Jaxy could not contend with that kind of horse logic, so he leaned back and asked, "Then what'cha wanna do?"

Over his head, Jillian looked down. "There's a great donut shop in The Dalles. After your run to Washington we'll join up and go to Las Vegas from there. It'll be fun!"

Jaxy slumped lower. "Not when I get back to 'Guindale'."

Done with separating what would fit in the Cooper from the bulkier items destined for the van, Jillian lit the gas log and fell into the sofa with her feet on Jaxy's lap.

Jaxy lifted them off to zip open the pack. "Rory's wedding ring. You want it?"

She moved them back on. "Keep it. Keep them both. Our wedding gifts to you."

"How special."

"And what makes the angel so special?" she tickled the fanny pack with her toes.

"It's a major piece of Russian history."

"—to you."

"Me? Nothing. To the Antique Mall manager Klav Lovorsky, it could mean, at a minimum, his job."

"But you said it came from my 'sister' in Canada."

"Also correct. I'm free to move about. She cannot, so wished to connect with you through a nice reproduction, but in her foggy state of mind sent this—the original Fabergé—by mistake."

"She's an invalid?"

"An old head injury has her hooked on pain killers."

With questions growing by the minute, in no way would Jillian let the angel leave town in that fanny pack until she got the answers straight from her godfather's shoulder. So, up she rose to pour a cognac, put on mood music and lights, and take the cushion next to Jaxy.

"Have I mentioned I'm spoken for?" He scooted against the sofa arm.

"Once or twice." Jillian lit and swirled the amber liquid, snuffed it with a ceramic coaster, and gave it to him saying, "Want to hear a funny? One night Rita showed-off with the palm of her hand but the sugar stuck it to the rim, so she jerked like this—and the snifter flew across the saloon and flamed some poor guy's accordion in the middle of 'Hey Baby Que Paso'!"

Jaxy came back with one of his own. "I microwaved a shot glass once, and 'ping!' it snapped clean off at the gold stripe. Apple schnapps ran everywhere. Guin said, 'Why not do the other three? They'd make a nice set of napkin rings!'"

When the laughter died, Jillian scooched closer in the mellow dark. "Know how the betting went on our last match?"

Jaxy nursed at the spiced brandy. "From the cheering, I'd say half went with you and half with me."

"Nope." Jillian took a satisfying sip of water and hooked a leg over his. "They all went down on me—they were betting on the spread."

Jaxy stared far into the red firelight. "They'd lose tonight."

CHAPTER 24

The Hill House, Glendale, CA
9:00 p.m. Thursday, January 4

When Guin fell to bed she felt more out of sorts than ever. She needed her dad, but it was too late to call. Booker would have little to give if she did, not because he came off uncaring, but because he liked Jaxy. Her father believed the bohemian not only was good to Guin, he was good *for* her, and kept his daughter's hardnosed ways in check. But Booker had also predicted music and politics would not mix, and the closer she inched toward the nation's capital, the further they would drift apart.

Guin saw it otherwise. Her dad's love of hearth and home may have worked for him, but she embraced the voting community, not individuals, as "family". The Hill house felt more like a watch high above her vassals, than a seventies construct in want of new paint and dry rot repair. In this castle Jaxy served as the dependable jester, while the engagement ring presented an air of respectability in the venue of realpolitik and held unwelcomed suitors at bay. Still, with an abundance of well-heeled and willing saps out there to fill the void, why could she not bear losing Jaxy?

Guilt.

Guin had pledged to walk the aisle if Jaxy made up the tuition shortfall her father denied—a brokered union she'd put off, counting on him to drop the subject once she repaid the money—and now this!

"Stupid, stupid me—the fault is mine!" Guin flogged her breasts. Or is it? How many ports-of-call did the boy have on his milk route? How many others wore his promise ring? No, no—stop thinking like a jilted, love junky! This wasn't the Jaxy she knew, and nobody knew him better.

She felt around the dresser for her diary, but for the first time since she took up journaling in the privacy of her playhouse, Guin had nothing to say. She locked it away and found "Pillow Talk" on a classic movie station, but the party-line mishaps didn't help. She resorted to laundry; to climb on the dryer with her teddy the way she did as a girl, to let the rumbling warmth lull her to sleep. Guin poured in detergent, started the fill, and shook Jaxy's duffel into the tub.

Clunk.

Guin's shoulders sagged to see what else in this hagalaz-stricken washing machine had come apart. To her astonishment, out she fished a white-fringed miniskirt and Cowgirl hat. Next came a vest glutted with mushy tissue, alligator boots, and underneath everything a signed, soggy glossy of J.D. Avlon in a soaking wet Tee.

"What?" Guin turned the duffel inside and out. *"No panties ?!?!!"*

Wide awake, into the house she tore, stubbing her toe on the step-up to jerk the laptop from the wall, sending the power cord flying. Back to the garage she rampaged, to patch into a monitor speaker and fire up Alanis Morissette. With the volume bar slid all the way Guin pulled at her hair screaming out the lyrics, and on the last "You Oughta Know!" shattered the microphone into a Fat Pipes poster, then tore it down and ground it into the slab with her heel, pulverizing it into confetti. Physically exhausted and emotionally spent, Guin slumped, shaking violently in the dark with her head between her knees waiting for bitter drops to fall but they would not. For, a drought had struck her tear ducts long ago, and in their place poured from her pores, streams of sour sweat.

CHAPTER 25

The Klapakis Parsonage, Minnehaha, WA
9:30 p.m. Thursday, January 4

No sooner had Fr. Michael reclaimed his recliner than the telephone sounded off again.

"Why can't simple, underpaid, servant of God, watch ten minutes of golf without interruption?" Fr. Michael wondered out loud.

"Are you asking, or is that the title of your next book?" Camille handed over the phone.

"Doctor! I forget!" Fr. Michael slapped his head.

"If you don't come soon, it's going in the icebox," said the surgeon.

"I hate frozen fish! No, I come now, or Camille."

"Oh—no—she's—not!" Camille yelled across the house.

"I be right over—dat's okay?"

"Dat's okay!"

Thirty minutes of dicey driving later Fr. Michael stood on the welcome mat of Dr. Helen Leshenko's hulking, Goose Hollow home. "Your driveway is wider than street!" he said when the double doors opened to receive him.

"Envy does not become you," replied the surgeon in a rubber apron smelling of fresh catch. Then standing tall, out to the car she asked, "You came alone?"

"Camille—yes—she no fun after nine."

"But Presbytera called about the church potluck, and a young lady she hoped Drew might meet."

Fr. Michael shed his coat saying, "I can't keep up with every eligible female my wife hopes your son finds interesting."

The doctor stood higher. "Don't be a spoilsport. Call her in for a look at the foot."

"Oh, dat one! I let Yillianz' out downtown. Besides, she older than she look—and married."

Helen's face fell, and then her nostril wrinkled as it'd caught a whiff of warm compost. "Did you say 'Jillian'?"

"Yes, Zh-zyllians!" Fr. Michael beamed with pride at the attempt. "I gave up trying to talk to that *cowgirl*."

"Yilli' going through rough patch. Keep saying she need friend, but when I ask her over? She run faster than you on 'Pledge Card Sunday'." The priest wiggled his fingers.

"She gets one last chance," said Helen, staying all expectations with a stink face.

"WHO'S CALLING?" JILLIAN HANDED off her phone, too pooped to look herself.

"FrMk."

"Give me that!" Jillian sat up ladylike to speak into the phone, "Hi Father Michael! . . . No, not much. Rory's climbing, so it's quiet. . . The Hotel? A prospect from Los Angeles wants to display my work at his mall, and our restaurant hosts thought we made such a cute couple they gave us free drinks . . . Gracious no!!! I'm home washing clothes. Must we video chat to prove it? . . . *TONIGHT???* We can't have church people over to bless the house, Father! it's not presentable and the roads are terrible, and Rory would miss out . . . Shoot! I'll be at an arts fair so tell your wife oyster stew another time . . . Uh-huh, uh-huh, bacon bits, chives, braised celery, pepper sauce but not too much, and heavy cream not half and half . . . Yes, I'm dying to meet the Leshenkos too—Huu! Dryer stopped, gotta run!"

"Hoo, the dryer stopped. Do you use that line on passengers too?" asked Jaxy.

"Only loudmouth musicians," Jillian unloaded a basket of warm apparel on the sofa. "Fold these."

Jaxy picked around the lingerie and rolled a pair of My Little Pony socks.

"Like this," Jillian spread them flat and tucked the ends. "Father Michael—he's nice—wanted me for lunch Sunday."

"Sounded like the entire church wants you over Sunday."

WITH NO SIGN OF the Canadian connection, Rory left the Electric Avlon shop at halftime to follow through on Rita's flower advice. He wanted to set them out as a surprise for his wife and then hurry back to meet Yan. He left the Bronco idling on the street and made a quick dash through the garage, but Jillian had already beat him home! Darn. He couldn't go in because he couldn't stay. Rory started to head out just when the dryer cycle ended. He heard conversation. He cracked the garage door leading into the house and listened. *It was that joker he met on the plane!* Back to the shop he then went for a pair of light ankle weights he'd discarded under the metal workbench. He located a single, but it would do. He rummaged some more, but for one item found everything required for tonight's boundary-setting illustration.

"Yo Brad, got any five-inch worm drives?" Rory asked over the shop phone.

"Let me look. Jillian get home okay?"

"Sure did. Throwing a shirt folding, pant pressing, sock rolling rave. Didn't want to walk in on her little clambake uninvited."

"And you said she didn't have any girlfriends in Portland."

"She doesn't. Have the clamps?" Rory asked again.

Brad went to his tool crib. "Five and five eighths do?"

"Bring two."

"Shoot, I missed it!" griped Brad, "Gordon banked a three and drew a foul at twenty-three seconds!"

Rory growled, "I said she doesn't have any *girlfriends* in Portland."

"Tell her to get out more—Yes! A technical could make this a five-point play."

"And bring the JFK Colt."

"What?" Brad turned the game down. "First hose clamps and now my gun? I don't like the sound of this."

"For effect."

"Chill. If my lady had company I'd want to march in and boot his sorry ass too. But think it through, Cap."

"I'm done thinking about it. I want that S.O.B. out tonight!"

"The nelly's folding clothes. What's he look like?"

"It's that same pomp-a-doo I sat with on the airplane."

"You know him?"

"Hell—I introduced them!"

"Bummer. Catch what they were saying?"

"Through the garage door . . . a little."

"And?"

"They were talking about Church." Rory hated to admit.

"Sweet Jesus! But when you share a stein with some Fräulein to go spelunking down her lederhosen, that's different?"

"I don't paw through her hamper."

"Brutus was an honorable man."

"You're spouting Shakespeare at *me*?!"

"Listen. He's helping with clothes. What kind of guy does that? Go over and maybe he'll show how to fold yours too. If not, take him by the seat and pitch him into the snow. There! A simple solution for a simple problem, or you can forget it and finish out family night here with Pepper and me."

"If you bring up that game one more time . . ."

"Whoa! They ejected a fan for throwing a cup!"

"Great. I'll pick out a sweetbriar for him too."

SIDE BY SIDE, JAXY and Jillian watched the yellow and blue flames flicker and flit in a night of steady falling snow, disturbed but by the crackling of fire, branches shuttling along the eaves, and the irregular banging of a distant mailbox.

Jaxy set the cooling liqueur aside while Jillian scrunched to pull her bra through a sleeve and let it fall on his toe asking, "Where did you grow up?"

Jaxy kicked the cup away. "Arroyo Seco."

"Sounds exotic."

"It's a dry, rocky riverbed littered with trash and graffiti. And you?"

Jillian fell to rest on Jaxy's arm. "Third base."

Jaxy worked a square pillow under her head to say that that was where she would stay.

"What you said in the elevator," she faltered, "you meant it."

"Jilli', I think you're swell, but tomorrow's a big day and I need my shuteye."

Jillian took the stemmed glass to refill it.

"No more, thanks. Got a—."

"Big day. I heard you."

Locked in the bath Jillian squinched at the mirror, "What's his problem?" She sucked in her stomach, "What's my problem?" Her machinations, bumpy as executed, had worked except that when she set out for the mansion, Jillian expected this Rockabilly character to willingly swap a hard night's work on the mattress for a day's use of his van. But no—not Jaxy! He had to spoil everything with his monogamous principles. Never had she encountered such intransigence! Indisposed to a second brandy, he'd sidestepped her at every turn: The blonde bimbo, the frightened prey, the despairing wife, the vulnerable mother, the starving artist, the abandoned daughter, and the playful pussycat. She'd even let him handle her Victoria Secrets! How sexy is *that*?

Plumb out of ways to loosen him up, Jillian resorted to the medicine cabinet. In theory Ambien would work, but taken with alcohol it could have adverse side effects, and she needed him alert in the morning.

"Too bad Rory doesn't need Viagra!" Jillian slammed the vanity, wondering what Jaxy saw in that highfalutin fiancée that he didn't see in her. Catching her crabby reflection, Jillian abruptly ceased her snit.

"Aha!! That's what he likes," flexed the Cowgirl.

The stone cold bitch.

"Know something, Jaxy?" Jillian brayed into his napping face, then tuned in a pop station, brought up the lights, and stalked off to dump the cold brandy down the wastepipe. "I don't like being called 'Jilli'!"

Startled awake, Jaxy blinked and put on his glasses. "I appreciate the honesty J.D., I really do, because I *despise* 'Jaxy'."

She wheeled about. "My name is Jillian Danja Anders-Avlon!"

"Thaaaat's my name tooooo . . ." sang Jaxy.

"You're not funny!!!"

"Neither was growing up with kids calling me, 'Jackson Five', and chasing me around singing, 'A-B-C'."

"I can see how it scarred you."

"It shaped me into the Rockabilly I am today."

"Well—I like Michael Jackson."

"You would."

Heaven knows Jillian tried. Truly she did, but she could not stay mad at Jaxy. She had thrown everything including the kitchen sink at him, yet there he remained, the infuriating, straitlaced, Jackson Thrie.

"Then how about a nice bubble bath?" Jillian made her last play to part Jaxy from his trousers.

Jaxy hung his wingtips off the couch. "How about a nice blanket? And another top-up of that brandy. No need to warm it."

"What. Did. You. Say?" seethed Jillian, finding nothing charming about him anymore.

Jaxy corrected his manners, "Brandy, *please*? Half this time."

"Do-re-me, one-two-" sang Jillian on her way to the sideboard, and on the count of three laid hold of the cognac by the neck and splashed it up and down Jaxy as if watering a flowerbed.

"Mmm, orangey good." Jaxy ran his fingers through the sticky bangs and licked them clean.

"Men are gross!" Jillian whammed the bottle on the sideboard, caring not in the least for his feelings or the furniture.

"Existentially speaking, that is true. It's what ladies like you envy but for morphogenetic reasons can't have, so you keep following me around singing that song hoping it rubs off. Equal pay and opportunity? Nice, twenty-first century perks, but deep down it's not what a woman like you truly wants."

"How would a morpho-genius like you have a clue what I want??"

Jaxy held up a finger and delivered his point. "A woman of your breeding can get gross—you just can't *be* gross. Can I have that shower?"

"Breeding!" From her mom that would have come as a compliment, but from Jaxy this was as the last straw. "You Pretentious! . . . Punctilious! . . . Plebiscite!!"

"Plebeian."

"*I know the difference*!" Insulted beyond imagination by this rock-a-know-it-all Jillian turned away in unbridled indignation, and in that instant her outrage morphed into exultation. She had done it! She had made the grade and reached Queen Bee status. She merely had to boss him around for the next ten minutes and the rest was academic.

Jillian threw at him a wad of wet paper towels. "Clean it up and give me your pants to run through the wash. You're not crashing on my couch like that."

Jaxy cringed, "Then can I shower?"

"No. You'll clog the drain." Out the patio door Jillian poked her head and stated, "Hardly takes a minute to warm the Jacuz'."

Jaxy unbuttoned his shirt. "Didn't bring trunks."

"Too bad." Jillian dropped a beach towel on his face and started the bubbles.

Jaxy scowled at the stereo. "Got any Elvis?"

"I'll put on something we both like," said Jillian, and brushing out her hair slipped off to prepare for bed . . . or so she said.

Down to his boxers Jaxy stripped to cleanse off a day of sweat, a flagon of brandy, and a face-full of cheap shots. Pleased in finding Jillian's piss-off button, he intended to push it all the way to Las Vegas.

"Ah, that's more like it," Jaxy clapped his happy feet in the foam to the sedating sound of a bass horn descending the scales with a clippity-clop banjo introducing . . .

Lady Godiva!

Jaxy's eyes flew open wide as out the French doors and down the patio steps pranced Jillian in her birthday suit astride a My Little Pony stick-horse. Then his glasses fogged up.

CHAPTER 26

The Avlon Home, Clackamas, OR
10:00 p.m. Thursday, January 4

"Margarita, anyone?"

Jillian yelped, spun around, caught her heel on a webbed chair, and toppled onto Jaxy with a splash.

"Snap", Rory's phone camera flashed.

They required no reintroduction, for even with clouded vision Jaxy could tell a mean, ex-Marine from five feet, and an ugly one just showed up clutching a tequila bottle by the neck, and a rose by the teeth.

"Funky doo," Rory cast the bud to his wife.

It bobbed in the water as to the other side Jillian glissaded with knees bunched to her chin.

Jaxy's heart raced, no longer from erotic palpitations, but petrifying fear as his glasses cleared bringing Rory into focus leaning against a Tuscan pillar.

"Like theatre?" Rory glanced up from the photo.

Jaxy said, "a li-little."

"I like it a lot!" Rory popped the cork and took a long pull before continuing. "The corps put on 'Romeo and Juliet' for the Colonel. Guess who I played?"

"Ro-Romeo?"

"And kiss Brad? Hell no, I played Tybalt. Know what he did?" Rory rested a boot on the pool edge.

"He as-assinated somebody?" Jaxy took a stab through chattering teeth.

Rory hammered in the cork and placed a hand on his hip. "No sirree! He ran that dog Mercutio through in a fair fight. LIKE THIS!" he shouted with a hop and bottle thrust, then smiled down upon his invisible, dying foe.

Jaxy sat as still as death while the water churned and silence descended, disturbed by shuddering trees and a swinging, mailbox door.

"Ever heard: 'He who fights and runs away . . .,'" led Rory with a roll of a calloused finger.

"Lives to fight another day?" Jaxy eked out, not sure if a show of bravery would help, but certain more stuttering would not.

Rory turned to Jillian, "Woman. Can you tell us who said that?"

Shivered Jillian, "No," in the warm water.

"Of course not. Demosthenes. Heard of 'm Jack?"

"The orator?"

"And fucking ARMY DESERTER!" Rory swung the bottle, nearly busting it over a knee-high statue of St. Francis feeding a bunny.

Jaxy moistened his mouth. "You remember my name."

"You left your wallet in my bedroom," Rory stressed the pronouns. Then ordering his wife out to cover up with a long sweater, took Jaxy's shorts as security and shut down the jets with a warning: "Don't even think about going AWOL, Jack. I'm watching."

While Rory kept an eye on the patio, the unhappy couple got into it with animated bursts, pleas, tears, and some colorful vocabulary in the mix. After a while he called Jaxy in to towel off by the gas log and flopped a boa constrictor over his bare shoulders advising, "Don't worry, son, Bonita already ate. Don't move around though, or she might throw up."

Below the Black Forest clock Rory pushed his wife onto a dining chair where he could watch them and the front door, making it understood that if one bolted the other would pay the penalty. He plugged in the clock and opened the face to move the hands while bellyaching about the housecleaners, "Damn 'Maid Grenades' wreck more things around here." Satisfied with the time, he returned to the point at issue. "Jillian tells me you're here for a wedding."

Jaxy nodded.

"That's not what these say," Rory produced the sheets he found spread out on the table. "How long have the two of you been plotting this?"

"I talked her into it," Jaxy took the chivalrous fall.

"Daddy—you got bark," Rory chewed sunflower seeds into a woody ball, and spat the shells into the glass. From his boot he extracted a combat knife to clean his fingernails while flipping through the charts. "Last Summer we talked about having a baby. Said you weren't ready. Jack talk you into that too?" Like a copperhead Rory unwound, sticking the knife into the carpet an inch from Jillian's foot.

Jillian screamed, tipped over, and came down hard on her temple.

"Get up," snarled Rory, retrieving the knife.

Jillian righted the chair, cradling her head in quivering hands.

He put the erased smudge to Jaxy's face, "What's that say?"

Jaxy hesitated, "No aah-doption."

"Stop me anytime, but it reads like you planned to have the baby in Vegas, but couldn't agree on what to do after that." Rory wadded the paper and let it fall to the floor.

If not for a snake weighing him down, Jaxy would have squirmed off the ottoman. "I'll give you what I have and go away forever."

"What you have, dead man, is mine already, but carry on."

"My van. All leather and teak interior. Door needs work."

"Five hundred tops to a chop shop. What else."

"An Olympus camera with lenses, and a Gretsch guitar with a TV Jones pickup and a sweet pedal board."

"Another five."

Jaxy came alive, "Hundred? Try thousand! Duane Eddy recorded 'Forty Miles of Bad Road' on that guitar! It should be in the Rock and Roll Hall of Fame."

"So should your hair. What's this—something sweet for Jillian?" Rory sized up the jeweler's gift box from the fanny pack.

The color ran straight from Jaxy's face into Jillian's.

"How much?" asked Rory, tearing away the heart stickers from the tissue.

Jaxy stared off into the corner.

"How much money did you spend on my wife?" repeated the Captain.

"A hundred bucks or so."

"Didn't mean to ruin the surprise, babe." Rory said raising the lid. He rubbed his chin stubble with doubt at the contents and then back at Jaxy. "You spent *what*?"

"Okay. Two-fifty." Jaxy bumped it up.

From the box Rory held aloft a bronze, state fair medal by the wide, white ribbon. Then lolling his head to the side, without a change in expression said, "Sorry babe, but you came in third."

The doorbell chimed.

Rory cracked the blinds and threw open the door. "Brad—what took—?"

"Lumber truck tipped. Christ, looked like a barn exploded. Nobody's crossing Sellwood tonight" On the dining table Brad set a bivy bag, and a bright, yellow coil with a chain of carabiners, ice screws, and an ice axe. Then, crossing over to warm his hands at the fire, from the side of his mouth he said to Jaxy, "When I told you to drive the lady safely home, dipshit, *I didn't mean here.*"

"Peps!" Rory stepped aside as a Wolador dusted with snowflakes forced its way through the door. From her jaws he dislodged the remnant of a mahogany wood pinecone and confronted Brad. "See what she did to my clock the last time she came indoors? Put her out."

Brad shook Pepper gently by the ears. "Is this where you got it? Bad doggie."

"It's a *wolf* and belongs outside." Rory thrust her haunches toward the door.

In disregard Pepper dug in, then slipped between his legs and plopped down on the carpet next to Jillian.

Rory gave up trying to turn sixty pounds of pure obstinacy outside and went back to chatting about Hubba Hubba and the blowing snow advisories before getting around to the California floater he found in the hot tub and his bizarre gift. As Rory retold the tale it so vexed him, that he unzipped his wife's carry-on and dumped it out to see what else she had squirreled away.

"The heck's this—a used birthing blanket?" Rory shook out the bulky, blood-crusted corset, and when he did an exotic assortment of gold, precious stones, amber and pearls spilled onto his feet. "Whoa babe, that's some high-end stuff! Been working the casinos harder than I knew. About time you contributed to the nest egg."

Saltwater fountains sprang from Jillian's eyes as her husband scooped the loot into a kitchen trash bag. All but the guardian angel which Pepper snatched by the chain. Flaring her nostrils, she dared him to go for it.

"Nice doggie—in here," Rory opened the sack.

Pepper ducked under and nosed it into Jillian's hand.

"It's okay," Jillian petted her head and surrendered it.

"Thanks babe. This one's a keeper." Rory wore it down his shirt adding, "let's raise a toast to our newfound wealth!"

Demolished, Jillian declined.

"What was I thinking? You're pregnant! Pour a brandy for our guests, woman. A round for everyone," celebrated Rory.

While the marines laughed at an off-colored joke, Jillian filled glasses, stopping to give Jaxy the sorriest look.

In reply, Jaxy returned the dirtiest one possible then nudged the bulge of her sweater pocket saying below his breath, "Hide your phone in your sock."

When Jillian returned to her chair, she petted Pepper with one hand and did as told with the other.

Hard knuckles rapped on the door.

Rory hushed the room and backed to the wall drawing the knife.

The strident knocking persisted.

Rory lifted the blind. There stood Yan with a carnation pinned to his pinstripes and a hardback in his hand.

"Can't you understand American?" asked Rory. "It says meet at the shop!"

"What is your deal??? I scored at a good price, so I'm going door to door, you know, selling eight-balls like Kit cookies," Yan let the whole neighborhood know.

Rory dragged Yan in by the collar and kicked it shut. "Listen jerkwad, I said not here, not tonight, so shove off and don't stop till you reach Saskatoon!"

"I'm not here to deke ya', Captain, I take my cut like every . . . one . . . else." Yan's wide eyes roamed from person to person: a blonde in a Mighty Ducks jacket, a man watching Warrior basketball, and a timber wolf giving its undivided attention to a boa constricted about an Elvis impersonator in a bath towel quaffing a brandy.

"Groovy party," Yan hoisted a gun from his waistband. "Little lady know about this?"

CHAPTER 27

The Avlon Home, Clackamas, OR
10:30 p.m. Thursday, January 4

Couple's counseling began with the television off and everyone in a semicircle facing the group leader. Yan stayed on his feet keeping a .38 trained on the snake and talking over a partnership-building primer: "The association I represent upholds traditional mores—ones that have made our lands the great bastions of basketball and hockey that they are. The disintegration of these grassroots values now threatens our ability to conduct business in North America and its' Commonwealths. To reverse this trend our sponsors have asked me to hold what we call an 'intervention'."

"Jesus Christ," mumbled Brad.

"And where two or more are gathered, there He is, so no cussing. It's counter-productive," cited Yan from the handbook.

Jillian nodded in hearty agreement.

"The rules are simple. We go around each relating without relating on anyone else's relating, and then we hug—are we good?" Yan waved the barrel up and down until they related. "I go first. I used to run around with a constant, umm, I mean, well you know what I mean, looking for love in all the wrong places . . ." Yan wrapped up his five minutes by relating how he'd 'seen the light' and settled for a butter tart from North Van who couldn't bake one to save the queen, but 'who da hey!' he'd eat them all day if it made her happy, and then lowered the boom saying, "You're up, sugar pie."

"I grew up not far from my fiancée. She went to a catholic girls' school, so we didn't meet there," Jaxy laughed uncomfortably.

"Where did you meet?" asked Yan.

"On the boulevard shopping. Her—not me. I played requests on the corner. Guin tipped me fifty for La Bamba and then another for an original, so I wrote her one and followed her home," Jaxy showed off his lyrical prowess.

"Pop the question on the spot?"

"Said she'd take the plunge after she passed the bar."

"When's the big day?"

"Haven't set it."

Yan made more entries then continued, "Why not?"

"Too busy running for city council. Not me—her, so I made up my mind—."

"So have I—Brad?" Yan cut Jaxy off, "You and wolfie skookum?"

"We're good," replied Brad with a scratch of the dog's ear.

"And you? Into the lapel mic please."

Jillian and Rory nodded to each other, "We're good."

Yan shut off the recorder and crammed the gun into Jaxy's neck, "Good, 'cause intervention's over. Sugar pie's coming with me."

"Let him finish!" Jillian butted in.

"Honey—*we're skookum*," sternly spoke Rory from where he sat cross-legged at foot of her chair.

"What *I* heard him relate," said Jillian, "is that he's made up his mind to dump that high and mighty attorney."

"It's why I invited Jack here!" Rory joined in, "to cash and carry your entire stash of opiates home to show who's the major wage earner in the house."

Yan silenced the room to hear Jaxy's response.

"I'd say there's enough in that sack of jewels to pay for it."

Yan leveled the gun. "I'm selling meth man, not Manhattan."

All eyes fell on Jaxy, whose future hinged on his ability to draw sufficient funds from thin air for enough high-grade, Canadian crystal to make more friends at Ted's Pool Shed than he could deal with.

"Take plastic?"

Since Yan trusted no one to be left alone in the house, nor wished to be caught pulling Jaxy's savings by an ATM camera, to the closest one they went packed three to a seat. When they returned Pepper gave Jillian a slow, happy wag and dropped the slobbery pinecone on her lap.

"Thank you," Jillian took the gunky cone by two fingers and rolled it.

When Pepper laid down with crossed paws, and that, "Woladors don't play fetch" attitude, Jillian handed back, "Oh yes they do" and pointed until they reached an understanding.

"How do you do that?" asked Brad in amazement.

Jillian rolled it again. "Breeding."

At the dining table Rory counted out bills while Yan picked through the jewels. When he did not find a particular one, he carelessly lobbed the kitchen bag back to the Captain and began ransacking the house as the last in a night of poor decisions he would make.

"The hell you do that for?" cried Rory at the shamble of cushions and magazines.

Against the clock Yan pushed Jaxy with a hand on his throat and the gun in his face. "The Feodorovna—where is it?"

"In my husband's shirt!" screamed Jillian.

"This?" Rory raised the sparkling, angel medallion, baiting Yan to go for it.

When he did, with lightning speed and a frightening "hi-yah!!!" Rory burst the sack in the drug dealer's face, scattering gemstones across the room. In one, fluid, follow-up move he took the gun and bashed Yan into the door with an open-fist chin jab. From the table he snatched up the ice axe and propelled it through the Canadian's gut and deep into his lungs. The arc of the swing lifted Yan off the ground, where Rory watched him convulse and wriggle like a worm on a hook. Not done, the Captain pinned Yan's neck by the forearm, then using the jam for leverage, wrenched on the shaft to split his ribcage.

Rory held the Saskatoonian's flopping head by a handful of hair to have the last word, "Inflation's a bitch. Eh?"

CHAPTER 28

The Avlon Home, Clackamas, OR
11:00 p.m. Thursday, January 4

"Good as new!" Rory lauded the quick-dry fill and varnish repair to the door gouge. Then, with irritation said, "Jillian! Didn't I ask you to boil water and mop this down with peroxide?"

After scooping Yan's entrails into a dustpan and swabbing the spattered walls and floor with disinfectant, Jillian ran the spilled entrails down the disposal, then retched her own with violence into the sink.

"Dang, now I have two bodies to dispose," Rory thought aloud.

"Two?" Brad asked in distress.

"Not done with him," Rory looked over at Jaxy.

"Pep—let's go," called Brad.

Rory latched onto Brad's arm.

Pepper did not roll her eyes and thump. Pepper dropped her tail, humped her shoulders, and laid down her ears to tell Rory to move a hand, or lose it.

The Captain eased off with the reassurance that he had more "scaring" prepared for Jaxy, but no harm would befall, and taped the California hipster in a fitted sheet and the Canadian stiff with less care in the twin. After dousing the outside lights, he slid Jaxy across the cooling corpse laid out over the thrashed motorcycle, followed by some weighty things dumped on the floorboards with a thud.

Brad took the wheel with Pepper riding shotgun. Rory sat behind with the seat pushed forward and Jillian at his side. When Brad signaled to merge onto the freeway, Rory leaned forward and said something that ended with the words "Sellwood Bridge".

"Rory!" protested Jillian.

"Hey babe, I have to toss a couple things first."

"But you said."

"Refresh my memory, Madame, I was drinking," Rory opened the window to spit a shell.

"That you don't want to go to jail and give up everything you worked so hard for!"

"Well, Yan didn't follow the script, did he? So, if I'm to hang for one, I might as well for two."

"You killed him in our defense. You have witnesses!" pled Jillian for sanity.

"To a drug deal. But why should I worry? Who'll miss a dope man from Saskabush. anyhow? They should pay me for cleaning up their town," touted Rory, organizing his camera photos. "So, Jillian, compared to the others, how does Jack stack up?"

"I took first," Jaxy piped up.

"We never—!" Jillian tried to spare him, but it did no good.

"You were going to!" Rory back-fisted Jaxy, splitting a lip and breaking off a crown. With the pistol jammed between the Californian's teeth he swore, "For that Jillian's having an abortion tonight, pal, and you're going to watch."

The wagon slowed to a crawl along Tacoma Street until it came to a stop by a boatyard from where Rory instructed Brad to scout the bridge on foot. In the meantime, he counted down the reasons for doing away with the homewrecker: First, Jaxy might turn him in. Second, he might seek payback. Third, he knocked-up his wife. And fourth, but foremost: Jaxy bore no respect for institution.

Jillian rose to the defense, "You have him wrong, he's harmless! It's not his baby! None of this was his idea! Let him go. You said!"

"Like I give a damn whose baby." Rory closed the door with a bang to meet Brad jogging down the bridge.

Chalk it up to top-shelf tequila, cocky self-confidence, or the underrating of his captive's grit and determination, Rory would long regret not having put a gag on Jaxy and frisking Jillian before leaving them in the vehicle.

"'*I took first*'?" Jillian repeated Jaxy's smart remark. "You and your big mouth! Now we're both in big trouble!"

Jaxy spat blood and dished back, "Mine? Yan was about to escort me out."

"And shoot you in the neck for the Fabergé."

"Not if I still had it on me."

"I'll get it back for you. I promise."

"You won't if you don't make a run for it *right now*!"

"No way! You heard what Rory said he'd do."

"He will anyway, so do me one favor," Jaxy clenched his loose crown between the front teeth, "Hang on to thith as a promith you'll make it. It may be all that's left of me to bury."

Jillian reached across asking. "I smell gasoline. Do you smell gasoline?"

"Another reason to go. Fumes aren't good for the baby."

Jillian knelt on the seat and rolled the bodies aside to expose the flattened, road racer that followed her from the bridge. "That does it. This whole thing stinks!" she exclaimed taking the phone from her sock.

"No Jillian—not here!" Jaxy bounced up and down like a jumping bean, trying desperately to knock it from her hands. Call for help after you get away. Rory can't watch us both. I keep cutters in my fanny pack. Take it and run Jillian, Run! Oh, for God's sake woman, what are you doing?"

"Texting Father Michael."

"SPEAK OF Z' DEVIL. Maybe she come for soup after all!" Fr. Michael grinned when Jillian's name lit the screen. He handed off the phone, "Doctor, can you translate? I can't read her yibberish."

"My word!" Dr. Leshenko put her hand to her cheek. "It says, 'R killed a man and I'm next! Help!'"

Fr. Michael went back and forth from the phone to Helen, "What to do? What to do??"

With hands trained to not shake during surgery, Dr. Leshenko keyed in, "WAY."

"Oh no!" Jillian burst out. "Someone wrote back on Father Michael's phone!"

"You're sure?" asked Jaxy.

"Father can't text! He'd have written, 'where are you' with a question mark."

"Dammit Jillian! Stop analyzing and GO!"

From the passenger side Jillian sprang straight into Rory's arms.

"Leaving so soon, babe? Party just started."

"I have to 'go'," said Jillian squashing her knees together and sliding the phone into her sweater pocket.

"You'll have to hold it." Rory pushed her back down on the seat then strong-armed her leg out the door. "Dang it. Would you cooperate?"

"What are you doing??" resisted Jillian as her husband strapped an ankle weight to her calf, cinched it tight with hose clamps, and mashed the screws with pliers. To wires protruding from the top he rigged a detonator. The trigger he placed in his vest.

"Relax. Hardly enough boom-boom there to remove a foot. A

little invention from my time in Iraq when I found myself with too many mischief-makers like you to watch and needed more beer. Should patent it. Now stay put like a good kitty, and when I get back, I'll take it off."

Jillian's shoulders heaved uncontrollably, breaking Jaxy's heart. Nevertheless, the irrefutable miracle that she had moved the phone from her sock to the sweater moments before Rory took her leg bolstered hope, so he asked, "Are you wearing a belt?"

"Yes," said Jillian, "A white, weave one with round, little dealie—,"

"Good! Tie it above the knee, but don't let Rory see."

"Do wha-aaaa . . .?"

"Then forget cops and priests and find a doctor fast."

"But Rory said he'd take it off!"

"Exactly."

When the appalling truth sank in, Jillian melted into a pool of mucus.

"If it makes any difference!" Jaxy lofted the last Hail Mary with no time on the clock, "think about the baby instead of your goddam foot!"

It would be inaccurate to say that at the stroke of midnight, Jillian transformed from a trepid housecat into a fierce lioness. Nevertheless, her terror channeled into righteous anger when she undid her belt with the doodads and looped it above the knee. Bent on his own purpose, when Rory came around to the driver's seat and took over at the wheel, he gave no notice to the change that had come over his wife.

The snowfall lightened, and the moon showed through a crack in the clouds as the wagon approached the sloping bridge. Through a gap made by Brad in an unattended blockade of orange, warning lights they passed to stop fifty yards out over the water, far from the cleanup activity of a tipped over lumber truck on the other side of the deserted, concrete span. The decorative LED strips along the Suburban gave Rory enough light to slice off a short length of rope and tie it to Yan's legs. When Brad caught up he gave his friend the other end to thread through the motorcycle frame. In one, deft move Rory hefted the chassis as Brad boosted Yan over the rail. The double splosh-splosh sounded back, as the dead Canadian sank to the Willamette mud.

"Your turn, Jack," Rory slid Jaxy onto the fresh powder, and ramming the gun barrel into the Rockabilly's mouth a second time ordered Jillian out. "Over here, babe! Watch Jack's brains blow out the top of his head."

Staring off, Rory tilted the last drop of tequila reciting: "Life's but a walking shadow. A poor tale. A tale told by an . . . by an . . . ah hell, so long, Jack!"

Click.

"Idiot," prompted Jaxy.

"Yes, you are Jack, Ha-ha-ha! Just seeing if you could finish the line," Rory swatted Jillian's tush. "Good one, huh, babe?"

At that moment the accident cleared bringing the bridge to life. Brad spun about and yelled, "Rory! The plow!"

Rory cut and handed more rope to Jillian. "Here! To Jack's feet."

"We should go!" Brad looked to Pepper for reinforcement, but the Wolador had gone off for more pinecones.

Behind the bickering men, Jillian switched ropes and tied Jaxy's feet together by the long piece, then took his glasses and double knotted his feet. "Tuck," she forced his chin down, then softly whistling Pepper over pried a cone from her teeth and waved it before the dog's nose before stuffing it down Jaxy's front and rolling him to a fireman's carry.

Brad finally had his fill of tonight's drunken mayhem and split on foot for the far shore, trusting Pepper to find her way home. Without backup, Rory was pleasantly surprised to see his wife acting in helpful obedience. He raised an iron barbell plate above his head and signaled, "Ready babe, when you are."

With an "A-B-C, One-Two-Three", over the snow-capped rail

she hurtled Jaxy, and then dropping to the ground she commanded Pepper to "Fetch!"

With eyes on the river Jaxy rotated into a head dive to cushion the impact. Down . . . down . . . down he descended into the water holding his breath to postpone the inevitable in an instinctive fight to survive. Suddenly the rope went taut. Then, instead of being dragged by an iron weight to the river bottom, with a jerk he stopped, reversed direction, and torpedoed backwards toward the bridge, wingtips first, out of the water!

Jaxy sputtered and took in great gulps of oxygen, then his upward flight stopped, and he plunged again for another chilly dunking. This cycle repeated several times, except Jaxy did not dip as low, and on the return did not fly as high. When this yo-yo madness ended his hair skimmed the surface of the water as Jaxy swayed feet first from Rory's long, climbing rope, snagged by the climbing hardware to the bridge railing. The exhilaration of the ride, and the thrill of being alive, soon gave way to the bleak awareness that Jaxy dangled upside-down in a January blizzard at half past midnight where no one could see or hear him under the Sellwood Bridge, to freeze slowly by degree in a Martha Stewart designer sheet for the world to find stiff as a board in the morning.

Thank you, Jillian.

CHAPTER 29

Tomsk, Siberia, October 1917

Whatever blame history may lay on Tsar Nicholas II at Imperial Russia's curtain call, few find fault in him as a family man. While controversy flies over why he chose to overstay his welcome for love of country, over seeking safe harbor for his loved ones abroad while they had the chance, most say he held out too long in the faith that brighter days would arrive. They did not, and in an effort to deliver the Romanovs from imminent fate, an ally in the transitional government snuck the royal family out on a Red Cross train to a safe house in Tomsk, Siberia, halfway to the eastern coast. By October plans fell through under a new authority, and this port in a storm became a bleak incarceration.

Winter came.

The uninsulated confinement gave meager shelter from the jarring cold, and it became a group effort to stay alive with nothing but green sticks that barely took fire on the drafty, sub-zero nights. By day the close-knit Romanovs kept their blood circulating by chopping wood, taking exercise in the closed-off yard, reading, putting on skits, doing schoolwork, practicing music, journaling, and sending and receiving letters from the outside. How much treasured mail their captors tossed nobody knows, but some made it through. One package in particular, sent in care of Grand Duchess Olga from her grandmother Maria Feodorovna, contained a special gift—a guardian angel set in blue, sparkling sapphires with a poem of hope.

Spring came.

The snow melted and the ice thawed just as the mosquitos hatched, but nature's annoyances came as the least of the family's concerns. With Cossacks skirmishing in the hinterland, Moscow could ill afford to let the loyalists free their figurehead to serve as a rallying flag. Ergo, the mandate came to transfer the Romanovs to a stronghold in the Urals. However, an obstacle disrupted a smooth transition. The Leninists could not carry the Tsar's son Alexei, suffering from a hemophiliac setback, across the room without causing him excruciating pain, to say nothing of a long voyage down river. Anxious to whisk the parents away, the Reds sent them ahead with daughter Marie to Yekaterinburg, leaving the others to care for their ailing brother.

Summer came.

Which is worse? To shiver before the polar blasts of a Siberian winter, or the leers and jeers of an uncouth crew that brought the girls and Alexie, now sufficiently recovered, partway by boat to join their parents in Yekaterinburg. Made to sleep with their cabin doors open, they never knew when they might be passed from sailor to soldier with no way to fight back and nowhere to run! And the deckhands might well have, had they known that underneath the women's garments lay a wealth in jewels in order that, should they split up, the duchesses would have assets to pawn.

The last leg of the journey the children took by train, thankfully untouched to disembark during a torrential rain in the black of night. Under strict command not to lend the girls a helping hand lest the guards appeared sympathetic to the Tsar, the Cheka looked the other way. Rain-soaked and chilled to the bone, the sisters trudged their way through the mud, dragging trunks along the ruts, and helping Alexei to the cart that would take them to their final home on 49 Ascension Avenue.

CHAPTER 30

The Leshenko Home, Portland, OR
1:00 a.m. Friday, January 5, 2018

"Yilli! Where are you!" quavered Fr. Michael, with Helen crowding the phone.

"On a fixie!" yelled Jillian, darting between cars, and running stops as fast as her legs could pump the single sprocket bicycle with handlebar ribbons and a five-pound bomb strapped to her foot. Between huffs and puffs she briefed what happened and how she broke away. "I'm headed for the hospital. Go look for Jaxy!"

"You call 911?"

"No way! They'll send me back to jail," panted Jillian, jumping a curb to miss an opossum.

"Good! Because bad guys tossed Reuben's looking for angel. They infiltrate everywhere—even police."

"Oh no!! Is he okay?"

"Tank God he go to Mexico. Hide somewhere and I come get you."

"Can't! Rory's right behind me!"

"But—."

"Don't 'but' me—go find Jaxy! Huu—here it comes. Gotta go!"

"Should I go?" asked Helen of the hospital.

"Yillianz' beyond human aid," replied Fr. Michael, "but guy under bridge need it bad, so bring your doctor tings!"

"Let's take Drew's," she offered her son's wheels.

"He here?" asked Fr. Michael.

"Winter break. Drew? Drew!" Helen scurried across the house to her son's room where she found him busting heads on "Barroom Brawl".

"You're killin' me." Helen stood in the doorway with hands on hips.

"Take that—and that!" Drew yelled at the computer.

"We need your truck."

"Mine's a disaster. Use Dad's! Ha! See that?" He called out the score, and then paused the action for someone with clout. "Hey, Father K., what's a-crack-a-lackin'?"

"We'll tell you on the way to the marina!" Helen put her toe on the power bar bringing down the room.

The young man pawed around for his keys. "Warning you, Mom. Didn't have time to clean it before the rain let loose."

"The park gave you more hours?" Helen asked as her daughters, stirred from bed by the commotion, came tearing down the hall for a jellybean handout.

Drew pinched his sisters out of the way, "And combat pay to shoo-off little kids playing 'hide n' seek'!"

When they reached Dr. Leshenko's fishing boat docked near the bridge Helen marshalled the search: "Look for a man wrapped in a sheet tied to a rope. I'll take the *QP Doll*!"

"Who came up with this fat idea, you or Mom?" Drew swung his flashlight under the bridge

"Yillianz'," said Fr. Michael.

A party of badges led by Sergeant Tank Pantzer marched up. "Pretty late for a walk, gentlemen," Tank stopped to say.

Drew sauntered uphill so they all would face him, and not his mother's boat sliding by in the misty water. "I dropped a tri-fold along here today. Dark blue. Anyone see it?"

"We're hunting a body. Notice any activity on the bridge?"

Fr. Michael crossed himself, "Mercy! Not another jumper?"

"Caucasian male thrown in around midnight after a holdup. The tip came from a hospital phone where I sent my men to arrest *your goddaughter*."

"Golly??"

"No. The other one."

"Uh-oh. What Yilli' do?"

"Nothing yet. I'll be in touch."

A team of paramedics came by with an inflatable raft to join the police in the search downriver.

"What now?" asked Drew after the rescuers disappeared into the night fog.

"Pray your mom finds Yackzy before Tank does," said the priest.

A splash on the riverbank halted their talk. Drew redirected his beam, catching two green, opalescent orbs and gleaming fangs in reflection. "It's a wolf!" he cried, falling back into Fr. Michael.

Fr. Michael flicked his pipe lighter to ward off the beast.

At the flame the canine shrank to its haunches and howled at the bridge. Then snorting with excitement, swam fifty feet out to come back and shake water on them.

Fr. Michael squinted down the sandy bank. "I thought we look for dead man on rope, not wet dog on leash."

Drew shined his light on the tag and whooped, "Pepper! Something out there, girl?"

The Wolador nipped at Drew's thumb, then up the slope she bayed, turning as she went. Halfway to the bridge she stopped and waited stock-still, splaying her muscular legs.

"I'm going topside with wolfie!" Drew clung to the collar.

Along a snowbank thrown aside by the plow Pepper sniffed until she stopped to attack a mound with all fours. Drew fell alongside and dug until they uncovered the climbing rope, caught taut on the rail. Drew tugged, but it didn't give.

Down to the *QP Doll*! Drew called out, "Mom! Pepper found him!"

CHAPTER 31

The Royal Martyrs Chapel, Totum, WA
2:00 a.m. Friday, January 5

Vigil lamps that flickered and burned twenty-four/seven, softly lit the lofty chambers of the snowcapped, pink granite chapel of The Holy Royal Martyrs of Russia Monastery, tucked deep in the forests of southern Washington. There, a thick, barrel-chested, full-faced, balding Abbot, and a moccasin-shod, desiccated Archimandrite with a grey, wispy beard and long, tangly strands that fell from a hemp headband, faced the back, whitewashed wall.

The Abbot snapped at drawings rolled tight by a rubber band. "Inside are the dimensions. The bishop asked us to place the royal family here, from baseboards to molding, by the centennial celebration—and the Guild wants fireworks."

The shriveled monk read down the attendees' names, including bigwigs from the synod and a state senator off the pastoral letter. "Dear me, this is ambitious, but it won't happen. Not by July. Tell him Nicky and Alix. I'll fill the children in later."

The Abbot pinched his bushy salt and pepper beard. "He'd throw a 'hierarchical fiturgy'."

"Then we must scale it down."

"By George, that's it! Enlarge and transfer the icon on canvas and decoupage straight to the wall. In this lighting his Grace will never know."

"Absolutely not," the Archimandrite rejected the suggestion outright with his good arm, keeping the withered one out of sight under his cassock.

"Then it's the Klapakis godchild option."

The iconographer flinched, "Jillian Avlon? Saints preserve us."

"Not that one. Her brother Jean."

"Didn't know there was another painter in the bunch. Have him send his portfolio."

"Roche don't 'do' portfolios." The Abbot handed the Archimandrite the fall edition of *Art Colloque*.

"Jean Roche!" the monk gasped at the feature article exhibiting a self-portrait of the young savant standing before the Arc de Triomphe with half a head.

"The explosion left him deaf in one ear."

"Right or left?"

"Father Michael says it depends on which side you're standing." Abba Aldo's phone cut short the tête-à-tête with the Ninth Ode to the Nativity. He held it at arm's length and exclaimed, "Oh my soul. It's Klapakis now!"

"What has him up at this hour?"

"Golf."

UP THROUGH THE PINES from the granite chapel the wrought iron gate squeaked and squealed as it creaked on rollers. "Twice have I asked someone to lube that chain, but does anyone listen? No, they do not," the Abbot clutched and shifted onto Widowmaker Road. Minutes later the flatbed spun through a break in the fence, coasted past ice-coated, fruit trees, and skidded to a stop behind a Victorian cottage. From the kitchen sprang the metrical pommeling of hazelnuts on a cutting block, and a woman's voice croaking, "Oh Lord, won't you buy me a Mercedez Benz…"

Up steps bordered by two shoulder-high, cone-trimmed, juniper sentries, the Abbot mounted. He ran his fingertips along the fresh, daffodil yellow trim, then rapped his burly knuckles on the door thrice, then once, and then two more times.

"Aldo, it's late!" chided Grandma P. as she removed her embroidered apron, undid the chain, and relieved him of waxed, baking apples.

The Abbot hooked his jacket on the coat rack and opened the parlor fireplace screen to stoke the flames in a throwback room from the roaring twenties that smelled of cedar and mothballs.

"And make yourself at home! Since you have nothing else to do in the dead of night than to try to convert a feeble, old hippie," she said from the kitchen coming with black tea and ginger cookies.

"Father Michael called," began the Abbot.

"Lovely!" chirped Grandma, "should I set out another cup?"

"He has a situation with a…erm, 'lost sheep'."

Grandma P. stirred in a cube. "And how many does that make for him so far this year?"

"Someone nobody's heard of," said the Abbot.

"Nobody's ever heard of," repeated Grandma P. "This does sound exciting. Like Radio Mystery Theatre!"

"And she needs someplace to stay."

"To 'the old woman who lives in a shoe', he said."

"Tonight."

Grandma looked around. "Well…where is she?"

"Don't exactly know."

Grandma Pearson crossed her white rabbit tats. "Honestly, Aldo, between a parish of homes and a monastery with empty guest rooms, the two of you want me to take in one of your lost lambs—that you can't even find?? Hmph! Must be a real doozy."

Time passed, and again the secret knock disturbed Grandma P.'s predawn nap, waiting for her lost lamb to show up.

"Got her, Grandma!" Fr. Michael said through the screen. "Basement ready?"

"You black shirts will be the death of me," the widow replied unfastening the chain.

Across the threshold the priest bore his eldest goddaughter clothed in hospital scrubs. "Remember—nobody to know!"

Grandma P. inspected the cherubic face and squared off. "Have you men gone bonker-bins? Tricking me into dumping her here. I'll be rolling over in the grave with Whitman before the night's through!"

"Easy, Grandma—not who you think. This is beeg sister Yillianz'."

"You're joking. There's more?"

Jillian stirred, "Is Jaxy okay?"

Into her apple green eyes Grandma breathed easy. "Magnifico. Now back to sleep, lamb chop."

"Yilli' to have no telephone, no internet, and no TV," said the priest.

"Cookies?"

"Cookies okay."

"Anything else?"

Father Michael inched up Jillian's pant leg. "Do you have bolt-cutter?"

CHAPTER 32

Moosburg Motel, Leavenworth, WA
6:00 a.m. Friday, January 5

A fist came down on the upper deck door of the Moosburg Motel at sunup.

"And here come the cops," Brad rubbed his bloodshot eyes and went to face his doom. Coming back to Leavenworth was his best alibi, since in a hurry they hadn't checked out. A slice of pepperoni pizza lay hardening on the dresser.

"Captain. It's you, you moron! What happened?" Brad asked with relief, and then anger when Rory tumbled in.

"Going to kill the bitch," said Rory, on the verge of passing out.

Brad pulled a water-soaked hoodie from a blackened eye, cut cheek and busted schnoz. "Dude . . . lucky she didn't kill you."

As the story broke across police bands, the climbers caught up on the disappearance of Canadian agent Pierre de Chavoie, whose Chevrolet Suburban was found half submerged in the Columbia River with a quantity of blow and bloody belongings on the floor, and a Heizer extended magazine stuck between the seats. A Vancouver book vender confirmed the Mountie's last known location. No suspects had been questioned.

Rory filled in the gaps saying that after his wife flattened his face to give him the slip, he set Jaxy up for the murder by salting the place with cash, made a final entry in Yan's log about arranging a meet with the Californian at the Avlon house, and then dumped the Suburban for the cops to find. Knee-deep in mud, Rory hiked upriver and swam from there to the union motor pool to take a service coach to the shop.

"They won't think twice about it. I borrow their trucks all the time," said Rory.

"But your fingerprints!"

"All I touched outside the house without gloves was Jaxy's wallet and the car window with my face. Man, she cracked me good." Rory examined his cheekbone in mirror.

"Your wife knows where we go. It's a matter of time before they smoke us out."

"That's the weird thing! By the time I circled around the heat was out in force with her acting more afraid of them than me. Probably to do with that hoard of jewelry. So, now I lay me down and catch some z's."

"Looking like you went gliding without a kite? You were seen pretty sharp buying roses in Clackamas last night, I might add."

"If I buy flowers for the girls at the office while you help Jack into his fucking truck, that's my fucking business."

"But to say you broke your nose night-climbing after the fact is a fucking stretch."

"Faking a fight isn't." Rory balanced the pizza on his shoulder, "I dare you."

"Hey, that's mine!

Rory bumped his knuckles together. "Come, Brad. You can do better than that."

"Give it here thou gluttonous swine!" Brad splintered a flimsy chair over the Captain's back.

"Turn thee, Benvolio. Look upon thy death!" Rory split Brad's ear with a porcelain lamp, shattering it to pieces.

Around the room they hooped and hollered, smashing mirrors, and busting beds. In a minute, two squad cars pulled up, drawing night-clad, Leavenworth, holiday folk outside.

"Break it up! Break it up!" The policeman pounded with his baton.

Brad meekly came to the door, holding a bloody towel to his neck with one hand, and the pizza box by the other. "Sorry officer. Were we disturbing the peace?"

"Were you disturbing the . . . !!!!"

Rory butted his bashed face through the door whining, "Doofus took the last slice!"

"I.D.s now!"

Rory shook out his driver's license while Brad munched on the crust.

"You're Captain Rory Avlon?" The officer recorded the name.

"And former Chippendale," flexed Rory with a winsome smile.

"Should see him in a bow tie," Brad completed the picture.

"We've been looking for you! Heard from your wife?"

Rory stepped away wearing a fearful look. "No. Did something happen? Is she okay?"

The officer of the peace went over the course of events while Rory interjected in dismay, "I can't believe it . . . She didn't . . . Not possible . . ." Onto the bed he then fell, shocked to hear that his wife had thrown in with the vilest of criminals, Jackson Thrie.

"You gentlemen will have to pay for damages, but in the circumstance, I'll ask the motel to not press charges Mr. Avlon, because we need your assistance. How those two got the better of a ranking agent three years in deep cover with the Canadian mob has the Mounties floored. If your wife tries to get through call us. Do not attempt to corral her. Jillian Avlon is a wily one, and when cornered, extremely dangerous."

Rory gingerly brushed his bumps and bruises. "I would not have guessed."

The junior partner spoke up. "Hang tough. And next time fellows? Spring for a second pizza."

As the cars pulled away Rory leaned over the rail, "Better catch that California P.O.S. before I do, or I'll rip his head off!"

Asked Brad munching down the last bite, "How long have you been moving drugs for that Canadian anyway?"

"I didn't know he was an undercover cop. God this is messed up."

"No. What you did to your wife—that's messed up."

"Boy, this shall not excuse the injuries thou hast done me." Rory dabbed an ear.

"No wonder Pepper likes her better than you."

"Cork it. Let's go get stitched up."

Back from having their heads patched, Rory picked up an angry message from Rita. Since she fancied herself an ace counselor, and had a soft spot for flattery, Rory prepared his plea and radioed back.

Rita called his bluff: "Out with it, Rory! J.D.'s face is everywhere. I want the straight poop and if you short me, the world will hear about it."

Rory recapped that when he came home with roses on Rita's advice, he surprised his wife making it with Jaxy in the Jacuzzi. Before he could pitch the interloper into the snow, Jaxy's contact showed up with a gun. Rory didn't realize the dealer was a plain-clothed narc, but somehow Jaxy saw through the guise and stabbed him. When Rory tried to get a call off for help, Jillian clocked him with an aluminum bat. In and out of consciousness Rory overheard talk of dumping the body in the river.

"But you didn't go for police help after," said Rita.

"I was drunk, dazed, and to tell the truth? Pretty embarrassed. Her conking me—how would that make me look?"

"Like an innocent man."

"Right. Didn't consider that. Still, had Bradley not driven me to Leavenworth I might have expired there on the floor. The clinic here dresses Hubba battle wounds every day. Nobody questioned it."

"You guys are idiots."

"Can't argue that, but she's taken up with a rough crowd, Rita, running with a sicko who doesn't give a hoot about anything but making statements by killing defenseless citizens and swaying softheads like Jillian to perform his chicken-shit work. So—," Rory paused to set the hook, "—what should I do?"

Rita hemmed and hawed, "If Jaxy's gang is as bad as you say, stand down and let the pros do the heavy lifting."

"It'll be hard. The woman needs help."

"Wow Rory, after what she did? That's pretty big. I told Jillian she'd have a hard time finding a better man than you."

"Roger that."

CHAPTER 33

The ROMAR, Totum, WA
11:00 a.m. Friday, January 5

Warm water lapped, soothing and delightful. A spicy aroma wafted. Low in the background, an acapella chorale cantillated a rich composition. Astounded at how sensations on earth were heightened in heaven, Jaxy anticipated a dazzling new body with rock solid pecs, six-pack abs, bulging biceps, and nicer legs than those on the statue of David at Forest Lawn. Unable to wait any longer, he had to see this place! His eyes flew open to marvel at how celestial fonts resembled glazed, ceramic stand-alones with chipped edges and rusty claw feet, wrap-around, seahorse shower curtains, caked soap trays, and crusted aluminum window casings with torn screens set in cracked, yellow tiles last grouted during the Hoover Administration. The clock on the toilet tank read 11:05.

Holy Humbucker! Jaxy splashed. He hadn't washed up on the shores of paradise for Saint Petey's sake—no, he lay thawing inside some religious fanatic's bath in desperate need of a makeover. Questions raced through his head: Where was he? How did he get here? And what had become of Jillian?

With a meritorious effort Jaxy raised up on his forearms only to create a tidal wave sliding back. A hollow-cheeked, narrow nosed, twig of a man in a light grey robe with stringy hair and beard cackled from the hallway. "Don't go anywhere Jackson. I'll be back in two shakes."

Jaxy tried his extremities. He could not wiggle his toes. Perchance feeling would start again, but even if frostbitten, he had beaten the odds and should not complain.

"Juice?" the elder brought Jaxy a boxed drink and plastic straw.

"Thank you." Jaxy took a sip, then howled, "my tooth!"

His host brought denture paste to plug the missing crown, then on the toilet lid, across from Jaxy he sat saying, "Welcome to The Holy Royal Martyrs of Russia Monastery—."

"Where's Jillian?"

"—at the base of Mt. Adams. Half day from the city," replied the old monk, fingering a string of black prayer knots.

"She is?"

"No, Jackson. You are. I'm Archimandrite Photios, but you can call me 'Father'."

"Nice to meet you, ah . . . Father." Jaxy replied with hesitation, for he had never addressed anyone by that except his own pop. "My fan base calls me Jaxy."

"Your base has grown."

"Can't have enough. What day is it? Did I miss anything?"

"Friday. You missed Matins."

Jaxy winced as his toes began to tingle. "How did you find me?"

"Wasn't easy. We were told you'd be floating like a leaf—not swinging like a tractor tire. Right, Deacon?" the elder asked of an immense man filling the doorway.

The wide-body introduced himself in a resonant baritone, "Hello, Mr. Jaxy, I'm Matthias the camp cook. After the doctor sees you, break the fast at the trapeza."

"What's a trapeza?"

"The refectory," made plain the cook with a nod of his flour-flecked, panther black dreads, before clumping back to the kitchen.

Jaxy saw he would need a dictionary to find his way around this place. "And a refectory is . . . ?" he asked for further clarification.

"The mess hall. His fans call it 'Café Matthias'."

OVER THE GROWLING OF his gut, Jaxy leafed through a monograph on local, fire-mountain lore in the infirmary while waiting for the doctor to finish golf lessons with the Abbot. It's how the Abbot paid her for house calls.

Eventually Dr. Leshenko came by, and upon administering a reflex check, assured by a toe tickle Jaxy wouldn't lose a one. To set the rest of his body in motion she recommended a light regimen of exercise, and a round at the community three-par if so inclined.

Jaxy drew back the curtain. The only green to be seen was in the treetops. "You golf in this?"

Helen cemented the crown onto his tooth, tightened the screws on Jaxy's black glasses, and retook his blood pressure while making light banter. "Where it snows, some courses lay down this oily, putting surface. It's not ideal and neither is your diastolic. Take one capsule each morning and I'll see you in three days."

Jaxy read the warning on the sample pill card and toyed with the tooth. "Does the name 'Jillian Avlon' mean anything?"

Helen shot a sideways glance. "Patient records are strictly confidential."

"If you run into her, you should know that she's going into her second trimester. That's all."

With a look capable of freezing every green to Palm Springs the doctor raised her voice asking: "Think back, Jaxy, to yesterday. In confidence, where were you from six to ten?"

"Ramblin' down the Old Oregon Highway."

"*At night.*"

Jaxy ruffled his hair. "That's a bit foggy."

"And the rest of your recall? Any other lapses or gaps?" asked Helen, slathering camphor over the red marks on his neck.

Jaxy shrank back. "It's 1998, Bill Clinton's the President, and I did not have sex with that woman."

"Rub this on your gums," Dr. Leshenko slapped foul-flavored, oral anesthetic in Jaxy's hand and went to demand an extra thirty minutes of the Abbot's time for having to deal with that California smartass.

CHAPTER 34

Grandma P.'s Cottage, Totum, WA
1:00 p.m. Friday, January 5

Through the cottage screen Grandma P. snatched a candle bundle from the Abbot's hand. "Lost little lamb? *That nobody's ever heard of?*"

Abba Aldo held his stocking cap in contrition.

Past his head Grandma said to Helen, "Lock them both in the tool tidy for a week, that's what we should do."

From the basement Fr. Michael came offering up his defense, "People go missing around our blessed country every day, and this story goes national!"

"Did I not say, 'no television'?" asked the Abbot.

"Too late." Grandma P. shepherded them to the cellar calling, "Jillian? Meet Aldo de Torquemada!"

"And I'm Helen!" Dr. Leshenko gave Jillian a fun wave from the top.

Jillian met Helen halfway with an ardent embrace and led her by the hand to show off Grandma P.'s basement: an expansive, wall-to-wall carpeted game room, with a stainless, cabin cooking range, and modern half-bath that bore no semblance to the main floor décor.

"Feeling better?" The Abbot eventually asked

Jillian flung her hand at the 70-inch plasma newscast. "Not true!

Not one word!"

The Abbot held up a finger.

"Yes. I'm fine," Jillian settled down. "Is Jaxy?"

"He's-a walkin'."

"And-a talkin'," added Helen with her signature stink face.

"And asking too many questions!" finished Fr. Michael.

To the hutch Grandma called them, "Jillian did this this morning. Isn't she something?"

"It's Thunder Roll! Or pretty close. Didn't get the blaze quite," basked Jillian in the praise of the chestnut stallion, with his black mane and stockings splashing through a pasture stream bordered by wild grapes.

Helen said, "That's not a drawing, Jillian, that's a photograph."

"Grandma thinks all I can do is shoot pool and pass out peanuts."

"In addition, Lamb Chop has talent," said Grandma P.

Abba Aldo reached for the corner. "May I? A local art critic should see this."

Jillian took a safety razor to the pencil. "Not until I sign it."

"When you're finished," the Abbot tactically retreated.

"As if one eccentric artist around here wasn't enough," clucked Grandma P., striking a new round of talk amongst the ladies as the men took their hats to go.

ON THE MUDDY DRIVE Fr. Michael sat defrosting the windshield before heading home to Minnehaha, debating if he should delve further into the guardian angel when a tap on the glass opened the way.

"Grandma's washer's on the fritz and my butt will not fit her dresses. I cannot believe how thin she is for the amount she bakes," said Jillian in a comical pair of Whitman's pinned-up, ink-stained overalls and holding out a laundry basket.

Fr. Michael invited Jillian inside the car. "Since her husband die, Grandma gives away her goodies. She no belief in God, but she sure belief in fattening His people."

With the basket, Jillian passed along a shopping list of sundries. "Tell Camille I take size seven."

"My word, Yillianz'! Whole world knows you take size seven, but before I go—are you absolutely certain angel snap free of your husband's neck?"

"Told you! When I went for the switch I grabbed onto the angel too, but it broke off the chain and slipped through my fingers. It has to be there on the ground somewhere. Can you look again?"

"I will, but unless good Samaritan take to lost and found, I'm afraid it gone."

"How I wish I had not put it in that bloody rag with the other jewels from Denmark. Been meaning to ask about that," Jillian snuggled close for warmth.

"'As in British 'bloody'?"

"No, as in real, human blood! It's the most hideous, moth-eaten thing with slashes and rips out of a Hitchcock film. Did you ever see *Dial M for Murder*? Princess Grace still gives me gooseflesh, but give me one name in Hollywood today who can . . ."

Fr. Michael had no concept where Jillian might take this but chose not to derail her diatribe on how they don't make scary movies like they used to, to ponder why a Guild insider would route crown jewels cached in St. Olga's massacred remnant to Jillian instead of her brother Jean, the family head by birthright, unless he needed her for substantiation. For Jean, a naturalized French citizen, to step out of obscurity as the nearest, descending grandnephew to the Tsar saying, "Here I am!" with nothing for to show but a dog-eared, baptismal certificate would not convince the naysayers. What the heir had going for him were his sisters' mitochondrial markers transferrable from mother to daughter. That Jillian and Golly could trace their genes six generations to Queen Victoria of England along female lines, as could Olga through her mother, the Empress Alexandra, meant the corset's DNA match to either sister would validate Jean as the closest scion to the Russian throne by extrapolation.

The bad news? By the time Jean Roche left for America he didn't want the job, preferring the introspective life of a painterly hermit to a figurehead of state with a target on his back. He thus left the twin holding a Doctorate in Evolutionary Biology with the expertise to run an underground weapons research facility funded by an assassins' corporation, and the four-year, political science graduate from Colorado State able to go yard in fast-pitch and demonstrate the form, fit and function of an Airbus oxygen mask to duke it out.

With Jean sidelined, and Jillian's reputation gone to the dogs, Golly Gee had her first realistic shot at wringing enough Guild votes to make her prepotency stick if she could land a hand on the royal garment. But if going through the Avlon homestead, forensics bagged the blood-caked corset as evidence in the high-profile murder of a Canadian Mountie embedded in her association? God only knows what would happen.

Jillian concluded her thoughts as Fr. Michael did his and so he asked, "Would you like other jewels? They are not same, but tell me where and I go look."

"Under the snake tank. Mostly I want my angel."

"Now who be watching out for who? Maybe keeper angel put Yilli' in safe place! He's a busy little fellow lately. When you need him, he will show."

Jillian made a moue, "I can't imagine any angel with half an angel brain would have anything to do with me."

From the cottage a voice yelled for Jillian, ending their talk.

"Huu! Gotta run," Jillian hugged her godfather, then footslogged her way across the tire-churned drive for her turn at a medical checkup by Dr. Leshenko.

AFTER THE BASEMENT CLEARED out, the doctor strained to hear Jillian's heart over the pumping of Grandma's parlor organ through the ceiling boards. "In residency I played marimba in a chick band. When this is over Grandma, your boyfriend, and I should plan a jam," Helen made light conversation.

"Jaxy is *not* my boyfriend," replied Jillian.

"Understood. And I'm no O.B. either, but I pushed out four of my own and . . . sweetheart, what's wrong?"

"That . . . that . . . ," Jillian dug her nails into the pool table felt.

"Yes?" Helen eased a pillow under Jillian's neck.

"*Blabberface*!"

"It's good I learned of this, even if by an improper channel."

"Please don't tell anyone," asked Jillian.

"Junior will make itself known soon enough. Hold your breath."

Jillian ceased fussing while the doctor carried on, "Your husband must be pure evil."

Jillian exhaled, "He thought it was Jaxy's. That's what set him off."

"Then whose baby is it?"

"I'm not sure."

"Oh boy! Well dear, stress can affect your health and the little one's," cautioned Helen as she wrote "Jane Doe" and took the tray to leave. "Here is my prescription: Avoid news, eat ice cream, and watch something funny."

"You'll call again, won't you, doctor?"

Dr. Leshenko gave Jillian her private number. "Call me 'Helen', and you can call me anytime."

ON HIS WAY TO Clackamas, Father Michael stopped by the parsonage for the purpose of picking up his wife's new, knitted purple shawl, over which she squabbled and squalled: "But Mike, not everyone in the circle is done! Can't it wait to be blessed with the rest before you give it willy-nilly away to someone who won't participate?"

"*Economia*," Father Michael waved his hand over the basket, and with an abbreviated prayer rolled in two pounds of jellybeans, brought his pocket calendar up to date, and headed for the Avlons.

"Move along, reverend. No loitering," said the night-watch from the yellow caution tape that cordoned the domicile.

"Heavens! What happen?" Fr. Michael stretched forward.

"You don't know? It's all everyone talks about."

"But Avlons invite me over for house blessing," Fr. Michael offered the officer a jellybean and a look at his calendar.

The officer noted the time and occasion. "Father Klapakis? You gave these out at Miracles in Recovery House! Your message so moved my son—I believe you saved his life."

"No. Tank God and his sponsor. I just yack for an hour." The priest produced a phial of holy water, and lifting the barrier proclaimed, "But this evening I bless Avlon home, for more than ever they need miracle too!"

"You'll have to bless it from here."

Father Michael flicked a few drops at the paunchy statue. "Saint Nick maybe, but porch too far. For miracle to work everything must get wet. Living room, bedrooms, kitchen, halls, snake tank—."

"Snakes too?"

"Especially snakes. So, I make deal and stay out of house and hit what I can from garage."

The yard guard checked the time. "Be quick."

A minute later Father Michael came out to present himself for a quick frisk. If the uniform noticed the shawl had miraculously changed from a plush purple to crusty rust brown, he didn't mention it.

CHAPTER 35

Beaver Island, B.C.
2:00 p.m. Friday, January 5

Through the coastal pall that rolled up to laze the weekend on Bargain Bay, Golly Gee couldn't see to the boathouse with a surveillance system that cut out in the mist. But neither could one spy in to where she sat snug as a castled queen with her foot compressed and elevated.

She missed Yan. Not as the guard dogs did, for the section head mostly exasperated her. Yet no Beaver worked harder than him, and it showed when she needed beetroot juice, or someone to wipe the optics when the coms blurred. But surpassing this, the premier person on the planet to unpack the data surrounding Yan's enigmatic disappearance was Yan himself. Without her right hand, Golly Gee struggled in the solitary effort, but after a day of dead ends and red herrings on little sleep the postmortem left her stumped at how she had so grossly misread Jillian's willingness to hit back.

With a newfound respect bordering on admiration, Golly Gee taped a picture of her diabolic double to the whiteboard to capture second impressions: Ravishing—Resourceful—Artistic—Athletic—Ruthless—Calculating went up with a dozen other gushing accolades. Golly also explored a variant theory that Jillian secured Jaxy's help, not the other way around, to take this bold stroke and gain a publicized following in the process.

After brainstorming her primary suspects, Golly moved on to other potential perpetrators with means and motive. Klav "Loverboy" Lovorsky rose head and shoulders above the field, for the Russian Antique Mall manager hated her for understandable reasons. Consumed, however, in making preparation for a conference on World War I armaments, Klav lacked the occasion, imagination, and wherewithal to finesse the job. A more dangerous Siberian on the other hand did, and after Rat Catcher's failed attempt on Jean Roche's life in Paris, the possibility that this sworn, family foe formed a temporary alliance with Jillian to pick clean the Romanov family tree from within bore consideration.

After this the list grew short. Nobody wanted to stretch Jaxy Thrie's hide wider than Sergeant Tank Pantzer for the embarrassment this brought to Portland's Criminal Intelligence and leaving him open to criticism. The grand God-daddy of all, Fr. Michael Klapakis, she kept wound around her pretty finger. This left the "Switzerland" in the imbroglio: Remarkable Reuben Reisenschein.

For a man whose backbone wouldn't show on a CT scan, the artisan argued at length on the courier's behalf, then when the proverbial fudge hit the fan, ran for Cabo San Lucas. The thought of that two-faced jeweler siding with her sister sent Golly over the edge, literally, tripping on the whiteboard and crashing into the turret. "Owch—owch—owch!" She pounded at the one-way window through tears of betrayal and searing pain, "Ice and a Motrin!!!"

But no one heard, and nobody came.

Golly hobbled to her wide executive chair, donned the sash rife with perfume, and over the secure line invited Sergeant Tank Pantzer to the Lodge. As she reached for her datebook the mist thinned and the cameras started again. She joggled the joystick along the track to where she and Jaxy originally tangled. For a man practiced in the fighting arts, he went down easy. Too easy. Would he let her take him to the mud again? With lids at half-mast and head tossed back, Golly indulged a forbidden fantasy riding the Sunshine Coast of the imagination, hair whipped by salty sea air, the musky smell of a Mighty Ducks jacket, and the easy squeeze of a Rockabilly's knees around them breezy motorcycle chaps...

AFTER REHASHING FOOTAGE SHOWCASING Moby with bullet holes at an international airport, a purloined bicycle in a hospital dumpster, an abandoned forklift at the hotel, interviews with a host, custodian and skycap, Jillian barefoot in a Mighty Ducks jacket drinking punch at a posh restaurant, Jaxy barefoot in a bath towel punching buttons on a bank machine, a Chevy Suburban dripping with chrome, river weeds and an impressive drug stash and no mention of the Sellwood Bridge, Guin Hill had had enough. So off she went to whip up Jell-O salad, the only food she could keep down.

Unmoved by the unfolding drama, Roosevelt kicked back taking in the koi pond with the same "I'm Hip" T-shirt and noncommittal expression he had worn all week.

"To get the fine points and arrive at such inane conclusions? Unforgiveable!" said Guin.

Her teddy bear had nothing to contribute.

Countless concerned calls and texts went unheeded as Guin deactivated her social media profiles, unhooked the kitchen line, and darkened the house. While posting a "PLEASE DO NOT DISTURB THE COUNCIL-WOMAN" sign in the yard, she took note that the bland, green sedan had not moved since morning. On her street, an unfamiliar Jaguar wouldn't have given a moment's pause.

From there Guin called up everything on-line that mentioned her name. It went for pages. The fallout of being engaged to a wanted fugitive for the grisly murder of a Canadian law agent over a botched, narcotics bust, presumably to finance the terrorist activities of his suicide bomber accomplice, WWA flight attendant Jillian Avlon who overnight shot the moon as the nation's leading sex symbol, had wreaked political havoc. How could she show her face at City Hall?

And then came Jaxy.

Fat Pipes page hits had skyrocketed with "Glottal Catch" singles selling like hotcakes and spawning a new line dance in Tulsa. Guin's blood boiled to the point of tungsten to see art bloggers pouncing on Jillian Avlon's "Steeds and Studs" gallery with rave reviews, flooding it with orders. Then to complete the hat trick, WWA stock closed at an all-time high with the expansion of new travel routes and pink grapefruit drinks flying off the shelves.

To her interest, Guin then learned that joint North American agencies had set two point five million dollars apiece for information leading to the apprehension of Jackson Thrie and Jillian Avlon.

"Roosevelt? I do believe I see a silver lining. Behave yourself while I go to Oregon and make Jillian-ade. I'll take you someplace nice when I get back."

"No?" she rubbed foreheads while listening to the stuffed animal's reply. "How if I set you up with your own Match profile? 'Handsome teddy looking for cute bearfriend. No strings attached. Enjoys bounty hunting and bed jumping. You like that?"

Roosevelt liked that.

CHAPTER 36

The ROMAR, Totum, WA
3:00 p.m. Friday, January 5

With a clean bill of health, Jaxy found his way to Café Matthias at the north quad of the Royal Martyrs Monastery main assembly house. There the husky, camp cook greeted him with hands as knobby as coal on the knuckles, and pink as a newborn hamster on the palms. Deacon Matthias may have put on an innertube working kitchen patrol, but those were the surest arms Jaxy had ever held. Bellied up to a long, community table with bench seats built of quality wood and workmanship, Jaxy dove into a basket of buns and whipped butter. As he devoured a bowl of delicious lentils, through the window he took in the postcard-perfect lie of snow out beyond the woods to a patchwork of tilled land and rocky rills and wished for his camera.

After lunch the monks set him up in a visitor's trailer parked between pines downhill from the headquarters. The modern mobile came with every amenity a guest could want, and away from the main house activity. The dynamite heater had the place toasty within minutes. Still nauseous and weak, Jaxy dreamt upon snippets from the night before as he tossed and turned mumbling, "Keep staring . . . forget cops . . . A.B.C . . . 1.2.3 . . .

Hours later, he emerged to knock about the gift store. Walled off from the main house at the end of the long, front porch, the quaint space came stocked with jams and jellies, crosses, incense, candles, softbound and hardcovers, sheet and recorded music, and all manner of prayer-ware. The pewter, revetment icons reminded Jaxy of those they hawked at the Antique Mall. He purchased a bar of pine tar soap leaving a little extra in the honor system, cash box. Coming back into the big house gathering room, he crossed paths with the aged monk who had helped him in the bath, tending a blackened kettle on the potbelly stove.

"Your van is in the barn," The Archimandrite handed over Jaxy's keys. "You are the Abbot's guest—not prisoner."

Flabbergasted Jaxy blinked at the ring. "How?"

"Wasn't easy. Had to move his golf cart outside. Go. Pick out a tea bag," the elder shooed Jaxy to the kitchen where he engaged the cook shredding a defenseless lettuce head with massive fingers.

"Excuse me, where do you keep cups?" asked Jaxy.

Deacon Matthias showed him the mug tree. "So, what brings Mister Jaxy thisaway from sunny Southern California in dread winter?"

Jaxy spied the urn, "The coffee."

Approved the Deacon, "Back in the day an Ethiopian brother saw how the beans jazzed up his goats, so gave one a try. Been keeping monks awake in church since."

"Forgive me, but the older gentleman in charge . . . ?" Jaxy tilted out a cup of black brew.

"Hieromonk Archimandrite Photios," Deacon Matthias reverently dragged out, "is not in charge. But don't tell him that."

"Oh. Everyone's in black except him, so I thought."

The Deacon tugged at his side. "Father can wear any color cassock he wants, but for me it's black or nothing."

"Aye, that'd be cold." Jaxy took a seat at the long, cafe table.

"Know what sounds colder? Extreme winter sports—like bungee

jumping into the Willamette River."

"Enough!" a voice censured the idle talk unfitting for a monk from over their shoulders.

The Deacon resumed with the salad chanting, "The armies of angels trembled when they saw you baptized . . ."

A white mouser jumped to Jaxy's lap and arched her tail for a hiney scratch. The Archimandrite joined them at table, and again the golf subject came up.

"Not my game. Takes too much time and money," Jaxy offered his two cents.

"All have time and money for things that matter. Take Jillian for example."

Jaxy let the spoon go with a clatter and looked into Photios' pale eyes.

"You owe your life to that woman," said the Archimandrite.

Jaxy clenched his fists. "Darn it, Father, did she make it? I keep asking and everyone keeps changing the subject."

"Long enough."

"To bring me here with my busted crown and eyewear?"

"You can thank the Leshenkos for that."

Time passed with nothing forthcoming, so Jaxy tried a different angle. "Don't take this wrong, the guest trailer's nice and the fare excellent, but I can go anytime?"

"Is that what the doctor said?"

"Didn't say I couldn't."

"And miss your next appointment? A weekend in our rarefied air might do your heart good."

"Then I'll start my search for Jillian here."

"Who says she wants to be found?"

"Then she did survive."

"Long enough."

AFTER SUPPER THE COLLECTIVE, numbering fifteen, assembled for vespers in the Holy Royal Martyrs of Russia Monastery chapel situated beyond the drive and downslope from the main house in the forest thick at the property's geometric center. As they entered the somber chamber, each bowed low to the floor before two icons. The first portrayed Tsar St. Nicholas II with his slain family bedecked in fine raiment, halos, and crowns. The other showed Christ, but for a loincloth standing naked on the Jordan River with fish swimming at his feet, and more serious angels looking on. As Jaxy passed by a sandbox of long, skinny candles, he sniffed at the honeybee scent.

"Psst!—this way," the Deacon showed Jaxy how to cross himself. "Close enough for a scoundrel—in you go."

Instead of cheerless, marble statues like the "Christ the Redeemer" hood ornament on his fiancée's mother's Fiat, meant to strike terror in the hearts of gentiles and pedestrians alike, Jaxy gazed in awe from tiles to squinches at the dazzling, colorful murals, triangulated and proportioned in the flat, eastern style from pigments applied with an egg foundation to the stucco. The fierce eyes of Christ bore down upon him from high in the dome. Out the cave-like apse, Mary cast her almond gaze over his head into the star-studded, indigo universe.

A rococo partition of vines and grape leaves screened the congregation from the raised sanctuary where the Archimandrite bossed the subalterns as they prepared the various elements for worship. At a four-station music stand the Deacon crooned a litany while others took turns with the Psalter. The rest echoed responses from the central area clear of seating. Folding chairs lined the wall for visitors where a monk with layered, surfer hair helped him find a seat.

"I can't imagine the money that went into this—it's splendiferous!" Jaxy complimented the handiwork.

"Scaffolds and paint," replied the monk. "The chickens donated the rest."

"Someone did this—for free?"

"Father Photios started from the north door—."

Jaxy twisted around but saw no door.

The monk turned him about, "Over there. Been working his way back ever since."

AT THE CONCLUSION OF this same service held at St. Maximos church in Minnehaha, Fr. Michael beckoned the Leshenkos to his office. "Tee-time one o'clock sharp at Coppice Creek Golf Course tomorrow. You and Drew leave after antidoran. I have two baptism, so start without me. You bring clubs?"

"In the car," said Helen. "But why Coppice Creek?"

"Grandma P. having us for pie afterwards."

"But Drew, didn't you promise the girls a matinee?" asked Helen.

Fr. Michael expounded, "Police let Rory off hook and Grandma not so good with shotgun anymore. Abbot needs extra eyes on Yillianz, and Drew would be perfect for the job."

"Oh no, he wouldn't!" Helen's shielding instincts kicked in, placing her hands across Drew's chest from behind.

It pays better than trimming city park trees," Drew furthered the argument.

"And Grandma pretty good cook," Fr. Michael tacked on.

"And I'm not!?" Facing a lost cause, Helen loosened the knot from her hair and put away the covering. "On one condition—Drew goes early with me. We need to set some rules."

"And miss how I work fishing into gospel lesson?"

"The one from last year?"

"And the year before?" Drew recollected.

"Fine. I give other one about golf."

CHAPTER 37

Grandma P.'s Cottage, Totum, WA
11:00 a.m. Saturday, January 6

To the observation balcony with a picturesque view of Mt. Hood beyond the snowy bolls dripping off the tips of Grandma P.'s fruit trees, the old lady brought Helen a paring knife and an apple crate. "Hope you didn't come to sit all day like Lamb Chop and do nothing."

Snapped from her reverie to the rhythmic "swoosh" of a faraway saw blade the surgeon replied, "Thinking how you and Jillian make a great team."

"If she stays any longer, I'll teach her to make a great cobbler," Grandma cut lard into the flour bowl resting on her lap.

Jillian stepped around rubbing sleep from her eyes. "If she made it look fun, I might. Are we expecting company?"

"You, dear, are the company."

"I can't eat all of this."

"Never asked you to."

"For whom then do you bake?" Jillian polished an apple and took a bite.

"For whom do I bake? Since Whitman went belly-up my pies go to soup kitchens, monks, and other unfortunates."

Helen placed a hand on Jillian's and said, "Whitman was

Grandma's husband of fifty years."

"We met protesting the war," said Grandma with pride.

Helen leaned toward Jillian, "Vietnam."

Grandma continued, "We dreamed big, Jillian—not as today's visionaries who think 'going green' is getting a smart car for graduation. And we worked hard. Marching on D.C., standing up to the blue meanies, spiking trees in Washington. That's why we came — but stopped after the Alexander incident."

"A blade broke on a spike and took the man's head clean off," the doctor filled in.

"It was meant to wreck saws, Helen, not people, but it got their attention. In the end the tractors won. Cut down the old growth, plant Christmas trees, and call it 'renewable resource'. It's the money. Always the money. Who do they think they're fooling? Guess everybody, like Tricky Dick. Bet Lamb Chop never heard of him."

Jillian squinted her apple green eyes 'help!' at Dr. Leshenko.

"And she should be happy for that," Helen kept it on neutral ground. "They say half the registered population can't name the Vice President."

"Gerald Ford." Jillian lobbed a core into the compost bucket.

Dr. Leshenko and Grandma P. halted to look at each other, while Jillian nonchalantly peeled away expositing, "The only head of state to ascend as Vice President—after Agnew, and President—after Watergate without being elected to either seat. Follow the money? Those political ambulance chasers, Woodward and Bernstein sure did, laughing their way to the bank. If McCord and Dean hadn't cracked under pressure, I think Richard Nixon would have weathered it . . . but Grandma probably voted for McGovern."

"Gus Hall."

"Bet she still writes him in," Jillian winked at Helen.

"No chance. Since your sister ran off to Canada with my husband's files, I'm done reforming the world," said Grandma.

"And for that we can all be happy." Helen winked back.

"Is it true? I have a sister?" Jillian veered off politics.

From the parlor Grandma P. brought out a scrapbook, opened it to an obituary, and went to roll out the crust.

After Jillian read about the capsizing of a houseboat on the Great Slave Lake, she put her head on Helen's shoulder. "How heartrending. This woman drowned one week after earning a doctorate from the University of British Columbia just before turning *twenty-four*! It took that for my bachelors."

"—and taught ballet, and raced motorcycles to put herself through," read Helen.

"What couldn't she do? Just because we share a birthday doesn't mean we're related. Molly Rune was talented, and smart, and pretty. I'm none of those things," Jillian shut the scrapbook.

Helen hugged Jillian tight. "Feeling ugly doesn't make it so, and you wouldn't be the first grown adult to discover she has a twin."

"Why didn't Father Michael say something?"

"It's not his place." Helen petted Jillian's head and then carefully broke the news. "Sweetheart—an obstetrician worked up the labs. Did you experience unusual discharge or spotting the night of the bridge?"

"Not that I remember."

"Because everything points to a miscarriage. I'm afraid you lost the baby."

From the kitchen Grandma called, "Drew! Lunchtime!"

"In a minute!" Drew answered and kept sawing on a fruit tree limb.

Grandma came around to Helen, "I'm not going to argue with that young man."

Before rising, Helen took Jillian's hand. "I hate to play helicopter mom, but everyone wants my son here on the job except me, so please . . . some distance?"

Jillian bit her lip and tagged behind to Grandma's half acre of mixed plantings where they found Drew cutting on a sagging plum.

"Can't leave this branch half done or it'll split the trunk," defended Drew sawing through. After dragging the limb into the row, he leaned the pole saw against the brush and pulled off his work gloves.

"Drew, come meet Jillian," began Helen.

In surprised recognition Drew blinked, "I believe I already have."

With a quizzical expression, Helen sought an explanation.

Mortified, Jillian hid her face, so Drew answered for her, "Trimming trees at the Pittock Mansion!"

After years of wandering a parched and barren sand in search of what promised land she knew not, Jillian had found paradise in Helen—the mother lost at birth who adored her art, stroked her hair, soothed her pains, calmed her worries, and who now saw her for the tramp she was. With tears of self-loathing burning grooves down her cheeks, Jillian tightened the hood under her chin, passed on lunch, and loped down the road to Thunder Roll.

J.D. Avlon could run.

Her little league, stolen base record not only stood the test of time, Jillian could stay in the pack of a marathon. Therefore, Fr. Michael didn't catch up until she'd reached the Columbia River Gorge.

"Yilli! Where you going? Get in!" the priest shouted out the window.

"Where I should have in the first place!" Jillian kept running along the river.

"Don't dehydrate!" Fr. Michael tossed out water and paced her until she got the message that they were on this journey together.

"Damn it," swore Jillian, slowing to cool down before climbing in to stew against the door. When the Honda passed up a place to turn around, in puzzlement she asked, "Where are we going?"

"I asked first."

"The Dalles?"

"Show the way!"

Jillian hugged and hugged her godfather's neck making him tap the brakes lest they crash.

"Now harder question," he eased into the lane. "*Why?*"

Jillian looked at her shoes. "Helen didn't tell you?"

"Helen has no idea! She keep asking, 'What did I say? What did I say?' And Drew keep saying, 'You didn't say anything, mom'!"

"Oh."

"Oh?" her priest lifted a bushy eyebrow.

Jillian started and stopped several times over, until with great labor she cleared the air, "Father Michael—I'm not pregnant."

"That's a relief."

"I never was."

"Even better."

"But that's what I told Jaxy, and Jaxy told Helen, and it was one big, fat lie."

"Oh . . ."

As they traveled Jillian imparted how she played Jaxy for the van, and he in turn put his life on the line for a baby she never had, yelling at her to not give up on it either. Helen then followed through, wasting another physician's time to determine what Jillian didn't have the guts to admit. Worst of all, her tall tale triggered a sequence of events that cost a man his life.

"Yes, Yilli you are beeg, fat liar. But for sport or vengeance Rory kill Yan, not you, and no court of law will try you for that. I know if you knew you would not have lied, but lie you did. Now my daughter, have you anything else to confess?" asked Father Michael as he pulled off at a wide spot on the road.

With a downward slanting smile Jillian sniffled, "I said, 'dammit'."

Upon completing the absolution, the priest agreed to the let the "miscarriage" story stand and put it behind them to motor on to The Dalles in tranquility.

DOWN THE PATHWAY VIV sprinted, nearly tackling her darling friend at the picket fence. After a hasty, but joyful reunion, Jillian took off for a longer one with Thunder Roll, while Fr. Michael caught Viv up anent Jillian's surfacing at her ranch. As a wrap-up the priest requested that should Rory pay a call, to disavow any knowledge and point the Captain toward Minnehaha.

"This place where Jillian's staying—does it have stables? Placing Thunder Roll into her care might be good for them both." asked Viv.

Bringing a half-ton horse to Grandma's did not fit into the priest's Saturday plans, so he cut short the idea. "Old lady garages her Pontiac, so I tink no."

Upon hearing this, Jillian came scampering. "The monastery does!"

"No, it doesn't."

Viv started for the truck. "I'll bring the trailer."

Toe to toe Jillian would not let up, "Please, please, please . . ."

"Alfalfa, oats, blanket, saddle, helmet . . ." Viv checked off.

"No! No! NO!" Father Michael put down his foot.

Not getting her way Jillian stopped imploring and commenced to chasten her godfather with silence.

"Stop sulking like Olga and climb in. It's time to meet your family."

Sore at her godfather, but happy to have taken Thunder Roll out for a trot, Jillian ceased her snit and let him spout about his next of kin while dying to meet moody Olga who sounded like her kind of gal.

"Ever hear of Greek Civil War?" asked Fr. Michael, rounding the corner to Widowmaker Road.

"I'm siding with Camille," Jillian rubbed the steamy window to see out.

"No. Udder one. You see, while everybody busy with Mussolini,

Greece divide. Some to go with U.S., some Tito, and meantime King George, he fight it out with his wife in England—and if you related to George? Nobody like you! So, Yaya pack-up kids and come to America. Everyone except momma—she stay."

Done with feeling sorry for herself, Jillian's heart stirred. "I never knew mine. Do you miss yours?"

"Pooh. She call more than you."

"So, you're related to George the Second?"

"You follow dat? Camille, she fall asleep."

"Watch it." Jillian wagged a finger.

"Today Greece have no king, but our reunions still serve finest wine!"

"That turpentine gunk?"

"Retsina! Nectar of gods. Your real father liked turpentine too. Niko could drink entire party under table. I show you." Father Michael slipped Jillian a Polaroid from his shirt pocket showing with a thin, fair-skinned man clenching a table by the teeth and a younger Fr. Michael photobombing.

"You knew my dad?"

"We're cousins!"

"That's crazy. I'm not Greek."

"Neither was King George."

After Fr. Michael pulled in to park behind Grandma P.'s house, he took a tube from the backseat and from it unrolled an elaborate family tree done in gold quill across Jillian's lap cautioning, "Careful, belong to Reuben."

At the top Jillian read off the names King Christian IX of Denmark, his spouse, Louise of Hesse-Kassel, and their issues. "No way! Maria Feodorovna? I looked her up. She's pretty." Down the branches Jillian's eyes zigged and zagged. "Huu, us Danes get around."

"No fooling. Go on," said Fr. Michael.

Intersecting lines led to the names of Grand Duchess Dagmar J.

Nikolaevna, June 18, 1986-, Grand Duchess Feodora M. Nikolaevna, June 18, 1986-, and Grand Duke Hendrik J. Nikolaevich, May 7, 1987-.

In wonderment Jillian pieced it together. "First my trip to Denmark. Then Reuben. Although he seemed to have me confused with someone else. But this is my birthday. And Feodora's too." She turned her eyes to Fr. Michael, "Father, we said no more lies. Right? Am I Duchess Dagmar and this my sister and brother? Or should I ask my mom?"

"Ask away! Adele will tell you that to save baby Dagmar, the Anders bundle and take her to America and change her name to Yillianz'."

Jillian snatched up the page, her eyebrows arching higher and higher as she counted the generations up the Romanov family bramble. "Huu! Maria Feodorovna is my great great great great great Grandmother????"

"And one more for Victoria of England." Fr. Michael traced a different line.

"Huu! Reuben wasn't joking."

"Don't get excited. For many a Romanov it bring nothing but heartache, and for some—as your father found out—a death sentence."

Jillian's short-lived elation evaporated. "The hemophilia?"

"Cause by lethal dose of rat poison administered by same off-scouring that killed the Tsar."

"That's horrible! Why?"

"Thirty years ago, as iron curtain fell, Niko made premature noise about bringing back the crown and paid price. If Anders no whisk you to Colorado you'd be goner too. This why until you build strong defense from this same Siberian assassin as your sister has, everyone must believe Duchess Dagmar no exist—*or you won't*! And I'm sorry for saying Yackzy left better off dead at bridge—."

"You should be!"

"But if he winds up in bed with Feodora? He may not realize what hit him till—looking deep into her cold, blue eyes with a steel rod in his head—he will wish he had."

Shivered Jillian, "Who is she?"

"Your northern twin go by many names: Golly Gee, Molly Rune, Marie at her baptism . . ." Fr. Michael grew sullen.

"Grandma said Molly drowned."

With a puckish grin Fr. Michael replied, "Newspaper say Molly drown."

Jillian wiggled on her seat. "Tell me about her. *Everything*!"

CHAPTER 38

Yellowknife, Canada

Born in Copenhagen, Feodora Marie retained uncommonly vivid memories of a mother that died in her first year, and whom she dreadfully missed in the horrifying ones that followed. Her recollections over the next decade were a near blackout.

Adopted and rechristened Molly Dora after a houseboat moored on the Great Slave Lake, unlike her luckier sister relocated to the south, the Rune family smothered their ward with love on those long Canadian nights. So much so, that by her fourteenth year Molly had been incestuously molested so many times over by her adoptive brother she began to show signs of acute, medical fatigue. To encourage their stepdaughter to smile for the cameras, the Runes would play footage from the Beaver Lodge department of Pest Control as a sneak preview of her fate if she didn't perform for dinner.

"It's how you earn your keep," they said. They also talked openly of Molly's heritage, and where the middle child showed on the Romanov racetrack behind her younger brother, and elder sister: Last—so forget about it.

Through it all, dirt bike and snow racing, her extremophile bug collection, solving complex, mathematics equations, and dance lessons kept Molly marginally sane. Able to get lost for hours mining microorganisms, or on her toes in graceful pirouettes, the gifted performer landed first in an all-Territories contest for a tails and top-hat routine that brought down the house, after which she did too, collapsed and bleeding backstage. When the doctors pled with her caretakers to tame the rambunctious girl's sexual exploits for the sake of her health, Molly decided to take matters of her own health in hand when the Runes left for a month in Italy.

Home with her babysitting stepbrother, Molly coaxed him to the studio where she hiked up her chaps, laced on red roller skates, and put on a "Bad" show that made Michael Jackson look like a Regular Baptist. This she did all as a ruse in order to velvet-cuff him to the ballet barre during the act. Afterward she took a sledge to the video cameras and a pad to her captive audience for him to write in explicit detail the beastly things he had done to her behind their parents' back, and that he could not go on living this way. Molly then left him manacled to make up his mind. He had no choice, for he either wrote it out or she would leave him stuck in the "glue trap" to die of thirst where he could shout until he went hoarse in the soundproof room. Two days later Yellowknife Municipal found the suicide note where he lay dead on the floor from a rat poison overdose.

Thereafter, such activity ceased. With years of coerced acting under her belt, Molly astutely guarded her innocence by backing the Runes' denial of knowing about their son's atrocious behavior, and impressing the therapists with her model, chin-up attitude. The brilliant student tested early out of school, spent four years at Concordia, then upon acceptance to the Evolutionary Biology Program at the University of British Columbia, cycled across Canada getting by on a needs-based scholarship and the meager earnings of Women's Pro Motocross. Amassing data for her doctoral thesis on tephritidae spheres, she canvassed the Pacific Northwest, sampling fruit flies from small, pesticide-free gardens to chemically controlled commercial crops. While touring an organic grower near Mt. Adams, she interviewed the "Fearsome Pearsons" of Totum, Washington for an addendum on ecological governance. Unsupervised at the printing press one fated afternoon, she spirited away Whitman's file on North American communist subversives with an anomalistic density on Beaver Island, B.C. and the plot for her political agenda hatched.

Upon receiving her tam and gown Molly Dora fell off the face of the planet, as did the remaining Rune family from the houseboat. Back to British Columbia she slept and slaughtered her way into the Beaver Lodge to render services under the nom de guerre of "Golly Gee" to advance the communist revival cause in Eastern Europe. Little did the resurgent socialists suspect that once this dyed-in-the-wool Monarchist used their resources to liquidate her rivals to the throne, she would succeed where her forebears had failed, and the Marxists would all die in the glue trap.

SHAKEN BY THIS DISTURBING tale, Jillian said, "Poor Grandma Pearson! No wonder the woman can't sleep. Is Helen aware?"

"No. And do not trouble Abba Aldo with this. He has enough concerns. Keep eyes open and lips closed. Trust nobody."

"Even you?"

"Especially me," smiled Fr. Michael, and then he went severe. "But most of all Yackzy. You must *never* see that skunk again."

"I see who I want."

"So did your father!"

More than anything Jillian hated when people yelled at her, but she kept cool. "Does my sister ride a motorbike with a beaver on back?"

"Yes, I belief so."

"Ooooo, that stinker's in bed with my sister."

At the irony Father Michael laughed, "She register same complaint about you!"

Jillian went pensive, "Feodora is jealous of me?"

"Like nobody's business."

Jillian took her godfather by the wrist. "Then she still has a woman's pulse. Isn't there anything we can do?"

"I have bent over backward to drive into that hardhead that power and might is not for the taking but receiving, but she no care. So, I pray fervently for someone—anyone—who can get through before her pulse is gone."

"Send me!"

"I cannot lose two goddaughters to 'Golly Gee'. When she comes—and she will—do not go soft. Strike first! Strike hard! Lest she take your heart and crush it beneath her heel."

"This makes no sense of what you preach from the pulpit."

"For spiritual soldiers when cornered, it is given to shoulder cross and lay down life, but for military to take up sword and fight for it! The Tsar failed spectacularly at the latter but rose to the former. Both take courage and faith."

"Huu," Jillian drank in the names of her cousins cornered in a dank, Yekaterinburg basement in 1918, "It's not easy being a Duchess."

Fr. Michael tucked Olga's shredded corset into her arms. "No Yilli, it isn't."

CHAPTER 39

The garage door lifted, and Guin Hill backed her Lexus down into the street. She checked the sleepy neighborhood from the sides of her turtle shells, primped the flowers on her felt cloche, and then making sure the green Buick saw her leave, let a sheet flutter to the ground that read: "PRIVATE DICKS REALLY DO DRIVE BRICKS."

A short time later she cruised onto the Honorable Leroy Booker-Hill's South Pasadena horseshoe pavers. She stopped beside the grass island clipped to precision and said, "Hey Judge! Fire the new gardener already?"

"If you want a job done right, Guin, sometimes you have to do it yourself," Booker held a sixpack while Klav Lovorsky twisted on the new pop-up, sprinkler head.

"That's why I'm here! Can I park in back?"

Booker opened the white, ornamental gate saying to his hardworking chum, "I got a feeling my daughter is about to ask for more than a Coors Lite."

Inside, where an NFL panel blared loud enough to be heard from the mailbox, Guin came for precisely that and more. She kicked back in her oversized, Raider Nation varsity jacket (technically not hers, but

Booker had long given up hope of ever wearing it again) and listened to the talking heads go on about the wildcard race while buying a square on the men's football betting pool.

"Prefer news?" asked Booker coming in with Klav to clean up.

"Saturated." Guin's pumps fell to the floor, allowing her toes to expand and breathe through the black hose.

"For a person with a big job, you're not making much headway," remarked Lovorsky.

"Daddy?" Guin rubbed her arches together.

Booker glanced over to Klav. "Oh joy, here it comes."

"How long does it take to fly to Portland?"

"Gee Guin, I give up. How long does it take to fly to Portland?"

"In your plane?"

Ahead of the Monday trash pickup, Booker rolled the green can to the street where he traded a carton of menthols for a pack of Klav's disposable phones. As his friend drove away, Kansas City bound, Booker monitored the drab four-door loitering beneath a shade tree, then came inside where Guin paraded her mother's dated hot pants.

"Sedan man's still there," he peered outside.

"That job must be a drag."

"Like this outfit you picked out for me," Booker pulled on a wig her mother had worn in her final year of life and secured it in place by Guin's hat and sunglasses.

"Don't break 'em!" laughed Guin, "They're classics."

"See you tomorrow, you crazy daisy!" Booker bussed his daring daughter's cheek, dropped a cigarette pack down the deep pocket, and took up his go bag.

"You have to tap the garage button twice. Call when you're inside—but I won't answer—*and don't smoke in the house*!" said Guin.

"And don't smoke yours in mine."

⤜⟶⟵⤛

GUIN WATCHED THE SUN-PEELED green automobile tail her Lexus home to Glendale, then found her mother's trimming tools and took the shears to her hair. Over the shaggy bob, Guin put her father's fedora on at a jaunty angle and "Tic, Tic Tacked" to Los Angeles in her mother's Fiat with Jesus leading the way.

At the Wilshire office, Guin hailed the Abbot. "Provost? Sorry it took so long. Paparazzi won't give a minute's peace. You can reach me on this burner while I'm in Vegas. Lose that other number."

"They bugged you?" asked Aldo.

"Can't take any chances," Guin minimized the concern, spreading out a gallimaufry of travel necessities on her desk.

"Seeking a little R&R away from L.A.?"

"No, for a little gun, actually," she replied heading for the bookkeeper's cigar box that he thought nobody knew was, in truth, a pistol case.

"Ever heard of pepper spray?"

"Afraid it won't deliver the same message." Guin sat at the edge of the bookkeeper's chair to gingerly slide the small-bore gun from the holster with two fingers and sniff at it like some unknown substance pulled from the breakroom refrigerator.

"To who?"

"Rita—the missing link—whoops!!" Guin released the cartridge with a loud click, ejecting it into her lap. Guilty excitement washed over. She blew at a bullet tip before reloading because it seemed the thing to do and then continued, "Jillian Avlon's roommate from college, and the last person Jaxy saw before going to Oregon."

"Why not let the feds look into it?"

"Collusion. Rita has to step forward before they make her, or they'll call us to the carpet for why we didn't. I doubt your people would appreciate that news banner any more than mine," stated Guin carrying the single-action rimfire with fifty rounds in a wicker tote past plaques of commendation and endorsements conferred on her by the anti-gun bloc.

"Then why flirt with more scandal?" The Abbot questioned her judgment. "Board up plywood and weather the storm."

"Your plan failed, Provost. Do you want to keep babysitting those two waiting for Rory to give himself up? Do whatever it takes to make Jaxy believe the marine ground his wife into 'Jilli con carne' and leave the cleanup to me."

"I agreed to keep them apart by leaving Jillian at Grandma's house, but dead? If you want payback for Jaxy's philandering that's between you, but what you're asking is mean and dishonest and I won't be a party to it."

"Let me tell you about the man you're dealing with. He's slow to commit, but once he takes ownership—stand back. He may not strike you that way because Jaxy comes off aloof, lost in his music or reading all day until he locks onto some harebrained idea like saving some wench from her well-earned fate, then goes apeshit binary, not accepting zero for an answer."

"All to say if Jillian ate it at the bridge, he won't go half-cocked looking for her."

"But caution—the less said, the better. He's the juror you wish you dismissed at selection but didn't and screwed the poo—."

"Then nothing said would be best of all."

"If he doesn't bring up Jillian, of course. Please, just try to find ways to fill his days till I can fix this."

"Does he golf?"

"Refuses the game. I don't suppose you have a praise band?"

"No, Guin. I don't suppose we do."

"Surely you have bells."

"Well yes, but—."

"Then make him the official bellringer! He thrives on recognition. And books! Jaxy eats up books—and peanuts, so stock up."

"Books are us! Thanks, Guin—for that you have till Tuesday to fix this—or I will. Then you can take your lumps in the court of law, and I'll take mine in the church."

"Wednesday, and I'll drop a healthy contribution in the charity box of your choice."

"I will not take blood money from a spiteful—."

"Woman? Is that it? Ha! Hiding out in a monastery can't protect you from us females."

"*Au contraire* we have scads," the Abbot locked horns, "we don't need Joan of Arc."

Guin fired back, "Well you're in luck then, because I don't possess any of Ms. Arc's finer qualities. But goddam it, Provost, Jillian played Jaxy for a fool, and now she's gone and eff'ed everybody. It's time someone put a stop to this Good Samaritan baloney."

GUIN HILL HAD SEEN every identity scam out there, and represented clients on both sides of the room, but never in her wildest imaginings had she foreseen exploiting her knowledge of this seedy underworld to reinvent herself as "Rose Vandervelt—BEA". In the supply closet where Guin's law firm kept nefarious widgets appropriated for research, she designed a cattle-branding monogram for the RDoubleV Bail Enforcement Agency and took a self-portrait for a laminated I.D. card. Given another day "Rose Vandervelt" would have left town with a functional bank and credit card. To complete the makeover, Guin then dropped in at the Screwed and Tattooed on Sunset Avenue for a pirate earring and onyx stud, a set of black letters she could apply and remove depending upon the *emo-esque* feel of the day, a torn Siouxie Sioux camisole, and a Nine Inch Nails used compact disc.

CHAPTER 40

Arroyo Seco, Pasadena, CA
1990

The milk crate rocked in time to the strike of the hobo's thumbnail on a sun-bleached, Gretsch guitar. An instrument he swapped for the rights of an original composition to Jamie Records, or so the mangy migrant claimed. Note for note on jute twine stretched over a hubcap fixed to a slotted slat Jaxy copied and perfected the technique at their homeless camp in the shade of the Pasadena Freeway. The withered rail-rider eventually died, leaving the Gretsch to his promising student. From that solemn moment Jaxy babied the six-string, protecting the hallowed, hollow-body from the elements, and getting into the crevices and crannies with a cotton rag.

As the cloudbursts of that dreary day broke, out from under the overpass came Jaxy with guitar and crate to ply his trade. By three o'clock he had seven and change, holding out two bits to buy a carnation for his departed friend. To the audiences drifting down Colorado Boulevard, the sprout played outside an appliance shop that aired daytime dramas about well-off adolescents navigating day-to-day difficulties quite distinct from his. In sympathy to the producers, how many conscientious parents would let their impressible darlings sit through a pilot about a guttersnipe whose hooker mom locked him out of her graffiti-effaced tenement for his dispossessed dad to deal with? Not many. Yet between medleys Jaxy couldn't resist watching these charmed, fatuous lives through flyspecked windows until his pop yanked him away by the ear, saying they would get a TV as soon as they landed a place with electricity.

"PENNY FOR YOUR THOUGHTS," offered the Deacon as he approached Jaxy near the trailer shaking out the cobwebs.

"That's '*thought*'," replied Jaxy, "and scaled to inflation, since the coining of the phrase, the going rate is two bucks."

Deacon Matthias slipped a ten into the Rockabilly's hand. "I'll take five. But, please, not at once."

"How television has changed since the nineties."

"For the better?"

"Except for more hockey, no. How has the monastery changed?"

"Since the nineties? A lot. Let me show you."

To orient Jaxy, Deacon Matthias snapped a brittle, pine branch, and outlined the property in the snow. He divided it into three sections stacked south to north but narrowing at the top and fanning out at the base, bounded by Widowmaker road coming due south off the mountain, and Coppice Creek sluicing off to the east.

Of the agrarian setting Jaxy asked, "Aren't monasteries usually walled-off or set high on cliffs?"

"In the old country to keep rascals out like you. But the occasional brown bear tearing off a trailer door to get at the butter is as dangerous as it gets here," teased the Deacon. He then expanded on how the Archimandrite inherited the farm as a young man when his parents perished beneath an avalanche. Alone on the hop plantation, he whiled away his time at the neighbors, "The Fearsome Pearsons"—Vietnam-era activists, and far-left publishers of *The Red, White and Red* socialist weekly. There he befriended Aldo Escobar, a freethinker who came to interview the radicals for a seminary paper on "Eco-terrorism; an Orthodox Perspective".

Photios convinced the young theologian to give it a rest by helping erect trellises and train bines for a season which turned into two. In turn, Aldo convinced Photios to convert the microbrewery into a monastic skete. An exceptional craft, the grog put them on the map, but a price came with economic success when the bishop told them to spin-off the business or disband. The timing coincided with the Romanov canonization, so they retooled the farm and took the passion-bearers' name. Deacon Matthias came from Alaska to assist in the transition and the rest was history.

From a stereophonic sound system, the monastery bells called all to the blessing of the waters, thus ending the circle tour.

WITH POMP AND FANFARE, the chorus line processed through the woods to the banks of Coppice Creek where the Abbot knelt in full regalia on a footbridge over the cascading snowmelt. At the close of the festal hymn, he dipped a wooden, tri-bar cross into the stream, and by the other hand drew up clear water in a golden bowl. He then sent a request to the Deacon, who passed it on to Jaxy.

"He wants me to what???" shivered Jaxy.

"Peel down to your skivvies, swim out and bring it back. It's a high honor to be chosen. You got this."

The Rockabilly needed to hear no more, and off came the shirt and shoes. When ready, the Abbot launched the cross far up current for Jaxy to plunge in after and catch as it floated by. The Deacon helped Jaxy out to pat him down as the Abbot received the cross, dipping a shock of basil into the bowl to go down a row of hatted heads, slapping them with Coppice Creek, ice water.

Warm and dry in a gym suit, Jaxy broke away from the picnic of smoked fish and cured cheeses to take his camera fitted with a wide-angle lens to the upper side of a maturing apple orchard that butted against a nature preserve, accessible by foot for hiking and recreation. The Gifford Pinchot National Forest spilled off from there, and behind that rose the flat-topped stratovolcano, Mt. Adams, in hues of rouge and violet.

During his intake at the infirmary Jaxy had learned from autochthonous lore how a throw-down went down in this neck of the woods: Long ago Mt. Adams—called "Pahto" by the indigenous population—stole across the river and claimed her neighboring sister's deer, fruit, birds, and flowers. Thereby she, the youngest of three, grew richer and more beautiful than the other mountains. When Mt. Hood, or "Whyeast", nicely asked for half of her things back, Pahto would not share a berry, so the two fought and Whyeast knocked Pahto's block off, flattening the summit.

In awe, Jaxy photographed the immense volcano, volumetrically the largest in the state. Rounded like a white beluga, Pahto's gentle form didn't fool him. Down deep a fire still burned, and Jaxy hoped to be far away when she blew her stack again.

He gave the temperamental mountain space by taking Widowmaker Road back to the southern clearing. Enclosed by a deer fence, two commercial greenhouses stood between the furrows. Up from there, the central cluster of monastery buildings were shaded by a handsome stand of Douglas Firs. Downwind from the main house by Coppice Creek sat an immense barn where they kept four goats, two milking cows, a greying jenny named Spooky, and a dozen hens. A "No Vacancy" sign hung on the coop.

Jaxy entered the garage jutting out from the barn like the short leg of a "T" to inspect his van. New cracks in the fiberglass fenders added to the concave dent and bullet holes. He opened the back. Other than the cell phone, his possessions, including the fanny pack of tools, made the trip. Someone had rifled his music, so Jaxy hit eject and out popped St. Louis to Liverpool. Indeed, the Rockabilly had no particular place to go, and little to go on, except that Jillian had lived long enough to tell them where to look for him at the bridge; a heroic act for which, the Archimandrite hinted, she sacrificed herself.

That they brought him here and not to a conventional hospital bothered Jaxy—enough to chance calling home without the Archimandrite's permission. The only landline he knew of at Café Matthias afforded no privacy during the waking hours, so he would have to wait for lights out to try. Until then to the trailer he lugged his amp and guitar to relax the truss rod, polish the head and tailpiece, and restring it. Upon fingering spider scales, he slipped into "Devil's Dream", gaining speed with each pass, wondering about the Pelt Peddlers and how well the Dam Mother played the gutbucket.

A buzzing noise disrupted practice.

Jaxy set the guitar up and stepped outside. Against the dipping sun he saw topping a rise a fast-moving, gasoline powered golf cart with balloon tires operated by someone in a poncho. At a bend in the road, it kicked snow through the fence, eventually coming to a stop at the mudroom that doubled as the Deacon's overflow pantry. Jaxy hiked over to a young man hoisting a fruit pie from a five-gallon paint bucket buckled to the seat and depositing them on the stoop.

"Hi," the enthusiastic, smooth faced youth in black jeans and harness boots spoke, "I'm Drew. The new guy."

"Thought I was," said Jaxy trying to place the face. "I've seen you."

"On the boat. You came to for a bit," Drew cranked the starter and turned a figure eight before sliding the cart into a lean-to where they stacked fuel against the barn. The novice emerged hauling split logs and kindling on a toboggan. Jaxy joined in to replenish the front porch crib. As they worked, a flatbed blew through the wrought iron gate fanning pebbles as it bounced down the gravel drive, sending chipmunks scurrying for safety.

Jaxy caught a glimpse of the driver in a trapper hat and sheepskin coat. "Who's that? A handyman?" he asked.

With amusement Drew replied, "The Abbot!"

Deacon Matthias came out banging a cowbell calling every monk to his place at the supper table. With faces in their bowls, the fellowship supped in silence while a volunteer intoned the narration of John the Baptist from a colossal tome teetering on a lectern half its mass. Afterward, they stood as one and headed out for Vespers. The cat followed behind, pouncing on tassels as they swept by. A bed of brands in the potbelly stove begged for s'mores, so Jaxy went to the larder for ingredients. He roasted a marshmallow on a splinter, then fetched more wood to stoke the fire. There he met the surfer-hair brother coming in bearing journals tied by a string.

"Don't you stock the warehouse?" Jaxy remembered from his walkabout.

"And the gift store, and the library, and the woodpile when Drew knocks it over," added Philip on his way to the study hall.

Jaxy noticed the tan, scarred hands beyond the sleeve line. "Work the fields too?"

"Roofer by trade. Shingling a gingerbread down the road with heartwood dressed by the Abbot."

"He makes 'em. You shakes 'em!" Jaxy couldn't resist finding the rhyme and followed the librarian of all trades past the woodstove to a tight, narrow room with stout, metal shelves facing a plastic, picnic table running the center with a computer at the end spilling a rat's nest of cords to the floor. There, Brother Philip enlisted Jaxy as his assistant, showing him the catalogue system and how to mark bindings and input titles. Upon completion, Jaxy unhooked, straightened, and secured the cables to the table leg while the brother rounded up bric-a-brac from the gift shop to fill an order.

Alone at the computer Jaxy tried to hack in to see if the Ducks won, but locked out, he browsed the stacks instead. After music and hockey, he treasured books. Of the texture and aroma of the bound page, and the stuffy, narrow aisles of independent booksellers piled high to the ceiling, he couldn't get enough.

In his element, Jaxy dimmed the ceiling light and pulled up a hammock chair with a bowed back to a reading lamp to crack a volume on the last Romanovs to rule Russia; the singular work with a dust jacket that shouted, "Read Me First!" In the shadows of these rich texts Jaxy sat engrossed, matching the daughter's names to their fetching faces when an eerie creak and swish of cloth stood his hackles on end. Jaxy whipped around, and springing from his chair fell back to the wall, holding out his hands in holy terror at the towering veil of the grim reaper brandishing a scythe with an outstretched arm.

CHAPTER 41

The ROMAR Library, Totum, WA
7:00 p.m. Saturday, January 6

"Holy humbucker! Don't sneak up that way!" Jaxy twisted the gooseneck lamp at a diminutive monk who had tiptoed up the hanging ladder to the oversize shelf in want of a particular study. From there the figure cast a long and menacing scythe-like shadow against the wall with a squirrel hair paintbrush from the top rung.

Shied off, the timid fellow fumbled the work and scurried out. Feeling responsible, up and down the halls Jaxy called to no avail, leaving him holding out a cumbrous text on medieval art and architecture and stammering before Father Photios' door.

"Jaxy! It's quiet time!" hushed the old monk from a cell that smelled of linseed and incense.

"Who was that little monk with the paintbrush? Scared the daylights out of me."

"Must have been Brother Jean, my new protégé. Like you, he just arrived, but unlike you, he doesn't make a sound."

"Tell your art student to come to me for all his classroom needs, because I'm the new assistant librarian! He can check out any picture book he likes. My way of saying 'thanks' for putting me up."

"Ptth! For putting up with you—and they're called 'icons'." The

Archimandrite tipped mail off a rickety, rattan chair onto a sagging, spring bed shoved against the wall and beckoned Jaxy to take a seat by an easel with a tray of brushes under a drip sheet. Photios sat on the mattress edge near a freestanding shelf with a candle flickering before a budded cross, and the likeness of his patron on concave basswood.

Jaxy started anew, "Yes. I know. When they said you paint these—."

"You 'write' icons, Jaxy."

"When Brother Philip told me you write icons, I was speechless."

"Speechless—you? Let me tell you what's splendiferous about the Royal Chapel. You'll appreciate this: the acoustics. An ant crawling on the solea can be heard all the way to the analogion," whispered the monk, dancing his fingertips on Jaxy's knee.

"You don't say."

"And that's why I could hear you two librarians gabbin' all the way from the sacristy!"

"Well Father, your work is magnificent."

"Poppycock. Ever look up at a mosaic from the ambon of a thousand-year-old cathedral?" he jabbed finger at the ceiling.

"No," Jaxy settled in with a sigh.

"Then you have yet to see a magnificent icon."

With his introduction to iconography under the belt, Jaxy broached the "other" topic and found himself more nonplussed than before: "You say the Captain emptied a gun into his wife's chest, but the magazine had no bullets. I should know. Jillian could not have gone for help then anyway—least not at the bridge. This doesn't add up."

Father Photios closed his eyes and went on, "If I must. At the hotel, when coming up from chaining the van Rory caught her with a phone to her ear. She ran and, you see, he had fastened this, ah, device to her leg—."

Jaxy flung his hands to cut short the story. "No more!!"

"Jillian went like that," the Archimandrite snapped his fingers, "she did not suffer long."

"How do you know?" spat Jaxy.

"It's on the coroner's report."

"Did it report how my tooth and glasses ended up in the doctor's bag?"

"The priest Michael claimed them at the morgue."

Jaxy nodded, "I want to attend the funeral. I owe her that. You said I can come and go as I please."

"Jillian Avlon was a card-carrying, organ donor. There will be no interment."

"A celebration of life?"

"Stick around. At forty days the Deacon will prepare a wheat berry koliva for the family."

Low into the chair Jaxy sank with a heavy heart. "And to think what Jillian wanted most was to have a family. No mother ever tried as hard to save her baby."

"Baby? What baby?"

"Going into her third month," Jaxy dried his nose on a sleeve.

"Dear, oh dear," tutted the Archimandrite, and then delivered up a clinic on why you should not play dialectic hardball with a world-renown monk and tore the hide off the ball: "Then you are family!"

Not wishing to stick around another forty seconds to contend the allegation, with Jillian gone and the guardian angel out of reach, Jaxy determined the time had come to patch things up at work and home the best that he could. On his way to ready Moby, he stopped at Royal Martyrs Chapel to deposit a personal check for their hospitality and to hum a low tonic to test the acoustics. There, in the unperturbed dark before the shrine to the defeated tsar, Jaxy felt a bit beleaguered himself, overcome by events beyond his control. Though leery of symbols of faith he permitted candles, so lit a taper on Jillian and her unborn's behalf and then glided through the trees to the garage.

"You're kidding me?" Jaxy tugged on the combination lock, then went around through the lean-to to do what he could in advance of an early morning start. As he passed by the golf cart, he gave the painter's pail a light nudge. It still had some heft! He wondered if held anymore fruit pie. The Deacon's ten-spot would cover the cost of one to take home as a peace offering to Guin. As he rotated the can for a better angle, the load inside shifted and the bucket snapped free, teetered on the edge of the cart seat, and tipped over onto the woodpile popping off the lid. Openmouthed, Jaxy gaped down at a length of blood-caked serpentine chain protruding from Rory's unexploded, ankle weight bomb!

Heavy boots crunched down the drive. With delicate handling Jaxy had the bucket back on the golf cart and was down checking the van tires when came Drew in.

"Hey there, Jax'—you alright?"

Jaxy slapped the fenders, "Better shape than Moby. Give you any trouble on the road?"

"Chains gave out. I can size up a new set on my next run to town."

"No rush. Using the time to write new songs and catch up on reading. I doubt by now my fiancée cares when, if ever, I make it home."

Sympathized Drew, "To go from two women to none in one week must be rough."

Jaxy erupted. "We were friends, Drew, if that! And, if you didn't hear, one that had a leg ripped off by a crude homemade bomb!!"

"A *bomb*? Mother said she got capped in the chest. Man, I should check my facts before shooting off at the mouth." Drew reacted with genuine surprise as he sprung for the golf cart.

Caught off guard, Jaxy charged the bucket as Drew peeled away. Covered from head to toe in a hash of wet wood chips and lies the Rockabilly pounded the ground at the missed opportunity for a second look at the ankle weight. For, the guardian angel could very well be wrapped inside at the other end of the gold chain. Then rising with an oath, he went to find Father Photios.

"SOLIDS TO THE SIDES, stripes in the corners," called the pool shark in Grandma P's basement, taking antes on trick shots. Over the hour Jillian had lost more in small bills than she raked in, and the house's respect in the process. She dithered until Fr. Michael walked away before upping the ante from a one to a twenty on a line of balls.

"No!!" said Fr. Michael coming back to the table, but the others had already thrown in.

"Father?" She waited for him to be a sport.

"I thought you say no more," he contributed under protest.

"*Air hockey*," Jillian chalked up.

"Bam!" the balls broke and rolled to their designated pockets. The bills flew into the air and Jillian snatched them on the way down.

"Put away! Pinochle anyone?" Fr. Michael shuffled two decks together.

"I don't know how," said Jillian.

"Piece of cake! I'll help," answered Drew descending the basement steps. Shedding his coat, he took the chair beside her.

Helen gave him the stink-eye. "Shouldn't you go check on Jaxy?"

"Give the man some space. He's right where we want him—self medicating on his guitar." Drew nudged Jillian to take three cards.

When Helen caught Jillian poking back, she looked her square in the face: "If I am your mother, then Drew is your brother. Understood?"

"Shussh! Talking to Aldo!" Fr. Michael passed updates as he conversed with the Abbot. "Yackzy go on full court press! He no belief shoots-girl-with-gun story, so Photios tell him bomb blow off leg."

"No!" said Jillian horrified. And, having just been given a carte blanche to treat Drew like dirt, drove her nails deep into his forearm to show what a big sister is like. "That's not funny, you brat!"

"OUCH! Mom, tell Jillian—."

Without taking an eye off her cards Helen ordered, "Drew, apologize and go fix two hot chocolates with marshmallows."

Jillian stuck out her tongue while Fr. Michael continued, "But Yackzy no buy that either, so with your allowance, may they use cutesy photo to spruce up practice icon of Saint Olga?"

"I suppose," replied Jillian.

"To paint 'Saint Yillian'z' New Martyr'!" grinned Fr. Michael over the top of his phone. "Say 'cheese'!"

With a harried smile, Jillian said, "Cheese."

"Mmm, can't wait for the troparion," hummed Helen.

WHILE JAXY SHELLED NUTS in the Archimandrite's cell waiting for the complete and unabridged explanation, he heard a distant, whirring hairdryer and wondered who would have need of one here. In time the elder returned with a draped canvas.

"The priest Michael commissioned an 'homage'. Care to see it?" asked the monk.

"Not specially," Jaxy replied.

"Indeed, I think you would." The iconographer set the painting on the easel and plucked away the white cloth saying: "Behold Jillian!"

Bowled over by the flawless rendering of her apple green eyes and demure smile, done in the same eastern style as those adorning the chapel walls, less the halo, Jaxy could not praise it enough.

The Archimandrite chuckled, "Beautiful, wasn't she? In my opinion, woman is the splendiferous grand finale of creation. God was just practicing on Adam."

"So why that grisly thing?" Jaxy asked of the ice axe, dripping bright, red droplets from her hand.

"Martyrs are sometime portrayed with the instrument of torture that claimed their lives."

Jaxy massaged his tooth. "Not to sound skeptical, but good people die in the worst of ways every day. I don't see you writing icons of them."

"In my book, Jaxy, laying down a life for the likes of you would make anyone a saint. I tried to soften it by saying she went in a hail of bullets or instantly by bomb, but you asked . . ."

Fr. Photios left off, ". . . for it", but when the message sank in it sat Jaxy down hard as he imagined the fight the expectant put up to save her cub. "It's an absolute ten, Father, you done good."

"It's acrylic, for heaven's sake. A 'ten' would take weeks, and lots of gold leaf. Go on—take it—it's yours until the forty-day memorial. But don't kiss it," the Archimandrite cautioned, "until it's dry."

CHAPTER 42

The ROMAR, Totum, WA
9:00 p.m. Saturday, January 6

As a cross, Jaxy bore the painting to the trailer, facing it to the wall. He felt terrible for Jillian, for the broken serpentine chain supported a bloody struggle. He must find the angel at the other end and prevent further bloodshed. He pulled on the hoodie and hiked the route taken by the golf cart to where it continued past the mill into the forest deep. At this point Jaxy turned back to wait for daylight and poke about the garage for clues. On the bed of the Abbot's truck, he happened upon a crinkled, olive-brown golf bag, with recent grass pulls and stains. A strange temptation beset him. Persuaded that a little exercise might do him good, Jaxy lined a row of chewed-up, practice balls on the rubber mat in the lean-to. Then, imagining each one as Rory's head, proceeded to smack them over Coppice Creek with tremendous zeal and lack of care.

"Jaxy!" The blinding lights came on. "For someone who says he doesn't golf, you've got a mean swing."

ALONG A PRECIPITOUS INCLINE above the moonlit rush of

Coppice Creek, the grizzled Abbot led the way to where high on a knoll, a three-story structure, fringed by a spindly apron of western larch, soared over Totum Valley.

"What once was a mill, is now my woodshop. Thought you should see it before you leave," the stocky Spaniard let the clubs go with a clack to swing open the doors and invite Jaxy into the warmth of a workspace with ample headroom. Furnished with top-of-the-line jigs, table saws, lathes and drills, church furniture in various stages of assembly filled the floor. A wide, solid, foot-worn staircase led to an expansive loft with racked pine, poplar, oak, and hardwoods of every grade. From there, a short ladder provided access to the attic from where forced air kept the lumber at a balmy, seventy-six degrees and proper moisture content.

"Neato! I'm Jackson Thrie by the way. And excuse me for getting into your clubs without asking. Been a long week. Lost a dear friend," he added with sincere emphasis.

Two inches shorter than Jaxy and sprouting a bushy beard cropped long enough for authority, but short enough not to catch in a press, the fit, barrel-chested Abbot gave Jaxy a crushing bear hug. "In that one survived, we exult! And after prayer I can't think of a better way to lay aside earthly cares than on a golf ball. I'm Abba Aldo Escobar, Provost of the Holy Royal Martyrs of Russia Monastery, by the way."

Down the yawning cavern of an unfinished coffin Jaxy stared. "For anyone I know?"

"Me. Preparing for this is what we do," said the Abbot. Then shifting to a lighter topic he boasted of the new fire suppression system with a hotline to the district firehouse. While Abba expatiated on the advances in smoke and heat detection, Jaxy ambled over to a spacious spray booth to scan for paint cans. Not seeing the one from the golf cart he returned to the conversation, lackadaisically leaning into the handle of a bright yellow, free-standing, solvents closet, springing the latch.

"YELLYBEANZ!" FR. MICHAEL LOOKED up from his phone to thwack Drew on the head. "What you do? Leave the bucket where Yackzy could find it? He'll know for certain there's more to the story and won't believe another word we say!"

Under his elbow Drew ducked, "Like I taped a sign on it 'Hey big guy—don't look in here'!"

Helen cast out a low trump. "Why didn't you take it to the Abbot first thing?"

"He didn't have time for me when he got back, and yes, I left it sitting out in a dumb spot, and no, I shouldn't have left Jaxy alone for two minutes, but I can't watch him and Jillian at the same time."

"Then you should have brought it straight back," said Fr. Michael.

Grandma P.'s eyes bugged out. "And blow up *my* house?"

JAXY PULLED THE ABBOT away from the phone and onto the immediate problem, "You should know that explosive plastics comingled with cleaning solvents would fail a hazmat audit. You should let me remedy this."

The Abbot slammed the metal door on Jaxy's foot in reply.

Jaxy put his fingers in his ears and shut tight his eyes. When it didn't erupt, he continued, "I offered, as a favor, to take and disarm the bomb outside. You refused. I'd like to know why."

"It's not what you think."

"Oh, it's exactly that, and I'm not budging from here till I get what I came for."

"Great! The choir could use a first tenor, and anything I can get for the trailer—books, puzzles, roasted peanuts—speak up."

"Stop the runaround. If this is about money, name your price."

"Jaxy, I have no idea what this is about."

"Almighty God! Why is everything so hard? My pretty angel! The one you took from me!" Jaxy indicated the bucket.

His ire rising, the Abbot snubbed the proposition. "Sorry Jax'—not for sale, and don't take this as rude, but it's closing time." He reached for the light breakers.

Jaxy hopped up to the workbench allowing the door to the chemicals cabinet to automatically spring shut. "Then goodnight."

To the saints keeping watch over the shop the Abbot appealed, "What must I do to make him go away?"

"You lock the garage so I can't leave, and then don't want me around."

"Poking your nose where it doesn't belong? No." The Abbot secured the flimsy handle with a punched key that couldn't keep out a determined toddler.

Jaxy braced the shimmying cabinet. "The three-pin looked fairly basic, so let me defuse it in the field. If I succeed? I take what's rightfully mine and go.

The Abbot reopened the cabinet, set the bucket on the floor, and ripped the lid off. "Don't bother, it's a dud. Jean already checked."

"The new guy? Some initiation rite you have."

"Miho lost half a face and most of his hearing to a similar one in Paris. He came hoping to overcome his fear of mail. Providence provided."

"Let's see how close he came to losing the rest," Jaxy drew out the ankle weight with the wires snipped and stripped. He eased the flaps to expose lead bars and a sheared, serpentine chain adhering to the fabric by congealed blood. Inside out he shook it clean, then palming the gold chain returned the rest to the bucket.

"Happy the world is safe from exploding latex?" The Abbot put back the troublesome pail.

"You bet! And since I helped make it that way, I'll take my angel and be gone."

At that the Abbot lost his cool. "Your sweet little angel has a name, and it is *Jillian*! And she is certainly *NOT YOURS*!!!"

"Did I say that?" Jaxy's retracted his hand.

"And I don't have her!"

"I think I see the problem."

"It's about time!"

In jubilation Jaxy jumped to the floor, "Then she IS alive!"

Schablamm! Failing to heed Guin's warning, the Abbot had fallen for the gambit and pooched the plan. Jaxy's face said he'd better contain the smoldering fire, so he shouldered his clubs and led the way to an attached, modest apartment with a bed and bath at one corner, a den at the other, and a wainscot finished kitchenette in between. Without ado, the Abbot seated him at the tidy table covered by a gingham oilcloth and offered an apéritif to pair with what Jaxy already knew of his fall and rescue.

Hopping mad at everyone, Rory had gunned the Suburban over the bridge to retrieve Jaxy's van from the hotel and run it off the marina. Not conceiving that Jillian would bolt with a bomb on her leg, he crawled under the van to hook the snow chains. Left unwatched she crouched behind the Suburban door to tighten the tourniquet. When Rory poked his head inside to see where she had gone, Jillian sprang into action pinning his arm to deliver a penalty kick to the groin and take him out. The dud did not detonate, and Rory crumpled to the ground.

"Scooooooooore!!" Jaxy pounded out.

"Never underestimate the power of adrenalin, Jaxy," demonstrated the Abbot by reaching for the side knob that opened onto a frost blanketed deck. "Instead of running, Jillian took the door when her husband lunged again, and smashed the glass into his face blowing out the window!" the Abbot slammed it shaking the room.

Down went Rory a second time. Jillian wrestled the bomb switch from the vest but couldn't reach the keys, so she swiped a bicycle from the hotel rack and broke for the hospital. With Rory closing the gap in the Suburban, Jillian pedaled to emergency pointing at her leg screaming, "It's a bomb!" The attendants fled leaving her vulnerable and open to attack.

Omitting how Jillian went on to attain international fame as a suicide bomber by eluding a SWAT team through the Portland hospital after announcing that she had explosives strapped to her leg, the Abbot picked up the cliff-hanger starting at street level:

To not make a public scene with a mashed face, Rory kept going while Jillian popped the batteries out and smashed the detonator to bits. Dressed in hospital scrubs, she slipped out the basement and stole through back streets and alleys to the L&C Hotel to take the spare key from under the mat, and the van to the safety of the church. But, when she pulled onto the avenue up came Rory, so she stopped at a busy, all-night filling station forcing him to double-park down the street. There Jillian drew a large sum from a teller machine to pull off the final caper.

Along the curvy 84 she took it slow with Rory shading by a half dozen cars. At the city limits, Jillian accelerated onto the northbound exchange. Down the straightaway to Portland International she flew, blowing stops, and tearing up the tire chains on the final leg. By the time Rory saw her intent, he had fallen too many lengths behind and couldn't overtake her. At the unloading zone Jillian handed off the key to a skycap with a tip he could retire on, to stow the van in long-term, unlocked, with the spare under the mat. Sizing up the serious disadvantage, this time at a major airport, Rory slipped on by, no more to be seen.

To a happy conclusion the Abbot brought the escapade, "Jillian took the next flight while Drew retrieved your van."

"One more thing," Jaxy started up again.

"There are none. Now be gone—you can't sleep here."

"The ankle-weight. Jillian waltzed it through the metal detectors then shipped it back in a bucket?"

"Father Michael caught up to her at the airport. He keeps tin snips in his car. Don't ask why."

"To custom fit his golf clubs?" speculated Jaxy, and left the Abbot laughing.

AFTER YEARS OF ZERO-SUM gain in the circus of anarchist advocacy, Grandma P. adopted the motto, "The less involved, the better," and before the sod settled on Whitman's grave, shredded the files, sold the press, joined the Libertarians, learned to duck hunt, and stopped voting. Finding herself once again drawn into in a conspiracy involving the word "terrorism" spelling disaster with the government, Grandma slipped off to check on the cookies when the next emergency call hit.

"Jaxy smashed the lock off the garage!" The Abba Aldo's voice carried over the phone.

Grandma fired over her shoulder, "Didn't anyone think to syphon the gas from his tank?"

"Too late."

"Huu! He left for California?" asked Jillian.

"Not yet. Put your thinking caps on people, we haven't much time."

"Tell Jaxy she came back to Oregon, but we don't know where," advised Helen.

"That will only serve to encourage him! *Do you know what he called her*??"

"No, no, please no . . ." Jillian buried her face in her hands.

"His 'sweet little angel' and he wants her back."

Jillian locked eyes with Fr. Michael then brushed it off. "He's not that into me. He'll get over it."

Said the Abbot, "Because you're not into him! You creamed what little home he had to bail you out of a bum marriage, then skipped without a goodbye."

"I nearly got creamed saving that ingrate!"

Helen put her arms around Jillian and spoke into the phone. "She's right Aldo. What you say isn't true. Well . . . not entirely."

"But that's entirely what Jaxy thinks, and if he hears what his fiancée's up to while he's picking out pies to take home? He may drive on to Mexico for spite, and not care if the federales beat the tar out of him."

Helen encouraged him to keep trying. "Aldo, you're good at sweet-talk. If a little honesty puts him at ease, go for it."

"Sweet-talk? Huu," Jillian snuffled into Helen's sleeve, "should practice on me."

"Or use the frat house method and keep pouring till he passes out," Drew contributed from his well of experience.

"That won't work. Leave a trail of peanuts that goes around in circles," said Jillian.

Unable to bear another word, Grandma P. boomed down the stairs, "Lamb Chop!"

The cottage went quiet.

"Did you not see Jaxy as he lay dying at the monastery?"

"No . . . I fell asleep before he arrived."

"And did you not go out to the porch to mourn his passing?"

"Told you. Father brought me here."

"And did you not wander up to the road to hitch a ride to Colorado?"

"*Whatever are you talking about*?" Jillian burst into tears.

Grandma gathered her apron to march back to the kitchen, "That's how I remember it."

CHAPTER 43

Memory Eternal
11:00 p.m. Saturday, January 6

"No hard feelings. I appreciate all that you did," said Jaxy tearing a clean edge off the butcher paper cutter when the Abbot came through the Café pantry door.

"You're taking that?" Aldo asked of the painting.

"Mine till the memorial," Jaxy tested the tackiness at the canvas edge.

"You should stay till they catch Rory."

"No worse than catching it at home." Jaxy spread the sheet over the commons table. "But I have a bright future waiting for me. I need to get out there before the offer expires."

"Grab some bench, amigo," the Abbot motioned for him to sit.

"Tape?"

"Second drawer."

The abbot gazed upon Jillian's portrait. "Care to know what actually happened?"

With a stony face Jaxy wrapped hers in reply, "No. Can you put a finger there?"

The Abbot pressed down for Jaxy to apply tape adding, "You owe her that."

"Look. She—all of you—saved my life and I appreciate it. But if that places me in your debt, then throw me back in the river."

"Jillian didn't fly to Las Vegas." The Abbot would not let it go.

"I know. She flew the Cooper to Fort Collins—her plan from the start. Makes sense, baby and all." Jaxy gathered up the acrylic and headed for the door.

The Abbot stopped him midway. "What's this you say? Jillian has a child?"

"The doctor? Photios? They didn't mention it?"

"Nobody tells me a thing around here!"

"Coming this summer to a delivery ward in Colorado."

"Eh? So, rocking it in Fort Collins as the stay-at-home dad. That's the big future?"

Jaxy collapsed over the table's end. "We'll invite you to the shower."

"Be honored. Can I fix you a PBJ for the road?"

"Why not," agreed Jaxy, feeling famished at the suggestion.

As the Abbot sliced into the loaf, he resumed the story from the fishing boat, "Did Helen tell you that you had totally shut down before she reached the Bonneville Dam locks?"

"With huckleberry jam."

"Jillian was inconsolable, so the doctor ran a hot bath—more for her than you, truth be told—and kept working while the monks kept vigil. After a time, Helen announced that your pulse returned. You were alive!"

"And milk if you have it."

"Finger of scotch? Cuts the cow flavor."

"Thanks—no. Driving."

"I went to pass on the news to Jillian but couldn't find her. Miho had last seen out on the porch, but by then the storm kicked up and she was gone—and not for Colorado! A total whiteout, Jaxy. Could not see my hand before my face. At a pause in the storm Brother Jean, bless his soul, went and found her at the orchard's edge, half buried against the fence. I'm sorry, Jaxy, but he arrived too late. And I'm sorry for you, and the baby too."

Jaxy downed half the glass and wiped away the milk moustache. "Tragic. Truly tragic. But since we haven't begun to exhaust the ways by which Jillian could have bought the farm, you'd better have a good answer for trying to foist one more on me."

"I agree. You deserve it. Father Klapakis is better suited for the hard ones. Ask him," punted the Abbot.

"Take a shot."

"Helen couldn't predict how stable you'd be coming around, so pinned the death on Rory until she could help you work through it."

"Work through *what*?"

"The loss of your first conceived."

"Doctor Leshenko told you that?"

"No. You just did. How else would I have known?" The Abbot measured whiskey into Jaxy's milk and brought his voice to a hush. "Weigh carefully what you are about to hear: If I know every inch of these grounds and could not fight my way to the road, no way could Jillian have made it that far into the wood carrying your baby, unless she left *before* the ice storm hit."

"You're saying she walked off on purpose."

The Abbot went to the wine rack to select an apropos rosé for himself. "I prefer to think she got lost in her mourning. You'd be surprised how fast things get turned around in the dark."

Had Jaxy not already tasted the Abbot's scotch he would have walked out with the portrait and driven straight to Minnehaha to ask more hard questions. But the hour grew late, and the single malt Highland went down smoother than any from Booker's cabinet. Therefore, Jaxy unwrapped the portrait and stood it on a chair with gardenias from the bay window.

"To Jillian," The Abbot raised a toast.

"Occasional blondes everywhere," they clinked glasses, and over the next hour talked about Jack Nicklaus, Gordie Howe, and Jaxy's travails with the opposite sex.

Summated the Abbot, "I'm stumped. First Jaxy Thrie won't stop obsessing on 'teen angel' while making plans to marry his childhood sweetheart. Then all he talks about is how some country bar owner digs his music, and a Canadian tart that can't follow a Tiffin recipe. So, between us, which one does Jaxy like the best?"

"Fair question. I do love Guin, but she's a bear to live with."

"Love 'bears' all things," quipped the Abbot. "But jokes aside, I put my money on Jillian. You care a great deal for her, correct?"

"Let's get down to brass tacks. I lost something of importance to her on New Year's Eve, and I came to Portland strictly to get it back. I knew the woman for less than a week and she was not carrying my baby."

"If you say so."

"But if Jilli' walked off to the happy hunting grounds . . . ," slurred Jaxy with sagging eyelids.

The Abbot laid a condoling arm along the Rockabilly's shoulder, "Then there's no reason to go to Colorado."

What spilled next from Jaxy's mouth, whether from the mawkish effect of alcohol, or if he really meant it, would remain a topic of debate not settled in their lifetime: "First thing when I get home, Abba, I'm painting my van yellow. As yellow as the daffodils springing from her grave. And when people ask why? I'll say I did it for J.D. Avlon. The bravest blonde in the world."

The Abbot's eyes glistened. "Truly she was an organ donor, and that big heart of hers will go to a special someone in need. Rejoice Jaxy! Again, I say rejoice! Jillian did not die in vain. May her memory be eternal."

"Memory turtle," Jaxy dreamily repeated, and falling forward, planted his face in his third peanut butter sandwich.

PART TWO

CHAPTER 44

Mojave Desert, CA
1:00 a.m. Sunday, January 7, 2018

Gusty, Santa Ana winds buffeted the Spider Pininfarina as it fell behind an eighteen-wheeler going sixty in the fast lane, passing another in the slow with signals on, behind an RV doing fifty.

"How's this for my next campaign, Roosevelt: 'Stay in line you other trucker, or pay a fine you mother—,'" Guin left off the last word of her winning slogan, blowing by the temporary jam and spinning back gravel as her way of a hand gesture without lifting the top. Across the Mojave Desert Guin rolled down memory lane, maxing out her mom's speakers, and flashing back to when behind in the polls she went to her father for a fresh idea and received a slap down. She loved to recount the story how poetic justice was served that Sunday when his parting wisecrack tipped the scales and won Guin the election.

"Try: 'Nice girls don't run for office'," said Booker through a disinterested haze of smoke.

"Guess I'm not a nice girl then!" Guin swiped the burning butt from his lips to crush it in an ashtray.

"Didn't say that," he lit another while staying ahead of his bossy daughter as they traveled through his South Pasadena brick bastion, turning clocks ahead by an hour.

Guin set and wound a lovelorn wristwatch hanging from the sewing machine where her mother last took it off. "Then what did you say? Nice girls grow up to hem skirts or style hair?"

"I object! The prosecution is leading the witness. There is nothing wrong with any of those nice jobs. At least your mother cared about her clients."

"Excuse me? You're the one who taught me how to be a soulless lawyer. Pepperdine just handed me the diploma."

"Law is a dirty, three-letter word, Guin, and why I didn't want you following my footsteps."

"And why you refused to pay one cent for my education!"

"Instead of guilt trips, missy, you could try giving me a haircut. Can't buy a good one." Booker rubbed his shaggy neck in the vanity mirror.

"Sure! Where're the scissors?" threatened Guin with a wicked grin sifting through the drawers in search of her mother's clippers that had sadly fallen into disuse.

"Bailiff? Restrain this woman!" her father fled to the terrace to tap out another smoke and offer up a mite of advice. "Go ahead and run, Guin. Run your little heart out. But if you lose, don't cry to me."

With impudence Guin slapped the pack to the ground and stormed out, rattling the garden gate behind her.

"Not your brand?"

"I won't lose!" retorted Guin, "and I'll start by banning Winstons inside five blocks of the San Marino Courthouse!"

"Along with Smith and Wessons in Glendale? You can't win on either platform!

Guin gunned the engine to drown him out.

Booker cupped his hands to his mouth, "Why not ban something we can all get behind!"

Into the street the gun control advocate slammed the brakes, and yelled back, "Like what?"

"Like Daylight Savings Time!"

AT THE KLINNICK'S BAR and Grill curbside, Guin Hill hunkered to find a morning deejay not yammering about Jillian Avlon or playing *The Very Worst of the Fat Pipes* while waiting for the owner to show.

"This clinches it. Stakeouts blow," Guin said to her partner as she peeled the cellophane off the compact disc. "Okay with this?"

Roosevelt didn't mind passing the time with "Head Like a Hole".

Guin's patience paid off when the saloon reopened at six after the nightly cleaning. So, with a palette-knifed coat of black make-up and raggedy hair, in she sauntered in a bra-less tank top, elbow length, satin gloves, go-go boots, and short pants rent to the rivets.

At the far end sat the bar owner silhouetted against the bright glare of the alley doorway. After a minute she shouted out, "Yo— could use a little help here!"

From where he stood wire brushing a barbeque pit the grill-master answered, "Go home Rita. You're sick!"

"Sick of this story," Rita sweetened a black coffee with honey liqueur and asked, "What'll it be, sailor?"

"Same, smaller." Guin uncomfortably adjusted her crotch.

Rita set down a cocktail square and yelled out again, "Pouring the lady a drink!"

"Save us some for your funeral!" the man hosing down the blacktop responded.

"*Pendejo.*" Rita filled the mug and returned the carafe to the hotplate.

"Looks like 'ladies' morning out'," remarked Guin, scooching in for a better angle at the television. When the Canadian Mountie de Chavoie's picture came on, she asked, "Any idea where Yan might be?"

With a downward look Rita bitched, "All of United States and

Canada can't find him and you think I know?"

Guin gave her a good look at the RDoubleV card and the gun in her bag. "As a matter of fact, yes, and you can start by saying how you know Pierre de Chavoie by that *name*."

CHAPTER 45

The New Palace, Darmstadt, Germany
1872

Born into the Grand Duchy of Hesse on the Rhine, Alix came up in a sumptuous, yet austere Lutheran culture. After her mother's passing, the frolicsome girl grew reserved, shunning play in preference to learning letters and the arts. Ministered by rigid tutors and nannies supplied by her maternal grandmother, Queen Victoria of England, Alix's upbringing came with the puritanical strictness and moral observance of the time.

For these reasons, the stoic princess turned out to be a good fit for the stiff and conservative Nicholas II when behind the scenes at her sister's wedding, the twelve-year old captured the teenage Tsarevich's interest. With eyes only for each other, Alix and Nicholas' enduring romance made for a rare one at a time when brilliant matchmaking, not lovemaking, prevailed. Their relationship brought on further disapproval from Tsar Alexander who loathed giving the Germans a toehold in his palace, and an Empress that took a low view on anyone that didn't party like a Russian. Nonetheless, young Nicholas stuck to his guns, and with the decline of his father's health forced a blessing. Despite all, in the way of a royal wedding stood one hurdle to clear: Religion.

Unlike her flexible and pragmatic mother-in-law Maria, adapting to the Romanov way did not come automatic to a devout Protestant who viewed balls and ballet as worldly, and their Russian brand of Sunday worship with a parlous Roman tilt. Insofar as Alix wished to please her beau, conscience came first and coronation second, and she could not convert in name to a foreign faith with fingers crossed in front and behind. Her turmoil lingered to the day Nicholas II formally proposed when, instead of reveling in joy, she anguished over the prospect of apostasy. This required the combined force of the Church of England and the German Lutherans to reassure the princess that putting Nicholas' ring on her hand would not place her Saxon soul in jeopardy. To the deadline she resisted, when at the parting of Tsar Alexander love won out, and in 1894 she and Nicholas wed.

At her elevation to the throne, Alix of Hesse claimed the title: Her Imperial Majesty, Alexandra Feodorovna, Empress Of All The Russias. A year later the dreamy Grand Duchess Olga Nikolaevna came on board, followed by the arrivals of steely Tatiana, angelic Marie, and the intractable Anastasia. On the Tsarista's fifth and final try for a male heir, she delivered her one sickly son: The Grand Duke Alexei, for whom the cannons rolled.

JERKED AWAKE, JAXY SAT up and scratched a bandaged wrist. The last thing he could recollect was taking a practice swing at the cuckoo clock with a fire poker.

"Church is starting. Coming?" Drew rocked Jaxy's foot.

Jaxy rolled into the pillow. "Didn't we do that yesterday?"

"Then get yourself up and have a cup of the Deacon's mud with me."

Enjoying the experience of growing a beard, not to fit in, but because he had no reason to shave, Jaxy showered off a restive sleep then met up with Drew contesting the consumer guide's findings on chainsaws. Holding no opinion, Jaxy took up where he left off in his book about the stir a baby Romanov could raise and said, "No one shot cannons across the riverbed the day I was born."

A shrill whistle cut through the mudroom, "Grandma's plum came down and your mother wants it sectioned for the smoker. Grab an axe on the way,"

"Can I come?" Jaxy sprang into action.

Drew rotated Jaxy's dressed arm. "Not unless you want my mother to come look at that sooner than later."

"Nah. Got church," said Jaxy, marking the page and putting up the book.

By the slanting light of morning, Jaxy observed the high-performance golf cart travel the service road it took the night before pulling a wagon of woodcutting tools. Since Jaxy could make out yesterday's footsteps crossing the furrows, it followed that he should find Jillian's ill-fated ones in the north. Not for a second did he believe she set out to die in the woods, leastwise not on his account, but falsehoods often contained elements of truth, and if the Abbot had something—or *somebody*—to hide, Jaxy had to know.

At the library he signed out a frayed prayerbook of needs, and skipping church hurried to the hothouse to snip a handful of blooms. Upstream he wended, skipping stones to pass idle time. At the barbed wire he went west, and crossing over two hillocks, descended into the apple trees.

Under the barren Braeburns and Granny Smiths the Rockabilly trod but found nothing – no deep drifts with disoriented footfalls, or a search party trampling the borders. One mucky path ducked under the branches to a derelict privy. At the end of a fruitless campaign, Jaxy concluded that if Jillian strayed, she did not do so here. To bring closure to the extemporaneous wake held the night before, he spread petals on a mound at the far corner and wrenched off a loose plank to carve Jillian Avlon's name. As he labored the sweat from his wrist made the bandage itch. He sat on his heels to peel it away, but the Abbot had applied a thick one that stuck fast. Aggravated, Jaxy hacked with the cutters until the wrap came off, spurting blood from the reopened wound.

Whizzzzzz—Bonk!

Bowled to the ground by a snow-packed, fist-sized rock went Jaxy with the wind knocked out. He sat up to see Brother Jean standing in the sparse shade of a leafless tree, three rows off with his heel on a trunk, wagging a 'bad dog' finger at the saturated bandage.

In anger Jaxy pressed the gauze to check the bleeding. "It was bugging me—that's all. Dang, I'm not *that* tore up about her."

The Mutc turned away in a snit.

"Then what? Because I yelled at you in the library?" Getting no response, Jaxy put his face to the sun, and with deliberation asked, "Can—you—read—my—lips?"

Side to side Brother Jean turned his veiled face, "No—no—no—no—no."

"Ha. Ha. Let's play twenty questions. Did you follow me here?"

The bashful Mute affirmed.

"Do you know why I came?" Jaxy held out the board.

The monk took it to scratch in Jillian's date of birth.

"June eighteen, eighty-six. Just how in blazes would you know that?"

The Mute stooped to array the blossoms in a pretty pattern.

"Is this the spot where Drew found her face down yesterday morning?"

Yes—the Mute indicated with sadness.

"That's funny, because Jillian died in your arms Thursday night—or didn't the Abbot tell you?" Jaxy flipped the board behind him and marched off in a huff.

The next rock struck him square in the back.

To Widowmaker Road Jaxy took his search singing the "gonna-find-her"s with the Coasters' classic playing in the ear-buds. At the iron gate he rootled for clues but could not make head nor tails of who came or went on the gummed-up drive. Hoping to detect telltale signs at the highway, Jaxy accessed the electrical panel and depressed the black button. The gate creaked three inches on rollers and stalled, making a terrific squeal. Jaxy punched the override and grinding stopped.

"Not your prisoner, am I?" Jaxy yanked at the stout chain, padlocked, and stretched tight between post and crook. Done looking for answers here, he stormed back to crash the gate, but turning the trailer over could not locate his keyring. Supposing he left them in the ignition, Jaxy raced downhill only to find the Dodge gone from the garage! Cutoff from civilization, he rushed to place a panicked call from the café, but the kitchen phone had walked off. Along the creek trail he then tore to seek out one at the mill, where coming through the double doors he stumbled upon the bubbletop parked in the paint ventilation booth.

"Stop!" he cried, "what are you doing??"

Beaming with pride, the Abbot peeled away the masking paper and there stood Moby styling a glossy, new coat of paint. "I Bondoed the doors and fenders too, in loving memory of 'J.D.' on the house! Turned out nice, eh? Miho can lay down some stripes if you'd like."

"But Moby . . ."

"But what?"

"But Moby isn't . . . , " stammered Jaxy.

"But Moby isn't what?"

"*A yellow whale*!!!"

With the guarantee that he would restore the van to its abalone white sheen when he returned from the greens, the Abbot left the Rockabilly to contemplate the perils of mixing two parts ethanol with one part conversation while rattling across the fields in his golf cart. From the booth that opened out onto the southern plane, Jaxy listened to the muffler of a vehicle that could not possibly be street legal. When the belches abated, Jaxy started up Moby and made it to the organic farm's service road end when the van sputtered, shimmied, coughed, and died.

The orange, fuel light went on. Empty.

"Gaw!!!" roared Jaxy, hoofing it to the mill where he could not scrounge up enough to prime a lawn mower. To the barn he then ran, hoping for enough gasoline to make it to Totum.

The Abbot's truck saved the day.

CHAPTER 46

Viv's Ranch, The Dalles. OR
11:00 a.m. Sunday, January 7

With his neck to the noonday sun, Rory loosened his collar and folded the sleeves as he approached The Dalles' ranch stables taking in a lungful of emergent bromegrass under the white oaks.

Viv shaded her eyes, and gave the unexpected caller a troubled greeting, "Well hello there, stranger! Isn't this whole thing terrible?"

"Haven't slept a wink."

"Omagosh, what happened?" Viv checked out his purple swollen nose and cheekbone.

"Took a nasty on the rocks. Lucked out—could've been worse," Rory shook it off as tough guys do.

"Umph! You've had a rough go all the way around, my friend."

"Not as rough as Jillian. Heard anything?"

"We were to ride Friday, but she never showed. Next thing . . .," Viv broke off biting on a knuckle.

"A word to the wise, Viv. If she comes along hide your valuables and call me."

"But drugs? Bombs? Now heists? How could she have gotten caught up in that?"

"To dig herself out of gambling trouble she turned to grand theft and threw in with Jaxy is my theory. How's Thunder Roll—mind if I see him?"

"Not here, but I caught a rat in his stall. Want the outlaw dead or alive?" Viv held the coffee can over the trough.

"Live," said Rory surveying the trees. "Is he out getting exercise?"

Viv punched air holes in the lid with a pitchfork. "Massage therapy."

"A horse masseuse?? I'm so through with that animal," Rory took a licorice bite then lent a hand in grooming Gem. As they brushed out the tangles, he carried on with his inquiry, "Can you think of any haunts out here on the range where Jillian would spend time?"

"She'd usually snag a donut on the way home, but that's it. Her friends all live in Vegas." Nuzzling Gem, Viv said, "Except you, dahling."

Rory quietly gagged, and putting the currycomb up, thanked Viv and took the rat to go.

Viv sprinted after the Bronco as it started down the drive. "Hey! There's a priest in Vancouver. Sometimes she'd leave on the early side to see him. Can't remember the name—sounded Greek to me. Good luck with that."

"Klapakis?

"You know him?"

"Had us take the Myers-Briggs. I'm an E.S.T.J.!"

"What's that mean?"

"Means that after one session with Klapakis, I was D.O.N.E."

CHAPTER 47

Evandell Golf Course, Minnehaha, WA
3:00 p.m. Sunday, January 7

Jaxy did not find Fr. Michael Klapakis at St. Maximos Church. He did not find him at the vicarage. He found him at Evandell Golf Course, gazing downrange in a white beanie visor, black slacks, and windbreaker to ward off the afternoon breeze.

"Yellybeanz," Fr. Michael said to no one, stroking his goatee at the drifting drive.

"Good afternoon," Jaxy approached head on.

"Afternoon," replied the golfer without taking his eye off the ball.

"Father Michael? I'm Jackson Thrie." Jaxy stuck out his hand.

"Yackzy!" the priest straightened away as from a phantasm.

"Abba Aldo said you're the one to see, so I came with something I found at the store."

"You went shopping? In Totum??" Fr. Michael's stress mounted.

Jaxy puffed out his chest. "I'm the Royal Martyrs' assistant librarian and gift shop book stocker! Here's one about the Romanovs all paid for. My gift to you."

Fr. Michael moved the wool cap from his to Jaxy's head, snugging the bill low to conceal the Californian's face. "And mine to you. Now off to library with you. Good day."

"That's it?" Jaxy juggled a cascade of three range balls he plucked from the basket. "No solace for the bereaved?"

The golfer snagged one in flight and held it to Jaxy's eye as the others bounced away. "Ever ask who consoles priest when he loses someone closer than daughter to likes of you? Nobody. Aldo say you knock ball pretty far. Want a go?"

"I'll watch."

The way Fr. Michael ceremonially placed the ball with the red stripe angled, brought to Jaxy's mind how Brother Jean took pains to arrange the red and white petals in the snow. However, for having lost someone closer than a daughter, Jillian's priest seemed to have flown through the stages of grief at mach speed, then off he went to counsel his balls to fly straight and true. Jaxy allowed a warm-up bump, and when Fr. Michael pulled back for the big one, the Rockabilly held the uncommonly short shaft fast against the sun and launched his salvo:

"Allow me, Father. Rory didn't shoot Jillian because the gun was empty. He didn't blow her leg off because the bomb was a dud. He didn't axe her at the hotel because she caved in his face and got away on a bike. Then, as I walked the apple trees to pay my respects, like a rock it hit me: Do you know why bringing back those rich cats preserved in cryogens will never work?"

"Wait. Don't say . . ." Fr. Michael worked it out, "because their assets are frozen?"

"No, darn it! Because the cell walls collapse! That means as a donation, Jillian's precious heart is worthless. *So, what really happened in the orchard?*"

"Do you not know I teach Anatomy and Helen surgeon? Donor Banks freeze tissue. It may have cooked some uses for Yillianz', but not all."

"Like what? Her hair?"

"Don't gets cute layman!" the golfer shanked fiercely, then retired the club, leaving the bucket for someone else. As a courtesy the priest walked Jaxy to the van where he stopped short exclaiming, "Oh dees bad!"

"I quite agree. The paint job sucks."

"No, *dat's* good! Your California plates, dummy!" The priest slapped Jaxy's head.

Fr. Michael had each license plate off before Jaxy turned the last nut from the Civic front Washington plate to bolt it to the rear bumper of van. Then shoving the Rockabilly's white ones under the back bench seat and Jaxy low into his car, the priest putt-putted down the hemlocks to his home in the suburbs, pounding the steering wheel as they went. "I-yi-yi! I tot you come in Aldo's truck! How could he let you drive all dees way in dat billboard? Incredible! Vat vas he tinking?"

Uncertain as to why Fr. Michael found such thinking incredible for the Abbot, but not himself, Jaxy simply said, "I left a note saying I'd be back by supper."

"More like midnight snack."

AT DEEP DUSK RORY stomped the brakes, fishtailed to a halt, and dropped down into a groomed, u-shaped lot for a closer look at the Dodge bubbletop. The same make, year, and model, this bus came to the party in yellow and no bullet holes. As Rory spun the Bronco about, he flicked the high beams and caught sight of Jaxy's bolo tie hanging from the mirror. He braked hard for a second look. No tags. He brushed his knuckles under the manifold. Warm.

Boxed in a canyon, Rory called for backup. When Brad caught up, the tow operator ran the numbers through the dispatcher and said, "Patched and painted with a Washington plate? Your wife's got friends you don't know about."

"Only one explanation for this," Rory scowled at the registered name.

"Just one? The van has stolen numbers screwed to the bumper and you have it worked out," postulated Brad as he fished for the door latch.

"I know the man. A parish priest—and he golfs." Rory made a move for the Ford.

"Wait a sec. Your wife wasn't the last one behind the wheel," Brad hopped from the cab and handed off a short task list curled inside a cupholder: 1) Repaint my van. 2) Find Jillian 3) And take my Angel back!

"*That son-of-a-bitch made it*?" Rory grabbed the scrap and stalked away.

Brad jumped between Rory and the Bronco. "We can't invade church property like some Afghani rat-hole. I plan to spend the night in my bed with Pepper, not on a pissed-stained cot next to you."

Rory tried to throw his friend out of the way, but Brad grabbed a handful of shirt impeding the way. "They have more than a Bible study on their team! A pro shop pimps Jaxy's van while he runs circles around the biggest manhunt in memory, then has the cojones to leave it in broad daylight. If I read it right, there's one thing left on his list to do," Brad tapped Rory's vest pocket, "—*and that's you.*"

To the voice of reason Rory gave in, activated the "Find a California A-Hole" app on his Electric Avlon field phone, and snuck it down the van seat pouch before driving home to Clackamas.

"EVENING OFFICER!" RORY HAILED from the street, hugging a coffee can.

"Crime scene, mister. Keep moving." The night watch angled his beam down the curb.

Rory passed his identification over. "Truth is, I live here. I'd like to collect my water bill before they cut me off."

"Take it up with the utilities or pay on-line."

"Good idea. Any new leads on the wife? If you ask me, no way could she mastermind anything this sophisticated. She had to have help."

"At the moment, everyone's suspect."

Rory shot Santa Claus a mistrustful look. "Him too? I'd rather get into my mail before he does."

Said the watchman, "Stay right there. I'll bring what I find."

"Terrific! And while you're at it, would you mind feeding Bonita?" Rory cracked the aerated, coffee can lid sending the trapped rodent into a frenzy.

The guard jumped away.

"Gosh officer, it's easy. Go slow. Be 'one with the snake' and she'll think you're alright. Watch the fingers around the rat, mainly."

Far from the can the guard frisked Rory and had him turn out the pockets. "Keep to the garage, Avlon. You have one minute—starting now."

On his return, Rory showed off his bills bundled in a pillowcase. "I helped myself to clean shirts and underwear from the dryer too, if that's okay."

The officer looked. If he noticed the wetsuit, fins, and snorkel at the bottom, he didn't mention it.

CHAPTER 48

The Klapakis Parsonage, Minnehaha, WA
5:00 p.m. Sunday, January 7

A ring of white smoke drifted to the ceiling, hit perpendicular to its vector of travel, and spread across the plane, increasing in diameter to disintegrate at the corners. After Fr. Michael showed off, Jaxy took a turn, passing a guitar pick through one ear to fall out the other.

"Easy for you! You have hollow head. Teach me one," said Fr. Michael.

To amaze the duffers at the nineteenth hole, Jaxy revealed how to conceal a coin and turn it into a golf ball. After the lesson in sleight of hand, Jaxy opened the Sunday paper and caught up on "Jax' the Ax" and "Jillian the Jihadist" sought for abducting a senior, Canadian intelligence officer on a blown drug raid. Were it not for a high-stakes Fabergé on the loose with lives on the line, Jaxy would have beat it to the nearest precinct to blow the whistle on Rory. Instead he stayed the course, and map-folding the paper to the sudoku asked, "Still waiting to hear your version of Jillian's death. And writing her into an icon? Holy Humbucker! How many commandments did *that* break?"

"Aldo say you no stay put if Yilli' survive bridge, and painting her pretty head without halo okay. It supposed to make you not feel so bad—like 'consolation prize'!"

"Didn't work."

"Not on a water witch with a stick in his britches, I grant'chu dat."

That they had a 'hot thing' going could not be commuted, so Jaxy played along to carry on with his mission to find the medallion. "Then why not put her up at the monastery?"

"Did you not see 'No Woman Allowed' sign?" spurned Fr. Michael.

"Neither did the doctor, apparently."

"There is beeg, Greek word, Yackzy, call '*economia*'. But not as on Wallstreet, it means we sometimes bend rules to accomplish greater good. Like Helen keeping you alive."

"Then the Abbot could econo-mo-date Jillian—in the other trailer, of course," reasoned Jaxy.

"Dat be more like stock market crash."

Jaxy slipped in the casual denial, "Come. We're just friends. *Platonic*. Say, there's a big, Greek word for you."

"*Baloney* is another! But I say no more," Fr. Michael puffed out a cloud.

"Oh no—my fiancée!" Jaxy blurted out. "Does Guin know?"

"My stars, Yackzy, everybody does! Read all about it!" Fr. Michael opened to an op-ed titled "Jack and Jill went up the Hill". Pieced together by some inventive writing, the article chronicled the wedding at the Pittock Mansion to a nostalgic, rock & roll reception at the L&C Hotel until they came tumbling down into a hot tub, replete with the splashy, stick-horse photo someone leaked onto the World Wide Web. Jaxy found another damning exposé with more spreads of a rumpled, honeymoon bed, and Jillian's powder blues hanging off the chandelier.

"Is nothing sacred?" Jaxy tossed the gossip column aside in preference to a televised news update on the principal cast of characters starring Jillian Avlon: Wild West Airlines Cowgirl, accomplished animal portrait artist and NCAA softball star; her husband, U.S. Marine Corps Captain Rory Avlon: International Brotherhood of

Electrical Workers Chapter Business Manager, mid-heavy weight, Savate kick-boxing champion, and decorated Veteran of Foreign Wars; Guinevere Hill, Esquire: Attorney-at-Law, Glendale City Council-Woman, Red Cross lifeguard, and gun control activist; and Jackson Thrie: Resale, antique furniture mover and Fat Pipes rockabilly band member.

"*Member*! It's my band! Jaxy popped a tube.

The report continued: "Last seen transporting drugs and explosives to Portland International in a white Dodge Ram with personalized plate MOBYD3 in brash reference to organized crime, it is believed the phantom couple have not left the basin where combined agencies have thrown an area wide dragnet. Meanwhile bottlenecks at ports of entry are turning the tide of public sentiment . . ." The sober, ending line announced: "In a statement released by narcotics division head, Sergeant Pantzer, it is feared that Mountie Agent Pierre de Chavoie, a key informant inside Jaxy's underground cell, was brutally silenced by Mister Thrie."

"SQUEAK!!" WENT THE BEAVER bathtub toy in the brisk, ocean night air.

From the braided branches of the Beaver Lodge fence, the loudspeaker required, "Identify."

"Tank," said the portly Police Sergeant filling his mackintosh with the air of important business.

"I can tell that from the lighthouse. Badge off the belt . . . higher."

"Do we have to do this every time, *fräulein*?"

A red, coherent dot danced on Sergeant Pantzer's jowls. "*Jedes Verdamnt.*"

Tank repositioned the badge holder and fed his card to the beaver reader to glide the motorized gates on lubricated bearings. After throwing treats to the dogs, and fruit-scented, dayglow markers to Golly, he elevated his massive arms in complaisance, doffing his trilby in salute to her black leathers.

Golly Gee wobbled his triple chin with the detection wand. "I am so not in the mood for you tonight."

To Golly's whiteboard they rode the lift to test the fruity, new pen colors where she added the Sergeant's surprise pop-in to her ever-growing list of undetermined, root cause questions.

"I came because you asked for me," Tank jogged her memory, "and for not putting it on your calendar, this one will cost you."

"By allowing my sister to flee at less than blinding speeds, your bungled, hospital containment already did."

On Tank's turn at the board, he diagrammed the Pittock attack scene with razzleberry x's and tangelo o's saying, "Let's compare. Earlier that day, you had J-Squared hedged between the mansion and the gate lodge to waste pot shots as the Fabergé angel slipped away. At least my flub has an uptick. In custody Jillian would have seized into the fetal position to play the hapless gull caught in the crossfire. On the lam, she's become an unruly part of it, and as far as the Romanov Guild is concerned, toast."

Golly plucked the pen from his hand. "I could not disagree more. If you thought more like a Cossack than a Kraut, you would know my people want a leader with brass balls. Thanks to you Jillian grew a pair!"

"If you fought like one, maybe you would too. Tell me—is that one there?" asked Pantzer with incertitude of her splashy, whiteboard doodle.

"Whooo—no free bug-spray for you! Chrysanthemum *Asterales*. Means 'flower of gold'. From it you can extract environment-friendly, Diptera repellent straight from the garden."

"If it works on maggot musicians, I'll take a case and rest mine, although 'why' I can't say until you secure the room."

Golly leaned out with her crutch to throw an industrial, four-way, Frankenstein switch to flood the bomb shelter access to the beaver float with pond water, jam RF activity on the island, and power off everything but refrigeration, lighting, and air flow. After banishing all personal communication devices to the faraday bucket outside the sealed chamber she demanded, "What's so stinking sensitive we have to close the float?"

"*You*, my dear. For as much as you love to hate her, Jillian is not the problem. Your slippery Californian is, and I need a hand in bagging him."

"The gall to come on bended knee after leaving me up shit creek with your 'rules' *when I could have prevented it*!!!" Golly drew a hangman game on the whiteboard placing in a frowny face inside the noose.

"Quit acting like a five-year-old. The less you help the more it will appear that you sent Yan to the front lines to rid the Beaver Lodge of a government plant the day Jaxy Thrie conveniently rode into town," said Tank.

Golly's lips pinched white in concentration. "You, Sergeant, are looking for the wrong person. This my boy did not do. Too sloppy."

"You would recognize sloppy work, for I had no idea you went anywhere near the mansion until I dug this from a tree." Tank rattled a bullet inside a clear, plastic box.

"Crap. Give me that." Golly's fingers shot out.

"I collected it when neighbors complained of kids shooting rockets over the roofs again. I told them that with no planets in retrograde the ghosts had grown restless. I'd think you want them to remain that way," the Sergeant pulled it from reach.

"Blackmailing me now?" Golly Gee wiggled her bum.

"I detected other signs of paranormal pranking. Did you know it is unlawful for any person, disembodied or otherwise, to enter a public museum without first paying admission?"

"Sorrrry. I thought five-year-olds got in free."

From his notes Pantzer pressed on: "Nor shall any apparition bathe, dive, wade, or swim in any natural, or artificial fountain or water feature. What do you have to say for yourself, my immaterial girl?"

"Can I come after school and pick up trash?"

"Damn right you will, on the Fourth of July with that tree trimmer. Say, there's a thread to pull on," he wrote "Leshenko" in the eight hangman spaces.

"Leave him alone. The kid's clean." She wiped away the name.

"Then why the same night, on yet another wild goose chase orchestrated by your sister to spread thin my resources, did I bump into Drew with goody-two-shoes under the Sellwood Bridge?"

"His mother rents a boat slip there."

"And the day after they golf Totum when superior courses abound closer to home?"

Before a wall map Golly took her time answering, "Father's cheap."

"I keep losing sight of that."

"And your reason for coming. I could be watching the Golden Globes."

"Councilwoman Hill."

"The forever fiancée? What did she do?"

"Fall off the map without a trace last seen in the company of your man Lovorsky."

Clapped Golly Gee, "You should have led with that."

"I'm warning you. Guin Hill is an elected official. I can't look the other way if you had anything to do with that," said Pantzer facing out the blackened window.

"Then arrange a meeting with Klav. That's Loverboy's territory."

"Can you set one up?"

Golly jangled the red, Bakelite rotary phone built to survive a nuclear blast. "You had me disconnect. *Remember*? Besides, in my hour of need he went to Kansas City for a convention talk on turn-of-the-twentieth century war tech. Klav's quite the rusty gun collector."

"I thought you owned his antique Russian ass."

"The mall, not his worldview. He talks a big game of old Tomsk and Yekaterinburg, so I bought out the family store on a hunch it would lead me to Rat Catcher. It didn't play out, and he's tired of me all up in his business about it."

"Intriguing. You say Klav is a *Yurovsky*?"

"Ha! To hear him speak, you'd think he chambered the bullet that killed the Tsar himself."

CHAPTER 49

The Ipatiev House, Yekaterinburg, Russia
July 1918

On the spine of the ore-rich Ural Mountains sprawled the muddy, storm-drenched industrial camp of Yekaterinburg; Russia's fourth largest city and Sverdlovsk District administrative seat. White Army cannon fire fell across the plain. On 49 Ascension Avenue sat the august Ipatiev House, enclosed by a four-meter, plank fence constructed in haste, and tagged "The House of Special Purpose". On the upper floor slept eleven prisoners of state – the deposed Tsar, his wife and five children, a doctor, maid, cook, and valet – and the family spaniel. Under a coarse woven corset, near the heart of the eldest daughter Olga, lay hidden a guardian angel passed to her from her grandmother, the dowager Empress Maria Feodorovna.

With separatists and Romanov loyalists advancing in superior numbers on the stronghold, by order of Moscow the Cheka Commandant, Yakov Yurovsky, came at midnight to awaken and move his eleven charges to the bunker on the basis that there they would be safer should fighting commence on the streets. Across the inner courtyard he marched his stoic detainees, single file, down twenty-three steps to a plastered basement with barred windows and positioned them to be photographed for proof of existence. But instead of cameras and lights, Yakov called for an armed detail and assigned each squad member to one of the condemned. On the alleyway above, a diesel transport started to drown out the noise.

Without a trial or hearing, Commander Yurovsky stood before the Tsar, drew a missive from his pocket, and read the death sentence.

"What? What??" Nicholas bent a confounded ear forward, as if he had misheard.

"In view of the fact that your relatives are continuing their attack on Soviet Russia," restated the Commander, "the Ural Executive Committee has decided to execute you."

"You know not what you do . . ."

CHAPTER 50

The Beaver Lodge, B.C.
6:00 p.m. Sunday, January 7

"Seventy pock holes?" asked Sergeant Pantzer in amazement. "At the gun club we call that amateur hour."

"From the slugs that ricocheted off the bling layered into the girls' bullet-proof clothing, hitting the cellar walls," said Golly.

"Christ, that must have hurt."

"But they still wouldn't die, so short on time and ammo Yurovsky finished them off with rifle butts and bayonets to create a blood lake the size of this office."

"Uck. How much jewelry did Yakov pull out?"

"Six kilos shipped to Moscow—all but the Guardian Angel of Maria Feodorovna. This he returned to the dowager on the run in the Crimea. Some say to gloat, others to express regret. I think the commandant grew afraid of it."

"Or of being caught with it."

"Whatever the motive, Maria read into it a sign that by the angel's might, the Romanov crown would rise from the ashes to rest on the most deserving head at the hundred-year jubilee."

"Your brother," the Sergeant took an informed guess.

"Close," the Russian heiress clapped in anticipation.

"Duchess Dagmar?"

"You're getting warmer," trilled Golly, filling in the letter G. "Care to buy a vowel?"

"U."

"Whooo! Outstanding." Golly finished out her name and flipped the whiteboard to the Failure Mode and Effects Analysis table.

Tank reassessed the figures of merit, uncapped a black chisel-tip from his pocket protector, and scaled back the degree given to the senior sister as the eminent threat to realizing Golly's dreams of Eurasian hegemony, while upping the likelihood of occurrence, and the impact severity of Jaxy Thrie's next move to scuttle them.

"Would you mind not using a Sharpie?!!!" Golly furiously rubbed at the fixed stain. "A ton of number crunching went into these values."

Argued the sergeant, "In the course of one week a no-name busker infiltrates the lodge, smokes two key personnel, cuffs the hottest crown jewel on the planet, sweeps the highest-ranking Romanov duchess off her feet, *and you score him a four*??? Show me his charts again."

"'Highest ranked' does not convert to 'best qualified'," replied Golly as she unrolled a scroll of ink squiggles from the drum. "You don't suggest Jaxy Thrie is Rat Catcher, do you?"

Over his bifocals the Sergeant focused in on Rockabilly's electrodermal response to the butter tart question and said, "Infinitely worse."

Golly squared up, "I'm listening."

"After running hundreds down the garburator and contaminating our ground water for years, I'll be a monkey's uncle if I didn't realize it until now. You feed your people noxious butter tarts on purpose to separate a genuine bad one from your legion of ass-kissers. Nice work, Golly, you found your star-crossed match. One that that tomfool from Saskatoon helped interview for his own replacement.

Golly bluntly boxed the pens to adjourn. "You truly think we teamed up to take Yan out, don't you? Sorry, Sarge, I make calculated moves, not dumb ones, and I'll be as pleased as punch when they throw Jackson Thrie in the hole without parole for freelancing without an assassins' permit and poormouthing my baking."

"That's so? Jaxy gave the division a shiner in my own backyard because you shot high and wide. I don't want him put away for life. I want that Rockabilly cur put down for good." Pantzer shook the bullet.

"A death sentence isn't an easy stick," said Golly playing with the music-note earring.

From a stainless rack Tank chose a silver crowbar and slid it down the bench. "It will be with this rammed through his cranium at the moment of climax. This way I will know it was you that fucked the man's brains out, and not one of your lickspits."

Golly slid it back. "Paragraph two point two of Beaver Ethics Code 218 categorically forbids uninvited advances, untoward talk, unseemly language, coercion, or acts of violence against a coworker resulting in mental stress or physical harm. And no lodge member is above compliance, including their C.E.O."

"Then fire him first for offing Pops in contempt. I'll kick in for the severance," offered Pantzer from his billfold.

"Put it away. You couldn't afford a squirt bottle of my fly spray."

Into the pen can the contribution went anyway. "For Counsel Hill if she shows up. Or are sending chrysanthemum to the surviving fuck-buddy an infraction of BL218 too?"

With an *"ARSCH@L#!!!!"* down came the board with a mighty crash as Golly Gee kicked the Sergeant out with her good foot while hurling German epithets into an inoperative, red telephone.

CHAPTER 51

The Klapakis Parsonage, Minnehaha, WA
6:30 p.m. Sunday, January 7

Five minutes into a lively, televised debate on the merits of polyamory, Jaxy jumped to a Bonnie and Clyde movie marathon. Tiring of that, at a commercial he came to the kitchen to ask more hard questions. Before Jaxy could begin, however, Fr. Michael headed off the inquest with one of his own.

"Yilli' say you meet over air hockey," prompted the priest, cracking an oyster jar and stirring braised celery and half and half into the stew.

Jaxy wedged a salad tomato. "We had a friendly game and talked about music and horses."

"Happy couples don't pass the time with strangers at bars and arcades, Yackzy," Fr. Michael hit head on.

"On business they do. Besides, the Avlons aren't too happy with each other these days if you believe the stories."

"And Guin—she okay with that?"

"Now there's a real fairytale," Jaxy set down the kitchen knife in resignation.

Fr. Michael raised his bushy brows. "Once upon a time . . ."

ON A MAUNDY THURSDAY morning, Guinevere Rosa Hill made her grand entrance into the world smack in the middle of her mother's Lamaze class. A pushy thing, from A's in algebra to the best cannabis in town, Guin knew how to score. Her father, a judge of Welsh descent, while stringent with others' juveniles went easy on his own, giving Guin's schoolmarms fits as the fiery speech and debate team leader routinely trounced her opponents and aced her AP exams half stoned while being found in possession only once. Suspended, grounded, and confined to her upper story room, Guin airlifted supplies to her best friend three houses away until she crashed her dad's radio helicopter into the ivy-covered chimney, strewing her mother's convertible with Panama Red and rolling papers.

Across the thoroughfare, through leafy park trees the sly, and exceedingly shy Jackson Mason Thrie took note, and in the hope of crossing paths with the brassy brunette, struck camp and moved farther down wash, closer to her house. For all of that, Guin kept to the sunny side of the street, and Jaxy, incapable of working up the nerve to cross the dotted yellow line, stayed on his to minister to a dad too impaired to care for his own underage flesh and blood. Over time Jaxy gave up on the exotic, older-girl-next-door until one smoggy, August day a clowder of co-eds piled two high in a Spider sidled up to the corner on Colorado and De Lacey to where he sat on a milk carton playing requests for tips.

"Hey kid! How old are you?" the leader in cat shades called out the top.

"Seventeen," lied Jaxy, slicking his mop and trying not to look sixteen until he couldn't stand it and corrected, "—almost."

"Have you lived outside your whole life?"

"I-I don't live outside," he tried to deny.

"Do too!" Guin Hill stood on the seat, and screwing her fists into binoculars showed her friends, "I watch him from my bedroom window 'swiiiiiiinging in the rain'," she warbled.

Aghast, Jaxy retreated in embarrassment.

"Like Jungle George without a breechcloth!" she said, while her companions singed Jaxy's ears with coarse laughter and crude compliments.

The light changed and the self-conscious street performer waved them on, "Go away! You're stopping traffic."

Contrary to his wish, Guin set the brake and shot a fifty-dollar wad into his guitar case requesting, "La Bamba!"

Slack-jawed, Jaxy smoothed out the largest tip he'd ever taken and said, "Excuse me, mmm, but didn't you mean to give me a five?"

"Who shops with fives?" laughed the hot-blooded, half-Brazilian with a hip-bump and a tilt of her glasses. "Bossa nova style."

Guin's friends piled out to form a samba line, and drawing strangers from their occupations, and passersby from the stores, Carnival broke out that sultry, summer day in Old Town Pasadena.

IN A SUDDEN SHIFT from facts to feelings, Jaxy opened up as the priest ladled out the creamy soup. "So, I moved in with the Booker-Hills, tested out of high school, and got my class B trucking license to pay down Guin's tuition. For her part she said after graduation we'd marry, but ring shopping is as far as it went. Now every time I press for a date, she gives one more flimsy reason for putting it off!"

"Like blessing goddaughter's house!" segued Fr. Michael into the mealtime prayer.

"Amen, Father," closed Jaxy with an emphatic fist. "Ten years, I tell you! Ten Years I played her anti-gun marches and 'Don't Turn the Clocks Back' campaigns, staking signs, and giving out 'Stick with the Guinners' buttons and magnets, and never considered this until Jillian touched on it with her hurt-bird-in-the-dugout story."

Father Michael patted his breast, "Consider what—Guin treats you like rescue?"

"Yes. And I'll never overcome it."

"Bosh. They all treat us that way. With Hill at least you have future."

"As our nation's 'first fiancé'? We're pulling in different directions, Father. It's not working, and what do I get for trying?" he pointed at Jillian's face filling the television. "That."

"You know, tings not always smooth here either. Camille keep saying 'golf–golf–golf', or 'quit dropping indefinite article, Mike'! Even so, when Yillianz entered my life, I chose to love her as my own daughter, not mistress."

"But you're a priest."

"Tank you for noticing! And do you know why priests never fool around with pretty woman half their age seeking little TLC?"

"Tell me. Why do priests never fool around with the younger set looking for 'a' little TLC?"

"Because we say so!" Fr. Michael laughed and laughed, snapping his fingers like marionettes, and turning a dance with a towel.

"And us good, little lay people are supposed to believe you."

"Congratulations, Yackzy! You are now official catechumen." Fr. Michael loaded the dishwasher and broke out the ice cream.

"Great. I'll hang the certificate next to Guin's law degree."

To his recliner Fr. Michael took a bowl of rocky road, and from it command of the television. "There are two schools," he commentated on a golf advertisement, "one say save money on castoff equipment, but I say it make game harder to master and discourages student. A proper shaft should be correctly sized, weighted and balanced with enough loft to get airborne first day out."

"Same with guitars! Start a kid on a cheap laminate and he'll play for a day. Give him one with solid tone and feel and he'll stick with it for a lifetime," said Jaxy, settling into the sofa.

"Practice is what the catechism of life is all about. Learning from mistakes or repeating them over and again until we do. What you learn on?"

"A '56, Chet Atkins with a touch smoother than buttermilk after crisscrossing the country with a drifter that swore to his grave Duane Eddy recorded 'Forty Miles of Bad Road' on it. I believe him. Listen. You can tell."

"That's some story, I like to hear it."

"I'll dedicate the request to Jillian. May I ask how you know her? Because, even though I haven't all that long, I think long enough to say she doesn't strike me as, ah, the church-going type.

"And you know this how?" Fr. Michael shook his spoon at Jaxy without turning his head from the lay of the ball.

"Guin. Not her so much, but her mom was fanatical to the point of paranoia. She read significance into everything. I set a guitar pick on the family Bible once. Holy humbucker! Didn't make that mistake twice. Jillian doesn't even own one."

"A guitar pick?" asked Fr. Michael, not listening that closely.

"A Bible! Why do people answer questions with questions?"

Fr. Michael shrugged while reading the grain for a long putt from the collar.

"Because they don't want to answer them!" Jaxy filled in.

After the ball rolled by Fr. Michael proceeded, "At the start of the year, your secular humanist friend bought on eBay what you describe as 'superstitious' keepsake with lettering she took for Greek, so she looked me up and ask for translation."

"That's what she told you?"

"Why, I belief so. Yes."

"She didn't buy it."

"No! She steal it?" Fr. Michael grew tense.

"In a roundabout way. I started out the day with two identical medallions. The one she showed you and a cheap version. But I passed off the wrong angel—the expensive one—over a hockey bet which she promised to give up if I came to Portland to help her move."

Fr. Michael sat erect. "*Give it up*! That was the deal?"

Jaxy took the clicker and shut off the golf match. "I am talking about the Fabergé Jillian said she found on eBay! The little thief then changed her mind causing me to nearly lose mine!"

"Horseradish!" cursed the clergyman as holy men do. "You, sir, are the thief! To woo and seduce any wedded woman is shameful. But to use angel to steal into marriage bed of such beautiful thing as my spiritual child Yillianz' is worse! It is beyond comprehension! It is!! You . . . You . . . *Paliánthropos*!!!" Father Michael pounded his hairy fist, tipping the bowl off the armrest.

Jaxy jumped to catch the dessert before it hit the carpet. "I saw the hot tub photos, Father, and I can't deny. But I gave the guardian angel away to her before you met. According to you, it's *how* you met. And frankly, I'm having a hard time seeing how anyone could grow this close to anybody, regardless of how 'connected' they feel, for having known each other for one goddam week!"

"Good Yackzy, good! Since it took you only one goddam, game of air hockey to get my goddaughter of thirty-two years pregnant!"

Jaxy flinched and excused himself to the backyard to stargaze.

By the time Fr. Michael came to seek pardon for losing his cool, Jaxy had regained his, having grown intrigued by where the priest stood in the hierarchy.

"I'm not up on how this 'godfather' stuff works, but it seems this puts you in the crease of a family faceoff pitting Jillian Avlon and her sister 'Chaps', against the Beavers of Canada, the Russian Antique Mall, and a watchmaker over this hot bit of Romanov history. Are you familiar with these partners?"

"Don't forget Berlin."

"That's right because Berlin won't forget you. Connecting the dots, wouldn't that make you top dog—like a Greek don, or something?"

asked Jaxy staring out at Canis Major.

"Something like. In Athens they call me *'Nonós of the Night'*," said the priest with gravelly emphasis.

"Ooo—catchy. Can I call you that?"

"No! I am not your *Nonó*."

"Still, I ask—who mandated the bad-ass, biker hit at the mansion? Because if it flowed from you, I wouldn't have made it off the hill, would I?"

"I have beeg plans, so I send bad-ass biker to break you two up and send Yilli' home."

Jaxy snapped to. "Then hear me out, Sir! I take no side, nor came I to Oregon in want of a one-night stand or bucking for a promotion. I am three days past due getting that elusive medallion to Beaver Island and fear that my employer and dear family will become casualties of a war I helped start if I don't. So, do with me what you will, but leave them out of it."

Front to rear Fr. Michael inspected Jaxy's dress, straightening the gig line and flicking lint from the shoulder. "At ease, catechumen. Speak truth and nothing befalls your beloved."

Jaxy relaxed his stance.

"As Orion is witness," Fr. Michael identified a different constellation, "how tight are you with Yillianz'?"

"I belong to an attorney from Glendale, sir!"

"And her leetle sister—what you call her?"

"Chaps! Would be in violation of corporate ethics policy BL218 godfather sir!"

"Principled to a fault."

"You say that as if it's a bad thing!" barked Jaxy.

"It can be fatal. Come."

Inside the house Fr. Michael collected his car keys and overcoat and gave the Romanov biography back to his understudy.

"For me?" asked Jaxy in perplexity.

"Go, find quiet place with these girls and forget about z' rest. Ask not what their death meant for Russia in 1918, but what their life means for you. Right here. Right now, catechumen. For without that there be no Romanov saint—just martyrs to their father's lofty principles."

The Klapakis front door opened with a flurry, and the parish matriarch in raspberry sweats waded in with groceries.

"Talking of lofty principles, here comes one now," Fr. Michael began the introductions. "Camille, meet . . ."

Jaxy removed his glasses while Camille set the bags on the kitchen floor.

"I'm Mason." Jaxy offered a polite hand.

"And I'm Presbytera Camille. I don't mean to sound rude, but you look like that madman on the news. Take a wrap to cover your dimples if you go out," she said, giving his fingers a fragile shake for a sturdy woman, then dipped them into the knitting basket.

"Mason here for golf symposium from . . .," Fr. Michael deferred.

"Chicago," Jaxy jumped in.

"Where are you staying? We have a spare room," she crossed the scarf high above Jaxy's neck.

"Monastery—but thank you."

Fr. Michael guided Jaxy toward to the door, "Mason's car at Evandell. They lock at nine."

"Hold up! The clock shop set out the feast day raffle items, so I stopped on my way home. I can't imagine who selected this one—certainly not Father Michael—isn't it stunning, Mason?" She opened a gold, paper jewelry box.

Jaxy read the tag hanging off the guardian angel medallion, "Remarkable."

"Tank you, Ca-miiiiiiille." Father Michael brusquely lidded the box and left with Jaxy for the golf course.

On the way to his van Jaxy asked about the serpentine chain he found at the monastery. Fr. Michael said that after Jillian broke the medallion from Rory's neck, the chain must have fallen into the ankle weight.

"Jillian then took the angel in for cleaning and repair?" Jaxy pried for more details.

"You could conclude that," replied her priest.

"And since Reuben works for the Beavers, he would entrust it to you."

"Naturally."

Jaxy pumped his fist. "Then my people are safe from retribution."

In a sotto voice Fr. Michael said, "In this business, Yackzy, nobody is."

"So said Yan. Then permit me to see the Guardian Angel of Maria Feodorovna back to the island."

Fr. Michael moved it to the dash. "Why—when twice you carelessly let it get away?"

"To bargain for Chap's release since that seems pretty low on your priorities."

"I don't know anything about that."

"The heck you don't. Without Yan's watchful she will bolt, and it will not go well."

"Did I not say I have plan? When you retired Pops Lang you took his spot in the Beaver organization. If the association belief you to take down even more treacherous mole Yan, what that make you now, catechumen?" asked the priest.

"Chap's bodyguard? How does that solve anything?"

"By making it easier. But first let this blow over and go finish book. With world on alert best place for Feodorovna angel is under ROMAR chapel altar. Nobody dare look there."

"Including me," said Jaxy with dread.

"Brother Jean can. In meantime nobody can know we talk so

name some place you go today."

"The fish hatchery."

"You suck gas to have cappuccino with Herman Sturgeon? Use head!" Fr. Michael gave it a slap. "What besides golf would drive man to break out of monastery for lark on town?"

"Hockey?"

"Bingo!" proclaimed Fr. Michael, and to help sell the sports bar cover story bought him a tallboy and a bag of salted nuts from the snack shop.

CHAPTER 52

The Totum Pole, Totum, WA
10:00 p.m. Sunday, January 7

The smell of dead animal grew overpowering. Nonetheless, abiding by the letter to not brake "even for moose", Jaxy pressed on with the scarf over his nose and the windows down. At the four-way coming into Totum he made a California stop, then stomped on the gas for the homestretch. Moby lurched, cut out, lurched again, coughed, and died. The orange dash light came on.

Empty.

"Gaw!!!" Jaxy column shifted to neutral and came to rest on the gravel lot behind the only place open for business.

The threat of being fingered in public seemed less precarious than the five-mile walk in wingtips against a bracing wind sloughing off the ridge. So, upon finding nothing odoriferous wrapped around the wheels, Jaxy let Moby air it out as into the Totum Pole he stole in a golfer's beanie and carded, wool scarf bunched around his mouth and chin. By the window, stout locals played foosball next to two tipsy barflies flicking popcorn to ruin the game. Over the entrance, lit by the obligatory, stained-glass advertisements a poster of Chief Seattle dispensed a cautionary word:

"Be just and deal kindly with my people, for the dead are not powerless".

The roadhouse came with all the trappings except for the one thing Jaxy needed: A payphone. Down on options, he presented his plight to an alfalfa farmer styling a straw-hat, checkered shirt and suspenders giggling at a Golden Girls' episode showing from the television above her forty-something, Irish red hair. Rather than lend a phone, the helpful farmer siphoned enough fuel from her Volvo through a keg hose to get Jaxy down the highway to a filling station. Since the regulars paid them no mind, for the kindness Jaxy bought the next round and chanced a "whatever she is having" for the road. One celebratory rye on the rocks led to two, and as the whiskey hit Jaxy's self-preserving sense of public mindfulness, they locked elbows and with gusto sang, "Thank you for being a friend . . ."

When the segment ended the alfalfa farmer went to take a turn at foosball, so Jaxy switched the station over to hockey. During a pause in the action, following a tussle along the boards, he played with the wet rings over a collage of brown and white, vintage photographs pressed flat beneath the glass bar top that served as a window into Totum's rustic past when automobiles shared the roads with wagons and buggies. From snapshot taken of an Oregon Trail marker, Jaxy read the unhappy fable of Princess Wahatpolitan who, luckless in love, leapt to her death from Beacon Rock.

The fair alfalfa farmer came back for a top-up, interrupting Jaxy's moment. "Tell me your name, lad, and I'll tell ye mine."

Jaxy brought a napkin to his cheek. "Friends call me 'Mason'."

"And mine call me Shea-o. Shea O'Sullivan of BZ Corner," said the farmer looking over Jaxy's shoulder at the photography. "You go all emotional over sad cases too?"

"One more and I'll be over her," Jaxy set the napkin down to knock back a third.

Shea-o pulled his ear to her mouth, "Who—Jillian Avlon?"

Jaxy pulled his scarf higher and flagged the bartender for the tab, but Shea-o ordered two more ryes instead and in a low voice said, "What's the hurry man? Your secret's safe with me."

"People say that. Few mean it," replied Jaxy.

"I'm wanted in Londonderry for shooting a Garda. Not anyone can say that. Now we each have one on the other, don' we? Shall I keep going?"

"Holy humbucker. You killed a policeman?"

"Shot. Not torn open and drowned like yours, you twisted fuck. Plus, I know where you hide the bodies. That's our other dirty secret."

"You seem to know more about me than I do. How is that?" Jaxy wrapped the scarf higher.

"The van. I took a gander when you went to the men's room. You really should have locked it. Don't see many conversions like it anymore. Really sticks out in a crowd. The best place to hide that hot mess is *not* in the open. I know a place. "

"So do I. Time to hit the road." Jaxy started to raise his hand a second time to pay up, but Shea-o pushed it down.

"Next time," she said.

"I still owe you for a tank of gas."

"And I shall hold you to it, Jaxy. Hear what happened to the bloke that missed three payments to his exorcist?"

Jaxy shook his head.

"He was repossessed! Ha-ha. You're turn. Make it good."

"Lessee if I can remember one from today," Jaxy screwed his face until the haze thinned and he started in, "I have it, Shea-o! Know why . . . know why . . . bringing back those dead, rich cats bottled up in liquid nitrogen will never work?

Shea-o shrugged.

"Because their asses are frozen!"

Shea-o didn't get it, but she let go with a hearty har-har regardless, spraying the bar with lemon and ice. "Well, thankee for a fine evening out with 'the deadliest musician alive'. Here's something to remember the most dangerous farmer by," Shea-o handed Jaxy a carved token with her name and addressed burned into the side.

Jaxy made out the letters "Wooden Nickel" on the other.

"Don' e're take one from an Oerish, it'll bring seven years o' bad luck," warned Shea O'Sullivan.

Jaxy tried to resist, but she balked, "It's yours now, Jaxy!"

Jaxy loosed the ribbon from the gold paper, jewelry box and showed off the guardian angel while grasping tight the chain. "Tonight, this fella brought me seven years of good, so I broke even."

"Look at that." Shea-o reverently cupped the medallion and then flipped it around to ask, "Camille—she the wifey or the girlfriend?"

Jaxy grabbed the angel and gawped at the words: "Happy Birthday to the Remarkable Camille—God Grant You Many Years. January 2018."

"Bartender! Check!! Now!!!" Jaxy slapped the copy on the counter.

From the door a gruff voice commanded, "Bartender! I suggest you take Jackson Thrie's money before calling the sheriff."

Jaxy froze in place at the mean ex-Marine closing in from ten feet.

"I saw him first!" yelled a local hero vaulting the foosball table to make a million-dollar tackle.

"He's mine!" Shea-o swept the most wanted man in America catawampus off the barstool as Rory went sailing by.

While tumbling backwards in her freckled arms, the Rockabilly watched heads collide as they went down in heap of sawdust and shells.

"Go-Go-Go, ya stupid yank!" She kicked Jaxy to his feet, as out from under he scooted to grab a handful of nuts from the barrel and flee to the van.

"Where did those donut-eatin' cops come from?" asked Jaxy, shifting into overdrive and spraying a rooster-tail of mud and gravel at the gawkers who'd come out of the pub to watch him blow through the traffic light. In the mirror, he saw a flashing cherrytop turn in while two others bore down on his tail. Coming upon a construction site for a winery expansion with earthmovers parked for the night, Jaxy downshifted, killed the headlights, cranked the wheel, and emergency braked into the graded area.

The van skated over a film of black ice, clipped a skip loader, and caromed into a row of seedlings planted at the back of the lot. Through the hedge of sage and softwoods the van chomped its way to slam sideways against the winery's aging barn. The muffled crash of magnum bottles prefaced the structural creaking, until a louder rumbling started, and a season's worth of snow slid off the roof to bury the van under rotten ice from tires to bubbletop.

With his heart pumping triple-time, Jaxy set out his driver's license and registration with fumbling fingers, and then meekly waited for the nightsticks, stun guns, and other state-sanctioned thuggery. For openers, they would book him for running a red with a stolen plate and an open container, followed by reckless driving and evasion, destruction of property, and instigating a bar fight under the influence of cheap rye. From there, they would move on to the more fascinating charges of drug trafficking and terrorism in cahoots with a Wild West Cowgirl, and the abduction and homicide of a Saskatonian Mountie.

Blurry, bright searchlights streaked about. They seemed to be waiting for back-up before accosting a stewed fugitive, armed and dangerous in a van full of guns, drugs and dynamite. Jaxy hardly dared to breath lest, misreading his intention, they open fire. After twenty minutes, the deputies crossed the highway to beat about a bed and breakfast, then cut the spotlights, stopped shouting, and exited the scene. Dumbfounded, Jaxy held his breath for another five minutes, all the time thanking his lucky stars that a K-9 unit didn't show, or they would have had him in their jaws before their paws hit the ground.

Panting for fresh air, Jaxy kicked out through the side door into a night of mixed blessings. The Dodge had taken out none but the smallest of shrubs, while the limber saplings and leafy shoots had rebounded, obscuring him from his pursuers. The avalanche of snow off the barn roof concealed the rest. With the rear dug out, he reorganized things. The Glenlivet bottle had rolled forward. In need of a nip to calm his jitters, Jaxy closed the back, came around to the side, and reached for the scotch.

"Jillian!" he recoiled, hitting his head, and breaking off the mirror. With a stomach still churning from the putrid stench and teacup ride, it took all Jaxy had to keep his dinner of oysters and ice cream down. A butchered body sat buckled behind in a scissor-cut miniskirt and poofy, polka-dot top. Blackened and mud-caked strands of hair held down by a watch cap plastered the once fine face. Tacked to the bloated torso a tagboard read, "Your Turn Jack".

In tortured agony, Jaxy brushed the clotted bangs aside and stared, not into Jillian's eyes, but at the missing Mounted Policeman Pierre de Chavoie.

"Eee-yuck! Rory, you depraved animal!" shrilled Jaxy through alternating waves of revulsion and relief. After a refreshing jog around the winery and a hand scrub of snow, he backed up the van, forming a makeshift igloo where he dragged the Mountie's decaying remains, burying it under the snow and ice. Then, up the vintner's drive, Jaxy stealthily drove with lights off. A new parade of black and whites went screaming by. In the shelter of a pumphouse, he stopped to throw open the van doors to let the rancid odor fade while tuning in the radio.

It did not take long to find a station buzzing of the near capture of Jackson Thrie in Totum, Washington, who, after a thrilling, high-speed chase in and out of side streets evaded law enforcers to inexplicably disappear on the edge of town. Evidence left at the pub sent the Klickitat Sheriff to a nearby monastery in search of the desperado.

"Side streets?" Jaxy looked up and down the empty roadway. "What side streets?"

Had he a phone, it would have been hard to resist letting them know that Totum boasts a population of twenty-eight, and a third of them were at the bar. Just as well, for up against that polished federation of byzantine liars, Johnny Law had no chance at a straight story from the monastery either. They would leave with nothing to show for their efforts but a wall calendar of martyred saints and jars of apple chutney. Meanwhile, Jaxy passed the time with roasted nuts and ale, singing the bass line in "Red Cadillac and a Black Moustache," not sure who was who in the song anymore.

CHAPTER 53

The ROMAR, Totum, WA
11:00 p.m. Sunday, January 7

Scarcely had the Klickitat County Sheriff left the Holy Royal Martyrs Monastery when a pressing call from Guin Hill tore the Abbot away from offering up an Akathist of Thanksgiving.

"Provost! I found out why baloney butt went to Portland. It excuses nothing, but this is super important, so do not, I repeat, do not let Jaxy leave the ROMAR for any reason."

"Too late, Hill. He's gone," said the Abbot.

"Noooo!!!! You said you had ways to keep him occupied!"

"We're a monastery, Guin, not an amusement park. I chained the gate and drained his tank, but you called it, he found more and a way out. We think to look for Jillian. He was spotted in Totum and the Sheriff just left the ROMAR looking for him."

"Darn it. Baloney Butt's after something hotter than Jillian—an old, gold Fabergé angel worth gazillions that he carried from his place of work and that got away from him unleashing this unholy mess. It's easy to spot—solid oval loaded with diamonds and sapphires."

"He made mention."

"I confronted Klav Lovorsky who manages the antique's business. Some time ago he cut an unfavorable deal with a Canadian cartel he can't back out of, and they are holding him and anyone near and dear accountable for the angel's loss. To gain his help, I had to give away all I know about Jaxy and Jillian, where they went, and how I got involved. Using this information with what muscle he has, Klav bargained for extra days. See if Jillian has it. I have got to get this guardian angel in the mail to the mall before the Beavers torch us all."

"To go through Jillian's belongings, I must have her here, at the ROMAR."

"Shoot. Moving her isn't part of the deal."

"Can't have it both ways, Counsel."

"Not the deal I'm talking about," she agonized.

The Abbot grew dark. "The one you cut with the Canadians?"

"If the angel doesn't show by Tuesday move Grandma out too—and have her fire policy paid up."

To the stony silence at the other end, in broken words Guin confided, "I'm sorry, Provost, I truly am, but it was either her house . . . or daddy's."

At half past the hour Deacon Matthias' tired baritone crackled through the box hanging from the iron-gate: "Welcome to The ROMAR. How may we assist you?"

Jaxy ran the van window down and pushed the "talk" button. "Large coffee. Sugar, two creams."

The Deacon said something not to be repeated outside confession and put the Californian in a five-minute timeout to reflect on what it meant to be the biggest one in Washington before creeping the gate as slow as it would go.

This gave Jaxy time to prepare for the sell job of his life. Unaccustomed to taking scotch straight from the bottle, he plugged his nose, opened his throat, and gulped the remainder down, chasing the woody taste with the pilsner. Then having found the perfect place from The Best of George Jones, he boosted the speakers and patted the dash saying, "Okay, Moby, strut your stuff." Down the drive he shimmy-shook in low, timing it so that when he passed by the Cafe window, from the depths of his lovesick soul he howled, "If drinking don't keeeell me—her memory will."

To the garage Jaxy sashayed without mashing a single tree, from where he spied Philip's surfer hair in the mudroom light. For the finale he went face down over a branch to make a snow angel, then staggered his way to the main house, munching on peanuts and spitting out the shells.

"Back by supper? It's almost midnight!" Father Photios pressed the grey cassock with fidgety fingers. "Did you get lost?"

"Easy to do. Roads here all look the same. Should do something about that," Jaxy belched a piquant bouquet.

"Pew! Jaxy, you've been drinking!"

More exhausted than inebriated, Jaxy recounted his daytrip to the Columbia River. "You know, the hatchery makes a killer cappuccino."

"I'll keep it in mind."

"From there I drove on to a monument for some Chinook princess hitched to a chieftain that didn't impress her. So, she fixed the sitch' by jumping off that big ol' rock into the river with her baby!" Jaxy yawned. "Now *that's* love, father."

"It is?" the Archimandrite didn't follow.

Jaxy forged ahead with his authoritative ramble, "Do you know that the howling winds at night are the lost cries for her one, true brave?"

The archimandrite twirled a finger to speed it up.

"Up and down the gorge she goes! But chu-know what?" Jaxy paused for dramatic effect.

"What."

"She never finds him."

After a pause the Archimandrite said, "Well, I'm glad you didn't go in after her."

"Almost did! Because I couldn't stop thinking about poor Jillian in that awful storm with her wee one and I wanted to lay down and die too! But instead, father, I did the right thing."

"Do tell."

"And found a sweet, little sports bar and watched hockey to take her off my mind. Guess I lost track of time," Jaxy trailed off, growing drowsy.

"And how many you drank!"

"Only had one . . . , no make that . . . Hey! Does anyone know if the Rangers won?"

"You're a lost soul."

"That hurts but makes me think. Ever hear of that Indian maiden—."

"Yes!" The room shouted as the cuckoo jumped out to announce midnight.

"Holy humbucker!" Jaxy realized the time, "it was ten when . . ."

"Precisely, Jaxy! What happened after the Totum Pole?" the Archimandrite pushed the story along.

Jaxy pulled close, shifting from side to side. "Ever watch the *X-Files*?"

Photios poked his chest, "As I imagined. You're an alien."

"Wait! I got it. It grew stuffy inside, so I went out for air and heard Princess Who-zee-wat calling me to follow, and we slid 'round and around till it came pouring down to bury us under at least fifty feet of—."

"Stop right there! *We* slid? Buried *us*?"

Jaxy thought long on that before saying, "Yes . . . we did."

"Who was with you?"

"Not a living soul."

"But you said 'we'."

"Arrr! Me and Mowbly," spake Jaxy in pirate talk.

"Who's Mowbly?"

Jaxy spread his arms wide with exasperation, "You know! Dick—

the whale!"

"Enough!" Father shutdown the arcane rantings of a wet brain. "No more of your pickled hallucinations! Now to bed with you—and quit cryin' about Jillian."

As Jaxy hit the bare mattress he could scarcely believe that for once he had controlled the narrative and pulled it off. After a life of confusion over how people, without batting an eye, could say one thing and mean another, he finally understood that it's not the conservation of angular momentum, but the liberal dispensing of malarkey that makes the rockin' world go around.

CHAPTER 54

St. Maximos Church, Minnehaha, WA
8:00 a.m. Monday, January 8

From the terra cotta hallway Rory gave a crisp greeting, shut the church office door securely behind him, and took the tufted camelback opposite the parish priest.

"Captain Avlonz'—good morning! Terrible tings happen. How you holding up?" welcomed Fr. Michael as he fished around the desk drawer.

"On top where I can see them," Rory directed a suppressor-equipped SIG Sauer at Fr. Michael's chest.

"No bang-bangs in Church, okay?" Fr. Michael disregarded the danger, pulled out his pipe, and aimed the stem at Rory. "Puts away! Obviously you come for something, so shooting me before you get that something does no good."

Rory holstered the gun. "You know what I want."

"Yackzy." Fr. Michael lit the bowl.

"I know where he went. He'll keep."

"Then why Klickitat Sheriff no capture. Hmm?" Fr. Michael blew a neat circle around Rory's face.

"Because Klickitat Sheriff don't have 'Find A Mo-Fo' on his phone. You have Jillian. I want her. *Where is she?*" Rory waved off the smoke.

"Try Colorado?"

"The authorities have, for all intents, taken up residence at the Anders, while my father-in-law looks for a new line of work. Try harder."

"Shush! Ladies overhear deal."

"Not bartering for what's mine you nincompoop."

"You drop in empty-handed to call me neencompoops?"

"I am not," Rory peeled back his jacket, "empty-handed."

"Ever hear of Greek Civil War?"

"Christ. Where can I find fresh coffee around here?" Rory unscrewed the lid from his travel cup and emptied the grounds into the Ficus.

Fr. Michael yelled down the hall, "Amelia!! Two espressos!"

"Said, 'coffee'."

The priest tamped the ash and continued his yarn, "It was terrible! Like General Sherman on Atlanta. Entire villages level in single day and if you live in mountains? Tings worse. One day soldiers take my aunties and uncles and line them against wall, and if no switch sides? They shoots and dumps 'em down well!"

"Land it, Klapakis."

"All perish but mama," Fr. Michael dabbed an eye.

"Don't like traitors," said Rory.

"Mama no traitor. She one tough lady and climb up hole to take revenge and a leetle something off that dead Albanian. A guardian angel with twelve blue sapphires—one for each aunt and uncle. Like fool I kept it for years right here on shelf until one day—."

"My wife dopped in." Rory produced the guardian angel from his vest pocket.

"You—you have it?" Fr. Michael fumbled his pipe.

Rory retracted the pendant. "Your acting is worse than your syntax."

Fr. Michael set his jaw and cleaned the pipe while the coffees were served. Alone again, he continued, "See, your wife borrowed it to wear to some wedding, then put me on spot saying she give it back if I help hide her from cops. But then say she no have—that she give to you! Make me so mad."

"Hide where?—and don't use that confession line on me."

"Inferior ones circulate, so before I agree to a trade let us make certain this angel is mine," insisted Fr. Michael to an inspection. Together they viewed the date and inscription under a microscope. Then handing it back the priest concluded the meeting by saying, "Tank you, Rory. We have deal."

FOR THE FIRST TIME since facing her orals, Golly Gee couldn't sleep. Until now British Columbia's Combined Forces Special Enforcement Unit had treated the Eleemosynary Beaver Colony like any other society of benevolent varmints, but the winds of change had upset the apple cart. Recent trips made by Jaxy Thrie to Canada and Las Vegas were open to scrutiny. To top it off, on the heels of the Avlon marital implosion came her sister's rapid rise to fame, and it was not impossible for her adversary to breakaway and lead the pack by July.

To attain to this Jillian had banded with Jaxy to bushwhack and torture her righthand man Yan for vital, Beaver intel. As the Lodge leader she had to contain this security breach or lose the respect of former Stasi double agent Sergeant Pantzer whose experience and sway on continental Europe she prized. This made Golly Gee sad. Sad for having to deep-six the one person with enough chutzpah to insult her butter tarts. Someone who could find her funny bone and make her laugh. The only man to make her go weak at the knees. This paradox made Jaxy Thrie a liability. One she had to eradicate at once, and in a way so decisive and graphic as to solidify alliances and make enemies quake in fear.

But where did he go?

A van of those proportions would be hard to conceal without assistance. Find it—find Jaxy. Increased activity in the vicinity of Totum gave rise to suspicion. The sighting of him at the watering hole clinched it. State troopers would soon choke the byways with checkpoints. She had to move fast on cross-country mountain roads.

Over a night of tossing and turning on a haystack—the preferred choice of bedding for a quick mop-up of spilled blood—Golly enacted how the death scene would play out in the Organic Farms barn. But when push came to shove would she follow through? She had wished to offload the responsibility as Klav's to address, but while a whiz with numbers, in the field the man was a complete tool. In contrast, her more seasoned assassins had grown so petrified of Rockabilly's reputation she couldn't rely on them either. But whichever way she spun it, to retain Tank Pantzer's trust she could not get around hand delivering the fatal blow herself, face to face, while having sweaty sex.

That was the shittiest part of all.

And thus, soughing like the Little Red Hen, Golly torqued the oil drain plug, topped-off the sidecar reservoir, and pulled her chaps up by the straps to go do the whack job herself.

CHAPTER 55

The ROMAR, Totum, WA
9:00 a.m. Monday, January 8

But for a jar of instant coffee crystals, the Abbot had swept the trailer clean, shoving Jaxy's guitar under the chapel scaffolds when the Sheriff of Klickitat came knocking. So, skipping his Café Matthias wake-up cup, Jaxy stayed in, drank Folgers, and read how Russian life sucked in the First World War.

In 1914 the European pot of stew known as the Balkans had a meltdown. Ruled by the Austro-Hungarian court, Archduke Franz Ferdinand would soon replace his aging uncle Joseph at the helm with a "shared power" proposal unpopular with both the Austrians and their southern subjects. To extend goodwill to the disenfranchised, the Archduke paid a visit to the Bosnian capital where, while waving to the multitude that lined the streets, a factious Serb chucked a "welcome to Sarajevo" bomb at the limo. The alert chauffeur hit the gas and it bounced off the trunk taking out the trailing car. Later that day, the same driver neglected to exit the city by an alternate route giving the insurgents a second chance. This time the "Black Hand" didn't miss.

Twenty-twenty hindsight is better, so they say, and had Tsar Nicholas II foreseen the frightful toll, he might have reconsidered leaving the locals to slug it out. The Balkan Peninsula, however, was no tract of rural hamlets and fishing villages, but a proud cadre of nations the size of Texas fortified by forty million strong with military and religious ties to Mother Russia that harkened to the days of Byzantium. The Hapsburgs of Austria knew this but took the gamble, and by declaring war on Serbia they, in effect, did so on the Tsar.

Unprepared to mount a major offensive, Nicholas II preferred an immediate and peaceful resolution and persuaded the Serbs they should want the same and bend to Austria's demands. Not getting the fight he expected, Franz Joseph rebuffed the white flags hanging from the Belgrade windows, for he wanted just deserts for the regicide, and he wanted it now! The next day cannonballs flew over the blue Danube and Russia mobilized.

Not content to sit and watch his good friend to the south get waxed, and eager to try out his new boats, tanks, and biplanes, Wilhelm Kaiser of Germany did the neighborly thing and declared war on Moscow. Landlocked and blockaded with factories on strike, a pathetic railway, and ministers and generals who couldn't agree, Nicholas II made do with the munitions and supplies at his disposal. The one thing he had no shortage of was foot soldiers, yet his steamroller of fifteen million could not gain mastery over German tactical superiority. Warsaw fell and the fight spilled onto Russian soil. As the body count climbed and necessities dwindled, disgruntled workers took to the streets collapsing the government and paving the way for Marxism. In the end, the Tsar's call to arms achieved one strategic goal: it diverted the Kaiser's resources for the Allied Forces to get the upper hand and force the Treaty of Versailles.

While Nicholas addressed the quagmire on the battlefield, his family did so for the wounded at home, and in no small way. His mother, Maria Feodorovna headed the Red Cross, organized charities, and spent endless hours comforting the suffering. His wife, the Empress Alexandra converted the Catherine Palace to a military hospital and stewarded eighty-five other infirmaries around Petrograd. His daughters, Olga and Tatiana rolled up their sleeves as "Sisters of Mercy" to sterilize surgical tools and assist at the operating tables nursing the worst kinds of injuries, amputations, and extractions.

Too young for this type of exposure, the little ones, Marie and Anastasia, took turns at bedsides, playing board games and reading to infantry on the mend. To the graves of those who did not pull through they took flowers on days so frigid and through snow so deep that even the stoutest of heart wouldn't have braved a walk to the corner store, much less versts to honor the fallen at a national cemetery . . .

The cowbell clanged. Jaxy looked up from the book—12 o'clock!

Through the pantry he slunk to the end of the bread line, but the Archimandrite marched him to the fore where the lectionary stood opened and waiting. In quiet attention the order dined on beans and rice while Jaxy read to them the life and times of a fifth century, Carthaginian pagan who sailed for Constantinople, whereupon seeing the error of her ways repented like a champ. After the monks filed out to their routines, they brought Jaxy a cold bowl of beans along with a bucket and sponge, and orders to scrub the bathroom.

"Nobody loves me, everybody hates me . . ." lowed Jaxy, spooning down lunch and jotting prose into a spiralbound notebook. On a full stomach the poet laureate then tackled Photios' grimy tub, signing his name in pencil to the grout. After that he went for his guitar.

Drew caught up on the trail. "Jax'! Where you going?"

"Get Daisy."

"Chapel's closed when the 'arteests' are at work."

The door opened and Brother Jean beckoned them anyway. Up the scaffolds the Mute clambered with an enlarged photograph to the space on the wall reserved for five youthful figures bunched around two adults. As he went, Jean made light marks to balance the scene with a soft, measuring cloth.

"I scrubbed the tub," Jaxy said to the Archimandrite who knelt on the tiles below, transferring profiles onto a gridded sheet.

Past a cold shoulder, the Archimandrite spoke to Drew, "It's traditional to stand the parents in back and order their offspring by age in front. But the bishop wants them positioned as posed, so seat them we will."

"When will it be done?" asked Jaxy.

Without a word Fr. Photios went back to his work.

In a more conciliatory frame of mind Drew answered, "To showcase by July. But now Abba wants more down the sides for a special surprise."

"Four more to 'kiss up'," said the Archimandrite, spreading out vellums of the additional historic scenes with annotations to document the saint's lives.

"Wrong. Wrong. Wrong," asserted Jaxy.

The Archimandrite's neck strained with fury. Drew waited for the shootout to commence. Brother Jean floated above the fray.

"I mean it. It's all wrong!" Jaxy brazenly struck out the name "Marie" from the Sister of Mercy at a hospital sickbed and wrote in "Olga", and changed the name of the other to "Tatiana" rectifying: "Marie and Anastasia were too young to work in surgery, and Tatiana had dark hair so that's got to be her."

"When did you become the expert?" Drew dropped the peacemaking act.

"Do your research. If I'm wrong, I'll eat my beans from the deacon's hat," Jaxy said with confidence, and bidding the iconographers a good day, took his guitar, and walked out.

On a milk stool by the rippling waters of Coppice Creek, Jaxy put the finishing touches to the lyrics going between notepad and guitar. He plugged in, tuned the strings, and wishing he had Portnoy playing harp and Pinetop on keys, warmed things up at a walking pace backed by the percussion of the brook.

Monastery Bean Eatin' Blues

Refrain: *I got the nobody loves me, everybody hates me, going to the garden boo-hoos. (Choir: He's got the nobody loves him, everybody hates him, going to the garden boo-hoos.) I got the nobody loves me, monastery bean eatin' blues . . .*

Verse: *The life of poverty and the community way ain't for everyone, that's a fact . . . The only thing you own is the shirt on your back, you can wear anything you want, as long as it's long and it's black . . . I got the nobody loves me monastery bean eatin' blues.*

The snap of a twig distracted him. Jaxy preferred to create alone, but if the Mute couldn't hear what did it matter? So, he bridged into a guitar solo, full of soul and sorrow, ending with a crescendo and a bow to his audience of one. The monk returned the bow, and then retraced his steps to the chapel to carry on with his own masterpiece.

Under a clement sun Jaxy spread his coat over a cobblestone swale to bask in the rays. Soon after, Drew joined in a chipper mood carrying a picnic basket. "Nice catch, Jaxy! You won't have to eat from the Deacon's hat after all."

"Wow! He certainly went the extra mile!" Jaxy extolled the monster club with hickory cheese, candied nuts, and cranberries.

"Matti? Na, he's a cook. Could feed an army with two loaves and a fish, but Father Arsenios? He's a chef."

"Where *do* they get their names?" Jaxy asked with mild amusement.

"To Father Arsenios!" Drew held up his sandwich.

"Many years!" hurrahed Brother Philip approaching from the barn, and knotting his surfer hair in a bun added, "Arsenios oversees the Organic Farms food processing."

"Doesn't it grow old? Work all day—pray all night."

Brother Philip took a seat on the stool and noting the guitar replied, "Sweating out days in a furniture warehouse and nights in beer halls. Doesn't that? For my troubles I get three hots, a cot, and a cat. Can't beat that."

"Unless you're fasting," said Drew.

"Beats falling down over a log," remarked Brother Philip.

Jaxy chewed with his mouth closed.

The monk let up. "Sorry Jax', you owe no explanation, but before you leave this joint, you might try something that works for me."

Not receptive to unsolicited advice, Jaxy shut his eyes as well.

"Instead of singing the blues write out what you want most besides the Ducks bringing home the Stanley Cup and put it in a 'God Box'."

"You're talking to America's most sought-after man. What's left after that?" asked Drew.

"And when you're ready, share it with someone," finished Philip.

"Smells like confession," sniffed Jaxy.

"Or put a match to it and let the smoke carry it to heaven," the monk advanced a more palatable alternative.

On a torn, half page Jaxy wrote in bold, block letters: "I WANT MY ANGEL BACK!"

"Thar she blows again," said Drew, and settled into a nap.

CHAPTER 56

Sunshine Coast Highway, B.C.
10:00 a.m. Monday, January 8

The zebra-striped Ural trekked southbound on the Sunshine Coast Highway behind a lumbering line of cars in no hurry to make Hopkins Landing. At a window in traffic, the rugged, big-bore, backcountry bike jumped into the oncoming lane to pass eight vehicles in as many seconds. The sidecar nobbies didn't touch pavement until it reached the last gas bar in Gibson.

On the open road Golly Gee could concentrate. Dance let her escape the kerfuffle in her head. Riding helped sort it out. As much as her labor force despised the annual ethics refresh when they counted off in fives to role-play dilemmas in the workplace, followed by an impossible, on-line quiz which they had to take and retake until they scored a perfect twenty to renew their assassins' license, it kept things clean. Abiding by the Beaver code of conduct fostered respect at home, and on the frontline safeguarded them from entanglements with a mark.

Since Golly kept men at arm's length never had she given thought to how thorny BL218 conformance could be until dormant feelings of her own awoke. To fend them off she asked the hard question: Could Jaxy *be* Rat Catcher? Tank, called the courier "infinitely worse", but what could be more reprehensible than the Siberian ogre who murdered her father and left her orphaned to sex traffickers? By Seattle, Golly had forced open the rotten, boarded prepubescent memories of being sold at both ends by adults to whom she looked for protection—painful vignettes from a bruised and confused child, overpowered and constrained until release came and she went catatonic. For each repugnant scene the contemptable fiend would pay, one machined thread at a time.

And yes, she could, and should have waxed Jaxy at the mansion as Tank maintained, but Golly restrained for he had yet to act outside and against corporate interest. For the privilege of screwing her brains out she would now return the favor with an auger bit through his and write it off as an investment loss over a messy misunderstanding.

It had been this way all her days. What the family outcast saw as necessary evil to surmount life's obstacles, others saw as pure, plain evil. Instead of the competent one, the Romanov Guild wanted the decent one to seize the dynastic ring. Didn't they get it?—Golly's pulse quickened as the two-wheel drive left the paved roads for the gummy, mountain hairpins—nice boys and girls may cross the line first in the Kingdom of God, but they bring up the rear everywhere else! Nicholas and Alexandra bore that out. They say the Tsar hooped the crown through poor selection of ministers, mishandling the war, unaddressed labor unrest, consorting with shady characters, and so on. For sure none of this helped, but the indisputable weak link broke long before the war when he lost the populace's confidence because he commanded no *fear*, granting amnesty to enemies of state and hiding out on his yacht, fretting over the future when he should have stayed home in charge of the present! Nicholas II didn't go down with the ship—he sank it. Had Marx and Lenin not come along other ideologues would, as well they should, Golly adjudicated. Not because Vladimir Ilyich was the greatest thing since iced Smirnoff, but because Nicholas Alexandrovich couldn't squelch a rebellion, let alone squash a bug.

These were, of course, Golly Gee's impressions that in the end meant little. For come July the cameras would find her in Red Square, front and center at St. Basil's Cathedral leading the chorus, "Wise Nicholas and blest Alexandra, we praise you . . ."

CHAPTER 57

Pittock Mansion Portland, OR
12:00 p.m. Monday, January 8

Beneath the outstretched boughs of a mossy oak, Guin Hill sat at a Pittock Mansion park table trying to find Mt. Adams on the horizon. A white, wooly husky strained at the master's leash to see if she would spare a bite of cornbread. Guin broke off a corner for the sweet mooch, then had the vista to herself until a ponderous police sergeant showed up in a double breasted peacoat to block the view.

"Vandervelt . . . or do you prefer, 'Rose'?" Tank Pantzer filled the sagging bench.

"Either, or," Guin slid over a legal size manilla folder and a letter of introduction. "Thank you for meeting. My client sends his salutations from Kansas City, Missouri."

Pantzer consumed the juridical jargon, taking in the slinky gloves and N.A.F.R.A badge, black eyeliner, nose ring, and the "MAID OF ORLEANS" tattoo on her neck. "Solid work. Concise . . . thorough," he began.

Guin gushed smiling with hands in her lap and knees together.

"But headhunting is illegal in my town. Mr. Lovorsky should have thought about that before sending you here with that popgun in your purse."

"May he not seek fair and just compensation for the defamatory damages inflicted upon his enterprise as long as I don't interfere or engage the suspect?"

"Hell, I got everyone from gangsters to baristas interfering with my job, so yeah. Why not an antique store, what's one more? But something else bothers me," Sergeant Pantzer angled his bifocals down across his face as he poured over her resume.

"Excuse me?" Guin leaned forward.

"Says you were Valedictorian at Pepperdine School of Law. Commenced with Honors from the Catalina Academy of Crime Scene Investigation as a Fugitive Recovery Specialist. And, as a registered lifeguard, you snorkel and play polo."

"Starting wing all three years," bragged Guin.

"Then you would have the latest gizmos in shallow water rescue."

"Certainly. But strictly for work. Not recreation."

He straightened the page. "Then why not dive for the body yourself?"

"Put a third bounty on the marine captain and watch me somersault."

Tank Pantzer wore a disappointed look. "You're smart, Rose, but nothing next to that Glendale Commissioner. She'd say in the absence of new and forthcoming evidence, the waterlogged Mountie would have to float first, forcing Rory to skip. Then she'd go after him."

"To make that happen, the esteemed council would then tell the division sergeant where to look and leak it to the press," she brushed the folder.

Tank's visage greyed as his lips sank into his triple chin, puffing out his cheeks. Then coming to a decision, contracted Rose Vandervelt to conduct the reclamation and penned three figures on a slip—one for bringing up Yan, one for bringing in Rory, and his own private line.

"Normally I wouldn't negotiate with an attorney for a candy bar, hear me? But based on the statement that you extracted from Rita Klinnick," Tank tapped Guin's report, "I may have made a bad call on your fiancé, and you deserve a consideration. Keep an eye on your six and your hand by your purse—you're not the only woman gunning for the man that killed Yan."

Guin unclipped the bothersome nose pin and asked, "How did you guess?"

Tank pushed a pair of cuffs across the table. "I intended these for you to wear, not keep, but a prominent judge called worried sick I'd put his daughter up for the night. Have a nice swim, Guinevere."

CAPTAIN RORY AVLON HAD no intention of walking into an ambush. Thus, he gave the sneaky Greek thirty-six hours to produce Jillian at the monastery. This would give the marine a full day to learn the lay of the land, the buildings, the entrances and exits, and to number and know the Royal Martyr's platoon of monks from a safe distance. At a sporting goods store Rory stocked up on rations, an outdoor magazine, a birdwatcher's guide, and rifle cartridges to make his Mt. Adams camping adventure as pleasant as possible. By late afternoon he descended the six percent grade that ended at the wilderness north of the Organic Farms apple orchard to explore an unimproved parking area for day-use convenient to the monastery. A wide spot on the roadway with room for six cars and bounded by a tight ring of trees too narrow for the Bronco to work behind, as a base of operations it felt too exposed. Rory looked across the highway to an unkept, dirt road that led into a scraggy field of sedge and foxtail poking through the smattering of snow. Disregarding the "No Hunting" and "No Trespassing" signs, Rory finished off the tequila and pitched the empty down the berm to a cattle guard from where the trail looped toward the rim of a volcanic bowl cropping out over the lowlands.

A drainage ditch cut through the pasture, spanned by a ramshackle bridge with gaps in the roof and decking. A few hundred yards beyond, Rory peeled off the beaten track to crawl up a funnel wash to where the Bronco topped out over the saddle. Down the south facing scarp he established his position in the boscage over Totum Valley. He scoped the twenty-minute trek to the monastery and saw that it presented no difficulty to a fit outdoorsman of his ilk. With two jerrycans lashed to the bumper, Rory had fuel aplenty to run the heater, so he idled the engine and tuned in to an alarming update: Divers had spent the day dragging the river bottom under the Sellwood Bridge! He understood why Brad bowed out, but his friend would never give him up. The police had spliced it together some other way.

The radio show went on to regular scheduled programming of adrift and angry songs inspiring Rory to open his wallet to that Janus-faced backstabber he once called "sweetheart". He put Jillian's picture away and started for a new bottle but stayed his hand. Fortunate to have gotten free of the bedlam he created at the Totum Pole with no one recognizing his bashed face, his run of luck would end soon if he continued that way. So, instead of more tequila, he took up his field gear for a looksee.

Onto the bluffs Rory climbed for a top view of the Royal Martyrs Monastery, then down into the huckleberry meadow he slunk like a fox to the main gate taking distances and heights with a sextant as he went. By sundown he had an excellent description of the complex and a fair estimate of the Abbot's workforce. The workday over, Rory settled into the Bronco and a box of protein bars. A breaking news bulletin interrupted an otherwise dozy afternoon of grunge. A logbook had washed up in the wetlands from which lab techs reconstructed references made by the Mountie to a stolen Fabergé medallion confiscated from Jaxy days before the murder and attested by airport eyewitnesses. The investigation now included revenge as a motive, as a consortium of assassins had stolen the Guardian Angel of Maria Feodorovna from a museum to sell on the black market in support of the *raison d'être* to resurrect Soviet communism in Eastern Europe. The striking similarity of Jillian Avlon to composites of their seldom seen, drop-dead gorgeous mob queen catapulted the WWA Cowgirl to the most-wanted-in-extremis with a new price on her heinous head of a cool, five million.

And Jack? With no mention of him in the radio broadcast, melted down he had to be worth at least ten bucks. Yet beneath the surface of that dippy, hipster act swam a barracuda, well established in a corrupt and dangerous organization, and, as Rory firsthand twice witnessed, escape artist nonpareil. And what about that white elephant the Captain carried in his vest pocket? Without the right connection he could do with it little than bust out the sapphires and sell them piecemeal, which even to Rory seemed blasphemous. He could send it back to the museum using the monastery for the return address, or more fun still, sneak it into Klapakis' office for him to justify in court how his "mama's" angel found its way into a Prince Albert can!

More possibilities then appeared. Instead of exacting violent revenge, why not do it in a civil way and cash in? If Rory could bag and tag them with the famous Fabergé, like in his Marine heyday, he'd be the hero! With good representation, his sentence for getting swept up in a gang war, and the slaying in self-defense of a gun packing, Canadian dope peddler could be commuted, if not dismissed altogether!

Rory lowered the news, smiling anew upon his wife's picture. "I see you helped yourself to more than pastries at the family reunion, babe. What else did you bring home from Denmark?"

CHAPTER 58

The ROMAR, Totum, WA
4:00 p.m. Monday, January 8

The sanitized story of the martyr's final hour, recorded in scrolled gold at the Romanov shrine, missed what transpired at the Ipatiev House by a mile. Of the caps that rebounded. Of the barbaric stabbings on the basement floor. Of the mashed skulls, smashed teeth, and torn limbs. Of the acid bathed and fire-scorched body parts haphazardly dumped into a mineshaft that led a distinguished archeologist, who over the course of her anthropological career had unearthed many a savage site to say: "I had never seen such violation—it made me ill."

Jaxy put the book up. He couldn't read on.

The surfer monk's settling voice called from outside. "Taking flowers to Camille. Want to ride along?"

"I'm grounded."

Through the trailer door the brother passed a pair of baggy work-stained dungarees. "Abbot say's it's okay if you wear these. I'll help with the beard."

Jaxy stepped back from the monk's, clean-shaven, swashbuckling new look. "Whoa—watch out Zac Efron!"

Brother Philip kneaded spirit gum into Jaxy's whiskers to stick snipped tresses to the Rockabilly's face. "I learned this from a makeup channel. Hold still . . . let not your heart be troubled . . . I practiced on Drew."

Slate skies portended the coming of a new storm, but Brother Philip had not a care, for foul weather or fair mattered not to a monk with a cat, three hots, and a cot. "You'll meet some nice folk tonight, so what should you go by?" he asked as they turned into St. Maximos Church.

"Mason's my middle name," Jaxy played with the straggly tufts glued to his cheeks that didn't go too well with his mop pulled tight into a painter's cap.

"Nah, how about Max. Like the church, and it rhymes with Jax',"

"How about I stay in the truck." Jaxy spun the bill around.

Brother Philip repeated "Max" while slipping a worse for wear London Fog over a blue shirttail hanging out black jeans. Jaxy hid behind dark, bug-eye fit-overs and trolled along to a Sunday school wing where a handful of men congregated on the covered walk by a rusty can.

"Hey, slick! How's it on the holy hill?" one gave a thumbs up to the monk's neat mien.

"Divine," Brother Philip handed Jaxy off, "Ace meet Max."

Ace took over, "Getting a kick-start at the monastery?"

"Might say," said Jaxy, shucking like a bum straight off Lincoln Avenue.

"How long?"

"Four days—seems like forever."

Ace fanned the resins from Jaxy's neck. "It gets better."

"Doubt that . . . Phil?" Jaxy checked around, but the brother in street clothes had gone off with the hothouse flowers. "What's going on?"

"Didn't he tell you? We're friends of Bill," Ace muscled the newcomer into a choking warm classroom to take a seat crammed around a buckled and stained foldout table with a spritely crowd for a

Monday night with no football.

"Welcome to Professor Langley's Flying Machine Men's Meeting of Alcoholics Anonymous. My name is Ace and I'm an Alcoholic," began the leader when the hand ticked the top of the hour.

"Hi Ace" everyone voiced.

Thoroughly regretting his falling-down-over-a-log act, Jaxy hoped to course correct in one session without the need for a follow-up. Years had passed since he had accompanied his dad to a similar gathering in the park on Saturdays for the promise of a cupcake. The thing that stood out in his mind was the way sober alkies turned on a dime into sticklers with time, never starting late or ending early. At the conclusion of a lengthy reading Jaxy looked over to the clock above a literature rack that wobbled whenever the door opened and shut with a bang.

7:02.

To sit it out in the butt-numbing cold held less appeal, so in his chair he stayed, avoiding eye contact by staring into a foam cup of store grind coffee. As a last resort, Jaxy turned to his Higher Power for a citywide, grid failure which he knew would go unheard, like his many invocations for the Ducks.

The door opened and Fr. Michael beckoned him outside.

His prayer had been heard!

In the breezeway Jaxy thumbed, "Are you . . .?"

"Me? No. I'm what they call 'friend'. Sorry, I meant to catch you before meeting start."

Jaxy bit into a mint cookie. "And I thought you held back on purpose, so I'd be overjoyed to see you."

"I wish this such happy occasion," the priest showed Jaxy to his office, and there sat Guin and Helen.

Jaxy did a one-eighty. "I think they want me at the stag meeting."

Fr. Michael shut the door, trapping him inside.

"An explanation is in order then," said Jaxy, with a weak smile.

"Save it for the trip home," Guin lipped off.

"Easy does it," Fr. Michael intervened to focus on the immediate need: His encounter with Rory and the timeframe within which they had to work. Since Rory had pinpointed the monastery hideout, Booker would now fly Jaxy and Jillian out of harm's way to Colorado. Fr. Michael would then invite Rory to the ROMAR and into the long arm of the law.

Dr. Leshenko opposed the plan as overly simplistic, having too many variables, and fraught with peril to the peaceable monks who had risked enough already.

Beyond this, counseled Guin, she had yet to pull Yan from the river to support Rita Klinnick's story and pin the murder on Rory. Without that Sergeant Pantzer was hamstrung.

"Can I say something?" Jaxy seized the opportunity.

"No!" everyone shouted and went on to dis him as if he were not there.

Guin insisted they stick with her initial plan. "Dad can rope a puptent within a short morning's walk from the bridge where boloney butt will lay low as bait. As soon as I bring up the body, I'll tip off the press of a Jaxy sighting while Tank waits for Rory to make his move!"

"By Dog Park?" Helen backchatted with Guin.

"He'd fit right in," they laughed together.

"No," said Jaxy.

Guin's eyes reached to her ears. "Excuse me?"

"I'll camp anywhere you say *in the van*, but not on the cold, wet ground."

"You will camp where I say."

Again Fr. Michael refereed, "Let's find safe place for him to bunk tonight and resume with clear heads in the morning."

"Not safe bunking with me," said Guin, grazing on the candy dish.

"Yackzy wore out his welcome at the ROMAR, and he no stay here," the priest checked off the options in a room of sober contemplation under the boisterous singing of "Happy Birthday" floating in from the Sunday school room.

Without thinking it through, Helen broke the silence: "I know! He can sleep on the *Q-P Doll*!"

Jellybeans flew everywhere.

TO THE PARKING LOT emptied of meeting goers, Camille carried a pink, bakery box sealed tighter than Fort Knox intended for Brother Philip, but the monk had already gone for Tex-Mex with his chums in recovery, so she pushed it on Helen. "It's what's left of Phil's five-year cake made of low-fat, Swiss cocoa."

"Matushka, it's still not calorie free." Helen patted her tummy.

"Not you—for Aldo! Shussh. It's our secret. I've been counting points longer than him, but you can't tell."

"I'll take no part in this treachery. They need me at the hospital."

Camille would not let up on her mission to sneak a piece of chocolate decadence into the monastery when Jaxy came ambling along. "But how will Mason get back?"

"Who is Mason?" asked Helen.

With a wink, Jaxy took the cake and responsibility by saying, "Doctor, let's go! Don't want to miss compline two nights in a row."

From far down the classroom wing, the A.A. leader's voice rang out, "Keep coming back Max—it gets better!"

"Who's Max?" asked Camille.

"And what gets better?" followed up Helen, transferring her golf clubs to the trunk to make room for cake.

"Let's hope the coffee," replied Jaxy, wedging the cakebox in the seat behind.

Jaxy settled into the surgeon's turbo Saab where "HP" stood for horsepower, and away they purred to the *Q-P Doll*. When Helen signaled for the cutoff he reached over to nudge the wheel toward state 14, and on went her stink face.

"My guitar. I need it," said Jaxy in an off-handed way, as if requisitioning a convenience store run.

"Can't you get by a single night without?" Dr. Leshenko blinkered anyway.

"Your golf bag goes everywhere with you."

"I don't *sleep* with it," she decelerated into the turn.

Jaxy unhooked his belt, preparing to make the jump.

Helen child-safe locked the doors and up the ramp she zoomed.

"Doctor, please. The Gretsch guitar isn't the issue. There's something far more important in Totum I left behind."

"We told you Jillian went to the monastery because you are *never, ever* going back!" Helen sped down the fast lane.

Snapped Jaxy, "Did I say 'monastery', Helen? Did I?? But does anyone pay attention? No! Not ever, because I'm only good at music trivia and dumpster diving for French fries."

Helen tapped the brakes and powered on her emergency sat phone. "Peace. Tell me and I'll have Aldo send this essential item down immediately."

"He won't have the slightest notion where to look."

"For crying out loud, Jaxy! What on earth did you leave behind in the town of Totum, so vital to the plan, that we must go and bring back tonight, in my car???"

With a crooked smile Jaxy said, "Yan."

After Helen tired of using Jaxy's head for a boxer's speed bag, it took little to convince her they should cart the rotting corpse to Sellwood in the van, so on to Totum and the theme of the Spring golf tournament they moved. To a starving Rockabilly, sponsoring her at ten dollars a cup sounded generously steep, but ungratefully cheap to a doctor that had gone out on a limb to save said Rockabilly's life. With the assurance they would immortalize his name in a clay-fired fellowship hall brick, Jaxy said he'd go halves with Brother Phil. He then asked for ideas on golf equipment. The voice of experience recommended that for ease of use and smart looks on the fairway, he pony-up for a deluxe bag on wheels, stretch trousers, and quality gloves and spikes, but to go middle of the road on clubs and buy used balls in bulk. After adding up the escalating costs for this new hobby they'd sucked him in, Jaxy reached back to dig a thumbnail into the heavily taped, baker's box.

"Stay out!" Helen slapped his hand adding, "You're as bad as Drew."

"It's picked over, A.A. birthday cake, Helen."

"Men," Helen made her classic face. "Bottom feeders to the last one."

Jaxy peeled back the tape, raised the flap, took one eye-popping look, and shut it tight saying, "You're right. Camille arranged it just so. Shouldn't mess it up. But if we have time, I'd like to share a piece with the Abbot."

With Helen's consent he rested his tired head on the door with the pink box balanced on his knees. A care package that indeed contained a square of delicious, Swiss chocolate cake sealed inside an airtight food container alongside a stack of ladies' slacks, polo shirts, balled up My Little Pony knee socks, and a beaded, silver jewelry box atop size seven bikini briefs, fanned out in decorative pink, white, and blue.

Jaxy almost saluted.

CHAPTER 59

Totum Hills, WA
10:00 p.m. Monday, January 8

From the andesitic buttes, a leather-clad figure took in the nightscape nursing a veggie cleansing juice and an aching ankle. Through the tall pines Golly Gee could see the Abbot's chapel—not as stylish as The Church on the Blood, but classy. If he played his cards right, someday he might get a decent relic. She popped her jaw.

By infrared she homed in on a white, hot Saab turning into the large garage by a cargo van, dark from sitting. Attaboy. There you are. Golly mapped her approach and retreat to the mill. Not that she came intending to take Jaxy to the proverbial woodshed—the barn had advantages, hay mainly. However, without warning Sergeant Pantzer called off the boff for reasons that cut no ice with her, and the Booker-Hills could thank her later. Having come too far to leave her past unavenged on the fool who tried to beguile her, there she would lurk until the morning bells when like a jackal in heat she'd lure that mongrel to the shop with her exotic, blue eyes, to open his throat with her exceptionally, white teeth.

With her mind thusly set, Golly gimped like an arthritic cat to the sidecar for her props thinking July couldn't come soon enough, "'cause I'm getting too old for this shit."

JAXY CAME OUT OF a luxuriant golf dream into a greasy garage with Helen shaking his arm from outside the Saab. "We lucked out. Aldo didn't mind the cake, so get the guitar before Pharaoh hardens his heart," she appealed.

"You took it?" Jaxy threw a tantrum, "I said I wanted to!!!"

"The world is so peaceful when you sleep, I hated to wake you. But cheer! The Abbot saved you some." Helen gave Jaxy his portion on a paper plate.

"No thanks!"

"Then prep the van for Yan." The surgeon ousted him from the car with a well-placed poke of the plastic fork.

Mostly mad with himself, Jaxy lined the berth with lawn and leaf bags, then raided the cafe pantry of gloves, towels, cleansers, stick matches and aerosols. On the final round he found the doctor dozing off at the wheel! No time like the present—as Brother Philip liked to say—so Jaxy gently laid the guitar case on the garage floor and slunk off to seek the Abbot's authoritative take on a topic of grave import.

"For Betsy's sake Jaxy, I lock you in and you tunnel out. And when I send you away, you won't leave!" The Abbot stood glowering on the deck.

"I am, I am! I came for my guitar. But since you're up, can we go over something from the other night?" Jaxy walked in uninvited, and going straight for the clubs, waggled the driver between his feet.

"Face it, she's not—."

"Like this?" Jaxy brought the head around. "Every golfer talks as if they are final say, but no two agree. So, before I throw my savings away on Gucci pants and titanium clubs, how much do *you* say a beginner should shell out for a starter rig?"

"Hold that thought," Abba Aldo ducked into the shop.

Alone in the quarters Jaxy looked high and low for the cakebox, taking care not to disturb a thing until he heard a door shut in the adjacent room and felt a draught. Out of time and luck, he foot-wedged a ball down the felt strip. "Hole in one!" he crowed when the Abbot walked in with a Sunday bag of sundry clubs.

"Did you go out?" The Abbot checked the deck.

"No sir! Here the whole time."

"Anyhoo, don't dump a ton of money into the name. Just take these," the Abbot handed Jaxy the half-set of mixed, dinged irons and weathered woods poking from a ratty canvas bag with cheeks bulging of hacked balls and old score cards. "Start with the nine and let up on the grip. Pivot—watch the lamp—that's it. Elbow straight. It's a pendulum, so speed, not strength. *Now* open the face . . ."

Two cups of decaf later, Jaxy completed his lesson and sank into the supple, sofa leather thrilled to learn he had to spend nothing!

"How did it go at Saint Maximos tonight?" asked the Abbot rubbing tired eyes.

"AA? That's one friendly bunch."

"Helen's boat's nice too. If you're concerned." Abba brought their time to a close.

"Mostly for my guitar. Would be hard to replace."

"But not impossible."

"Duane Eddy recorded—."

"'Forty Miles'! I heard."

"I heard Jillian's closer by than that."

"*Was.*"

"Oh? How did she die this time?"

"Adele Anders came for her."

"That'd do it."

"But she'll be back for the scramble and so should you! Till then invest your savings in good instruction. I mean it, you have potential," promoted the Abbot as he walked Jaxy to the deck.

"I'm sponsoring the doctor at ten bucks a hole," Jaxy said.

"That's strokes."

"You're shitting me."

"Would I do that?" The Abbot patted Jaxy's bearded face. "Love the look. Stay dry."

"Yes. You would," thought Jaxy circling the mill to seek a way in, but finding it battened tight for the night he retreated to the trailer to try again at Matins. With an over-the-shoulder look through flocked branches, a tinted glow from the third floor caught his interest. A curvaceous shadow glided behind the curtain.

Jillian!

Taken for a fool for the last time, to the Organic Farms warehouse Jaxy tromped for the roofer's ladder and drug it back to the mill. Up the downspout Jaxy slid the rail, then blowing on his palms for stiction, as a knight errant he ascended to steal back the guardian angel from the fair Rapunzel.

On the now darkened attic he tapped, but no light came on. Jaxy tried raising the window, but it had swelled tight. Prepared for this, he cranked on a long-shanked screwdriver and splintered off two inches of wood with a tremendous crack. The tool spun from his fingers and plummeted to the snow. Not wanting to bring down the Abbot's wrath by breaking the glass, Jaxy collapsed the ladder and returned it. He could not laze about for morning. He had to confront Jillian before she decamped with the medallion. Resetting the ladder against the office cage, Jaxy raised his eyes to the warehouse crossbeams for inspiration and found it.

A smoke detector and a big red bell.

Out to prove there is no faster way to empty a building at night than to stage an unscheduled fire drill, Jaxy allowed Helen her last minute of slumber as he stole into his van for a road flare. Up the ladder he scaled with safety glasses and facemask, bearing a flare taped to the end of his lucky nine iron. He struck the cap, and sparking, dirty sulfur enveloped him as he directed the plume like Lady Liberty straight at the detector.

"CLANG! CLANG! CLANG! CLANG" the alarm shattered the night. Jaxy made for the exit but got spun about in the smoky dark and wound up in the food processing area. Halfway across, the sprinklers kicked in. Gallons of rejuvenating Coppice Creek water drenched him as he leapt into the garage to get hit in the face with more ice water spewing from the scantlings, converting the place into a carwash.

Monks ran hither and yon shouting orders as the Abbot came tearing down in nightclothes to turn his charges out before the barn burned around their hooves. In the effort to save her hair behind a half open umbrella, Helen took no notice of Jaxy as he flew by on his way to the mill where, bursting through the Abbot's quarters a smile the length of the Northwest Passage broke across his face. Not the date he came expecting, her trippy twin he found instead, loafing about in red roller skates and them breezy, motorcycle chaps.

CHAPTER 60

The Abbot's Woodshop, Totum, WA
11:00 p.m. Monday, January 8

By the stroboscopic lights of a ghetto blaster churning out "Hi-Heeled Sneakers", Golly Gee exploded into an artful jam of sensuous shuffles and fluid tricks, gliding and spinning the toolbox around as a performance partner on casters to end upside-down in splits on a structural pole. On the fading note she cartwheeled off to fall with blind faith into the arms of Jaxy.

"Holy humbucker! What is the matter with you?" said Jaxy into the face shield of her motorcycle helmet.

"You didn't like it?" she asked dejected.

"Look around! This is a monastery woodworking shop—not a roller rink. And why are you even here? How did you escape the island?"

"I didn't—not yet. The Beaver Lodge will let me go if bring back the Feodorovna angel. I'll show you my bellybutton piercing, Jaxy and a lot more if you have it. You *do* have it?" Golly Gee pulled herself up by a firm clasp of his fanny pack.

"Yes . . . I do," Jaxy cast an anxious eye about, "Give me a minute."

"That's all you get," Golly Gee cut the conversation short, keeping her crowbar in reach. Men liked to fuck but more than that they liked to talk about it, which is why they never lived to tell their friends what it's like to die in the middle of it.

"Have I told you I'm engaged to be married?" Jaxy fought off her groping hands.

"Not for long!" Golly swung her knees to land seated on the pack with her legs wrapped around his back. She went to undo his belt buckle, but the fanny pack got in the way. Thwarted in this, she stretched high with the crowbar to drive home the point of her call through his coronal suture giving no thought in advance to what might happen when the target isn't fully engaged in rocking the canoe.

"Careful Chaps! You could hurt someone!" Jaxy caught her forearms on the downstroke. The crowbar whirled from her hands and into the metal cabinet with a deafening crash.

Valiantly Golly tried to kick away on the roller skates just as she had when a child, but Jaxy kept the featherweight at arm's length, laughing as cruel grownups always did.

"Are you on speed?" he asked in earnest.

"No!" She flailed. "Put me down!!"

"I know people in Minnehaha that can help with that."

Golly Gee came close to catching his chin with a skate wheel for that transgression, and then stopped struggling to catch her breath for a second try.

"If you're not high then unmask your face and tell me to mine why uninvited, sexual advances on the island or on assignment, are expressly forbidden by corporate ethics standard BL218, revision C, paragraph two point two, or I will lash you to the attic fan until you do,"

"I authored that!"

"Then you know it is grounds for immediate termination," he reminded adding, "and I can push it through tonight."

"No, you can't! I'm the Beaver Lodge C.E.O.!" defied Golly, spitting mad.

Jaxy threw her own smug words into the faceguard, "*Not . . . for . . . long.*"

A fragile butterfly, caught by a Siberian expatriate who could cite the association guidelines chapter and verse, Golly Gee would soon be rotating tits down from the ceiling fan for this sadomasochistic prude to take her life, and then her seat on the Beaver board. Childhood fears and piteous tears came washing over as they did on those interminable Yellowknife nights. Then succumbing to the inevitable Golly Gee went limp, retreating into a cocoon of survival.

"Chaps—wake up! I was only messing with you. I didn't mean a word of it!!" Jaxy tried to snap her from the paramnesia. Getting no response, he tossed the ragdoll on the bench to lift off the motorcycle helmet and tilt her head forward.

"I'm a bad girl." Golly dropped her jaw in compliance.

"Yes, you are." Jaxy slid a finger to the back of her tongue and pressed down.

Golly Gee gagged and spewed a complete meal of viscous syrup down his legs. Her eyes bulged, "What in the name of God are you doing!?!"

"Is that blood?? Dammit, I need to know what you took and when," said Jaxy, ready to take it all down.

Pale and shaken, Golly looked over her fully dressed and intact condition. "I don't get it. My clothing. I'm still . . ."

By a tender caress Jaxy upheld, "The Chief Executive Officer of all water-loving, woodland creatures."

She tilted her head, "Then . . . you're not Rat Catcher?"

"No, Chaps, I'm Rockabilly. The guy you rode to the airport."

"Call me Golly. Golly Gee."

"Okay, Golly Gee, this purple goop. Is it Codeine??" Jaxy removed his pants to mop the floor and rinse them in the sink.

Golly Gee wiped a pulpy drip and coyly said, "Beetroot juice. For hypertension."

"How much?" asked Jaxy handing her a glass of water.

"I usually start my day with one." Golly rinsed and washed her face.

" . . . or two, or five," continued Jaxy taking her pulse, then shined his penlight into those breathtaking, amber gold and glacier blues that appeared as two sides of the globe when viewed from space looking back at the Pacific Ocean in one iris, and the Atlantic in the other. "Your pupils look okay, but don't think that I don't think you aren't juiced on more than beets."

Golly pretzeled her legs around his waist. "You're a doctor too?"

"What did I just say about respecting personal space on the job?"

"That you didn't mean a word of it. Look closer. What else do you see?" She pulled in.

Far and wide into those wild, heterochromatic eyes Jaxy searched for the overarching meaning to her Kafkaesque existence, and took a stab, "Morphogenetics?"

"Take off!"

"Amen to that." Jaxy pushed away before the constable on patrol rolled in, but she constricted her thighs, cracking his back.

"Would you make up your mind?"

Golly Gee took pliers to his face, "Better not have hurt Father Michael finding out about my university research, or you're losing more than a nose hair, buddy."

"No way. Anything I have on you I got from Yan. What's more, as of yesterday your godfather dotted-lined me to senior staff," said Jaxy.

"As what?" asked Golly, taken aback.

In a placatory tone Jaxy apologized, "Sorry. Until I finish training, I can only give that out on a strict, need-to-know basis."

Golly Gee rammed the pliers up Jaxy's nose to pivot his head from side to side by the nasal septum demanding, "*I —need—to—know*!!!"

Under extreme duress Jaxy caved, "As your bodyguard!"

With a "Whooo!" Golly Gee flipped the pliers aside and mashing her Grand Tetons into his glasses, rode him like a two-stroke, pedaling backwards to crash into the tool chest. The bottom bin rocked forward and out popped the pink carton. Everything came to a grinding halt as Jaxy craned in felicity at the tiffany beaded box, and Golly in choler at the size sevens.

To the chest they dove with Golly Gee boxing him out, but Jaxy held her back by the chaps. Instead of resisting, she headbutted, bumping the drawer as they grappled to the floor. The chest lid fell with a definitive clang, and the horseplay stopped. The victor crawled forward, delivering a donkey kick into Jaxy's ribs as a final statement.

"Jesus Murphy!" Golly banged the toolbox up and down, but the drawer wouldn't open. "You jammed it."

Bruised and beaten, Jaxy tried to raise the top, but it wouldn't budge. Over a metal stool he leaned to massage his sore side gasping, "It's locked."

Golly unhooked the music dangle from her lobe. "I need the pliers, paper clip, and a ball peen hammer."

Jaxy didn't lift a finger.

"My mouse. How can I become a team player without you?"

"How do I know we're playing on the same one?" Jaxy brought the requested tools.

With a crimped and flattened earring Golly jogged the lock grunting, "If Father says then for suresies... next stop we salt your DNA at the Strategic Beaver Research Centrifuge. You can memorize the creed while we wait. Whooo! This one will not play nice," she passed the tension wrench to Jaxy. "Your turn, rookie."

Jaxy handed off his spectacles for a closer look. "I tested clean. Work has my medical records."

"For *indices*—not STDs. I can swab, though I prefer taking a blood draw."

"No thanks. I watched needles kill my old man."

"I watched rodenticide kill mine," evoked Golly with a forlorn face, and then perked up, "But that was ages ago. I have plans, Jaxy—big yacht plans! We'll sail the Sea of Finland on the Standart II without bugs in our business, and fly in gourmet hotdogs and sweet potato chips, and we'll dance in the ballroom, and swim in the heated pool. And I'll learn guitar and teach you to skate and make butter tarts and housefly repellant, and the many uses for ketchup, and—."

"And who's paying for this?"

"I'm loaded!"

"No kidding."

"So, if there be a trace of aristocracy in your arteries, we must find out.

"If that's a new stimulant you're pushing, I want nothing of it."

Loud voices from the barn suspended her proposal: "False alarm! It's a false alarm! Call the fire department and tell them it's a false alarm!" Unfortunately, the issue came too late. Sirens, the glare of lights, and blasts of horns filled the air on the road to the monastery for the second night in a row.

Golly dialed it back: "Stay. Find the key and bring the guardian angel to the Valentines Hoedown. We'll sample your blood there."

Jaxy wrapped the woebegone waif in his Mighty Ducks jacket and put his cheek to her ear. "Listen, I like you. I really do, but I spoke too soon. I have family obligations to consider before I commit."

"To me?"

"Yes, plus every year the Fat Pipes play Valentines at the Elks. It's our tradition and Guin's people come from as far as São Paulo—oh boy, oh boy. Please, don't get upset . . . Wait, Chaps, Wait! . . . My glasses!!"

But Golly Gee rescinded the onetime offer of a luxury Baltic cruise by making for the stairs with her mp3 boom box. At the landing she volte-faced to address him as queen from her balustrade:

"The name is *Feodora Marie Nikolaevna Romanova*!" Of the icons above his head she said, "these people are *my* family!!" and then at Jaxy with his own eyeglasses decreed, *"and do something about that fanny pack*!!!"

CHAPTER 61

The Abbot's Attic, Totum, WA
12:00 a.m. Tuesday, January 9

With the nine iron and shoes in hand, Jaxy tripped and stumbled after the sad husk of a human being that from all appearances, had gone up the stairs and around the bend under the delusional ravages of an addictive serum. If chemically enslaved by the Beaver laboratories as their test subject, then as her single source supplier it would explain why Golly could not go abroad for any length of time—the real reason why she could never leave the island. As Jaxy entertained these notions he fumbled myopically for the drop ladder to the third level loft. At the top rung he put his shoulder into the square cover, but it wouldn't budge, so he clutched the handrails by the upper arms and gave the access a powerful push with his soles, shoving off a bulky table dragged across to hinder his pursuit. Jaxy lifted himself into a space not large enough to hula-hoop and saw that the skillful skater had popped out the window, and with a "Whooo!" shinnied down the eavestrough. Out of breath, he conceded the chase, repositioned the table, and sat nearsighted as a mole on a ladderback chair.

"*Squeak*!!" Jaxy nearly jumped out of his skin. By moonlight streaming through the curtains, he saw what he had landed upon: A plastic, beaver, bathtub toy wearing his thick rimmed glasses with an invitation written in glossy red lipstick to the Valentine's ball. "Show this at the door, my mouse," it said, sealed by a kiss.

Jaxy straightened the frames in time to watch the oddball in quad skates hop-clop across the rise to Widowmaker Road. Except for the eye coloring, the sisters could easily pass for one another, and shared uncanny behavioral traits as well; the shameless manipulation of men not in the least. But where some might label Jillian a "soiled dove", Golly was a flat-out mud-hen. As her appointed bodyguard, Jaxy had the moral charter to liberate her from the crippling grip of "aristocracy" and into rehabilitation using the Guardian Angel of Maria Feodorovna as leverage.

Not to let moss grow, he slipped on his shoes and started with an attic recon for any place the Abbot might stash a key to the chest of tools. The penlight flickered, so Jaxy felt for a wall switch or string on the ceiling bulb to illuminate the space. Behind a power amp and subwoofer stack in the utility closet, he found a toggle attached to a timer.

"Eureka!" Jaxy exclaimed and flipped the switch.

"DING-Dong! DaDING-Dong! DaDING-Dong! DING-DING!" the festive bells woke Totum Valley with a sublime rendition of "Jesu, Joy of Man's Desiring".

In a frantic effort to shut down the sound and save his eardrums, Jaxy flicked the galvanized lever to and fro, but the handbells chimed on. He spun the timer, but nothing changed. Finally, he bunched a red and black wire pair in his fist, gave it a yank, and the ensemble stopped.

"Yesu! Time to go!" Jaxy dropped through the hatch and across the platform he bounded when the swinging doors flew open wide and on came the floods.

All stopped dead in their tracks: The Abbot and his entourage gaping up at Jaxy, and Jaxy back in his undershorts and wingtips, holding high the nine iron with a spent flare fixed to the grip.

"Put your pants on," ordered the abbot after sending the monks to their cells.

"They're soaked," Jaxy wrung them in the sink.

"Shouldn't wear them in the showers."

"Telling me! What kind of system did you install? Heat activated sprinklers should not come on all at once."

"Brother Philip said it would be better for the animals if . . . Hey! I'm asking the questions, *so start talking*!!"

To the steps Jaxy dropped to tell how he thought he saw Jillian in the dormer, so created the diversion to empty the shop for a long goodbye. The Abbot then ball-parked what the Rockabilly's quest for love in the attic would cost in damages and revenue. The ROMAR's greatest loss, however, could not be recouped. For in a shoebox cradled like a stillborn lay the sodden remains of the monastery's prized possession: A painting of Grigori Rasputin by the hand of St. Alexandra. As far as secondary relics went it wasn't much to brag about, Aldo admitted, but it was all they had.

"If you came clean on day one, none of this would have happened," Jaxy reversed the blame.

"Because the first words out of your mouth were, 'Where's Jillian?' and hers, 'How's Jaxy?' We feared if you knew she lived through the night you would go running after her like you did upstairs, putting yourself in harm's way and accomplishing nothing. So, when in her memory you wanted the van painted yellow, I skipped out on church to honor that in the event you'd bust loose on some quixotic crusade to save the girl, which is exactly what happened proving me right!"

"I did not say I wanted Moby looking like an elementary school bus."

"'First thing when I get home'—your very words."

"So what! Can't you tell when someone's had too much hooch to be taken seriously? I'm stone-cold sober now and having a tough time believing a thing I hear from you guys anymore, so maybe, just maybe, you don't want me snooping around because you want what's in the cakebox too!" Jaxy bumped the rolling chest.

At the flagrant insinuation and insolent disrespect, the Abbot shook a key from a baby food jar and unlocked the bin. "This care package contains Jillian's effects, and here it will stay till I know where to send it! You may lust after what's inside, but 'us guys' do not! You took advantage of ROMAR hospitality and put to ruin the organic farms warehouse and barn, so get a good night's sleep, Jackson, 'cause in the morning you're outta here!" The Abbot thrust a decisive, umpire's thumb at the door.

"As long as I take that cakebox along with everything in it, fine by me." Jaxy headed for the trailer.

"Stop right there! I have a different box for you."

"Mine at last!" Jaxy held out his hands.

"And if you ever step foot on these premises again, you Hollywood brat, I'll anathematize you for playing dormitory pranks at the expense of this holy place and destroying my cherished painting with no remorse!"

"Glendale. May I have it?"

"You bet. Behold Grigori!" The abbot raised the shoebox lid and mashed the soggy, gray-blue fragments into the un-housebroken pup's face, smearing Jaxy's nose and glasses with the runny slop.

"Take it—it's yours!" The Abbot pushed the carton until Jaxy embraced the gift. "But don't kiss it—until it's dry."

CHAPTER 62

L&C Hotel, Portland, OR
1:00 a.m. Tuesday, January 9

Roused from sleep, Guin bunched the blankets to her chin and answered, "What's up, Provost, besides me?"

"Good news—bad news."

"Only the good, *por favor.*"

"I intercepted the angel."

"Halleluiah! Overnight it to the Antique Mall. Now hit me with the bad."

"Jaxy came back for his guitar."

She sat up tall. "Baloney Butt's not on the boat?"

"Believe me everyone would love that, but after he touched off the fire alarm and flooded the barn—."

"*He did what?*"

"I'm worried for the boy. He's not thinking straight so I roughed him up and then sent him to the trailer with a round-the-clock watch. It gets worse. I found prowler tracks in the huckleberries, and another set I can't make sense of coming up to the mill."

"Should I call for backup?"

"Not until I clear the 'two-J's' out. So, with a last-minute change, can you fly them both from the Totum airfield instead?"

"Dad's gonna luuuuuv this," Guin signed off with a light touch. It didn't occur to her until halfway to his room that she hadn't thrown the phone all day. There's one for the diary!

STRETCHED ACROSS HIS PALLET, Jaxy balanced the guitar on his chest and tried to work the action to "Long Gone Lonesome Blues", but he'd found Daisy floating in an inch of greasy, garage water, and now she wouldn't play.

"Jaxy, you there?" Drew called from the outside.

"Can't say for sure," ached the Rockabilly.

"You'll meet your ride tomorrow at the public parking. Space is limited so pack light."

"I'm a complete reject," moped Jaxy hauling the mildewing shoebox, Jillian's apple eyed portrait, and the Gretsch guitar, rusting, warped, and checkered beyond repair to the far end of the trailer. Even if it fit, he'd have no use for it when tomorrow the Abbot unburdened the Rockabilly bum as far as he could in one direction and the pink, confectioner's box in the other. By Valentine's everything Jaxy cared for would be toast.

Jaxy emptied expendables such as hair gel and shoe polish, and all hopes of ever realizing a happy home or a rewarding music career into the wastebin. Harvest-ready dreams, ripe for the gleaning before Jillian came on like a blight to wipe them clean. Then, as fortune fell into his lap, in skated Chaps, juiced since breakfast making everyone think it was he who dangled like a crushed and flattened earring on the lunatic fringe.

Maybe he did . . .

Given a pass to do whatever the insane damned well please, Jaxy then turned his back on them as they had on him, took up his book, and crawled into bed.

CHAPTER 63

Yekaterinburg, Russia 1976

Where Yakov Yurovsky buried the royal bodies may have endured as one of the twentieth century's great, unsolved mysteries, in part because the Cheka commander by happenstance did a smashing job of covering his tracks, but more so because any Russky in his right mind wouldn't have risked a ruble looking into it. Any other that is, than the experienced criminal investigator, insatiably curious detective novelist, and successful movie producer Geli Ryabov with a surfeit of friends inside the Politburo.

Read-up on the spin that the Yakov Yurovsky dissolved, burned, and blew the Romanovs to smithereens in a mineshaft where nothing but a potpourri of buttons and bone fragments remained, in 1976, on location to film a revolution docudrama, Geli pried open the Ipatiev House cellar and what he found electrified him. Upon close study of the cramped cavity scored by gashes and bullet marks, and that no human teeth had been brought up from the shaft, doubt set in about the Tsar's final resting place. At which point Ryabov enlisted the aid of resident expert, geologist Alexander Advonin, who knew the region like the back of his hand to help hunt down the royal family, presumed exhumed and reburied elsewhere.

This chancy undertaking happened during a time when the communist party, reacting to a wave of sentiment for the old regime, dozed the infamous house of confinement to send a message not to loiter there. Undaunted, the men scrutinized accounts and interviewed witnesses to that tumultuous era in order to synthesize an alternate story—that having failed by acid and bonfire to scrub the evidence, and terrified White Army loyalists would find it, Yurovsky dug up the mangled and dismembered corpses to truck them to a faraway destination. Thirty minutes down the road, however, the lorry laden with a ton of gelatinous, scorched body parts mired to the axels in a bog and out came the shovels.

To nail down the second burial site, filmmaker Ryabov rooted out the commander's original unredacted register in the son's library in Moscow. Yurovsky's material provided detailed positions, landmarks, and distances to narrow the location, for which the geologist Advonin sleuthed over hill and dale comparing entries and photographs to geographical descriptions until one spring day in a shallow swamp he struck bone.

In the aftermath, they reassembled the skeletons identifying each member by computerized facial reconstruction, limb measurements, and age. Major strides in modern DNA theory and analysis came as the result of a fiercely competitive, international race to verify this fantastic, Romanov find by genetics. In the end, the astounding scientific irony of Yakov Yurovsky's botched job is that the sulfuric acid by which he meant to dissolve and obliterate the royal family from the face of the earth, leached into the soil, sterilizing the clay. This, in turn, inhibited bone decomposition, preserving the Romanov skeletons to make recovery possible.

"Now *that's* plumb crazy," Jaxy appreciated a real life, detective puzzler flying in the face of mortal danger. Then, happy he didn't have to do the same with Yan, closed the book and fell asleep.

CHAPTER 64

The ROMAR, Totum, WA
8:00 a.m., Tuesday, January 9

An anthill on the march after an unseasonable rain, the monks bumped along toting moist produce and canned goods to storage units rolled off that morning. Not inclined to hear the Deacon belt out one more hymn for his betterment, Jaxy snagged a banana and went to help. As he wiped down palettes, he heard the Abbot coming and braced for the worst.

"I am truly sorry for your guitar, Jaxy."

With astonishment, Jaxy took stock of the Abbot's unperturbed face wondering how someone could peg the amplifier needle into the red and return to naught overnight.

The Abbot opened his arms for a melancholic embrace, "'A non-possessive monk is lord of the world', but letting go of people? That's a hard one for me. Take five and enjoy the morning. Drew will walk you to the rendezvous after lunch."

With just an appendix about the legendary angel left to read, Jaxy required more material for the journey so felt around the van pockets and stepped out with the Electric Avlon field phone inside a Vintage Rock magazine. He transferred it to his camera bag and went to find a tripod.

"I'd like a group picture. May I borrow yours?" he asked.

"On the wall by my desk," said the Abbot.

To the mill Jaxy beelined. Coming up he espied Brother Jean at the open toolchest. The Mute sprinted off when from the trail the Abbot hailed, "Jaxy! I forgot! Tripod's in the library—return it when you're done." With a pleasant smile Aldo then locked the shop, sending him off to ninth-hour prayers.

Stymied again, Jaxy took the path blazed by Golly Gee to a thicket bordering the road. A raft of turkeys spooked from the vegetated slope on the north side of Totum Valley squawked and gobbled. He rested the camera's telescopic lens in a tree crotch and through the nettles scanned the forested ridge from where the birds took flight. A figure moved amongst the trees. Keeping one eye in the viewfinder, Jaxy speed dialed Rory on the Captain's own phone.

The form stood still.

"Thought so." Jaxy closed it up.

With the stops set, Jaxy methodically panned the hillside from top to bottom, and then legged it to the library computer where he ported the pictures, enlarging the copper brown Bronco's grainy grill. No tire tracks led in so Rory must have approached from the west. Jaxy printed a Totum Hills trail map before previewing an email from javlon@wwa: *Hey Jax—By the time you read this I'll be gone, but I'm super jazzed to have you as a friend. Thanks for being crazy you, and always cover the pond because fish are pets! Take care, Jillian.*" The note came with a thumbnail that Jaxy enlarged and pasted onto a template. He added flowery text and published a copy on folded card stock.

With the prime lens back on, Jaxy had the tripod in position outside the chapel when everyone spilled from prayers. Not camera shy, the monks fought for the best places on the steps while Jaxy set the timer and bunched in. Over Brother Jean's shoulders he rested an arm and spoke into the hood, "Stay out of the cake, Miho."

Brother Jean chafed mildly at the reprimand.

Up to the camera the Abbot stepped saying, "Hold that smile, Jackson."

"For your newsletter?" Jaxy smiled big.

"For your obit." The Abbot smiled bigger.

Not yet noontime, but waxing hungry, Jaxy went to Café Matthias to drop a slice of wheat into the toaster. When it popped out, the cat shot down the hall. He followed the tail to where the Mute sat meditating in the great room before the crackle of a dwindling fire. Jaxy peeled a page from the deacon's pad and rummaged the nook for a pen. It took ten, laborious minutes to write, and when finished he creased it tight before drawing near.

"Sorry I snapped at you, but I had to know. I had to know why you ran when the Abbot yelled up to the mill. I had to test if you hear better than you like to let on," Jaxy's voice went softer with each phrase.

Brother Jean rocked.

"I'll take that as a yes. So, inside the toolchest is a cakebox, and in that an estate piece that belonged to the Tsar's mother, Maria Feodorovna. A guardian angel about this big." Jaxy compared it to a shell in Ichthus the blue betta's fishbowl.

Brother Jean rocked.

"I need it taken and put under the altar, so it won't fall into the wrong hands while I'm away. Can you do that?"

Brother Jean rocked.

"See, there's this guy on Mount Adams, a real bad man that thinks —well, who cares what he thinks. To be blunt I might not make it back." Jaxy flipped the folded note up and down his fingers.

Brother Jean jabbed at the floor by his shoes.

"Pardon?"

The Mute would not let up until Jaxy knelt, facing the stove with his parting will and testament smoothed over the monk's lap. Brother Jean draped a floppy sleeve over the Rockabilly's head and waited for confession. He had all year.

"I can't believe I'm doing this," began Jaxy, slow and shaky, to read the scribbles: "I did not mean to hurt Jillian or bring harm to the monastery, and I should not have gotten involved with her in the first place. It was wrong and because of me, people are dead. If I live, I will rebuild the Abbot's barn, but if not, don't be too hard on me. And wherever Jillian may go, make sure she's okay, and her little sister Chaps, and—," Jaxy cleared his throat, "Guin too. Amen."

Brother Jean wept.

Jaxy then poked the note, long and thin, through the iron grates of the God Box to let the flames jump to lick it clean, and the smoke carry it to heaven.

ALONG THE PATH TO the old mill Jaxy meditated on the remainder of the day. Unlike those models of self-abnegating sacrifice read at table, he would not go down without a fight. If he defeated the Captain on the mountain everyone would live. But if not, to the end he would contend that Jillian was not at the monastery, and to leave the monks at peace. Jaxy put up the tripod and culled the Abbot's wall-mount of fine cutlery. The Viking sword with its decorative pommel and crossguard called to him, but he settled on a five-inch, folding, carbon steel, hunting knife with an elkhorn handle.

"Ride's here!" The Abbot said coming up the deck with a sack of apples.

Jaxy selected one. "Too bad grenades don't grow on trees—but I thank you."

"*De nada*. Anything else?" Abba asked when Jaxy did not move to the door.

Jaxy looked him steady in the eye. "Your forgiveness."

"You have that already."

"I will pay for the damages."

"Forgiveness means you owe nothing."

Jaxy twirled his key ring, "We'll see about that."

The Abbot stayed his hand. "Guin is coming."

"So is Rory. I must lead him away."

"God will defend us."

"I am not afraid."

"Then you are mad."

"Diagnosis acknowledged. One last question."

"Go."

"Photios, Arsenios, Matthias—where *do* they get their names?"

With fragrant oil from a brown, glass vial the Abbot dabbed Jaxy's forehead and pronounced: "Jackson Thrie, after a scoundrel that wrestled an Angel to the ground and lived, henceforth shalt thou go by 'Jacob'. *Via con Dios*."

IN PAYMENT FOR A novice's white robe, dusty snowshoes, and a resin bear tooth on a leather tie, Jaxy emptied his cash into the ROMAR gift store till. With the van packed, he guided Moby to Widowmaker Road where the monks gathered to send him off with icons, jams, and a pair of Sahaptin moccasins.

"How you crossing over?" asked one.

"He'll pull the fire alarm," said another.

Jaxy ignored the jests and asked for Jean.

Father Photios walked him out of earshot. "You upset him by not listening at the woodstove, so he will not say goodbye."

"I don't recall him saying a thing."

"He told you to STAY!" Photios pointed down to the ground.

"*That's* what he meant? Makes no difference. I'm still going."

"Patience," said the Archimandrite.

"No time," Jaxy hugged the human Bristlecone a brisk farewell as a thick mist settled in, and the deep creases on the aged monk's face smoothed out.

"I told you all creatures make time for what's important," the Archimandrite reminded.

Jaxy kicked at a stick and waited.

"My grandfather tamed a crow where you stand with walnuts and patience, because he believed this so," the timeless one went on.

"You grew up here?"

"Totum Valley," he curled a withered arm, "my ancestral home."

"Why a crow?"

"Black birds are cagey—more than the wolf. They do not—," he poked Jaxy's ribs, "make good pets. So why tame her? Because she had a crooked feather and could not keep up with the rest. They called her 'Bent Wing', and me after the crow—in prophecy maybe? Who knows, but I fear my days for writing icons are over. The time has come to pass the brush," the Archimandrite patted the useless limb.

"But you painted Jillian."

"I said, 'Behold Jillian'! You assumed the rest. That bird proved far braver than her brothers and survived them many years by bending her neck to accept a handout which the others refused with proud heads and fearful hearts."

"How long did she live?"

"Long enough. And how long do you plan to outlast Rory?"

"Long enough to convince him that Jillian's gone and to leave the monks alone."

"Seeing how well that worked on you, what's your story?"

Jaxy produced the announcement that he crafted at the library:

In Loving Memory of Jillian D. Avlon

June 18, 1986 – January 5, 2018

Ralph and Adele Anders invite you to join them in tribute at

St. Maximos Greek Orthodox Church, Minnehaha WA

7 p.m. Wednesday, February 14, 2018

For Jillian's   Contribution
in life as a living   angel, and in death
as a charitable organ donor, the family asks
in lieu of flowers to please send your
generous gift of love to: The
American Heart
Associa-
tion

.

"Your intentions are noble, but they are flawed," critiqued the Archimandrite. "To begin with Jillian is listed among the 'missing', not deceased."

"You can still conduct a memorial for the presumed dead, can't you?"

"And you misspelled Ralf."

"Phooey!" Jaxy dashed the flyer to the ground.

The Archimandrite retrieved the card before the breeze whistled it away. "Dear me, Jaxy! This is priceless! But enough tomfoolery—your ride awaits."

"Extend my gratitude for the pains the Abbot took on my behalf, but I made a wreck of the farm's economy and his cherished painting. Reasons to stay and set things right."

"Do tell. Why would he keep such a fine work of art in the barn?"

"Got me. But he did, and then shoved—,"

"The remains of a dissolute reprobate up your nose. The Rasputin oil meant nothing except for the Empress' signature he cut from the corner and placed at the altar. The rest he consigned in time for the great flood. By destroying it you did us a service. Take a walnut, Jaxy, your work is complete."

"Then why give me a warrior's name I cannot share, and skins I cannot wear?"

The Archimandrite rose tall to tie a band of hemp around the Rockabilly's forehead, and hook a crooked, black feather behind Jaxy's ear. "Since I cannot dissuade you I give you wing to tread lightly on Pahto. The feistiest of three, she has a short fuse—*do not provoke her*! Once you start the ascent, do not stop. Go all the way or do not go at all. Life and death are of no consequence to the one who contends with spirits of fire; only staying on to the end. Here is success, and here is failure—there is nothing more. Depart in peace."

CHAPTER 65

Totum Valley, WA
12:00 p.m., Tuesday, January 9

Against a Chevy Spark reclined Guin, shading her face against the
sun when the van blew by the visitor lot, accelerating up the mountain
road. With a frown she placed a call to the Abbot's mobile phone,
"Where does baloney butt think he's going?"

"On a fool's errand."

"By himself?"

"Yes. Jillian won't budge from the barn," said the Abbot.

"Tell her to draw a selfie of a mule."

"Her trademark piece, to wit. I'm sorry you came this way for
nothing, Guin."

"If I take the angel back with me, I won't have."

"Had I'd known you'd be heading straight home I wouldn't have
put it in the mail this morning! Hurry—you might catch the truck in
Totum."

"Let it go. Klav knows it's coming, so the cottage is safe. There is
nothing to fear."

"Excellent news, Counsel. Then Godspeed. Better go before the
storm."

"Hold a second..."

Caught up in talk, Guin had wandered to the trailhead at the end of the humble car lot. There, not far beyond the semicircle of trees and boulders that defined the zone she chanced upon a distinctive, Ural sidecar she had seen not long before under the flap of a camping tent in the deep, forest shade. She followed elfin steps to a tequila bottle ditched without care and not entombed with the older litter by a crust of snow. Guin smelled the cap. Fresh. She pulled up a snapshot of Rory's Bronco and compared the treads to those crosscutting the rancher's gate.

"Guin?" The Abbot's voice cut in.

"Provost. Tell the Sheriff to meet here at eight for the big roundup. See you then."

At lunch break Fr. Michael completed his hospital rounds to take a call from the monastery. "They up and away?" asked the priest, hungering for an encouraging word and a salty snack from the vending machine.

Aldo came on concerned, "No. And worse—that rascal Jaxy kept going up the grade to draw Rory into the open, leaving Guin to chase down something she saw in the picnic area."

"Chase what?"

"A muddy white sidecar with a beaver on board."

"No!" said the priest. "You tink Golly carjack?"

"Here's what I think: We pegged that Rockabilly wrong all along. That stunt he pulled in the shop? He didn't go seeking Jillian alone, and if those two are allied, why should he fear Rory?"

"I tell Yilli 'do not trust him', then I go and do just that! How I hoped Yackzy might be the one to turn her sister's wayward heart."

"I'm afraid he did. In all the wrong ways."

"How Leetle Pony-girl holding up?"

"Saying goodbye to the chickens and goats before going away."

"To where?"

"I didn't ask."

"That is not like you."

"Then nobody can force it from me."

"And that—my old friend—is just like you."

AT THE IRON GATE Jaxy had strung out his goodbyes to give Rory time to observe the van leading away from the monastery and onto the windswept moraines. Straining to see the Bronco bounce over the fields in pursuit, it occurred to him that the hunting knife was not the most potent weapon in his arsenal. No, the heftiest bat in the line-up was his trusty steed: Moby Dick.

At the pass Jaxy brought the van around to face Totum Valley, putting the buttercream buttes to his back. Under a gauzy sky, he pictured Guin in a smart blazer and pencil skirt strolling a dotted glen of laurel with the lily spray she would lay upon his closed oak casket, custom tailored by the Abbot in the shape of a guitar case who then would say a word of comfort and hope, calling him "Jacob", and royally confusing everybody.

Jaxy beheld the southern incline and braced himself for the showdown. With a vertical drop off the shoulder, and a sheer wall to his right, Rory had nowhere to go when he made the final bend but up the straight and narrow. By the time the Captain realized he had driven into a trap—wham! Too late! Moby would career down the runway and joust the Bronco onto the jagged crags below. There would be no winner in this deadly game of chicken—just the loss of two fine vehicles.

Thirty minutes later Jaxy gave up the wait to coast to the cattle gate and do it the hard way. One set of fat tires led into the flinty field, and none came out, so the fight came home to roost in the Totum Hills. Jaxy stomped at the ruts and determined they were firm enough to make the distance to a tumbledown bridge a stadion away.

Beyond that, passage grew too rugged for Moby's suspension, so he left the van under this provisional carport to proceed on foot. Before commencing his assault on Rory's flank, he belted the knife and fanny pack containing a powerful flashlight, the Electric Avlon flip phone, map, and energy drink. The book he brought as well, for if these gutsy gals could take one for the team, he wanted them on his side. To the elk skins Jaxy strapped the snowshoes, and for camouflage he slipped on the white muslin robe.

With the feather cocked for maximum lift, over the lava scab Jaxy darted from boulder to bush, the way he did as a kid playing army with stick rifles and dirt clods, the only training he received for today's operation. Past his shoulder that old dragon, St. Helens sneered down a fragmented snout in contempt at a showdown between inferiors. Up a cottonwood squirrels played, squeaking to each other on the circular stairway.

A distant rifle report echoed across the tableland. Birds stopped chirping. Seconds later Jaxy heard another. Clouds above knocked heads to dim the contrast. As fast as he could in those clumsy snowshoes, he hoofed it over the coulee to drop into Rory's camp devoid of anything but a cold firepit.

Two sets of skis approached from the monastery and departed in the direction of Totum. Finer footprints came from huckleberry meadow and circled to the road. A mid-size boot joined from the bluffs. What had he walked into? Beyond the Aspens, Rory's giant footfalls broke into a westward run toward yonder hills, paralleling the skiers, so quickening his pace Jaxy went after those. The snow lay deeper on the shady side making hiking a challenge as the chill rose and shadows lengthened. After crossing the Bronco tracks Jaxy slipped and slid down a crevasse to a broad clearing. There he stopped to knock snow from the roots of a fallen tree and to his joy found at the bottom of the fanny pack a PBJ wrapped with a note: "I'll keep the coffee on."

Over lunch Jaxy sped-read the appendix on the Guardian Angel of Maria Feodorovna and the dowager's Delphic wish. Not that he believed in destiny, but Jaxy believed in believing in destiny and the wallop it could carry. With the angel in the right hands at the centennial who knew what good may come. But whose hands? Those of nobody he knew.

Finished reading, he took out the map. His throat tightened when, plotting Rory's course, he saw it crossed the skiers' path. Monks in trouble? Or tattletale turncoats? Either way Jaxy decided the time had come for a reality check. With Moby blocking the only way out, Rory would be pinned down. Jaxy took the field phone and punched in 9-1-1.

"No Service," it said. Not one lousy bar.

"Blam!"

A spray of splinters stung the side of Jaxy's neck. Behind the hollow tree he ducked and released the blade.

"Stick 'em up baloney butt and throw me the knife!" Ordered the gunslinger.

From his cowering position Jaxy lobbed the hunting knife. A pair of handcuffs flew over in reply. He raised his palms above the trunk line. "Guin?"

"Jaxy??" The shooter came out from ambuscade with a small revolver at her lips, blowing away the smoke.

Jaxy stuck his nose over the trunk. "What on earth are you doing here?

"Me?? Didn't I see you drive away hours ago?"

"And didn't they teach you to say 'stick 'em up baloney butt' *before* you shoot?"

"Depends on the situation."

"What situation!? There ought to be a law. And look at you! Do your anti-gun constituents know you went from lobbyist to hobbyist?"

"My career is shot no matter what I do, thanks to you."

"Was not my intention," Jaxy rubbed at the creased bark. "Were you trying to miss me?"

Guin dropped in a shiny, new shell. "Wasn't mine, either."

Taking part in a common purpose—to stop Rory—down the hill they ran to a flat-topped boulder looking out on a peppering of buildings, miles off, marking the outskirts of Totum. Jaxy cased the area of sunflower shells and spent casings while Guin proceeded with caution onto the alluvial plain. One pair of skis and poles lay discarded where the tracks turned to hike to the Bronco along the valley floor.

Guin interpreted the scene: "No skirmish or blood. Signals fired from the notch?"

Jaxy raised his gaze to the cuesta. "Or a warning. I'm going after them."

A flake fell on Guin's shoulder. Softly she vetoed, "No Jaxy, we have the location. Call it in."

"Tried. I'm in a dead zone."

Guin checked her phone. "Shoot. Me too. Go wait at the van. I'll ski to Totum for help."

"Can I borrow that?" Jaxy asked of the gun.

"The van," Guin pointed.

"Take these," Jaxy gave up his flashlight and the energy drink. "I won't need them where I'm going."

"You are going to the van," she said.

"And you are going to stop telling me what to do."

Silence descended.

"Funny you say that," Guin warily proceeded, "because Dad asked if the Fat Pipes will play the Elks this year. I said that decision isn't mine to make."

At the hardest crossroad of his life Jaxy lowered his eyes. "Tell Booker I quit to go solo at the Beaver Lodge Valentine's hoedown."

"That so."

"Do we have to talk about this now?"

"I think we should."

When they finished Guin gave back the ring. She wouldn't compete anymore. From feather to footwear, she gave Jaxy one last go-over, brushing out the beard and preening the beanie. "There is one thing Jackson Thrie can do better than anyone else in the world."

"Misplace his keys?" Jaxy raised a brow, but it didn't seem funny.

"Make me smile. Even when I don't want to," Guin leaned in and kissed away a tear shed for them both, "and don't ever change."

CHAPTER 66

The Totum Hills, WA
3:00 p.m., Tuesday, January 9

To sniper's rock Jaxy hastened under diminishing daylight, then up and over the cleft he ducked into the dusky shadows until the Bronco came into range with Black Stone Cherry reverberating through the floorboards. Suddenly, the action plan looked easier than expected. Jaxy would simply shiver in his snowshoes till the Captain passed out and Guin Hill with her posse came crashing in, guns blazing, to cash in.

Everything changed when the sun dipped below the horizon and a hard wind whipped from the west. At that moment, Rory stepped out in monk's togs dressed as any other disciple of the faith except for the Nosler slung over his shoulder. He clamped on skis to glide toward the monastery giving Jaxy no choice but to jump him. When the Rockabilly left the ground, however, a powerful gust knocked him aslope into the filthy, wet firepit, charring his face and hands.

"In here!!" a voice sang out as he regained his feet.

Jaxy followed the cry to where he found the monk that tended livestock taped back-to-back to Brother Jean. "What are you fools doing up here?" asked Jaxy cutting through.

"Saw the Bronc' on the way to the Post Office. Thought it belonged to the neighbor, so we skied over to talk cows."

"Talk cows," said Jaxy with a laugh.

Continued the monk, "But all he wanted to talk about was his wife. Said I never heard of no Jillian. That I didn't know him by name made the man even madder, know what I'm sayin'?"

"You my good fellow, are lucky to be talking at all," said Jaxy when from the Mute's robe a carton addressed to the Russian Antique Mall fell out. "Whatcha' got Jean?"

Answered the first monk, "Abba didn't say, but it won't go today, sayin?"

"Nor any other," said Jaxy, shoving the familiar sized, shipping box into his fanny pack. He inventoried the camping staples and said, "Gents. Lie low and keep the motor running. I'll be right back."

"Where ya' goin'?"

"Canada."

To traverse the rock-ribbed ridge without stars or compass to guide him to the covered bridge seemed unwise, so Jaxy let the wintery blasts drive him to Widowmaker Road from where he could backtrack to the van. The wind, however, blew him offline into the huckleberry meadow where he inadvertently caught up to the Captain at the iron gate, occupied with something on the ground.

"*Go all the way or do not go at all,*" the Archimandrite's words stopped Jaxy in his tracks. The self-sacrificing ballyhoo he put forth to the Archimandrite on this spot then jumped to mind—a pact made on impulse before breaking it off with Guin and finding the Fabergé at the Ford. An unfettered future awaited him with the Booker-Hills and the Beavers behind him. But what of the brethren breaking bread in ignorance to the perils within the monastery walls and without— was theirs of lesser importance?

Jaxy placed a hand on the elkhorn handle. He and the angel had a history, and if Jacob of old could go the distance with one, then by the one in his fanny pack he could too—and then on to Canada! With the

Captain's collar turned Jaxy had a bead at the kneeling man's neck. A flip of steel from the upward grip to the reverse, the way the old hobo showed him with a popsicle stick would end it. Now came the harder question: Could he do it? Frozen in indecision, Jaxy watched Rory kick off the skis and scramble cat-like onto the monastery drive.

Jaxy tried to warn the Deacon on the iron gate's intercom, but the lines had been severed and the rollers jammed. In a foot race, he ducked through the barbed wire to place his feet on holy ground. The Abbot could damn him to Hollywood tomorrow, but tonight he had a job to do. The wind caught the cassock, sailing Jaxy into the briars as he stumbled in that cumbersome robe which snagged on every leaf and thorn on the way. Along the granite church he patted until the mudroom came into sight. Jubilant, Jaxy scampered up the stoop with seconds to spare, yelling for someone to bar the door and bring down the law. Sadly, the words never left his mouth, for he had forgotten about the snowshoes and an inch of webbed toe caught on the pantry sill, vaulting him into a metal, utility shelf of Organic Farms berry preserves and applesauce.

Glass jars exploded about his face and shoulders, followed by a fruit pie cooling in a fourteen-inch tin that slopped cherries, warm and gooey, around his neck. Jaxy pulled his knees to stand but crossed the shoes and face down he went into the juicy muck. Vocalizing muffled and unintelligible sounds, he attempted to rise a third time, but tripped and kicked the door closed, propelling him forward into more Mason jars, and slicing his outstretched hand. Toppings mixed with graham cracker crumbs caked his hair, coating the charcoal smudged robe. Swirls of red and purple jellies and jams splattered his cheeks and chin. Contusions and lacerations spurted blood to tie in nicely with the mangled mess making Jaxy the most delicious accident in all of Church history.

On his last attempt to stand, Jaxy heard crisp steps approach and an exasperated deacon bellow, "Who left the door open?" when through the front came the Captain accompanied by three rounds fired from a deer rifle and a roar from the top of his lungs: "*Where's Jillian?!?*"

The monks about-faced and forgot all about the raccoon in the pantry.

CHAPTER 67

Grandma P.'s Cottage, Totum, WA
6:00 p.m., Tuesday, January 9

"I'm going to beat you to the Pittock if you don't give me the key to the cart this instance!" Jillian threatened Drew with a cue in Grandma's basement.

"If you're so antsy, sister, why did you agree to come in the first place?"

"Told you! In *your* rush to go I left my cellphone with a box of clothes in the Abbot's toolchest. I have to have it. Try him again."

"He said not to bother him."

"Did the deacon?"

No one answered at Café Matthias either. An oddity for this time of day. Drew threw on his poncho and up the stairs he tore with Jillian on his heels. "Stay! I'll get it," he chocked the door from the outside with a chair against the knob.

"Drew! Drew!!" Jillian pounded and pounded then down the steps she bounded nearly kissing Viv herself through the mouthpiece of Grandma's phone when her riding bud from The Dalles picked up.

IN NO TIME JILLIAN heard the floor creak above. "Huu! That was fast!" she cheered skipping up to freedom.

The chair scraped away, and the door opened, but in place of Viv there loomed a man in a silver tonic suit smelling of stale cologne and wet cigarettes.

"Who are you?" retreated Jillian on shaking legs, but it didn't show.

"How big you've grown!" The stranger compared her to a baby picture.

Jillian tore it from his hand.

"Plucky too," he said, setting a copper cruet down with enough paraffin to light up the night and prodded her breast with the tip of a bayonet fixed to an antiquated, but serviceable rifle. He added with relish, "For old time's sake I brought a Browning—the type used in the Ipatiev root cellar, no less. How ironic. How rich! I think I shall stand you against the wall like your dear cousins—or are they saints? Do you miss them? Wish to join them?" The Siberian pressured her to back down until splitting the blouse, it bloomed bright red.

Jillian stood her ground and spat in his face. "If I am to die as them, at least have the courtesy to give me the name of my executioner!"

He wiped away the warm spittle. "Won't you guess? Your sister failed. Come, show who's the smart one . . . Tsk. Tsk . . . Not a try? Hint: I'm not Satan, just an old crony Klav Lovorsky. But rearrange the letters of the name and I become *Krysolov*—Rat Catcher!—and I am pleased to meet you."

"Huu-Huu," sang Jillian. "And do you know why the studio that recorded that song burned down to the ground?"

"Because God wanted to punish them," said Klav in sarcastic sureness.

"No. Hint: Because Mick Jagger got mad at Charlie Watts *and bashed his head in with an oil lamp!*"

"It will take less than that to burn your equipment—know why? Hint: Technology. Nobody will find the delicate bones of Duchess Dagmar—not in a thousand years because there won't be any. And nobody will pray to her when she's gone."

"My angel will protect me."

Klav's lip curled, "The one taken by my great Uncle Yakov from a dead girl's head? If it couldn't then, how can it now, hanging from a hook in the Yurovsky family store? Now turn and walk."

Jillian knelt at her archenemy's feet. "I am not worthy to die like Olga so shoot me here, and don't forget to use the ba...," Jillian's voice trailed off.

"What? The bayonet? You got it!" Klav shouted. And spreading his legs for a solid base, with a slight bend at the knee raised high the bolt-action rifle by the fore stock to drive the steel through the small of her back.

The moment his body stretched upward, off the balls of her feet Jillian shot like a breechblock, thrusting her head between Klav's legs to boost him from the floor. At the same time the copper cruet crushed down upon his nape, pitching him forward headfirst to the foot the stairs while the bayonet grazed harmlessly by.

Embracing Viv, over her shoulder Jillian spoke wide-eyed to the motionless form. "I said, 'use *the banister*'."

"Oh-ma-gosh!" fearfully Viv cried out, clasping the caved-in, paraffin can by the neck. "Did we kill him?"

With caution Jillian jostled Klav with her toe. The man's head flopped at an unusual angle. "Huu—I think the fall did."

Tugging riding boots on over her socks Viv asked, "Did Mick Jagger really do that?"

"Hell if I know. C'mon, we gotta ride."

CHAPTER 68

The ROMAR, Totum, WA
6:30 p.m., Tuesday, January 9

Before the assembly of monks Rory paced, breathing threats, and repeating the demand for Jillian.

"Who wants to know?" asked the Abbot.

"The 4-H club. You run this outfit?"

"Aldo Escobar. Provost of the Holy Royal Martyrs Monastery."

"I recall. And if you don't hand over my wife, you'll be on the news again."

To his retinue the Abbot put, "If anyone can take this man to his wife, please do so now."

All heads declined knowledge.

Rory replied, "Good soldiers! The memories of your spies I caught out in the open failed as well."

The abbot went deadpan. "Did they make it?"

"To town? No. But the mercury's dropping, so work with me."

"Death does not dismay a good soldier. A monk fears it no more than sleep."

"Let's find out. Everybody. Over there," Rory waved them to the corner by the potbelly stove.

Nobody moved.

"*Now!*"

The Deacon led and the others followed.

The Cafe telephone rang. It stopped. It rang again. From his hip Rory shot it off the wall. "Any more?"

The Abbot's Motorola tumbled to his feet and Rory put it out of service. Monk by monk he went down the line, turning up nothing but prayer ropes and pocket devotionals, and a bag of Cheetos.

"That's it, Al? Do I have to cavity search?"

"The brothers carried a two-way for emergencies."

"This?" Rory took it from the pocket and subtracting them from the head count still came up short. "Where's Poncho?"

The rattle-rumble of a golf cart provided the answer.

Rory flattened against the wall.

The novice stepped through clapping gloves to announce, "Grandma's new stovepipe is in and—,"

"And give me the key to the quad," Rory extended a hand.

Drew let it fall short making Rory reach, then taking hold of the outstretched wrist threw a clobbering roundhouse. Rory ducked causing Drew to connect with the back of his head, and both to lose balance. The rifle spun from Rory's hands, then springing off his shoulders came up with the ice axe filed to a wicked point.

"Captain," Drew respectfully spoke as he shed his ski cap and poncho. "I have no weapon."

"Boots and fists then," Rory set the axe aside, "but no limits."

Drew pulled the mittens off by his teeth. "Do you have any?"

"*Allez!*" Rory kicked away the chairs for a makeshift ring and the bout began.

Drew faded and blocked Rory's opening combination. Around they circled with feints and jabs and little hops, kicking low and high, warming up, stretching, and taking measure. Rory made the first serious strike to Drew's thigh that drove him to the wall. Drew bounced off like a whirling dervish and caught Rory's with a toe, setting the master down.

Quick as a catamount Rory pounced as Drew stepped in with a knee to the gut, bending him in half. Rory hooked Drew's calf going down, dumping the novice. As Drew slapped his arm to absorb the impact his fingers brushed the ice axe handle.

Rory lunged, sending the pick spinning along with the last vestige of a clean fight as they grappled for control. When Drew could not dominate at the power game, he broke free of the scissors lock and retreated.

Rory grabbed the axe with an evil grin that passed as soon as he saw his younger foe upright at the woodstove, holding his side with one hand and a grinder sharpened, hatchet with the other.

"You would have made a decent student," Rory said as they went at it with the striking of feet and clanking of battle-axes.

"I'll make a better teacher," replied Drew, followed by a flash of steel that nicked Rory's thigh drawing first blood. This so enraged Rory that he slashed Drew's abdomen but paid for this rash move by a hatchet butt to the funny bone. Rowling in pain, Rory shifted the ice axe to the other hand and went back to footwork and toe kicks. This flurry went on until rubber heel met blade, absorbing the strike, and wrenching it from Drew's hand.

HOLED-UP IN THE PANTRY, Jaxy opened the Electric Avlon field phone. One bar lit up! He pressed 9, and then blip-a-blip, the battery ran down.

Gaw! Beneath the hubbub he ducked out to tend to his injuries and on the way to the trailer collided with Brother Jean moving fast toward the house.

The Mute recoiled from Jaxy's shocking appearance.

"Miho!" Jaxy enunciated into the floodlight, "first, I tell you to put the angel in the chapel, and then to stay in the Bronco! You don't listen very well do you?"

Between his fingers Brother Jean peeked and shook "no".

"Still, I'm glad to see you. Have you a phone?"

Brother Jean pointed to the kitchen.

Jaxy then sent him off to hunt for a charger and then wait on the porch for the three-count signal.

WITH HANDS ON HER hips and leather leggings apart, Golly Gee admired her figure in the Abbot's shop window when the wide, side doors swung out. She pivoted to see a monk no larger than she was pull up before the rolling tool chest, pried apart, with the bottom ripped out, and a beaver bathtub toy balanced on top.

The monk seized the crowbar and brought it to a defensive posture.

"Too cute!" Golly Gee raised the Guardian Angel of Maria Feodorovna from her chest as an Olympic gold medalist and instructed, "If you're looking for this tell Jaxy I have it. What I need now is Olga's corset from the Ipatiev House and a blood donation. A drop or two of his will do, and all eight pints from my sister."

Through the swinging doors came Jillian with the corset saying, "Ask her yourself," then taking the crowbar from her brother said, "Go."

But Jean, who never listened very well, pulled away the veil to show what had been done to his once beautiful face.

"Whooo! What have we here—a family reunion?" asked Golly, going this way and that to reach her gun pack left by the chest. Jillian speared her away with surprising agility, so over her shoulder Golly looked for a cudgel. A rake to the neck told her not to do that again. Golly went then for the crowbar, but Jean threw the beaver toy at her head while Jillian skipped aside with a poke to the ribs that could have inflicted far more damage.

"Go play outside," Golly cruelly lobbed the toy back while stooping to lay her hand on a ten-gauge extension cord. With the makeshift whip she sent stinging lashes to the legs and sides, driving her siblings back. Emboldened by success, Golly tried once more for the crowbar but delivered a poor snap, and the cord wrapped around an arm that gave it hard yank. Golly let go to leave herself open to the twirling crowbar that hooked the serpentine chain and wheeled her around by the neck, driving Golly Gee crown first into the flammables cabinet, splitting her forehead open and knocking her out.

With the Guardian Angel of Maria Feodorovna at rest about the rightful heir's neck, the victor bound the vanquished by the power cord and sent Jean to the main house to find out what became of Drew.

Coldcocked on the floor Golly Gee couldn't field questions, so Jillian went to the den and signed on the Abbot's processor to call up Yakov Yurovsky and his cohorts. Repulsed, yet transfixed by the harrowing trail of intrigue that reached back to a Yekaterinburg root cellar, she sat trying to comprehend where Jaxy fit in, and how long this Siberian assassin wore the mask of a retro rock and roller filling kill orders on the sly out of the family store.

Jillian purged the search history apprehending why she came this way—not to take up the Archimandrite's filbert brush, but the Abbot's Viking sword, so strode into the shop to strike first and hard. Albeit, when she arrived to fulfill that which had been foreordained, Golly Gee had cut the binds on the table saw and fled broken and bleeding into the night.

At the crossroad, Jillian weighed giving aid to that Rockabilly skunk against chasing down her sister. Then counting on Drew to handle things at the house, girded the scabbard, and headed out through the double door.

CHAPTER 69

Mt. Adams, WA
7:00 p.m., Tuesday, January 9

A discharge of Hydrogen Sulfide from Piker's Peak preceded the seismic event that rocked Mt. Adams from an epicenter 20km north of the summit at seven p.m. on the ninth of January. The USGS scored Pahto 5.2 out of a possible 10, as the shockwaves from the quake sent the wide door swinging on its hinges into the side of Jillian's head, pitching her unconscious to the ground.

DOWNHILL FROM THE MILL, Golly Gee tottered on a leg stiffening at the joints, and clenching her teeth against a throbbing head and gamey foot. Should her rival catch up, Golly could fall back on the bullpup, but could she lean on the rifle for the half mile stump to the bike? The question no sooner posed itself than the answer came back negative, for the ground shifted beneath her feet and down she came on an unsteady rock to roll her unceremoniously off the lip into Coppice Creek.

Swift surges swept her along, and Golly couldn't get purchase on the slippery stones as she flailed and banged her way to the millrace.

There the flow slowed, but she could not drag herself up the slick, mossy sidewalls, or fight the swirling eddies on a lame foot.

With her godfather's warning ringing in her ears, Golly gainsaid, "I didn't touch the anointed one! . . . I didn't!! . . . I passed the test!!!" as the gurgling water drowned out Golly Gee's cries for mercy, to silence her mouth for good.

BY KNIFE TIP JAXY dug stinging, glass slivers from his flesh, cleaned and dressed the wounds, and refashioned the hemp headband and feather before returning to his post. As he crossed over the mudroom sill, heedful to lift high his feet, the ground heaved, capsizing him on a slip 'n' slide of deadly maraschinos and chocolate syrup. Blood gushing from new gashes to his shoulders, scalp and thigh saturated the fresh bandages. This time he didn't bother to get up.

And neither did Drew. Jounced to the slats as the final blow fell, he did as well, backwards over the potbelly to hit the wall and see stars.

WHEN THE AFTERSHOCKS SUBSIDED, several monks aided their subdued hero while the others went from wall to wall straightening pictures and books. By a miracle, Ichthus the blue betta stayed in his bowl.

The Abbot replenished the sloshed water and regarding the wet floor told Rory to "grab a towel or go."

Rory retrieved the SIG. "Not without Jillian."

"You think by waving that around you can call her up like magic? She's gone man! Gone! Come, let us reason together. What is mine is yours. What do you need? Money? A place to hide?"

"Ice water."

The Abbot passed over the pitcher and went for the port.

"Said water."

"It's a '97 tawny—or would you prefer something with a little more kick?"

Battered and breathing hard, Rory rested at the pine table. "Quit today. Cold turkey. Emptied out my tequila—all of it—on the ground."

"Just like that?" The abbot served up cold water with lemon.

"Just like that." Rory took a long draught and cooled his swollen check with the sweaty glass.

"Hungry? I can make up a sandwich," proposed the Abbot with one eye on the clock.

"Got anything sweet?"

The Abbot hollered out, "Deacon—did we eat the cobbler?"

"Look in the pantry!"

Jaxy had no idea he looked like the Shroud of Turin until the pantry door opened and the room recoiled from the ghastly specter. Unrecognizable under a blood-clotted mane and facial shag oozing from revolting cuts and abrasions, Jaxy angled the fierce hunting knife to let thick, dark, cherry juice drip to the floor. Then favoring his right hip from the crash landing, with the boldness of a battle-hardened brave, he backed them into the great room at knifepoint. Utterly grossing out the hall, Jaxy licked the blade clean up one side and down the other, and turning to Aldo with a wink and a low, satisfied grunt said, "The bear is dead, Abba."

"Poor Guin," despaired the Abbot.

With a touch of admiration, the Deacon added, "She didn't go down easy."

Rory swung the rifle to Jaxy's forehead. "Where's my wife?"

Jaxy swatted it off-line snarling, "You heard the man. Gone— Adios—Tchau! And she's not coming back."

"You son of a bitch. If you touched—."

"Not me!" Jaxy growled, "the bear! And once a bruin tastes human flesh . . . it wants more. So, I went after. All day we fought on the mountaintop. I brought a souvenir," Jaxy offered the resin tooth as proof.

"Need more than that."

"As did I. So, I sliced it open to see if I had the right one—you'd be impressed at what they'll devour—and dug this from the colon. Recognize?" Jaxy returned the wedding bands.

With a puzzled face, Rory gave the rings a meticulous shine before dropping them down the vest pocket. "Take a picture tough guy?"

Jaxy passed over the Electric Avlon field phone. "Second to the last is the best."

Rory flipped it out, and blip-a-blip the screen went dead and black as the bear.

On cue the Archimandrite presented Jillian's heartwarming, memorial announcement. "This one came today from Minnehaha."

After a thorough examination, Rory gave the card back saying, "Surprised Klapakis didn't spell Avlon with an 'f'! They always die by accident don't they, Jack? A plane crash here, header off a horse there. Eaten by bear shows some originality, I'll give you that. So, award the Muscovite an Oscar, Al! That was one helluva story. Really had me going. And the makeup!" Rory ripped a handful of chin beard from Jaxy's face. "Exactly how did you kill Jillian—roll the van??"

"W-what story?" stammered Jaxy having just confessed to the murder of a mean, marine's wife and desperate to fix it.

"I don't know when they do it in Siberia, Jack, but in America . . . bears hibernate in winter."

CHAPTER 70

The ROMAR, Totum, WA
7:30 p.m., Tuesday, January 9

In unspoken prayer the monks encompassed Drew as his lifeblood ebbed away through hardwood cracks from a puncture made to the small of the back. At room center Jaxy remained singled out, scrambling to convince the Captain that his wife was alive and well, having stayed a night to move on for destination unknown, leaving behind her wedding band on the nightstand.

Rory asked the Abbot. "On your collar, is this true?"

The Abbot checked the wall calendar. "In part. She stayed two, leaving behind a box of personal things. If we had a working phone, maybe you could ask the Anders?"

Sneered Rory, "Klapakis walks me through this same exercise and a day later here I stand no closer to Jillian than when I started."

Jaxy hopped on: "A day? Try a week. Try two! But from the bloodcurdling tales of torture and death read at every meal, I promise you, burn this house down around their feet they will never tell. Not me. Not you."

Rory grew excited, "Slow, agonizing death, he says! That kind of dedication is hard to find anymore, Al, even in the armed forces. How do you do it?"

"I compel no one. Those who follow the narrow way, do so voluntarily in the hope of reaping eternal rewards," illustrated the Abbot.

"And earthly ones too, I imagine," said Rory.

"We get by."

"By pulling off a few prayers here and some fingernails there while stashing a whole lot of cash and stolen goods inside those organic jars of jelly."

The Abbot's face grew dark. "What makes you think the Royal Martyrs Monastery could entertain such abominations?"

"By entertaining two of the most notorious ones outside Russia."

Jaxy started for the door, "Jig's up, Abba. It's been rad and it's been bad, but there's more to be had in Leningrad."

Rory dropped the hammer. "Sit your commie ass down."

Jaxy sat his commie ass down.

"I stopped in at dinnertime, Al, to take these two jailbirds off your hands, but there are more ways to financial gain, so listen up: Jaxy and Jillian stay on to hit more museums and mansions, and I take a quarter of what your operation pawns to the Antique Mall starting with this," from his vest Rory flashed the jeweled medallion, "or I shut this Russian pipeline down."

At the guardian angel Abba Aldo sputtered, "Impossible! That's ... that's ..."

"Extortion. But twenty-five percent won't close the doors. Consider it a luxury tax, and I'm collections."

Jaxy cut in, "No Rory. He means there are many angels in the God's universe, but only one made by Carl Fabergé. And since you can't get anything close to true, black market value without expert help let's play a parlor game. If the one that fell from your wife's bag into your pocket is the real thing, you keep every dime on the sell and we conclude our business. If the one I have addressed to the Antique

Mall is, then you win a cold stroll to the Bronco. But however it goes, this shit ends tonight."

"Or maybe you should shut the fuck up before I lose mine and go Yan all over you."

Jaxy trashed back, "Fool! You lost it when you gave up Yan for a laugh and now you don't know where he's buried. Play my game, and he stays that way."

A cloud came over Rory. "What distinguishes them?"

"The angels are identical, but the B-side displays the face of Empress Maria Feodorovna, and 1918 stamped in Roman numerals followed by a verse in Russian. Anything else is an automatic disqualification."

Confidence exuded from Rory's face, "Mine checked out yesterday under a forty-power lens. Did yours?"

Jaxy remained poised, "Check again."

Rory slipped the medallion out and read the back. His countenance blackened and contorted into an inhuman form. "Fucking gonna kill him."

"Is that what it says? Let's see." Jaxy read it and then his own face went slack at the one in profile:

To the Very Reverend Michael Klapakis
God Grant You Many Years
Her Imperial Majesty Dagmar Jillian Nikolaevna Romanova
EMPRESS Of All The RUSSIAS
July 2018

Not getting past the top line, Rory bounced it off the floor screeching, "He switched it on me! He switched in on me! The mackerel snapper switched it on me!" Not ready to concede, he bumped the Rockabilly's beltline with the gun. "What's yours say, Jack."

From the fanny pack Jaxy lifted the box he found in the robes of

Brother Jean, peeled off the wrapper, and hinged back the lid with aplomb.

"Sumbitch," drawled Rory, holding high the bronze medal by the wide, white ribbon, "look who came in third again."

CHAPTER 71

The ROMAR Totum, WA
8:00 p.m., Tuesday, January 9

With a carbon blade at his jugular, Jaxy breathed his last rarefied Washington air. He looked upon Drew, beaten senseless to the floor where he soon would join him. He glanced at the Abbot looking to the cuckoo clock to save them, and an Archimandrite resigned to come what may. At last, Jaxy saw his faithful pal barge in with an armload of cut wood from the crib.

"Damn son—thought I left you tied in the Bronco!" Rory put a headlock on, causing the monk to drop the bundle with a crash, except for a single stove length clutched tight to his chest like a Lady of Guadalupe candlestick.

Jaxy drearily addressed the issue, "Jean's a deaf-mute and the village idiot. He wouldn't understand a thing you said if he did. We played, I lost, so get to it."

Rory shoved the monk away and put the knife to Jaxy's lips. "Any last word before I cut your lying tongue out by the roots and carve it into a valentine for Jillian?"

"Just one," Jaxy tipped his chin at Brother Jean.

"Well?" Rory pricked his skin.

"Come on . . ."

"That's two," counted Rory.

"*Three*!!!!"

Ker-ACKKKK!!!! A log the size of a drugstore, devotional candle split over Rory's head, collapsing him like a calf in a slaughterhouse.

Jaxy kicked away the knife and picked up the SIG. "Back! He might be playing possum. Brother Jean! Did you find a charger?"

But the Mute paid no heed as upon Drew he fell, tenting him with his veil and trying to wake him up.

"Jean!" commanded the Abbot.

While the monks softly cheered on their heroic, little bro, the Mute shambled over to rest his forehead on his Abba's chest.

"I ordered you to Totum and you disobeyed. When you took the vow, you forsook the right to speak, bonds of friendship, and any form of violence! No more are you my Miho, and I am not your Abba. Go to the garage. Brother Philip will drive you to Minnehaha."

Up from the rocker the Archimandrite rose to enfold the expelled monk in his overcoat and escort him in dignity. In the midst of this solemn occasion the scream of faraway sirens on their way to the monastery for the third night in a row split the night causing Jaxy's heart to leap for joy:

Guin made it!!!

In that moment of distraction, Rory pushed off his elbows and took out Jaxy's legs, jackknifing the Rockabilly into the reset chairs. Between his legs flying high in the air, Jaxy squeezed the trigger hitting everything on that side of the room except Rory, who scooped up the key on his way out the door to hop the porch rail to make his escape in the golf cart. Jaxy followed, diving off the deck to miss the buggy as it peeled away and fly headlong into a snowman holding aloft a nine iron with a spent flare taped to the end . . . when out of the dark came thundering hooves.

The chestnut stallion rose to catch four feet of air, crashing the cart from top-dead-center and shattering the windshield. Out tumbled

Rory, rump over teakettle, to smack his head against a pine, putting him out for the night. Laying aside his own pacifistic vows for the moment, through the door barreled the Deacon to sit on, and keep the Captain down for good.

A wolf whistle from the saddle called Jaxy away from the porchlights and lanterns. Shrouded by whirling snow devils, the Rockabilly hurried to congratulate Jillian, but instead of a handshake a lasso upended him by a tug.

"Not again," Jaxy said with his head banging the ground.

"Jacob—or should I call you 'Yakov'? Should have left you to die at Sellwood, you barbaric son of a butcher."

"Butcher? Me??? Come on Jillian, I couldn't hit a barn from five feet with an automatic!" Jaxy made a shooting sign with his finger at the sky as Thunder Roll dragged him by his feet.

"Right. The same way my sister missed your head from point blank at the mansion on the afternoon your boss sent you to Portland? How did that happen? Tell me!"

"I don't work for Klav."

"Not anymore."

"Jillian? . . . What exactly do you mean by that?" asked Jaxy with concern.

"Klav Lavorsky is dead."

"Ohhh. If I'd only got the angel back to the island in time," said Jaxy, taking the blame and accepting the bumpy ride through the snow as his punishment.

"His neck would have snapped like a banty rooster's anyway. Like yours, and Golly Gee's, and everyone associated with the Canadian Beaver Lodge," said Jillian without emotion.

"Father Michael's too?"

Jillian threw Jaxy a hateful look. "Don't you bring him into this."

"For Chrissake, Jillian, your sister and I work for him. We have all along. He made me her bodyguard. Your godfather calls all the shots!"

The commotion caused by the Klickitat Sheriff breaking through the iron gate suspended the debate. Jillian stopped to listen. When no one pursued, she had Thunder Roll drag Jaxy out of view. At the lean-to she dismounted to unsheathe and press the Viking sword into Jaxy's Adam's apple saying, "You are a lousy liar. Father Michael has nothing to do with this. For years you worked side by side with the man that poisoned my biological father, until he became like one to you. You would say or do anything to save Klav Lavorsky's skin. You said so yourself."

"Klav's a great man, Jillian. He ponied up thousands to get my dad into rehab! Who fed you this line of crap?"

"Klav himself."

"When?" challenged Jaxy.

"Seconds before I threw him down Grandma P.'s basement. And do you know why he went there? Because my sick sister sent him."

From the garage a small, shaky voice said, "But I didn't. I didn't send him."

"Huu!" Jillian jumped, sword in hand, at the small, wet figure shivering and shaking against the lean-to door. Jean came out to step between them. "Stand down, brother," Jillian said.

But Jean, who never listened very well, would not.

Golly weakly continued with blue lips, "As I slipped into the creek, I remembered something. Did you ever hear Father Michael say: Learn from this, or you will be made to repeat the same lesson over—"

"—and over until you do?" completed Jillian.

From the woodpile Jaxy joined in, "I believe he said, 'over and *again*'."

"Hush!" said the sisters.

Golly Gee slumped to the floor, "Since I was little, I wanted to be you. First born with all the privileges. The apple of Father's eye. Since I couldn't, I set out to replace you. But each time I try to do you in things for me get worse!"

"You silly goose! Father Michael loves you more than anything. It's thoughts of you—not me—that keep him up at night. Only by doing yourself in could you destroy his favorite goddaughter! If you weren't wringing wet, I'd be the jealous one."

"Nice. Tell Father I completed the lesson. I passed the test," Golly Gee started to fade.

"Don't you dare die on me now." Jillian pushed by her brother to massage Golly's hands and face until color returned. She then turned the sword back at Jaxy seated on the cut wood with his hands tied before him. "If Golly Gee didn't send Rat Catcher to kill me then who did?"

"How would I know? I'm just the Antique Mall courier."

Golly chimed in asking, "The one who hand carried a letter bomb to Jean in Paris and then tried to frame me for the hit?"

"I know how it looks, but I didn't go to Paris. I had no reason."

"Then give up who did or give up your head." Jillian lifted Jaxy's chin with the sword.

"Beats me—ask your godfather Michael! I may not know him very well, but well enough to say that this is not how he would want my story to end."

"You're absolutely right. You *don't* know him," said Jillian.

Once again Jean calmed the waters by taking the sword out of her hands. In trade he gave Jillian her cake box of stuff so she could help Golly into a dry change of clothing. Behind the privacy of the lean-to door, the Nikolaevnas continued their discussion of Jaxy Thrie's close and long-standing relationship with Klav and the timing of events from the boathouse to the basement. Since things did not bode well for Jaxy, while the girls were out of view, Jean loosened the knots on Jaxy's wrists for him to slip away at the first opportunity.

After Jillian finished dressing Golly, she turned the Guardian Angel of Maria Feodorovna over to Jean asking, "What would Father Michael have us do?"

In charge for the first time, the Grand Duke went to the Abbot's truck and came back with golf pencil and a score card. He decreed in writing that the Antique Mall courier would stand trial in two days in Minnehaha. Having set a court date, the siblings prepared Thunder Roll for their ride on horseback to Grandma's. Golly was given the saddle and Jean climbed up behind to hold her steady. Jillian then tied the braided ranch rope to the horn, but when she gave the other end a yank Jaxy was gone!

"Huu!!!" Jillian ran about the lean-to in a dither, shaking the rope and yelling, "You're going to hang by the neck from this, Jaxy! Do you hear? The neck!" Then hearing boots crunch down the drive, up she mounted to whistle a command to Thunder Roll and gallop off to Grandma P's.

Brother Philip entered the garage saying, "My Gawd, Jaxy! You look like you could use a meeting. Have you seen Brother Jean?"

Jaxy looked up the monastery drive empty of squad cars. "No. I thought he'd be with you. Are the cops gone?"

Brother Philip said, "Yessir. They sent Rory to the cooler and Drew to urgent care. "

"What about me?"

"What about? The Sheriff has no idea you were ever here."

"Naturally," Jaxy laughed. "And Guin?"

"She's waiting for you, Jaxy. Time to go."

Jaxy could not agree more. Always have a backup plan, his dad told him. An escape with a place to go that no one would know. For this reason, Jaxy printed more than one map at the library that morning.

Out the side he then exited, going around the chapel away from the big house. Well acquainted with the woods, in no time Jaxy found Moby waiting for him at the covered bridge. He hooked the new set of snow chains around the tires and backed out to Widowmaker Road. Through the snowy night Jaxy made his way to the fork at B-Z Corner. He checked the address burned into the wooden nickel one more time, and a quarter of an hour later turned into the only farmhouse with a hay raker for miles around.

Up four, slick, icy steps of concrete Jaxy climbed to ring the chimes.

From inside came a happy voice: "Tell me yer name, friend, and I'll tell ye mine!"

ACKNOWLEDGMENTS

My wife Kathryn for her support and feedback on story development and artwork ideas.

My son Daniel, a writer of fiction as well, for attending conferences and workshops with me and giving encouragement along the way.

The Southern California Writers' Conference, Free Expressions' Breakout Novel Intensive (BONI) seminars, and the professional services of Erica Ellis at Ink Deep Editing.

Damonza.com for designing a great cover for this novel, and Kayla Toris for the attractive interior layout.

Mark Jobe Images for the excellent portrait photography used on the book cover and website.

Finally, I would like to thank the staff at Acorn publishing: Holly Kammier, Jessica Therrien, Leslie Ferguson, and editors Molly Lewis and Debra Kennedy for making this book possible.

ABOUT THE AUTHOR

A lifetime resident of California, Jerry moved to Santa Barbara after graduating from USC to work in the aerospace industry. Today, he designs night-vision cameras for everyday use. In his free time, Jerry likes to write and use his musical talent to compose original scores for piano and guitar. After his first loves—song and storytelling—Jerry enjoys hiking, spending time in the garden, and baking sourdough bread.

www.ingramcontent.com/pod-product-compliance
Lightning Source LLC
Chambersburg PA
CBHW021337310726
48971CB00001B/171